FROM

MAGGIE: A Girl of the Streets

and Other Writings About New York

A stone had smashed into Jimmie's mouth. Blood was bubbling over his chin and down upon his ragged shirt. Tears made furrows on his dirt-stained cheeks. His thin legs had begun to tremble and turn weak, causing his small body to reel.   (from "Maggie," pages 7–8)

The girl, Maggie, blossomed in a mud puddle. She grew to be a most rare and wonderful production of a tenement district, a pretty girl.
(from "Maggie," page 22)

"Teh hell wid him and you," she said, glowering at her daughter in the gloom. Her eyes seemed to burn balefully. "Yeh've gone teh deh devil, Mag Johnson, yehs knows yehs have gone teh deh devil. Yer a disgrace teh yer people, damn yeh."   (from "Maggie," page 39)

As the girl timidly accosted him, he gave a convulsive movement and saved his respectability by a vigorous sidestep. He did not risk it to save a soul. For how was he to know that there was a soul before him that needed saving?   (from "Maggie," page 64)

"I know he ain't th' kind 'a man I'd like t' have you go around with. He ain't a good man. I'm sure he ain't. He drinks."
(from "George's Mother," page 82)

He remembered Jones. He could not help but admire a man who knew so many bartenders.   (from "George's Mother," page 93)

For three days they lived in silence. He brooded upon his mother's agony and felt a singular joy in it.
(from "George's Mother," page 119)

From the dark and secret places of the building there suddenly came to his nostrils strange and unspeakable odors that assailed him like malignant diseases with wings. They seemed to be from human bodies closely packed in dens; the exhalations from a hundred pairs of reeking lips; the fumes from a thousand bygone debauches; the expression of a thousand present miseries.

(from "An Experiment in Misery," page 138)

"I have been told all my life that millionaires have no fun, and I know that the poor are always assured that the millionaire is a very unhappy person." (from "An Experiment in Luxury," pages 145–146)

"Humanity only needs to be provided for ten minutes with a few whirligigs and things of the sort, and it can forget at least four centuries of misery. I rejoice in these whirligigs."

(from "Coney Island's Failing Days," page 165)

And who should invade this momentary land of rest, this dream country, if not the people of the Tenderloin; they who are at once supersensitive and hopeless, the people who think more upon death and the mysteries of life, the chances of the hereafter than any other class, educated or uneducated? Opium holds out to them its lie, and they embrace it eagerly. (from "Opium's Varied Dreams," page 195)

The bicycle crowd has completely subjugated the street. The glittering wheels dominate it from end to end. The cafes and dining rooms or the apartment hotels are occupied mainly by people in bicycle clothes. Even the billboards have surrendered.

(from "New York's Bicycle Speedway," page 196)

MAGGIE
A GIRL OF THE STREETS

and Other Writings About New York

Stephen Crane

WITH AN INTRODUCTION AND NOTES BY ROBERT TINE

GEORGE STADE
CONSULTING EDITORIAL DIRECTOR

BARNES & NOBLE CLASSICS
NEW YORK

JB

BARNES & NOBLE CLASSICS
NEW YORK

Published by Barnes & Noble Books
122 Fifth Avenue
New York, NY 10011

www.barnesandnoble.com/classics

Maggie: A Girl of the Streets was first published in 1893, and George's Mother first appeared in 1896. The remaining sketches first appeared in a number of New York newspapers between 1894 and 1896.

Published in 2005 by Barnes & Noble Classics with new Introduction, Notes, Biography, Chronology, An Inspiration for Crane's Writings About New York, Comments & Questions, and For Further Reading.

Maggie: A Girl of the Streets and Other Writings About New York
ISBN-13: 978-1-59308-248-2
ISBN-10: 1-59308-248-7
LC Control Number 2005926185

Produced and published in conjunction with:
Fine Creative Media, Inc.
322 Eighth Avenue
New York, NY 10001
Michael J. Fine, President and Publisher

Printed in the United States of America
QM
9 10 8

STEPHEN CRANE

Stephen Crane was born on November 1, 1871, the fourteenth and last child of the Reverend Jonathan Townley Crane and Mary Helen Peck, a Methodist missionary. Stephen's interest in war and the military developed early, and he convinced his mother to enroll him in the Hudson River Institute, a semi-military school in upstate New York. On the advice of a professor who urged him to pursue a more practical career than the army, Stephen transferred to Lafayette College in Pennsylvania, to study mining engineering; however, he seldom attended class and failed a theme writing course because of poor attendance. His formal education ended after one semester at Syracuse University, where he was known on campus for his baseball skills. Despite his unimpressive academic performance, he wrote regularly while he was a student.

Stephen Crane became a prolific writer—of journalism and novels, short stories and poetry. By age twenty-three he had completed two major novels marked by an impressionism and a psychological realism that anticipated the "new fiction" of Ernest Hemingway, F. Scott Fitzgerald, and William Faulkner. His writing of fiction is informed by the keen, precise observation that also made him a journalist; for *Maggie: A Girl of the Streets* (1893), he shadowed a New York prostitute for weeks. Crane was born after the Civil War, and he relied on secondary sources and his own intuition and emotional insights in creating *The Red Badge of Courage* (1895), the story of a young recruit's experiences during one key battle. The book is often cited as the first modern novel.

While on assignment to cover the Cuban-Spanish conflict that preceded the Spanish-American war, Crane met his lifelong companion, Cora Stewart, a well-read daughter of old money who owned a brothel in Jacksonville, Florida. Crane and Stewart later lived in England, where they socialized with Henry James, Joseph Conrad, and Ford Madox Ford, who admired Crane's unique writing style. The young American continued to publish novels, stories, and articles for journals, which solidified his reputation.

Illness cut Crane's life short. In 1899, in Badenweiler, Germany, he collapsed with severe hemorrhaging of the lungs brought on by tuberculosis and malaria. He died in a sanitarium on June 5, 1900, five months before his twenty-ninth birthday.

In his short but brilliant career, Stephen Crane produced six novels, two collections of poetry, and more than one hundred stories, which were compiled in a ten-volume edition published by the University Press of Virginia (1969–1976). He is remembered as a pioneering writer who anticipated the styles that modernized American literature in the 1920s.

TABLE OF CONTENTS

THE WORLD OF STEPHEN CRANE AND
HIS WRITINGS ABOUT NEW YORK

1871 Stephen Crane is born on November 1 at 14 Mulberry Street, Newark, New Jersey, the last of his parents' fourteen children.

1878 Stephen enrolls in school. His father becomes pastor of the Drew Methodist Church in Port Jervis, in upstate New York.

1880 Stephen's father dies of heart failure.

1883 Stephen and his mother move to Asbury Park, a town on the New Jersey coast.

1885 Concerned about Stephen's digressions from Methodist teachings, his mother enrolls him at Pennington Seminary, a school where his father had once been the principal. He writes his first story, "Uncle Jake and the Bell-Handle." Stephen becomes intrigued by the battles of the Civil War and decides to pursue a career in the army.

1888 In January, Stephen enrolls at the Hudson River Institute, a semi-military school in upstate Claverack, New York. He works as a gossip reporter for his brother Townley's news agency; his vignettes appear in "On the Jersey Coast," a column in Townley's New York *Tribune*.

1890 In February, Stephen's first signed publication, an essay on the Christian virtues of Sir Henry Morton Stanley's African expedition, appears in the school magazine. In September, he enrolls at Lafayette College, in Pennsylvania, to pursue a more practical profession, mining engineering. He does poorly in his studies and fails a course in theme writing. After one semester, he withdraws from Lafayette. Rudyard Kipling's *The Light That Failed*, serialized in *Lippincott's* magazine, inspires Stephen to develop his own style of writing. *How the Other Half Lives*, Jacob Riis's groundbreaking exposé of the sordid living conditions of New York City's tenement dwellers, is published.

1891 Stephen's mother enrolls him as a "special student" in the Scientific Course at Syracuse University, where she hopes he will be influenced by the school's strict Methodist codes. He joins the baseball team and transfers his Delta Upsilon fraternity membership from Lafayette. He continues to write for the New York *Tribune* and publishes a story, "The King's Favor," in the *University Herald*, the Syracuse literary magazine. In June, Stephen leaves Syracuse and joins the *Tribune* as a seasonal reporter. In August, he meets Hamlin Garland, a radical-minded young writer and critic from Boston, after he writes a review of Garland's lecture on William Dean Howells at Avon-by-the-Sea, New Jersey. Garland will have a profound influence on Stephen's development as a writer.

1892 In July, five of Stephen Crane's anecdotal stories about his camping and fishing trips in Sullivan County, New York, are published in the *Tribune*. He is dismissed from his job when his report of a parade of workers in Asbury Park embarrasses Whitelaw Reid, the *Tribune*'s owner and a U.S. vice presidential candidate. In the fall, Crane moves to New York to work for the *Herald*.

1893 *Maggie* is published at Crane's expense, under the pseudonym Johnston Smith. The novel catches the eye of Garland and William Dean Howells, both literary realists, who befriend Crane. In April, Crane begins to write *The Red Badge of Courage*.

1894 In late February, Crane and a friend dress in rags, wait in a bread line, and spend the night in a flophouse—experiences that inspire the stories "An Experiment in Misery" and "The Men in the Storm"; these pieces are published in the New York *Press* and *The Arena*, respectively. In the spring, Crane begins another New York novel, *George's Mother*. An abridged version of *The Red Badge of Courage* is published in the Philadelphia *Press* and other newspapers in December. Crane writes "A Night at the Millionaire's Club," a mocking dig at the snobbish club members.

1895 He tours the American West and Mexico as a roving reporter for the Bacheller-Johnson Syndicate. He meets author Willa Cather in Lincoln, Nebraska. His experiences out West will inspire two of his best-known stories, "The Bride Comes to

Yellow Sky" (1897) and "The Blue Hotel" (1898). Upon his return from Mexico, he settles in Hartwood, New York. Appleton publishes *The Red Badge of Courage* in October. Cuba, rebelling against rule by Spain, declares "Independence or death." The United States increases its involvement in resolving the Spanish-Cuban conflict. *The Black Riders*, Crane's first book of verse, is published.

1896   *The Red Badge of Courage* receives critical acclaim—Crane wins recognition from Joseph Conrad and H. G. Wells. "The Veteran," a short story that features the protagonist of *The Red Badge of Courage* as an old man, is published in *McClure's Magazine* in June and collected in *The Little Regiment and Other Episodes of the American Civil War*. In November, Crane travels to Jacksonville, Florida, as a newspaper correspondent covering the Cuban insurrection against Spain; he tries to book passage on a vessel that will run the blockade of the island. He checks into the St. James Hotel under the name Samuel Carleton and arranges passage to Cuba on the *Commodore*. He meets Cora Stewart, the well-mannered, literary-minded owner of the Hotel de Dream brothel, who will become his common-law wife. *George's Mother* is published, and *Maggie* is reissued in its original form.

1897   On January 1, Crane embarks on the *Commodore*, which sinks on January 2. Crane and three others escape in a dinghy and reach Florida's east coast on the morning of January 3. On January 7 Crane publishes a newspaper account of the sinking. While recuperating, he composes "The Open Boat," which recounts the thirty hours spent in the dinghy; the story is first published in the June issue of *Scribner's Magazine*. Crane serves as a correspondent during the brief Greco-Turkish War. He and Cora move to England; he is welcomed into the literary circle of Ford Madox Ford and Henry James, and meets Joseph Conrad, who becomes a close friend.

1898   The United States declares war on Spain. Crane returns to the United States to become a war correspondent for the New York *World*. *The Open Boat and Other Stories* is published.

1899   In January, Crane returns to England and moves with Cora to Brede Place, an ancient manor in Sussex. The couple exchanges visits with Henry James, the Conrads, Ford, and the

Wellses, often at Lamb House, James's cottage in Rye. While working on his novel *The O'Ruddy*, Crane falls ill with tuberculosis. In December, he is debilitated with severe hemorrhaging of the lungs. His second book of verse, *War Is Kind*, is published, as is *The Monster and Other Stories*.

1900   Despite his deteriorating health, Crane continues to work on *The O'Ruddy* and other short pieces. In the spring, while in Badenweiler, Germany, he collapses. Cora checks him into a sanitarium, where he dies on June 5. *Wounds in the Rain*, a collection of Cuban war stories, is published after his death, as is *Whilomville Stories*, a childhood memoir.

1903   *The O'Ruddy*, an Irish romance completed after Crane's death by Robert Barr, is published.

1923–   A biography of Crane is published. Willa Cather and H. L.
1925   Mencken are among the writers who create introductions to a new twelve-volume collection of Crane's work.

1950–   Author John Berryman's biography and R. W. Stallman's
1970   anthology of Crane's best work are published, as is a complete edition of his works by the University Press of Virginia. Crane is generally recognized as one of the major forces in modern American literature.

INTRODUCTION

Poor Crane was . . . never properly appreciated. We were great friends from the first, after he arrived in England. But believe me . . . no paper, no review would look at anything I or anybody else could write about Crane now. They would laugh at the suggestion. . . . Mere literary excellence won't save a man's memory. Sad but true.

—JOSEPH CONRAD (1912)

Conrad wrote those words just six years after Crane's death, and, at the time, it seemed as if the great writer had written the epitaph of his "great friend." Less than a decade after his death, Crane's groundbreaking work in American letters was largely forgotten. "Who's Crane?" Conrad laments. "Who cares for Crane. . . . I hardly meet anyone now who knows or remembers anything of him. For the younger, on-coming writers he does not exist."

Conrad's lament may have been true at the time, but by the 1920s Crane's works had been rediscovered and his reputation began an inexorable rise. Crane's standing is now perhaps higher than it was when he was alive, and his contributions to American literature are confirmed and cemented in place. While he might never be as beloved as his contemporaries Mark Twain and Henry James, Crane is undoubtedly a pillar of nineteenth-century letters, far eclipsing popular contemporaries such as Francis Marion Crawford and William Dean Howells. There remains even now, a hundred years after his death, a whiff of danger and brimstone about Stephen Crane—though he would never claim the sentiment as his own, he may be said to be the first American literary figure to embody the ambitions of a later generation: Live fast, die young, and leave a beautiful corpse. While no one can attest to the last attribute, he exemplified the first two. As for the first—in just eleven short years Crane wrote novels, poems, short stories, and hundreds of pieces of reportage, including war correspondence—he even managed to find time to compile a book of songs. Had he written nothing more than the novels *Maggie: A Girl of* the *Streets*, *George's Mother*, and his masterpiece *The Red Badge of Courage*, his reputation would be secure. In addition, though, we have the racy facts of Crane's life. He consorted with those considered the lowest of the low—Bowery bums, prostitutes, crooked cops, con men, men of violence—but he was equally at home with the great and good, and he was as well-learned as the members of high society. He was at ease in stately homes in England, fashionable spas, and the watering places of Mittel-Europa, as well as tenement slums and opium dens.

By the age of twenty-four he was famous enough to rise in an open court of law and announce himself as "Stephen Crane, the novelist," confident, I would imagine, that everyone present knew who he was. It seems that they did. In any case, the judge asked for no further identification.

Stephen Crane was born in 1871 in Newark, New Jersey, the son of the Reverend Jonathan Townley Crane and Mary Helen Peck Crane, the last of fourteen children born to the couple. Both his mother and father were active, proselytizing Methodists, puritanical in the extreme. Reverend Crane wrote impassioned jeremiads against many popular pastimes—baseball was one of his particular bugaboos—and his wife joined the crusade against alcohol. Mrs. Crane enjoyed great success with a series of articles and lectures on the damage done to the human body by liquor, accompanied by a graphic magic-lantern show during her public-speaking addresses. Mrs. Crane was active in the New Jersey branch of the Woman's Christian Temperance Union and later became a power in the national organization.

It would seem that the young Stephen Crane had the perfect springboard to push against when he decided to abandon the restrictive values of his straight-laced family and launch himself into the louche world of the demimonde. But in the manner of many of the offspring of religious parents, it seems that Crane never quite lost his sense of sin, his genetically imprinted fear of God. As one of his champions, Amy Levenell observed: "He disbelieved it and he hated it, but he could not free himself of it."

Still, somehow he managed to tamp down the fires of self-damnation. He was not far into his teenage years when he made his first stabs at bohemianism. At a semi-military prep school in Claverack, New York, he was said to be given to outlandish dress, was "giftedly profane," and made his contempt for authority quite obvious. Cadet Crane did not make it through a single year at the academy.

At Lafayette College in Easton, Pennsylvania, he began to read widely—not the required texts, but contemporary literature, particularly Flaubert and Tolstoy, authors still a generation away from the curriculum of a small American liberal-arts college. He repeatedly voiced profound opinions on these writers and on any other matters of the day. The brief experience at Lafayette College was succeeded by a stint at Syracuse University. It was at Syracuse that Crane developed a taste for the slums and the police courts—a curiosity that would stay with him throughout his brief life.

It was darkly bruited about at Syracuse that the colorful Stephen Crane was writing a scandalous novel about a prostitute. Legend has it that he started the book as early as sixteen years of age, but surely that would have been too young, even for someone as precocious as Stephen Crane. Most scholars of Crane's works agree that he began the book at nineteen years of age, during his only semester at Syracuse University.

During his short professional life Crane traveled the world. He became an habitué of literary salons in Europe, covered wars in the Balkans, Mexico, and Cuba, and wandered the more remote corners of the western United States. But it was always in New York City that he found his métier; it was in the city that he was most at home. After Syracuse University, and a predictably brief stint on a suburban New Jersey newspaper, Crane gravitated to New York, the place that would shape his work, and, as a consequence, subsequent American letters.

Crane was determined to live in the city and to make his living with his pen. Living a bohemian, hand-to-mouth existence, he took to vanishing into the vast netherworld of the city, living among the whores, the drunks, the drug addicts, and the "b'hoys," the Irish gangster swells of the Bowery. Emerging from this underworld, Crane would have enough material for a freelance newspaper piece as well as other material that would become *Maggie: A Girl of the Streets*. Occasional newspaper work, a small but providential inheritance, and regular handouts from one of his brothers allowed Crane to cobble together a modest living—but it was *Maggie* on which he had pinned his hopes.

By 1892 Crane had finished writing *Maggie*. He approached the editor of *Century Magazine*, hoping his story would be serialized in the pages of that august publication. Almost immediately his hopes were dashed. The editor found the manuscript "cruel" and far too straightforward about the awful details of slum life. At the time there was no shortage of literature about the life of the underclass, but it was always couched in the safe terms of moral disapproval, sugar-coating the misery of the wretched, and suggesting that somehow the poor were responsible for their misery. Crane's matter-of-fact presentation of life in the gutter was, the editor of the *Century* felt, too harsh for its middle- and upper-class readership.

Crane then began that dispiriting trek, so well known to first-time novelists, traveling from publisher to publisher only to have his manuscript rejected again and again. Many of the editors who read *Maggie* had the same opinion: While there was much to admire in the book, the squalor of the story, the appalling degradation of virtually all the characters, and the coarseness of the language were bound to outrage the "Mrs. Grundys" of the world (the fictional Mrs. Grundy, introduced in Thomas Morton's 1798 play *Speed the Plow*, exemplifies the negative influence of conventional wisdom) and bring nothing but opprobrium down on the author and by extension his publisher.

Crane then came up with the idea of publishing his book under a pseudonym, and he chose the bland, almost forgettable name of "Johnston Smith." "You see," he explained, "I was going to wait until the world was pyrotechnic about Johnston Smith's *Maggie* and then I was going to flop down like a trapeze performer from a wire, coming forward with all the grace of a consumptive hen, and say 'I am he, friends'" (Stallman, *Stephen Crane*, p. 69; see "For Further Reading").

That Crane set out to *épater les bourgeois*—outrage the middle class— there can be little doubt. However, the intentionally scandalous nature of the book still left him with the problem of finding a publisher—a problem that seemed insurmountable. Following rejection after rejection, Crane was forced to suffer the ignominy of publishing the work himself, paying a house best known for medical texts and religious tracts to print the first edition of *Maggie*. In 1893 he paid $869 for 1,100 copies of a cheap-looking yellow paperback edition of the book. Johnston Smith, however, had ceased to exist—Stephen Crane's name appears on the title page. The publisher's name appears nowhere.

Even under the canopy of anonymity the publisher had insisted that the manuscript be bowdlerized to a degree. Some of the rougher language and more violent scenes were removed or toned down. But *Maggie: A Girl of the Streets* was still pretty strong meat for its day, and Crane now waited (one senses with a degree of gleeful anticipation) for the hue and cry, the fierce literary arguments, the denunciations from the pulpits of every denomination, that would propel *Maggie* to best-sellerdom and make the young man's fortune.

Instead, silence. No newsstands or reputable bookshop would take the book on account of its incendiary nature—the only exception was Brentano's, which took a dozen copies on consignment and returned ten. In desperation Crane took to giving away copies, dozens and dozens of them, and somehow, miraculously, the book found its way into the literary bloodstream, moving from one man of letters to another. When Crane's spirits and fortunes were at their lowest ebb, he heard through a friend that his book had found its way into the hands of the well-respected author and critic William Dean Howells, who admired the book and announced that he would review it. The friend who gave Crane this welcome news was Curtis Brown, who would later become a prominent literary agent.

Brown remembers: "If Crane had been told that Howells had condemned the book he might have heaved a sigh. But instead, given the welcome news, he seemed dazed. He looked around like a man who did not know where he was. He gulped something down his throat, grinned like a woman in hysterics and then went off to take up his vocation again" (Stallman, p. 71).

But even with the enthusiastic support of the powerful Howells, the 1893 edition of *Maggie* could only be considered a failure. Just the same, the praise of a literary man whose opinion Crane respected seemed to strengthen him and was enough, it seems, to make him "take up his vocation again."

This vocation led him to write his finest and best-known work, a novel that became an American classic: *The Red Badge of Courage*. Published in 1895 by the eminently respectable publishing house of Appleton and Company, the novel achieved huge sales and vast acclaim from the critics and reading public. Stephen Crane was suddenly thrust into the limelight he had sought, and had become, overnight, a literary figure to be reckoned with. He was also a rich young author, a guaranteed best-seller. As a result *Maggie: A Girl of the Streets* was reissued in 1896, and this time the manuscript was returned to its original state—all of the emendations and coy ellipses were removed. *The Red Badge of Courage* may have made Crane's reputation, but *Maggie* was first in his heart.

Maggie: A Girl of the Streets was the first American novel to render slum life with not only realism but with artistry as well. Late-nineteenth-century readers were no strangers to slum literature—be they crusading works like *The Dangerous Classes of New York and Twenty Years' Work Among Them* (1872), by Charles Loring Brace, or moralizing tracts like the Reverend Thomas DeWitt Talmage's *The Night Sides of City Life* (1878) and *The Abominations of Modern Society* (1872). But never before had a book about slum life been lacking in a moral judgment. *Maggie* is a simple story, nineteen vignettes of clear, almost photographic realism, and it never bows to the conventions of nineteenth-century literature of the underclass. That is, Crane never imposes any middle-class judgments on his characters, never condemns them, always refuses to judge them. Maggie's mother, Mary, her husband, Jimmie, Pete, Nell—virtually all of the characters are rendered square on, warts and all, and then Crane steps back as if to say: "Here they are. This is how it is down there. Judge them if you will. I won't."

But the slums imposed their own standards of morality. Mary, a drunken harridan, no stranger to the police courts, is counted a more "moral" character than her daughter Maggie. Mary, whose sins are myriad, cruel, even bestial, is a better person than her innocent daughter because Maggie evolves into a sinful fallen woman who has given up her chastity—a step she takes out of desperation, not desire, after constant cruelty and ultimately cruel betrayal.

By my count, Maggie—though she is the title character—has fewer than two dozen spoken lines in the entire book. She is passive and experiences few emotions beyond fear, grief, and anxiety. And yet it is her silence (while the rest of her world is a raucous cacophony of shrieks, oaths, curses, alarms, vendettas, and drunkenness), her tiny attempts to bring a little beauty into her drab world (the pathetic little lambrequin), and her attempts to flee her grim reality at the rough Bowery shows Pete takes her to that make her the most sympathetic character in the book. She is capable of love and yearns to be loved in return. The fallen woman, the reviled girl of the streets, is the moral center of the book.

One cannot help but imagine how far she actually fell. Apart from her brief cohabitation with Pete, Maggie is a most unenthusiastic, not to say inept, prostitute (unlike the accomplished, manipulative Nell). As we follow her through the streets in the final hours of her miserable life, Maggie (who has ceased to be Maggie and has become, instead, simply "the girl") has no luck in plying her trade—she is constantly rebuked or merely ignored. On the other hand, one man rejects her because she was neither "new, Parisian nor theatrical"—the "new" suggesting that she must have had enough customers in the past to be known to the visitors of the demimonde.

It seems that the only customer she can find who is remotely interested in her is her last. ". . . a huge fat man in torn and greasy garments. His grey hair straggled down over his forehead. His small, bleared eyes, sparkling from amidst great rolls of red fat. . . . He laughed, his brown, disordered teeth gleaming under a grey grizzled moustache from which beerdrops dripped. His whole body gently quivered and shook like that of a dead jelly fish. Chuckling and leering, he followed the girl of the crimson legions" (p. 66).

Who is this grotesque character? Is he merely Maggie's last trick, a figure so repulsive that after she has serviced him she cannot conceive of falling any lower? Suicide becomes her last and only option. Or, perhaps she didn't commit suicide at all but was murdered by this hideous character? Crane leaves this question unanswered.

The point is, Maggie dies, and we are shown the paltry effects of this tragic event. In the final chapter of the book, when Mary learns of her daughter's death, she weeps copiously—mostly for herself, it seems—but the only real detail of Maggie's short, brutish life she can recall has to do with a pair of shoes the girl wore as a child.

In the most ironic moment of the book Mary "forgives" her little daughter. But forgives her for what? Maggie should be alive to mete out the forgiveness. But she is not, and slum life goes on.

Crane's realistic replication of actual speech is a trademark of his writing. Modern readers might find the almost phonetic speech in *Maggie: A Girl of the Streets* a little distracting at first, but it is one of the factors that gives the book such impact. Once one has become used to Crane's rhythmic street patois, the device gives great verisimilitude to the narrative. This exact rendering of spoken English appears mostly in Crane's writings on slum life. It does not appear at all in "The Open Boat." And it appears to a lesser—but significant—degree in *The Red Badge of Courage*, where enlisted men speak like enlisted men—lots of dropped "g's", "yeh" for you, "jes" for just. But the officers speak as officers are supposed to: like members of the officer class. Their accents and vocabulary would not have been out of place in the drawing rooms of polite society in New York or Philadelphia. The difference in the two manners of speaking throws up a class barrier between the two factions of the same army that is hard to ignore.

But the characters of *Maggie* are all of the same class and speak in the same way. The book is rife with slang, contractions, hundreds of misspellings ("dat" for that, "taut" for thought, etc.), and a torrent of apostrophes acting as stands-in for dropped letters. There is nothing refined about the story, from start to finish, so it would be hard to imagine the tale being told in any other manner. Even the most famous line in the book, as the narrative rises almost to the level of poetry, is composed with strict colloquial realism: Jimmie, ". . . on a certain star-lit evening, said wonderingly and quite reverently: 'Deh moon looks like hell, don't it?'" (p. 22). One can't imagine him or any other character in the novel expressing this heartfelt emotion, this momentary appreciation of beauty, in any other way.

George's Mother was one of Stephen Crane's favorite pieces of writing, and he had hoped to achieve signal success with it. In the chronology of Crane's writing it comes just after *Maggie: A Girl of the Streets* and just before—almost simultaneous with—the publication of *The Red Badge of Courage*. Given the proximity in time of *George's Mother* and *Maggie*, as well as their similar New York slum settings, it is tempting to think of the former novel as some kind of flip side of the latter. It is certainly easy to draw comparisons between the two books. Indeed, *George's Mother*'s Kelceys and *Maggie*'s Johnsons live in the same building, the warren of tenement apartments situated in the filth of Rum Alley, only a few yards from one another. It's not difficult to imagine Mrs. Kelcey shaking her head and remembering in her prayers the unhappy Johnson family, just as it's easy to imagine George witnessing the brawling and drunkenness going on just a few feet from his front door. We certainly know that he is aware of Maggie, "sweet" on her—yet she is barely aware of his existence, a burden George finds difficult, and which is part of his final undoing.

The two novels are similar in other ways. Both books recount devastating falls from grace that, while heartbreaking, mean nothing to the world outside the fetid slums of New York's Lower East Side. George and Maggie suffer tragedies that go unnoticed except by those directly affected by them.

However, George's Mother is also quite different from Maggie, in tone if not in setting. In the Kelcey household there is none of the howling desperation that is a hallmark of life at the Johnsons, nor are we exposed to the unrelenting filth, chaos, destruction, or coruscating anger that characterizes Maggie: A Girl of the Streets. Also, the two main characters of George's Mother, Mrs. Kelcey and her last-born (of six) and only surviving son, George, are decent, hardworking, salt-of-the-earth types. It is difficult to see how they deserve the tragedy that will eventually befall them. While such a tragic forecast is easy to make for the Johnson clan, it is almost unthinkable for the Kelceys.

It is interesting to compare the two mothers: Mrs. Johnson and Mrs. Kelcey could not have been more different, but their stories are so similar. Mrs. Johnson drinks; Mrs. Kelcey is an active member of the Woman's Christian Temperance Union. Mrs. Johnson keeps a slovenly, disheveled household, filthy and strewn with debris; Mrs. Kelcey, to the degree that she can be in her mean lodging, is house-proud—wantonly destroying a piece of crockery or a piece of furniture would be completely alien to her, unfathomable. For Mrs. Johnson, smashing and destroying her few poor belongings seems to be something of a hobby, or at least her most powerful form of self-expression. It is all Mrs. Johnson can do to put a plate of potatoes on the family dining table, whereas Mrs. Kelcey is forever at the stove, cooking to satisfy her son, working over her pots and pans, wielding them "like weapons."

Of course, the most telling difference between the two women comes at the end of the two books: When Mary Johnson learns of Maggie's ignominious demise she cries, not for her "fallen" daughter but for herself, making a showy act of forgiveness. In Mrs. Kelcey's case, when George falls into drunkenness she remains moral and upright. George doesn't die—he takes to drink like many of the expendable workingmen in turn-of-the-century New York. But it is too much for Mrs. Kelcey to bear. It is a betrayal, and in that sense it represents the death of her sixth and final son. When George loses his job, Mrs. Kelcey takes to her bed and dies of a broken heart.

It has been widely and incorrectly assumed that Stephen Crane drank himself into an early grave, and that he was an opium addict. It is also thought that *George's Mother* was some sort of autobiographical broadside aimed at his proper, puritanical teetotaling parents, that *George's Mother* reflects a son's rejection of all that his parents (particularly his mother) stood for. None of this is true. Crane did drink, maybe on occasion to excess, but no more than the average male of his era.

While Crane has stated that Mrs. Kelcey was an exaggeration of his mother's own Woman's Christian Temperance Union advocacy, the comparison ends there. There is little else to connect the well-spoken, educated, suburban preacher's wife with the roughhewn, barely literate slum dweller Mrs. Kelcey—except that they both possessed a good heart and worried about their wild offspring.

Yet autobiographical connections do exist. Crane admired his mother while resisting her way of life and her manner of thinking. George, in his inchoate way, finds "correctness" in his mother's morals but experiences her unwavering uprightness as "maddening" nonetheless.

George's Mother may be another of Crane's cautionary tales, but, as with *Maggie*, he is not shoving his own sense of morality down the throats of his readers. Rather, once again, he paints the picture and lets the viewers decide the morality of the tableau for themselves. Whose fault is it, he asks, if the downfall of the slum woman is prostitution and the great abyss awaiting the workingman is the saloon, where all he owns or holds precious is drowned in a pail of cheap beer?

Crane did not turn his eagle eye only on the slum-dwelling New Yorkers of his age. As we read in "A Night at the Millionaire's Club," he was as attuned to the very rich as he was to the poor. If anything, he was more scabrous in his treatment of society's upper crust. Written in 1894, "A Night at the Millionaire's Club" takes place at the height of the gilded age, when vast fortunes were accumulated by a tiny percentage of the population. This was the era of the Morgans, the Vanderbilts, the Fricks, the Goulds, the Rockefellers, the Astors— those families who owned outright textile mills, railroads, shipping lines, vast tracts of land, mines, oil fields, and in the case of Morgan, virtually all of Wall Street itself. These vast fortunes—untaxed and unregulated—amounted to a significant percentage of the nation's economic worth. (According to material presented on economist J. Bradford Long's Web site, in 1900 one percent of the population held 45 percent of the nation's wealth.)

It is no wonder then that the smug, self-satisfied, rather desiccated millionaires of their eponymous club considered themselves far above mere mortals, even if the mortals in question happen to be the upright, though plain-speaking, figures of the early days of the American re-public: Ralph Waldo Emerson, Nathaniel Hawthorne, Alexander Hamil-ton, and George Washington—all men of intelligence and action who valued political commitment and democratic ideals over wealth and personal power. Essentially turning this fundamental American moral-ity and identity on its head, the millionaire families used their terrific fortunes to build huge "cottages" in Newport, Rhode Island, build-ings long on pretension but distinctly lacking in taste. Crane has end-less fun with their absurd pretensions.

When a club servant (wearing a suit of livery that would have cost at least three times George's yearly salary) enters this sacred space to announce some visitors, the millionaires show little more than a languid curiosity—never mind that the lackey has announced four of the greatest names in American history. It is of no conse-quence to the millionaires. When they further learn that these inter-lopers are Americans there is general consternation. "Don't bring 'em in here!" "Throw 'em out!" "Kill 'em!" (p. 132).

However, a cooler millionaire head prevails. Erroll Van Dyck Strathmore very calmly gives the orders. The newcomers are to be treated kindly, shown a cigarette end he happened to drop on the steps of the club, given a recipe for Mr. Jones-Jones Smith-Jones's terrapin stew and a gallery ticket for a theatrical show. Then they are on no account to return to the Millionaire's Club, because, it has been ex-plained, the millionaires don't know any Americans.

Crane's was the time of the Grand Tour, when wealthy Americans looked to Europe for culture, when American money was traded for the titles of Old European nobility (more often than not a nobility fallen on hard times and looking for an infusion of that railroad or steel money that only an American fortune could provide). But more than that, the millionaires refuse to see themselves as Americans, even when confronted by men far more noble and "aristocratic" than they will ever be. The millionaires here have ceased to be Americans at all and have joined a new nationality—that of the plutocracy. In this neat little sketch Crane skewers these plutocrats, holding them up to a scorn and derision that they can only be said to have brought on themselves.

Although "An Experiment in Misery" seems to be merely the musings of two young men on the life of a tramp, Stephen Crane and a friend, William Carroll, were actually hired by a newspaper syndicate to disguise themselves as down-and-outers and live as the indigent on the Bowery. Accordingly, the two men dressed as tramps, with just sixty cents between them, and set out to have a closer look at New York's underworld. As mentioned earlier, visiting the slums was hardly a new idea; it had been something of a tourist tradition for years. People of "quality" would be conducted, under guard and guide, through the dens and alleys to gaze upon and shiver at the filth and degradation in which their fellow citizens chose to live. Mostly these tours were merely a chance for the upper classes to indulge their taste for the pornography of human suffering. Surprisingly, some good came out of this voyeurism: Danish immigrant Jacob Riis caused quite a stir when Charles Scribner's Sons published his book *How the Other Half Lives* in 1890. He spent the next twenty-five years documenting slum life and campaigning for better living conditions.

Stephen Crane and William Carroll were actually going to live it. Carroll hated every minute of slum living: He reported that while he lay cold and scared and uncomfortable in a nickel-a-night flophouse, Crane reveled in the entire experience. He liked the needle beer and the "free lunch" the cheap bars served—soup they called it, watery and bland, with "little floating suggestions of chicken" (p. 136). Crane's account of a single night living in the rough is actually an amalgam of several such experiences—Carroll went once and one suspects that he had his fill of low living on that single occasion.

One gets the impression on reading "An Experiment in Luxury" that Crane liked to experiment with squalor. From the dismissive description of what was probably a very elegant brownstone house to that of the pathetic millionaire whose greatest pleasure in his delight-filled home comes from a simple kitten, Crane suggests in no uncertain terms that money is wasted on the wealthy. The journalistic standards of the nineteenth century were not as rigorous as they are today, and one cannot help but suspect that the "old friend" and "the youth" are two sides of Crane's own character and that it is the "old friend" who most reflects his true opinion of the rich. The old friend's jeremiad early on in the piece is the most telling. "I have been told all my life that millionaires have no fun, and I know that the poor are always assured that the millionaire is a very unhappy person" (pp. 145–146). Crane goes on to prove that millionaires and their off-spring have every reason to be happy, but that they choose not to be. The youth gets plenty of advice on how to be miserable. "Be sure not to get off anything that resembles an original thought. . . . Be dreary and unspeakably commonplace. . . . Be damnable" (p. 150). But even for all the gloom of the millionaire's home, Crane concludes correctly, "Wealth in a certain sense is liberty" (p. 154).

At the time of the publication of *The Red Badge of Courage*, numerous reviewers remarked that the battle scenes in the book were so true to life that they could only have been written by a grizzled veteran of the Civil War. Crane dismisses this story; he says that he had gotten most of his battleground ideas from watching football games. Even if this flippant remark is not true, Crane could not have fought in the Civil War; he was born six years after the cessation of hostilities. Clearly Crane was not above making up details. His exciting and tragic "When Everyone is Panic Stricken" is completely fictional, but that does not make it any less gripping. The story, which appeared in the New York *Press*, has a beautifully evoked "you are there" quality. The reader can smell the smoke, hear the comments of the passers-by, and almost feel the anguish in the cry of the mother who has left her child in the flame-engulfed building: "My baby! My baby! My baby!" (p. 182).

The heroic policeman who plunges into the flame to rescue the child, the thundering hooves of the fire horses, the nonchalance of the firemen to whom one fire is much like another—these are all figments of Crane's imagination, and yet it all rings true. Of course,

Crane must have witnessed fires in his time, and given that the rac-
ing fire engines of the day were one of the great street scenes of New
York City, he must have seen those as well. Still, it is all fiction. "The
facts are: there was no fire at all, no baby, no hysterical mother, no
brave policeman, no nothing, except Crane's magnificent and, in this
instance, impish imagination, and the great William Dean Howells was
so taken in that he pronounced Crane's article 'a piece of realistic
reporting.' It is fiction, not reporting. Anyone who consults the New
York newspapers around the date 25 November 1894 'will find nothing at all about any fire having taken place, much less anything about
any policeman rescuing a child from a burning building'" (John S.
Mayfield, *American Book Collector*: January 1957).

Edward Marshall, the Sunday editor of the New York *Press*, expressed himself years later about Crane's tenement-house fire report:
"It is one of the best things he or any other man ever did." And while
it is, the sketch is pure fiction. Crane later attempted to make amends
for his deception: While covering the Spanish-American War, he filed
a competing dispatch written by Marshall before his own, because
Marshall was wounded and could not to do so himself.

Crane's powers of invention find their way into a number of his
New York City pieces. "Coney Island's Failing Days," "In a Park Row
Restaurant," and "When Man Falls, a Crowd Gathers" are most likely
composites of sights and experiences that Crane witnessed over the
years, thought rarely at one time nor with the companions he claimed
to have been with. Of course, this does not make them any less valid.
To modern readers, the title "Coney Island's Failing Days" may sug-
gest the decline of the great American playground. Quite the contrary.
"Coney Island's Failing Days" is an account of the closing of the summer resort, which will reopen in all its frankfurter-and-music-hall
glory when the season begins the next year. "In a Park Row Restaurant" suggests nothing more than rush hour in a busy restaurant in a
part of the city that was, and is, the locus of city business. Restaurants
such as the one Crane describes are gone now, but such frenzied dining still goes on in many New York fast-food places. Lunchtime in the
Wall Street area may not be quite as frenetic as the battle of Gettysburg, to which the dining experience is compared, but it is still hec-
tic, even in the twenty-first century.

In the interests of truthfulness, Crane may have played fast and loose with the facts, but four of the pieces included in this edition present details of New York life largely as they were, without embellishment. In "Opium's Varied Dreams" he presents a methodical, almost clinical study of drug addicts in the New York City of his time. His writing here is almost as sympathetic as his slum reportage; he simply states the facts and lets readers draw their own conclusions. There is no doubt that Crane's observations were intended, in part, to titillate his readers, but one can also discern a certain sympathy for the drug user.

In the 1880s the United States was in the grip of bicycle mania—and New York City was no exception. "New York's Bicycle Speedway" is Crane's take on the craze; it notes that wheelmen and wheelwomen, as he called the cyclists, had taken over a number of thoroughfares in the city, including part of Broadway, the area around City Hall, but in particular an extension of Eighth Avenue, now Central Park West, from One Hundred and Tenth Street to Columbus Circle. The bicycle craze wreaked havoc with the already chaotic traffic in the city. The piece is a lighthearted look at a trend that did not last long; it is an interesting snapshot of the city during one brief moment.

It is said that a police precinct captain responsible for the Bowery heard that he was being transferred uptown, to the Tenderloin, an area on the West Side of Manhattan from roughly Twenty-third Street to Columbus Circle that at the time was rife with corruption. Referring to the bribes he had received downtown, he is known to have said, "All these years I've been living on chuck steak. Now I'm gonna get me some tenderloin." Crane's series of articles "In the Tenderloin" takes the reader on an anecdotal tour of this area, which had a high concentration of bordellos, music halls, bars, and clip joints. The area, known as Satan's Circus, was a natural stomping ground for Crane, who knew it well.

Far distant from the Tenderloin was Minetta Lane, a horseshoe-shaped side street off Sixth Avenue in Greenwich Village. In the newspaper headline that ran with the piece titled "Stephen Crane and Minetta Lane," Crane calls this tiny street "one of Gotham's most notorious thoroughfares. . . . Where the inhabitants have been famous for evil deeds, where the burglar and the shoplifter and the murderer live side by side" (p. 217). Again, Crane seems to be quite at home in this den of iniquity and on first-name terms with many of the most notorious burglars, shoplifters, and murderers.

Apart from having been the author *The Red Badge of Courage*, Stephen Crane was probably best known not for something he had written, but for an incident that occurred during his life. The Dora Clark/Stephen Crane episode tells us a great deal about Crane's character. It was a simple affair: While in the Tenderloin one night in September 1886, Crane observed a young woman (probably a prostitute) named Dora Clark being arrested by a policeman named Charles Becker. Becker claimed that he had seen Clark solicit two men on a Tenderloin street. Because he knew this not to be the case, Crane called the arrest "an outrage" and personally intervened, making the case a cause célèbre. That a man of his stature should step forward to defend a woman of such dubious reputation was just the sort of thing Crane would do. With intense press coverage and imputations against Crane's own character, he insisted on defending Dora Clark to the fullest degree. The case consumed the nation and briefly knocked the presidential election off the front pages of the newspapers from Maine to California. Ultimately he and Clark were vindicated and Becker reprimanded from the bench. The whole incident suggests Crane's career in a nutshell: His fascination with low life, his general sense of honor, and his tireless defense of the downtrodden.

Robert Tine is the author of six novels, including *State of Grace* and *Black Market*. He has written for a variety of periodicals and magazines—from the *New York Times* to *Newsweek*. He was educated at various schools in six countries (in addition to the United States: Bahamas, Wales, South Africa, Swaziland, and Argentina) and at Columbia University in New York.

MAGGIE

A GIRL OF THE STREETS

and Other Writings About New York

CONTENTS

Contents

4

MAGGIE

A Girl of the Streets

A VERY LITTLE BOY stood upon a heap of gravel for the honor of Rum Alley. He was throwing stones at howling urchins from Devil's Row[1] who were circling madly about the heap and pelting at him.

His infantile countenance was livid with fury. His small body was writhing in the delivery of great, crimson oaths.

"Run, Jimmie, run! Dey'll get yehs," screamed a retreating Rum Alley child.

"Naw," responded Jimmie with a valiant roar, "dese micks* can't make me run."

Howls of renewed wrath went up from Devil's Row throats. Tattered gamins† on the right made a furious assault on the gravel heap. On their small, convulsed faces there shone the grins of true assassins. As they charged, they threw stones and cursed in shrill chorus.

The little champion of Rum Alley stumbled precipitately down the other side. His coat had been torn to shreds in a scuffle, and his hat was gone. He had bruises on twenty parts of his body, and blood was dripping from a cut in his head. His wan features wore a look of a tiny, insane demon.

On the ground, children from Devil's Row closed in on their antagonist. He crooked his left arm defensively about his head and fought with cursing fury. The little boys ran to and fro, dodging, hurling stones and swearing in barbaric trebles.

From a window of an apartment house that upreared its form from amid squat, ignorant stables, there leaned a curious woman. Some laborers, unloading a scow at a dock at the river,[2] paused for a moment and regarded the fight. The engineer of a passive tugboat hung lazily to a railing and watched. Over on the Island,[3] a worm of yellow convicts came from the shadow of a grey ominous building and crawled slowly along the river's bank.

A stone had smashed into Jimmie's mouth. Blood was bubbling over his chin and down upon his ragged shirt. Tears made furrows on his dirt-stained cheeks. His thin legs had begun to tremble and turn

---

*Derogatory term for Irish people.
†Street urchins.

weak, causing his small body to reel. His roaring curses of the first part of the fight had changed to a blasphemous chatter.

In the yells of the whirling mob of Devil's Row children there were notes of joy like songs of triumphant savagery. The little boys seemed to leer gloatingly at the blood upon the other child's face.

Down the avenue came boastfully sauntering a lad of sixteen years, although the chronic sneer of an ideal manhood already sat upon his lips. His hat was tipped with an air of challenge over his eye. Between his teeth, a cigar stump was tilted at the angle of defiance. He walked with a certain swing of the shoulders which appalled the timid. He glanced over into the vacant lot in which the little raving boys from Devil's Row seethed about the shrieking and tearful child from Rum Alley.

"Gee!" he murmured with interest, "A scrap. Gee!"

He strode over to the cursing circle, swinging his shoulders in a manner which denoted that he held victory in his fists. He approached at the back of one of the most deeply engaged of the Devil's Row children.

"Ah, what deh hell," he said, and smote the deeply-engaged one on the back of the head. The little boy fell to the ground and gave a hoarse, tremendous howl. He scrambled to his feet, and perceiving, evidently, the size of his assailant, ran quickly off, shouting alarms. The entire Devil's Row party followed him. They came to a stand a short distance away and yelled taunting oaths at the boy with the chronic sneer. The latter, momentarily, paid no attention to them.

"What deh hell, Jimmie?" he asked of the small champion.

Jimmie wiped his blood-wet features with his sleeve.

"Well, it was dis way, Pete, see! I was goin' teh lick dat Riley kid and dey all pitched on me."

Some Rum Alley children now came forward. The party stood for a moment exchanging vainglorious remarks with Devil's Row. A few stones were thrown at long distances, and words of challenge passed between small warriors. Then the Rum Alley contingent turned slowly in the direction of their home street. They began to give, each to each, distorted versions of the fight. Causes of retreat in particular cases were magnified. Blows dealt in the fight were enlarged to catapultian power, and stones thrown were alleged to have hurtled with infinite accuracy. Valor grew strong again, and the little boys began to swear with great spirit.

"Ah, we blokies* kin lick deh hull damn Row," said a child, swaggering.

Little Jimmie was striving to stanch the flow of blood from his cut lips. Scowling, he turned upon the speaker.

"Ah, where deh hell was yeh when I was doin' all deh fightin'?" he demanded. "Youse kids makes me tired."

"Ah, go ahn," replied the other argumentatively.

Jimmie replied with heavy contempt. "Ah, youse can't fight, Blue Billie! I kin lick yeh wid one han'."

"Ah, go ahn," replied Billie again.

"Ah," said Jimmie threateningly.

"Ah," said the other in the same tone.

They struck at each other, clinched, and rolled over on the cobble stones.

"Smash 'im, Jimmie, kick deh damn guts out of 'im," yelled Pete, the lad with the chronic sneer, in tones of delight.

The small combatants pounded and kicked, scratched and tore. They began to weep and their curses struggled in their throats with sobs. The other little boys clasped their hands and wriggled their legs in excitement. They formed a bobbing circle about the pair.

A tiny spectator was suddenly agitated.

"Cheese it, Jimmie, cheese it!† Here comes yer fader," he yelled.

The circle of little boys instantly parted. They drew away and waited in ecstatic awe for that which was about to happen. The two little boys, fighting in the modes of four thousand years ago, did not hear the warning.

Up the avenue there plodded slowly a man with sullen eyes. He was carrying a dinner pail and smoking an apple-wood pipe.

As he neared the spot where the little boys strove, he regarded them listlessly. But suddenly he roared an oath and advanced upon the rolling fighters.

---

*Fellows, chaps; from the British slang word "bloke."
†Run away fast.

"Here, you Jim, git up, now, while I belt yer life out, you damned disorderly brat."

He began to kick into the chaotic mass on the ground. The boy Billie felt a heavy boot strike his head. He made a furious effort and disentangled himself from Jimmie. He tottered away, damning.

Jimmie arose painfully from the ground and confronting his father, began to curse him. His parent kicked him. "Come home, now," he cried, "an' stop yer jawin', er I'll lam* the everlasting head off yehs."

They departed. The man paced placidly along with the apple-wood emblem of serenity between his teeth. The boy followed a dozen feet in the rear. He swore luridly, for he felt that it was degradation for one who aimed to be some vague soldier, or a man of blood with a sort of sublime license, to be taken home by a father.

～◎ II ◎～

EVENTUALLY THEY ENTERED INTO a dark region where, from a careening building, a dozen gruesome doorways gave up loads of babies to the street and the gutter. A wind of early autumn raised yellow dust from cobbles and swirled it against an hundred windows. Long streamers of garments fluttered from fire-escapes. In all unhandy places there were buckets, brooms, rags and bottles. In the street infants played or fought with other infants or sat stupidly in the way of vehicles. Formidable women, with uncombed hair and disordered dress, gossiped while leaning on railings, or screamed in frantic quarrels. Withered persons, in curious postures of submission to something, sat smoking pipes in obscure corners. A thousand odors of cooking food came forth to the street. The building quivered and creaked from the weight of humanity stamping about in its bowels.

---

*Hit or beat up; short for "lambaste."

A small ragged girl dragged a red, bawling infant along the crowded ways. He was hanging back, baby-like, bracing his wrinkled, bare legs.

The little girl cried out: "Ah, Tommie, come ahn. Dere's Jimmie and fader. Don't be a-pullin' me back."

She jerked the baby's arm impatiently. He fell on his face, roaring. With a second jerk she pulled him to his feet, and they went on. With the obstinacy of his order, he protested against being dragged in a chosen direction. He made heroic endeavors to keep on his legs, denounce his sister and consume a bit of orange peeling which he chewed between the times of his infantile orations.

As the sullen-eyed man, followed by the blood-covered boy, drew near, the little girl burst into reproachful cries. "Ah, Jimmie, youse bin fightin' agin."

The urchin swelled disdainfully.

"Ah, what deh hell, Mag. See?"

The little girl upbraided him. "Youse allus fightin', Jimmie, an' yeh knows it puts mudder out when yehs come home half dead, an' it's like we'll all get a poundin'."

She began to weep. The babe threw back his head and roared at his prospects.

"Ah, what deh hell!" cried Jimmie. "Shut up er I'll smack yer mout'. See?"

As his sister continued her lamentations, he suddenly swore and struck her. The little girl reeled and, recovering herself, burst into tears and quaveringly cursed him. As she slowly retreated her brother advanced dealing her cuffs. The father heard and turned about.

"Stop that, Jim, d'yeh hear? Leave yer sister alone on the street. It's like I can never beat any sense into yer damned wooden head."

The urchin raised his voice in defiance to his parent and continued his attacks. The babe bawled tremendously, protesting with great violence. During his sister's hasty manœuvres, he was dragged by the arm.

Finally the procession plunged into one of the gruesome doorways. They crawled up dark stairways and along cold, gloomy halls. At last the father pushed open a door and they entered a lighted room in which a large woman was rampant.

She stopped in a career from a seething stove to a pan-covered table. As the father and children filed in she peered at them.

"Eh, what? Been fightin' agin, by Gawd!" She threw herself upon Jimmie. The urchin tried to dart behind the others and in the scuffle the babe, Tommie, was knocked down. He protested with his usual vehemence, because they had bruised his tender shins against a table leg.

The mother's massive shoulders heaved with anger. Grasping the urchin by the neck and shoulder she shook him until he rattled. She dragged him to an unholy sink, and, soaking a rag in water, began to scrub his lacerated face with it. Jimmie screamed in pain and tried to twist his shoulders out of the clasp of the huge arms.

The babe sat on the floor watching the scene, his face in contortions like that of a woman at a tragedy. The father, with a newly-ladened pipe in his mouth, crouched on a backless chair near the stove. Jimmie's cries annoyed him. He turned about and bellowed at his wife:

"Let the damned kid alone for a minute, will yeh, Mary? Yer allus poundin' 'im. When I come nights I can't git no rest 'cause yer allus poundin' a kid. Let up, d'yeh hear? Don't be allus poundin' a kid."

The woman's operations on the urchin instantly increased in violence. At last she tossed him to a corner where he limply lay cursing and weeping.

The wife put her immense hands on her hips and with a chieftain-like stride approached her husband.

"Ho," she said, with a great grunt of contempt. "An' what in the devil are you stickin' your nose for?"

The babe crawled under the table and, turning, peered out cautiously. The ragged girl retreated and the urchin in the corner drew his legs carefully beneath him.

The man puffed his pipe calmly and put his great mudded boots on the back part of the stove.

"Go teh hell," he murmured, tranquilly.

The woman screamed and shook her fists before her husband's eyes. The rough yellow of her face and neck flared suddenly crimson. She began to howl.

He puffed imperturbably at his pipe for a time, but finally arose and began to look out at the window into the darkening chaos of back yards.

"You've been drinkin', Mary," he said. "You'd better let up on the bot', ol' woman, or you'll git done."

"You're a liar. I ain't had a drop," she roared in reply.

They had a lurid altercation, in which they damned each other's souls with frequence.

The babe was staring out from under the table, his small face working in his excitement.

The ragged girl went stealthily over to the corner where the urchin lay.

"Are yehs hurted much, Jimmie?" she whispered timidly.

"Not a damn bit! See?" growled the little boy.

"Will I wash deh blood?"

"Naw!"

"Will I"—

"When I catch dat Riley kid I'll break 'is face! Dat's right! See?"

He turned his face to the wall as if resolved to grimly bide his time.

In the quarrel between husband and wife, the woman was victor. The man grabbed his hat and rushed from the room, apparently determined upon a vengeful drunk. She followed to the door and thundered at him as he made his way down stairs.

She returned and stirred up the room until her children were bobbing about like bubbles.

"Git outa deh way," she persistently bawled, waving feet with their dishevelled shoes near the heads of her children. She shrouded herself, puffing and snorting, in a cloud of steam at the stove, and eventually extracted a frying-pan full of potatoes that hissed.

She flourished it. "Come teh yer suppers, now," she cried with sudden exasperation. "Hurry up, now, er I'll help yeh!"

The children scrambled hastily. With prodigious clatter they arranged themselves at table. The babe sat with his feet dangling high from a precarious infant chair and gorged his small stomach. Jimmie forced, with feverish rapidity, the grease-enveloped pieces between his wounded lips. Maggie, with side glances of fear of interruption, ate like a small pursued tigress.

The mother sat blinking at them. She delivered reproaches, swallowed potatoes and drank from a yellow-brown bottle. After a time her mood changed and she wept as she carried little Tommie into another room and laid him to sleep with his fists doubled in an old quilt of faded red and green grandeur. Then she came and moaned by the stove. She rocked to and fro upon a chair, shedding tears and crooning miserably to the two children about their "poor mother" and "yer fader, damn 'is soul."

The little girl plodded between the table and the chair with a dish-pan on it. She tottered on her small legs beneath burdens of dishes.

Jimmie sat nursing his various wounds. He cast furtive glances at his mother. His practised eye perceived her gradually emerge from a muddled mist of sentiment until her brain burned in drunken heat. He sat breathless.

Maggie broke a plate.

The mother started to her feet as if propelled.

"Good Gawd," she howled. Her eyes glittered on her child with sudden hatred. The fervent red of her face turned almost to purple. The little boy ran to the halls, shrieking like a monk in an earthquake.

He floundered about in darkness until he found the stairs. He stumbled, panic-stricken, to the next floor. An old woman opened a door. A light behind her threw a flare on the urchin's quivering face.

"Eh, Gawd, child, what is it dis time? Is yer fader beatin' yer mudder, or yer mudder beatin' yer fader?"

⚜ III ⚜

JIMMIE AND THE OLD woman listened long in the hall. Above the muffled roar of conversation, the dismal wailings of babies at night, the thumping of feet in unseen corridors and rooms, mingled with the sound of varied hoarse shoutings in the street and the rattling of wheels over cobbles, they heard the screams of the child and the roars of the mother die away to a feeble moaning and a subdued bass muttering.

The old woman was a gnarled and leathery personage who could don, at will, an expression of great virtue. She possessed a small music-box capable of one tune, and a collection of "God bless yehs" pitched in assorted keys of fervency. Each day she took a position upon the stones of Fifth Avenue, where she crooked her legs under her and crouched immovable and hideous, like an idol. She received daily a small sum in pennies. It was contributed, for the most part, by persons who did not make their homes in that vicinity.

Once, when a lady had dropped her purse on the sidewalk, the gnarled woman had grabbed it and smuggled it with great dexterity beneath her cloak. When she was arrested she had cursed the lady into a partial swoon, and with her aged limbs, twisted from rheumatism, had almost kicked the stomach out of a huge policeman whose conduct upon that occasion she referred to when she said: "The police, damn 'em."

"Eh, Jimmie, it's cursed shame," she said. "Go, now, like a dear an' buy me a can, an' if yer mudder raises 'ell all night yehs can sleep here."

Jimmie took a tendered tin-pail and seven pennies and departed. He passed into the side door of a saloon and went to the bar. Straining up on his toes he raised the pail and pennies as high as his arms would let him. He saw two hands thrust down and take them. Directly the same hands let down the filled pail and he left.

In front of the gruesome doorway he met a lurching figure. It was his father, swaying about on uncertain legs.

"Give me deh can. See?" said the man, threateningly.

"Ah, come off! I got dis can fer dat ol' woman an' it 'ud be dirt teh swipe it. See?" cried Jimmie.

The father wrenched the pail from the urchin. He grasped it in both hands and lifted it to his mouth. He glued his lips to the under edge and tilted his head. His hairy throat swelled until it seemed to grow near his chin. There was a tremendous gulping movement and the beer was gone.

The man caught his breath and laughed. He hit his son on the head with the empty pail. As it rolled clanging into the street, Jimmie began to scream and kicked repeatedly at his father's shins.

"Look at deh dirt what yeh done me," he yelled. "Deh ol' woman 'ill be raisin' hell."

He retreated to the middle of the street, but the man did not pursue. He staggered toward the door.

"I'll club hell outa yeh when I ketch yeh," he shouted, and disappeared.

During the evening he had been standing against a bar drinking whiskies and declaring to all comers, confidentially: "My home reg'lar livin' hell! Damndes' place! Reg'lar hell! Why do I come an' drin' whisk' here thish way? 'Cause home reg'lar livin' hell!"

Jimmie waited a long time in the street and then crept warily up through the building. He passed with great caution the door of the gnarled woman, and finally stopped outside his home and listened.

He could hear his mother moving heavily about among the furniture of the room. She was chanting in a mournful voice, occasionally interjecting bursts of volcanic wrath at the father, who, Jimmie judged, had sunk down on the floor or in a corner.

"Why deh blazes don' chere try teh keep Jim from fightin'? I'll break yer jaw," she suddenly bellowed.

The man mumbled with drunken indifference. "Ah, wha' deh hell. W'a's odds? Wha' makes kick?"

"Because he tears 'is clothes, yeh damn fool," cried the woman in supreme wrath.

The husband seemed to become aroused. "Go teh hell," he thundered fiercely in reply. There was a crash against the door and something broke into clattering fragments. Jimmie partially suppressed a howl and darted down the stairway. Below he paused and listened. He heard howls and curses, groans and shrieks, confusingly in chorus as if a battle were raging. With all was the crash of splintering furniture. The eyes of the urchin glared in fear that one of them would discover him.

Curious faces appeared in doorways, and whispered comments passed to and fro. "Ol' Johnson's raisin' hell agin."

Jimmie stood until the noises ceased and the other inhabitants of the tenement had all yawned and shut their doors. Then he crawled upstairs with the caution of an invader of a panther den. Sounds of labored breathing came through the broken door-panels. He pushed the door open and entered, quaking.

A glow from the fire threw red hues over the bare floor, the cracked and soiled plastering, and the overturned and broken furniture.

In the middle of the floor lay his mother asleep. In one corner of the room his father's limp body hung across the seat of a chair.

The urchin stole forward. He began to shiver in dread of awakening his parents. His mother's great chest was heaving painfully. Jimmie paused and looked down at her. Her face was inflamed and swollen from drinking. Her yellow brows shaded eyelids that had grown blue. Her tangled hair tossed in waves over her forehead. Her mouth was set in the same lines of vindictive hatred that it had, perhaps, borne during the fight. Her bare, red arms were thrown out above her head in positions of exhaustion, something, mayhap, like those of a sated villain.

The urchin bended over his mother. He was fearful lest she should open her eyes, and the dread within him was so strong, that he could not forbear to stare, but hung as if fascinated over the woman's grim face.

Suddenly her eyes opened. The urchin found himself looking straight into that expression, which, it would seem, had the power to change his blood to salt. He howled piercingly and fell backward.

The woman floundered for a moment, tossed her arms about her head as if in combat, and again began to snore.

Jimmie crawled back in the shadows and waited. A noise in the next room had followed his cry at the discovery that his mother was awake. He grovelled in the gloom, the eyes from out his drawn face riveted upon the intervening door.

He heard it creak, and then the sound of a small voice came to him. "Jimmie! Jimmie! Are yehs dere?" it whispered. The urchin started. The thin, white face of his sister looked at him from the doorway of the other room. She crept to him across the floor.

The father had not moved, but lay in the same death-like sleep. The mother writhed in uneasy slumber, her chest wheezing as if she were in the agonies of strangulation. Out at the window a florid moon was peering over dark roofs, and in the distance the waters of a river glimmered pallidly.

The small frame of the ragged girl was quivering. Her features were haggard from weeping, and her eyes gleamed from fear. She grasped the urchin's arm in her little trembling hands and they huddled in a corner. The eyes of both were drawn, by some force, to stare at the woman's face, for they thought she need only to awake and all fiends would come from below.

They crouched until the ghost-mists of dawn appeared at the window, drawing close to the panes, and looking in at the prostrate, heaving body of the mother.

$$\text{IV}$$

THE BABE, TOMMIE, DIED.[4] He went away in a white, insignificant coffin, his small waxen hand clutching a flower that the girl, Maggie, had stolen from an Italian.

She and Jimmie lived.

The inexperienced fibres of the boy's eyes were hardened at an early age. He became a young man of leather. He lived some red years* without laboring. During that time his sneer became chronic. He studied human nature in the gutter, and found it no worse than he thought he had reason to believe it. He never conceived a respect for the world, because he had begun with no idols that it had smashed.

He clad his soul in armor by means of happening hilariously in at a mission church where a man composed his sermons of "yous." While they got warm at the stove, he told his hearers just where he calculated they stood with the Lord. Many of the sinners were impatient over the pictured depths of their degradation. They were waiting for soup-tickets.

A reader of words of wind-demons might have been able to see the portions of a dialogue pass to and fro between the exhorter and his hearers.

"You are damned," said the preacher. And the reader of sounds might have seen the reply go forth from the ragged people: "Where's our soup?"

Jimmie and a companion sat in a rear seat and commented upon

---

*Time of unemployment or being "in the red"; probably Crane's invention.

the things that didn't concern them, with all the freedom of English gentlemen. When they grew thirsty and went out their minds confused the speaker with Christ.

Momentarily, Jimmie was sullen with thoughts of a hopeless altitude where grew fruit. His companion said that if he should ever meet God he would ask for a million dollars and a bottle of beer.

Jimmie's occupation for a long time was to stand on street-corners and watch the world go by, dreaming blood-red dreams at the passing of pretty women. He menaced mankind at the intersections of streets.

On the corners he was in life and of life. The world was going on and he was there to perceive it.

He maintained a belligerent attitude toward all well-dressed men. To him fine raiment* was allied to weakness, and all good coats covered faint hearts. He and his order were kings, to a certain extent, over the men of untarnished clothes, because these latter dreaded, perhaps, to be either killed or laughed at.

Above all things he despised obvious Christians and ciphers† with the chrysanthemums of aristocracy in their button-holes. He considered himself above both of these classes. He was afraid of neither the devil nor the leader of society.

When he had a dollar in his pocket his satisfaction with existence was the greatest thing in the world. So, eventually, he felt obliged to work. His father died and his mother's years were divided up into periods of thirty days.[5]

He became a truck driver.‡ He was given the charge of a painstaking pair of horses and a large rattling truck. He invaded the turmoil and tumble of the down-town streets and learned to breathe maledictory defiance at the police who occasionally used to climb up, drag him from his perch and beat him.

In the lower part of the city he daily involved himself in hideous tangles. If he and his team chanced to be in the rear he preserved a

---

*Fine clothing.
†Person of no consequence.
‡Drayman, teamster.

demeanor of serenity, crossing his legs and bursting forth into yells when foot passengers took dangerous dives beneath the noses of his champing horses. He smoked his pipe calmly for he knew that his pay was marching on.

If in the front and the key-truck of chaos, he entered terrifically into the quarrel that was raging to and fro among the drivers on their high seats, and sometimes roared oaths and violently got himself arrested.

After a time his sneer grew so that it turned its glare upon all things. He became so sharp that he believed in nothing. To him the police were always actuated by malignant impulses and the rest of the world was composed, for the most part, of despicable creatures who were all trying to take advantage of him and with whom, in defense, he was obliged to quarrel on all possible occasions. He himself occupied a downtrodden position that had a private but distinct element of grandeur in its isolation.

The most complete cases of aggravated idiocy were, to his mind, rampant upon the front platforms of all of the street cars. At first his tongue strove with these beings, but he eventually was superior. He became immured like an African cow. In him grew a majestic contempt for those strings of street cars that followed him like intent bugs.

He fell into the habit, when starting on a long journey, of fixing his eye on a high and distant object, commanding his horses to begin, and then going into a sort of a trance of observation. Multitudes of drivers might howl in his rear, and passengers might load him with opprobrium; he would not awaken until some blue policeman turned red and began to frenziedly tear bridles and beat the soft noses of the responsible horses.

When he paused to contemplate the attitude of the police toward himself and his fellows, he believed that they were the only men in the city who had no rights. When driving about, he felt that he was held liable by the police for anything that might occur in the streets, and was the common prey of all energetic officials. In revenge, he resolved never to move out of the way of anything, until formidable circumstances, or a much larger man than himself forced him to it.

Foot-passengers were mere pestering flies with an insane disregard for their legs and his convenience. He could not conceive their maniacal desires to cross the streets. Their madness smote him with eternal amazement. He was continually storming at them from his throne. He sat aloft and denounced their frantic leaps, plunges, dives and straddles.

When they would thrust at, or parry, the noses of his champing horses, making them swing their heads and move their feet, disturbing a solid dreamy repose, he swore at the men as fools, for he himself could perceive that Providence had caused it clearly to be written, that he and his team had the unalienable right to stand in the proper path of the sun chariot, and if they so minded, obstruct its mission or take a wheel off.

And, perhaps, if the god-driver had an ungovernable desire to step down, put up his flame-colored fists and manfully dispute the right of way, he would have probably been immediately opposed by a scowling mortal with two sets of very hard knuckles.

It is possible, perhaps, that this young man would have derided, in an axle-wide alley, the approach of a flying ferry boat. Yet he achieved a respect for a fire engine.[6] As one charged toward his truck, he would drive fearfully upon a sidewalk, threatening untold people with annihilation. When an engine would strike a mass of blocked trucks, splitting it into fragments, as a blow annihilates a cake of ice, Jimmie's team could usually be observed high and safe, with whole wheels, on the sidewalk. The fearful coming of the engine could break up the most intricate muddle of heavy vehicles at which the police had been swearing for the half of an hour.

A fire-engine was enshrined in his heart as an appalling thing that he loved with a distant dog-like devotion. They had been known to overturn street-cars. Those leaping horses, striking sparks from the cobbles in their forward lunge, were creatures to be ineffably admired. The clang of the gong pierced his breast like a noise of remembered war.

When Jimmie was a little boy, he began to be arrested. Before he reached a great age, he had a fair record.

He developed too great a tendency to climb down from his truck and fight with other drivers. He had been in quite a number of miscellaneous fights, and in some general barroom rows that had become known to the police. Once he had been arrested for assaulting a Chinaman. Two women in different parts of the city, and entirely unknown to each other, caused him considerable annoyance by breaking forth, simultaneously, at fateful intervals, into wailings about marriage and support and infants.

Nevertheless, he had, on a certain star-lit evening, said wonderingly and quite reverently: "Deh moon looks like hell, don't it?"[7]

V

THE GIRL, MAGGIE, BLOSSOMED in a mud puddle. She grew to be a most rare and wonderful production of a tenement district, a pretty girl.

None of the dirt of Rum Alley seemed to be in her veins. The philosophers up-stairs, down-stairs and on the same floor, puzzled over it.

When a child, playing and fighting with gamins in the street, dirt disguised her. Attired in tatters and grime, she went unseen.

There came a time, however, when the young men of the vicinity, said: "Dat Johnson goil is a puty good looker." About this period her brother remarked to her: "Mag, I'll tell yeh dis![8] See? Yeh've edder got teh go teh hell or go teh work!" Whereupon she went to work, having the feminine aversion of going to hell.

By a chance, she got a position in an establishment where they made collars and cuffs. She received a stool and a machine in a room where sat twenty girls of various shades of yellow discontent. She perched on the stool and treadled at her machine all day, turning out collars, the name of whose brand could be noted for its irrelevancy to anything in connection with collars. At night she returned home to her mother.

Jimmie grew large enough to take the vague position of head of the family. As incumbent of that office, he stumbled up-stairs late at night, as his father had done before him. He reeled about the room, swearing at his relations, or went to sleep on the floor.

The mother had gradually arisen to that degree of fame that she could bandy words with her acquaintances among the police-justices. Court-officials called her by her first name. When she appeared they pursued a course which had been theirs for months. They invariably grinned and cried out: "Hello, Mary, you here again?" Her grey head wagged in many a court. She always besieged the bench with voluble excuses, explanations, apologies and prayers. Her flaming face and rolling eyes were a sort of familiar sight on the island. She measured time by means of sprees, and was eternally swollen and dishevelled.

One day the young man, Pete, who as a lad had smitten the Devil's Row urchin in the back of the head and put to flight the antagonists of his friend, Jimmie, strutted upon the scene. He met Jimmie one day on the street, promised to take him to a boxing match in Williamsburg,[9] and called for him in the evening.

Maggie observed Pete.

He sat on a table in the Johnson home and dangled his checked legs with an enticing nonchalance. His hair was curled down over his forehead in an oiled bang. His rather pugged nose seemed to revolt from contact with a bristling moustache of short, wire-like hairs. His blue double-breasted coat, edged with black braid, buttoned close to a red puff tie, and his patent-leather shoes, looked like murder-fitted weapons.

His mannerisms stamped him as a man who had a correct sense of his personal superiority. There was valor and contempt for circumstances in the glance of his eye. He waved his hands like a man of the world, who dismisses religion and philosophy, and says "Fudge."* He had certainly seen everything and with each curl of his lip, he declared that it amounted to nothing. Maggie thought he must be a very elegant and graceful bartender.

He was telling tales to Jimmie.

Maggie watched him furtively, with half-closed eyes, lit with a vague interest.

"Hully gee! Dey makes me tired," he said. "Mos' e'ry day some

---

*Nonsense.

farmer* comes in an' tries teh run deh shop. See? But deh gits t'rowed right out! I jolt dem right out in deh street before dey knows where dey is! See?"

"Sure," said Jimmie.

"Dere was a mug come in deh place deh odder day wid an idear he wus goin' teh own deh place! Hully gee, he wus goin' teh own deh place! I see he had a still on an' I didn' wanna giv 'im no stuff, so I says: 'Git deh hell outa here an' don' make no trouble,' I says like dat! See? 'Git deh hell outa here an' don' make no trouble;' like dat. 'Git deh hell outa here,' I says. See?"

Jimmie nodded understandingly Over his features played an eager desire to state the amount of his valor in a similar crisis, but the narrator proceeded.

"Well, deh blokie he says: 'T'hell wid it! I ain' lookin' for no scrap,' he says (See?) 'but' he says, 'I'm spectable cit'zen an' I wanna drink an' purtydamnsoon, too.' See? 'Deh hell,' I says. Like dat! 'Deh hell,' I says. See? 'Don't make no trouble,' I says. Like dat. 'Don' make no trouble,' See? Den deh mug he squared off an' said he was fine as silk wid his dukes (See?) an' he wanned a drink damnquick. Dat's what he said. See?"

"Sure," repeated Jimmie.

Pete continued. "Say, I jes' jumped deh bar an' deh way I plunked dat blokie was great. See? Dat's right! In deh jaw! See? Hully gee, he t'rowed a spittoon true deh front windee. Say, I taut I'd drop dead. But deh boss, he comes in after an' he says, 'Pete, yehs done jes' right! Yeh've gota keep order an' it's all right.' See? 'It's all right,' he says. Dat's what he said."

The two held a technical discussion.

"Dat bloke was a dandy," said Pete, in conclusion, "but he had'n' oughta made no trouble. Dat's what I says teh dem: 'Don' come in here an' make no trouble,' I says, like dat. 'Don' make no trouble.' See?"

As Jimmie and his friend exchanged tales descriptive of their prowess, Maggie leaned back in the shadow. Her eyes dwelt wonderingly and rather wistfully upon Pete's face. The broken furniture,

---

*Rube; person with no experience of city life.

grimey walls, and general disorder and dirt of her home of a sudden appeared before her and began to take a potential aspect. Pete's aristocratic person looked as if it might soil. She looked keenly at him, occasionally, wondering if he was feeling contempt. But Pete seemed to be enveloped in reminiscence.

"Hully gee," said he, "dose mugs can't phase me. Dey knows I kin wipe up deh street wid any tree of dem."

When he said, "Ah, what deh hell," his voice was burdened with disdain for the inevitable and contempt for anything that fate might compel him to endure.

Maggie perceived that here was the beau ideal of a man. Her dim thoughts were often searching for far away lands where, as God says, the little hills sing together in the morning. Under the trees of her dream-gardens there had always walked a lover.

～◎ VI ◎～

PETE TOOK NOTE OF Maggie.

"Say, Mag, I'm stuck on yer shape. It's outa sight," he said, parenthetically, with an affable grin.

As he became aware that she was listening closely, he grew still more eloquent in his descriptions of various happenings in his career. It appeared that he was invincible in fights.

"Why," he said, referring to a man with whom he had had a misunderstanding, "dat mug scrapped like a damn dago.* Dat's right. He was dead easy. See? He tau't he was a scrapper! But he foun' out diff'ent! Hully gee."

He walked to and fro in the small room, which seemed then to grow even smaller and unfit to hold his dignity, the attribute of a supreme warrior. That swing of the shoulders that had frozen the timid when he was but a lad had increased with his growth and

---

*Derogatory term for someone of Mediterranean descent; from the Spanish name Diego.

education at the ratio of ten to one. It, combined with the sneer upon his mouth, told mankind that there was nothing in space which could appall him. Maggie marvelled at him and surrounded him with greatness. She vaguely tried to calculate the altitude of the pinnacle from which he must have looked down upon her.

"I met a chump deh odder day way up in deh city," he said. "I was goin' teh see a frien' of mine. When I was a-crossin' deh street deh chump runned plump inteh me, an' den he turns aroun' an' says, 'Yer insolen' ruffin,' he says, like dat. 'Oh, gee,' I says, 'oh, gee, go teh hell and git off deh eart',' I says, like dat. See? 'Go teh hell an' git off deh eart',' like dat. Den deh blokie he got wild. He says I was a contempt'ble scoun'el, er something like dat, an' he says I was doom' teh everlastin' pe'dition an' all like dat. 'Gee,' I says, 'gee! Deh hell I am,' I says. 'Deh hell I am,' like dat. An' den I slugged 'im. See?"

With Jimmie in his company, Pete departed in a sort of blaze of glory from the Johnson home. Maggie, leaning from the window, watched him as he walked down the street.

Here was a formidable man who disdained the strength of a world full of fists. Here was one who had contempt for brass-clothed power; one whose knuckles could defiantly ring against the granite of law. He was a knight.

The two men went from under the glimmering street-lamp and passed into shadows.

Turning, Maggie contemplated the dark, dust-stained walls, and the scant and crude furniture of her home. A clock, in a splintered and battered oblong box of varnished wood, she suddenly regarded as an abomination. She noted that it ticked raspingly. The almost vanished flowers in the carpet-pattern, she conceived to be newly hideous. Some faint attempts she had made with blue ribbon, to freshen the appearance of a dingy curtain, she now saw to be piteous.

She wondered what Pete dined on.

She reflected upon the collar and cuff factory. It began to appear to her mind as a dreary place of endless grinding. Pete's elegant occupation brought him, no doubt, into contact with people who had money and manners. It was probable that he had a large acquaintance of pretty girls. He must have great sums of money to spend.

To her the earth was composed of hardships and insults. She felt instant admiration for a man who openly defied it. She thought that if the grim angel of death should clutch his heart, Pete would shrug his shoulders and say: "Oh, ev'ryt'ing goes."

She anticipated that he would come again shortly. She spent some of her week's pay in the purchase of flowered cretonne* for a lambrequin.† She made it with infinite care and hung it to the slightly-careening mantel, over the stove, in the kitchen. She studied it with painful anxiety from different points in the room. She wanted it to look well on Sunday night when, perhaps, Jimmie's friend would come. On Sunday night, however, Pete did not appear.

Afterward the girl looked at it with a sense of humiliation. She was now convinced that Pete was superior to admiration for lambrequins.

A few evenings later Pete entered with fascinating innovations in his apparel. As she had seen him twice and he had different suits on each time, Maggie had a dim impression that his wardrobe was prodigiously extensive.

"Say, Mag," he said, "put on yer bes' duds Friday night an' I'll take yehs teh deh show. See?"

He spent a few moments in flourishing his clothes and then vanished, without having glanced at the lambrequin.

Over the eternal collars and cuffs in the factory Maggie spent the most of three days in making imaginary sketches of Pete and his daily environment. She imagined some half dozen women in love with him and thought he must lean dangerously toward an indefinite one, whom she pictured with great charms of person, but with an altogether contemptible disposition.

She thought he must live in a blare of pleasure. He had friends, and people who were afraid of him.

She saw the golden glitter of the place where Pete was to take her. An entertainment of many hues and many melodies where she was afraid she might appear small and mouse-colored.

Her mother drank whiskey all Friday morning. With lurid face and tossing hair she cursed and destroyed furniture all Friday afternoon. When Maggie came home at half-past six her mother lay asleep

---

*Heavy cotton or linen fabric, usually brightly colored or patterned.
†Ornamental drape for a mantle.

amidst the wreck of chairs and a table. Fragments of various household utensils were scattered about the floor. She had vented some phase of drunken fury upon the lambrequin. It lay in a bedraggled heap in the corner.

"Hah," she snorted, sitting up suddenly, "where deh hell yeh been? Why deh hell don' yeh come home earlier? Been loafin' 'round deh streets. Yer gettin' teh be a reg'lar devil."

When Pete arrived Maggie, in a worn black dress, was waiting for him in the midst of a floor strewn with wreckage. The curtain at the window had been pulled by a heavy hand and hung by one tack, dangling to and fro in the draft through the cracks at the sash. The knots of blue ribbons appeared like violated flowers. The fire in the stove had gone out. The displaced lids and open doors showed heaps of sullen grey ashes. The remnants of a meal, ghastly, like dead flesh, lay in a corner. Maggie's red mother, stretched on the floor, blasphemed and gave her daughter a bad name.

~~ VII ~~

AN ORCHESTRA OF YELLOW silk women and bald-headed men on an elevated stage near the centre of a great green-hued hall, played a popular waltz. The place was crowded with people grouped about little tables. A battalion of waiters slid among the throng, carrying trays of beer glasses and making change from the inexhaustible vaults of their trousers pockets. Little boys, in the costumes of French chefs, paraded up and down the irregular aisles vending fancy cakes. There was a low rumble of conversation and a subdued clinking of glasses. Clouds of tobacco smoke rolled and wavered high in air about the dull gilt of the chandeliers.

The vast crowd had an air throughout of having just quitted labor. Men with calloused hands and attired in garments that showed the wear of an endless trudge for a living, smoked their pipes contentedly and spent five, ten, or perhaps fifteen cents for beer. There was a mere sprinkling of kid-gloved men who smoked cigars purchased elsewhere. The great body of the crowd was composed of people who showed that all day they strove with their hands. Quiet Germans, with maybe their wives and two or three children, sat listening to the music, with the expressions of happy cows. An occasional party of sailors from a war-ship, their faces pictures of sturdy health, spent the earlier hours of the evening at the small round tables. Very infrequent tipsy men, swollen with the value of their opinions, engaged their companions in earnest and confidential conversation. In the balcony, and here and there below, shone the impassive faces of women. The nationalities of the Bowery[10] beamed upon the stage from all directions.

Pete aggressively walked up a side aisle and took seats with Maggie at a table beneath the balcony.

"Two beehs!"

Leaning back he regarded with eyes of superiority the scene before them. This attitude affected Maggie strongly. A man who could regard such a sight with indifference must be accustomed to very great things.

It was obvious that Pete had been to this place many times before, and was very familiar with it. A knowledge of this fact made Maggie feel little and new.

He was extremely gracious and attentive. He displayed the consideration of a cultured gentleman who knew what was due.

"Say, what deh hell? Bring deh lady a big glass! What deh hell use is dat pony?"*

"Don't be fresh, now," said the waiter, with some warmth, as he departed.

"Ah, git off deh eart'," said Pete, after the other's retreating form.

Maggie perceived that Pete brought forth all his elegance and all his knowledge of high-class customs for her benefit. Her heart warmed as she reflected upon his condescension.

The orchestra of yellow silk women and bald-headed men gave vent to a few bars of anticipatory music and a girl, in a pink dress with short skirts, galloped upon the stage. She smiled upon the throng as if in acknowledgment of a warm welcome, and began to walk to and fro, making profuse gesticulations and singing, in brazen

---

*Very small, rose-shaped drinking glass, typically holding one ounce of liquid.

soprano tones, a song, the words of which were inaudible. When she broke into the swift rattling measures of a chorus some half tipsy men near the stage joined in the rollicking refrain and glasses were pounded rhythmically upon the tables. People leaned forward to watch her and to try to catch the words of the song. When she vanished there were long rollings of applause.

Obedient to more anticipatory bars, she reappeared amidst the half-suppressed cheering of the tipsy men. The orchestra plunged into dance music and the laces of the dancer fluttered and flew in the glare of gas jets.* She divulged the fact that she was attired in some half dozen skirts. It was patent that any one of them would have proved adequate for the purpose for which skirts are intended. An occasional man bent forward, intent upon the pink stockings. Maggie wondered at the splendor of the costume and lost herself in calculations of the cost of the silks and laces.

The dancer's smile of stereotyped enthusiasm was turned for ten minutes upon the faces of her audience. In the finale she fell into some of those grotesque attitudes which were at the time popular among the dancers in the theatres up-town, giving to the Bowery public the phantasies of the aristocratic theatre-going public, at reduced rates.

"Say, Pete," said Maggie, leaning forward, "dis is great."

"Sure," said Pete, with proper complacence.

A ventriloquist followed the dancer. He held two fantastic dolls on his knees. He made them sing mournful ditties and say funny things about geography and Ireland.

"Do dose little men talk?" asked Maggie.

"Naw," said Pete, "it's some damn fake. See?"

Two girls, on the bills as sisters, came forth and sang a duet that is heard occasionally at concerts given under church auspices. They supplemented it with a dance which of course can never be seen at concerts given under church auspices.

After the duettists had retired, a woman of debatable age sang a negro melody. The chorus necessitated some grotesque waddlings supposed to be an imitation of a plantation darkey, under the influence,

---

*Open gas flames used for lighting.

probably, of music and the moon. The audience was just enthusiastic enough over it to have her return and sing a sorrowful lay,* whose lines told of a mother's love and a sweetheart who waited and a young man who was lost at sea under the most harrowing circumstances. From the faces of a score or so in the crowd, the self-contained look faded. Many heads were bent forward with eagerness and sympathy. As the last distressing sentiment of the piece was brought forth, it was greeted by that kind of applause which rings as sincere.

As a final effort, the singer rendered some verses which described a vision of Britain being annihilated by America, and Ireland bursting her bonds. A carefully prepared crisis was reached in the last line of the last verse, where the singer threw out her arms and cried, "The star-spangled banner." Instantly a great cheer swelled from the throats of the assemblage of the masses. There was a heavy rumble of booted feet thumping the floor. Eyes gleamed with sudden fire, and calloused hands waved frantically in the air.

After a few moments' rest, the orchestra played crashingly, and a small fat man burst out upon the stage. He began to roar a song and stamp back and forth before the foot-lights, wildly waving a glossy silk hat and throwing leers, or smiles, broadcast. He made his face into fantastic grimaces until he looked like a pictured devil on a Japanese kite. The crowd laughed gleefully. His short, fat legs were never still a moment. He shouted and roared and bobbed his shock of red wig until the audience broke out in excited applause.

Pete did not pay much attention to the progress of events upon the stage. He was drinking beer and watching Maggie.

Her cheeks were blushing with excitement and her eyes were glistening. She drew deep breaths of pleasure. No thoughts of the atmosphere of the collar and cuff factory came to her.

When the orchestra crashed finally, they jostled their way to the sidewalk with the crowd. Pete took Maggie's arm and pushed a way for her, offering to fight with a man or two.

They reached Maggie's home at a late hour and stood for a moment in front of the gruesome doorway.

---

*Poem meant to be sung, not recited.

"Say, Mag," said Pete, "give us a kiss for takin' yeh teh deh show, will yer?"

Maggie laughed, as if startled, and drew away from him.

"Naw, Pete," she said, "dat wasn't in it."

"Ah, what deh hell?" urged Pete.

The girl retreated nervously.

"Ah, what deh hell?" repeated he.

Maggie darted into the hall, and up the stairs. She turned and smiled at him, then disappeared.

Pete walked slowly down the street. He had something of an astonished expression upon his features. He paused under a lamppost and breathed a low breath of surprise.

"Gawd," he said, "I wonner if I've been played fer a duffer."*

VIII

AS THOUGHTS OF PETE came to Maggie's mind, she began to have an intense dislike for all of her dresses.

"What deh hell ails yeh? What makes yeh be allus fixin' and fussin'? Good Gawd," her mother would frequently roar at her.

She began to note, with more interest, the well-dressed women she met on the avenues. She envied elegance and soft palms.† She craved those adornments of person which she saw every day on the street, conceiving them to be allies of vast importance to women.

Studying faces, she thought many of the women and girls she chanced to meet, smiled with serenity as though forever cherished and watched over by those they loved.

The air in the collar and cuff establishment strangled her. She knew she was gradually and surely shrivelling in the hot, stuffy room. The begrimed windows rattled incessantly from the passing of elevated trains. The place was filled with a whirl of noises and odors.

*Fool or dolt; victim of a trickster.
†Kid- or dove-skin gloves favored by upper-class women of the era.

She wondered as she regarded some of the grizzled women in the room, mere mechanical contrivances sewing seams and grinding out, with heads bended over their work, tales of imagined or real girlhood happiness, past drunks, the baby at home, and unpaid wages. She speculated how long her youth would endure. She began to see the bloom[11] upon her cheeks as valuable.

She imagined herself, in an exasperating future, as a scrawny woman with an eternal grievance. Too, she thought Pete to be a very fastidious person concerning the appearance of women.

She felt she would love to see somebody entangle their fingers in the oily beard of the fat foreigner who owned the establishment. He was a detestable creature. He wore white socks with low shoes.

He sat all day delivering orations, in the depths of a cushioned chair. His pocketbook deprived them of the power of retort.

"What een hell do you sink I pie fife dolla a week for? Play? No, py damn!"

Maggie was anxious for a friend to whom she could talk about Pete. She would have liked to discuss his admirable mannerisms with a reliable mutual friend. At home, she found her mother often drunk and always raving.

It seems that the world had treated this woman very badly, and she took a deep revenge upon such portions of it as came within her reach. She broke furniture as if she were at last getting her rights. She swelled with virtuous indignation as she carried the lighter articles of household use, one by one under the shadows of the three gilt balls,* where Hebrews chained them with chains of interest.

Jimmie came when he was obliged to by circumstances over which he had no control. His well-trained legs brought him staggering home and put him to bed some nights when he would rather have gone elsewhere.

Swaggering Pete loomed like a golden sun to Maggie. He took her to a dime museum† where rows of meek freaks astonished her. She contemplated their deformities with awe and thought them a sort of chosen tribe.

---

*Traditional sign of a pawnbroker's shop.
†Freak show.

Pete, raking his brains for amusement, discovered the Central Park Menagerie and the Museum of Arts. Sunday afternoons would sometimes find them at these places. Pete did not appear to be particularly interested in what he saw. He stood around looking heavy, while Maggie giggled in glee.

Once at the Menagerie he went into a trance of admiration before the spectacle of a very small monkey threatening to thrash a cageful because one of them had pulled his tail and he had not wheeled about quickly enough to discover who did it. Ever after Pete knew that monkey by sight and winked at him, trying to induce him to fight with other and larger monkeys.

At the Museum, Maggie said, "Dis is outa sight."

"Oh hell," said Pete, "wait till next summer an' I'll take yehs to a picnic."

While the girl wandered in the vaulted rooms, Pete occupied himself in returning stony stare for stony stare, the appalling scrutiny of the watch-dogs of the treasures.* Occasionally he would remark in loud tones: "Dat jay has got glass eyes," and sentences of the sort. When he tired of this amusement he would go to the mummies and moralize over them.

Usually he submitted with silent dignity to all which he had to go through, but, at times, he was goaded into comment.

"What deh hell," he demanded once. "Look at all dese little jugs! Hundred jugs in a row! Ten rows in a case an' 'bout a t'ousand cases! What deh blazes use is dem?"

Evenings during the week he took her to see plays in which the brain-clutching heroine was rescued from the palatial home of her guardian, who was cruelly after her bonds, by the hero with the beautiful sentiments. The latter spent most of his time out at soak in pale-green snow storms, busy with a nickel-plated revolver, rescuing aged strangers from villains.

Maggie lost herself in sympathy with the wanderers swooning in snow storms beneath happy-hued church windows. And a choir within singing "Joy to the World." To Maggie and the rest of the

---

*Museum security guards.

audience this was transcendental realism. Joy always within, and they, like the actor, inevitably without. Viewing it, they hugged themselves in ecstatic pity of their imagined or real condition.

The girl thought the arrogance and granite-heartedness of the magnate of the play was very accurately drawn. She echoed the maledictions that the occupants of the gallery showered on this individual when his lines compelled him to expose his extreme selfishness.

Shady persons in the audience revolted from the pictured villainy of the drama. With untiring zeal they hissed vice and applauded virtue. Unmistakably bad men evinced an apparently sincere admiration for virtue.

The loud gallery was overwhelmingly with the unfortunate and the oppressed. They encouraged the struggling hero with cries, and jeered the villain, hooting and calling attention to his whiskers. When anybody died in the pale-green snow storms, the gallery mourned. They sought out the painted misery and hugged it as akin.

In the hero's erratic march from poverty in the first act, to wealth and triumph in the final one, in which he forgives all the enemies that he has left, he was assisted by the gallery, which applauded his generous and noble sentiments and confounded the speeches of his opponents by making irrelevant but very sharp remarks. Those actors who were cursed with villainy parts were confronted at every turn by the gallery. If one of them rendered lines containing the most subtle distinctions between right and wrong, the gallery was immediately aware if the actor meant wickedness, and denounced him accordingly.

The last act was a triumph for the hero, poor and of the masses, the representative of the audience, over the villain and the rich man, his pockets stuffed with bonds, his heart packed with tyrannical purposes, imperturbable amid suffering.

Maggie always departed with raised spirits from the showing places of the melodrama. She rejoiced at the way in which the poor and virtuous eventually surmounted the wealthy and wicked. The theater made her think. She wondered if the culture and refinement she had seen imitated, perhaps grotesquely, by the heroine on the stage, could be acquired by a girl who lived in a tenement house and worked in a shirt factory.

～⍟ IX ⍟～

A GROUP OF URCHINS were intent upon the side door of a saloon. Expectancy gleamed from their eyes. They were twisting their fingers in excitement.

"Here she comes," yelled one of them suddenly.

The group of urchins burst instantly asunder and its individual fragments were spread in a wide, respectable half-circle about the point of interest. The saloon door opened with a crash, and the figure of a woman appeared upon the threshold. Her gray hair fell in knotted masses about her shoulders. Her face was crimsoned and wet with perspiration. Her eyes had a rolling glare.

"Not a damn cent more of me money will yehs ever get, not a damn cent. I spent me money here fer t'ree years an' now yehs tells me yeh'll sell me no more stuff! T'hell wid yeh, Johnnie Murckre! 'Disturbance'? Disturbance be damned! T'hell wid yeh, Johnnie—"

The door received a kick of exasperation from within and the woman lurched heavily out on the sidewalk.

The gamins in the half-circle became violently agitated. They began to dance about and hoot and yell and jeer. Wide dirty grins spread over each face.

The woman made a furious dash at a particularly outrageous cluster of little boys. They laughed delightedly and scampered off a short distance, calling out over their shoulders to her. She stood tottering on the curb-stone and thundered at them.

"Yeh devil's kids," she howled, shaking red fists. The little boys whooped in glee. As she started up the street they fell in behind and marched uproariously. Occasionally she wheeled about and made charges on them. They ran nimbly out of reach and taunted her.

In the frame of a gruesome doorway she stood for a moment cursing them. Her hair straggled, giving her crimson features a look of insanity. Her great fists quivered as she shook them madly in the air.

36

The urchins made terrific noises until she turned and disappeared. Then they filed quietly in the way they had come.

The woman floundered about in the lower hall of the tenement house and finally stumbled up the stairs. On an upper hall a door was opened and a collection of heads peered curiously out, watching her. With a wrathful snort the woman confronted the door, but it was slammed hastily in her face and the key was turned.

She stood for a few minutes, delivering a frenzied challenge at the panels.

"Come out in deh hall, Mary Murphy, damn yeh, if yehs want a row. Come ahn, yeh overgrown terrier, come ahn."

She began to kick the door with her great feet. She shrilly defied the universe to appear and do battle. Her cursing trebles brought heads from all doors save the one she threatened. Her eyes glared in every direction. The air was full of her tossing fists.

"Come ahn, deh hull damn gang of yehs, come ahn," she roared at the spectators. An oath or two, cat-calls, jeers and bits of facetious advice were given in reply. Missiles clattered about her feet.

"What deh hell's deh matter wid yeh?" said a voice in the gathered gloom, and Jimmie came forward. He carried a tin dinner-pail in his hand and under his arm a brown truckman's apron done in a bundle. "What deh hell's wrong?" he demanded.

"Come out, all of yehs, come out," his mother was howling. "Come ahn an' I'll stamp yer damn brains under me feet."

"Shet yer face, an' come home, yeh damned old fool," roared Jimmie at her. She strided up to him and twirled her fingers in his face. Her eyes were darting flames of unreasoning rage and her frame trembled with eagerness for a fight.

"T'hell wid yehs! An' who deh hell are yehs? I ain't givin' a snap of me fingers fer yehs," she bawled at him. She turned her huge back in tremendous disdain and climbed the stairs to the next floor.

Jimmie followed, cursing blackly. At the top of the flight he seized his mother's arm and started to drag her toward the door of their room.

"Come home, damn yeh," he gritted between his teeth.

"Take yer hands off me! Take yer hands off me," shrieked his mother.

She raised her arm and whirled her great fist at her son's face. Jimmie dodged his head and the blow struck him in the back of the neck. "Damn yeh," gritted he again. He threw out his left hand and writhed his fingers about her middle arm. The mother and the son began to sway and struggle like gladiators.

"Whoop!" said the Rum Alley tenement house. The hall filled with interested spectators.

"Hi, ol' lady, dat was a dandy!"

"T'ree to one on deh red!"

"Ah, stop yer damn scrappin'!"

The door of the Johnson home opened and Maggie looked out. Jimmie made a supreme cursing effort and hurled his mother into the room. He quickly followed and closed the door. The Rum Alley tenement swore disappointedly and retired.

The mother slowly gathered herself up from the floor. Her eyes glittered menacingly upon her children.

"Here, now," said Jimmie, "we've had enough of dis. Sit down, an' don' make no trouble."

He grasped her arm, and twisting it, forced her into a creaking chair.

"Keep yer hands off me," roared his mother again.

"Damn yer ol' hide," yelled Jimmie, madly. Maggie shrieked and ran into the other room. To her there came the sound of a storm of crashes and curses. There was a great final thump and Jimmie's voice cried: "Dere, damn yeh, stay still." Maggie opened the door now, and went warily out. "Oh, Jimmie."

He was leaning against the wall and swearing. Blood stood upon bruises on his knotty fore-arms where they had scraped against the floor or the walls in the scuffle. The mother lay screeching on the floor, the tears running down her furrowed face.

Maggie, standing in the middle of the room, gazed about her. The usual upheaval of the tables and chairs had taken place. Crockery was strewn broadcast in fragments. The stove had been disturbed on its legs, and now leaned idiotically to one side. A pail had been upset and water spread in all directions.

The door opened and Pete appeared. He shrugged his shoulders. "Oh, Gawd," he observed.

He walked over to Maggie and whispered in her ear. "Ah, what deh hell, Mag? Come ahn and we'll have a hell of a time."

The mother in the corner upreared her head and shook her tangled locks.

"Teh hell wid him and you," she said, glowering at her daughter in the gloom. Her eyes seemed to burn balefully. "Yeh've gone teh deh devil, Mag Johnson, yehs knows yehs have gone teh deh devil. Yer a disgrace teh yer people, damn yeh. An' now, git out an' go ahn wid dat doe-faced jude* of yours. Go teh hell wid him, damn yeh, an' a good riddance. Go teh hell an' see how yeh likes it."

Maggie gazed long at her mother.

"Go teh hell now, an' see how yeh likes it. Git out. I won't have sech as yehs in me house! Get out, d'yeh hear! Damn yeh, git out!"

The girl began to tremble.

At this instant Pete came forward. "Oh, what deh hell, Mag, see," whispered he softly in her ear. "Dis all blows over. See? Deh ol' woman 'ill be all right in deh mornin'. Come ahn out wid me! We'll have a hell of a time."

The woman on the floor cursed. Jimmie was intent upon his bruised fore-arms. The girl cast a glance about the room filled with a chaotic mass of debris, and at the red, writhing body of her mother.

"Go teh hell an' good riddance."

She went.

X

JIMMIE HAD AN IDEA it wasn't common courtesy for a friend to come to one's home and ruin one's sister. But he was not sure how much Pete knew about the rules of politeness.

The following night he returned home from work at rather a late hour in the evening. In passing through the halls he came upon the

---

*Traitor or sneak; from the name Judas.

gnarled and leathery old woman who possessed the music box. She was grinning in the dim light that drifted through dust-stained panes. She beckoned to him with a smudged forefinger.

"Ah, Jimmie, what do yehs tink I got onto las' night. It was deh funnies' ting I ever saw," she cried, coming close to him and leering. She was trembling with eagerness to tell her tale. "I was by me door las' night when yer sister and her jude feller came in late, oh, very late. An' she, the dear, she was a-cryin' as if her heart would break, she was. It was deh funnies' ting I ever saw. An' right out here by me door she asked him did he love her, did he. An' she was a-cryin' as if her heart would break, poor t'ing. An' him, I could see by deh way what he said it dat she had been askin' orften, he says: 'Oh, hell, yes,' he says, says he, 'Oh, hell, yes.'"

Storm-clouds swept over Jimmie's face, but he turned from the leathery old woman and plodded on up-stairs.

"Oh, hell, yes," called she after him. She laughed a laugh that was like a prophetic croak. "'Oh, hell, yes,' he says, says he, 'Oh, hell, yes.'"

There was no one in at home. The rooms showed that attempts had been made at tidying them. Parts of the wreckage of the day before had been repaired by an unskilful hand. A chair or two and the table, stood uncertainly upon legs. The floor had been newly swept. Too, the blue ribbons had been restored to the curtains, and the lambrequin, with its immense sheaves of yellow wheat and red roses of equal size, had been returned, in a worn and sorry state, to its position at the mantel. Maggie's jacket and hat were gone from the nail behind the door.

Jimmie walked to the window and began to look through the blurred glass. It occurred to him to vaguely wonder, for an instant, if some of the women of his acquaintance had brothers.

Suddenly, however, he began to swear.

"But he was me frien'! I brought 'im here! Dat's deh hell of it!"

He fumed about the room, his anger gradually rising to the furious pitch.

"I'll kill deh jay!* Dat's what I'll do! I'll kill deh jay!"

---

*An insult; the derivation is unclear.

He clutched his hat and sprang toward the door. But it opened and his mother's great form blocked the passage.

"What deh hell's deh matter wid yeh?" exclaimed she, coming into the rooms.

Jimmie gave vent to a sardonic curse and then laughed heavily.

"Well, Maggie's gone teh deh devil! Dat's what! See?"

"Eh?" said his mother.

"Maggie's gone teh deh devil! Are yehs deaf?" roared Jimmie, impatiently.

"Deh hell she has," murmured the mother, astounded.

Jimmie grunted, and then began to stare out at the window. His mother sat down in a chair, but a moment later sprang erect and delivered a maddened whirl of oaths. Her son turned to look at her as she reeled and swayed in the middle of the room, her fierce face convulsed with passion, her blotched arms raised high in imprecation.

"May Gawd curse her forever," she shrieked. "May she eat nothin' but stones and deh dirt in deh street. May she sleep in deh gutter an' never see deh sun shine agin. Deh damn—"

"Here, now," said her son. "Take a drop on yourself."

The mother raised lamenting eyes to the ceiling.

"She's deh devil's own chil', Jimmie," she whispered. "Ah, who would tink such a bad girl could grow up in our fambly, Jimmie, me son. Many deh hour I've spent in talk wid dat girl an' tol' her if she ever went on deh streets I'd see her damned. An' after all her bringin' up an' what I tol' her and talked wid her, she goes teh deh bad, like a duck teh water."

The tears rolled down her furrowed face. Her hands trembled.

"An' den when dat Sadie MacMallister next door to us was sent teh deh devil by dat feller what worked in deh soap-factory, didn't I tell our Mag dat if she—"

"Ah, dat's anudder story," interrupted the brother. "Of course, dat Sadie was nice an' all dat—but—see—it ain't dessame as if—well, Maggie was diff'ent—see—she was diff'ent."

He was trying to formulate a theory that he had always unconsciously held, that all sisters, excepting his own, could advisedly be ruined.

He suddenly broke out again. "I'll go t'ump hell outa deh mug what did her deh harm. I'll kill 'im! He tinks he kin scrap, but when he gits me a-chasin' 'im he'll fin' out where he's wrong, deh damned duffer. I'll wipe up deh street wid 'im."

In a fury he plunged out of the doorway. As he vanished the mother raised her head and lifted both hands, entreating.

"May Gawd curse her forever," she cried.

In the darkness of the hallway Jimmie discerned a knot of women talking volubly. When he strode by they paid no attention to him.

"She allus was a bold thing," he heard one of them cry in an eager voice. "Dere wasn't a feller come teh deh house but she'd try teh mash 'im. My Annie says deh shameless t'ing tried teh ketch her feller, her own feller, what we useter know his fader."

"I could a' tol' yehs dis two years ago," said a woman, in a key of triumph. "Yesir, it was over two years ago dat I says teh my ol' man, I says, 'Dat Johnson girl ain't straight,' I says. 'Oh, hell,' he says. 'Oh, hell.' 'Dat's all right,' I says, 'but I know what I knows,' I says, 'an' it'ill come out later. You wait an' see,' I says, 'you see.'"

"Anybody what had eyes could see dat dere was somethin' wrong wid dat girl. I didn't like her actions."[12]

On the street Jimmie met a friend. "What deh hell?" asked the latter.

Jimmie explained. "An' I'll tump 'im till he can't stand."

"Oh, what deh hell," said the friend. "What's deh use! Yeh'll git pulled in! Everybody 'ill be onto it! An' ten plunks! Gee!"

Jimmie was determined. "He t'inks he kin scrap, but he'll fin' out diff'ent."

"Gee," remonstrated the friend, "What deh hell?"

❧ XI ❧

ON A CORNER a glass-fronted building shed a yellow glare upon the pavements. The open mouth of a saloon called seductively to passengers to enter and annihilate sorrow or create rage.*

---

*To get drunk and maudlin, or drunk and belligerent.

The interior of the place was papered in olive and bronze tints of imitation leather. A shining bar of counterfeit massiveness extended down the side of the room. Behind it a great mahogany-appearing sideboard reached the ceiling. Upon its shelves rested pyramids of shimmering glasses that were never disturbed. Mirrors set in the face of the sideboard multiplied them. Lemons, oranges and paper napkins, arranged with mathematical precision, sat among the glasses. Many-hued decanters of liquor perched at regular intervals on the lower shelves. A nickel-plated cash register occupied a position in the exact center of the general effect. The elementary senses of it all seemed to be opulence and geometrical accuracy.

Across from the bar a smaller counter held a collection of plates upon which swarmed frayed fragments of crackers, slices of boiled ham, dishevelled bits of cheese, and pickles swimming in vinegar. An odor of grasping, begrimed hands and munching mouths pervaded.

Pete, in a white jacket, was behind the bar bending expectantly toward a quiet stranger. "A beeh," said the man. Pete drew a foam-topped glassful and set it dripping upon the bar.

At this moment the light bamboo doors at the entrance swung open and crashed against the siding. Jimmie and a companion entered. They swaggered unsteadily but belligerently toward the bar and looked at Pete with bleared and blinking eyes.

"Gin," said Jimmie.

"Gin," said the companion.

Pete slid a bottle and two glasses along the bar. He bended his head sideways as he assiduously polished away with a napkin at the gleaming wood. He had a look of watchfulness upon his features.

Jimmie and his companion kept their eyes upon the bartender and conversed loudly in tones of contempt.

"He's a dindy masher,* ain't he, by Gawd?" laughed Jimmie.

"Oh, hell, yes," said the companion, sneering widely. "He's great, he is. Git onto deh mug on deh blokie. Dat's enough to make a feller turn hand-springs in 'is sleep."

The quiet stranger moved himself and his glass a trifle further away and maintained an attitude of oblivion.

---

*A dandy and a ladies' man.

"Gee! ain't he hot stuff!"

"Git onto his shape! Great Gawd!"

"Hey," cried Jimmie, in tones of command. Pete came along slowly, with a sullen dropping of the under lip.

"Well," he growled, "what's eatin' yehs?"

"Gin," said Jimmie.

"Gin," said the companion.

As Pete confronted them with the bottle and the glasses, they laughed in his face. Jimmie's companion, evidently overcome with merriment, pointed a grimy forefinger in Pete's direction.

"Say, Jimmie," demanded he, "what deh hell is dat behind deh bar?"

"Damned if I knows," replied Jimmie. They laughed loudly. Pete put down a bottle with a bang and turned a formidable face toward them. He disclosed his teeth and his shoulders heaved restlessly.

"You fellers can't guy* me," he said. "Drink yer stuff an' git out an' don' make no trouble."

Instantly the laughter faded from the faces of the two men and expressions of offended dignity immediately came.

"Who deh hell has said anyt'ing teh you," cried they in the same breath.

The quiet stranger looked at the door calculatingly.

"Ah, come off," said Pete to the two men. "Don't pick me up for no jay. Drink yer rum an' git out an' don' make no trouble."

"Oh, deh hell," airily cried Jimmie.

"Oh, deh hell," airily repeated his companion.

"We goes when we git ready! See!" continued Jimmie.

"Well," said Pete in a threatening voice, "don' make no trouble."

Jimmie suddenly leaned forward with his head on one side. He snarled like a wild animal.

"Well, what if we does? See?" said he.

Dark blood flushed into Pete's face, and he shot a lurid glance at Jimmie.

"Well, den we'll see whose deh bes' man, you or me," he said.

The quiet stranger moved modestly toward the door.

Jimmie began to swell with valor.

---

*Mock, make fun of.

"Don' pick me up fer no tenderfoot. When yeh tackles me yeh tackles one of deh bes' men in deh city. See? I'm a scrapper, I am. Ain't dat right, Billie?"

"Sure, Mike," responded his companion in tones of conviction.

"Oh, hell," said Pete, easily. "Go fall on yerself."

The two men again began to laugh.

"What deh hell is dat talkin'?" cried the companion.

"Damned if I knows," replied Jimmie with exaggerated contempt.

Pete made a furious gesture. "Git outa here now, an' don' make no trouble. See? Youse fellers er lookin' fer a scrap an' it's damn likely yeh'll fin' one if yeh keeps on shootin' off yer mout's. I know yehs! See? I kin lick better men dan yehs ever saw in yer lifes. Dat's right! See? Don' pick me up fer no stuff er yeh might be jolted out in deh street before yeh knows where yeh is. When I comes from behind dis bar, I t'rows yehs boat inteh deh street. See?"

"Oh, hell," cried the two men in chorus.

The glare of a panther came into Pete's eyes. "Dat's what I said! Unnerstan'?"

He came through a passage at the end of the bar and swelled down upon the two men. They stepped promptly forward and crowded close to him.

They bristled like three roosters. They moved their heads pugnaciously and kept their shoulders braced. The nervous muscles about each mouth twitched with a forced smile of mockery.

"Well, what deh hell yer goin' teh do?" gritted Jimmie.

Pete stepped warily back, waving his hands before him to keep the men from coming too near.

"Well, what deh hell yer goin' teh do?" repeated Jimmie's ally. They kept close to him, taunting and leering. They strove to make him attempt the initial blow.

"Keep back, now! Don' crowd me," ominously said Pete.

Again they chorused in contempt. "Oh, hell!"

In a small, tossing group, the three men edged for positions like frigates contemplating battle.

"Well, why deh hell don' yeh try teh t'row us out?" cried Jimmie and his ally with copious sneers.

The bravery of bull-dogs sat upon the faces of the men. Their clenched fists moved like eager weapons.

The allied two jostled the bartender's elbows, glaring at him with feverish eyes and forcing him toward the wall.

Suddenly Pete swore redly. The flash of action gleamed from his eyes. He threw back his arm and aimed a tremendous, lightning-like blow at Jimmie's face. His foot swung a step forward and the weight of his body was behind his fist. Jimmie ducked his head, Bowery-like, with the quickness of a cat. The fierce, answering blows of him and his ally crushed on Pete's bowed head.

The quiet stranger vanished.

The arms of the combatants whirled in the air like flails. The faces of the men, at first flushed to flame-colored anger, now began to fade to the pallor of warriors in the blood and heat of a battle. Their lips curled back and stretched tightly over the gums in ghoul-like grins. Through their white, gripped teeth struggled hoarse whisperings of oaths. Their eyes glittered with murderous fire.

Each head was huddled between its owner's shoulders, and arms were swinging with marvelous rapidity. Feet scraped to and fro with a loud scratching sound upon the sanded floor. Blows left crimson blotches upon pale skin. The curses of the first quarter minute of the fight died away. The breaths of the fighters came wheezingly from their lips and the three chests were straining and heaving. Pete at intervals gave vent to low, labored hisses, that sounded like a desire to kill. Jimmie's ally gibbered at times like a wounded maniac. Jimmie was silent, fighting with the face of a sacrificial priest. The rage of fear shone in all their eyes and their blood-colored fists swirled.

At a tottering moment a blow from Pete's hand struck the ally and he crashed to the floor. He wriggled instantly to his feet and grasping the quiet stranger's beer glass from the bar, hurled it at Pete's head.

High on the wall it burst like a bomb, shivering fragments flying in all directions. Then missiles came to every man's hand. The place had heretofore appeared free of things to throw, but suddenly glass and bottles went singing through the air. They were thrown point blank at bobbing heads. The pyramid of shimmering glasses, that had never been disturbed, changed to cascades as heavy bottles were flung into them. Mirrors splintered to nothing.

The three frothing creatures on the floor buried themselves in a frenzy for blood. There followed in the wake of missiles and fists some unknown prayers, perhaps for death.

The quiet stranger had sprawled very pyrotechnically out on the sidewalk. A laugh ran up and down the avenue for the half of a block.

"Dey've trowed a bloke inteh deh street."

People heard the sound of breaking glass and shuffling feet within the saloon and came running. A small group, bending down to look under the bamboo doors, watching the fall of glass, and three pairs of violent legs, changed in a moment to a crowd.

A policeman came charging down the sidewalk and bounced through the doors into the saloon. The crowd bended and surged in absorbing anxiety to see.

Jimmie caught first sight of the on-coming interruption. On his feet he had the same regard for a policeman that, when on his truck, he had for a fire engine. He howled and ran for the side door.

The officer made a terrific advance, club in hand. One comprehensive sweep of the long night stick threw the ally to the floor and forced Pete to a corner. With his disengaged hand he made a furious effort at Jimmie's coat-tails. Then he regained his balance and paused.

"Well, well, you are a pair of pictures. What in hell yeh been up to?"

Jimmie, with his face drenched in blood, escaped up a side street, pursued a short distance by some of the more law-loving, or excited individuals of the crowd.

Later, from a corner safely dark, he saw the policeman, the ally and the bartender emerge from the saloon. Pete locked the doors and then followed up the avenue in the rear of the crowd-encompassed policeman and his charge.

On first thoughts Jimmie, with his heart throbbing at battle heat, started to go desperately to the rescue of his friend, but he halted.

"Ah, what deh hell?" he demanded of himself.

~~ XII ~~

IN A HALL OF irregular shape sat Pete and Maggie drinking beer. A submissive orchestra dictated to by a spectacled man with frowsy hair and a dress suit, industriously followed the bobs of his head and the waves of his baton. A ballad singer, in a dress of flaming scarlet, sang in the inevitable voice of brass. When she vanished, men seated at the tables near the front applauded loudly, pounding the polished wood with their beer glasses. She returned attired in less gown, and sang again. She received another enthusiastic encore. She reappeared in still less gown and danced. The deafening rumble of glasses and clapping of hands that followed her exit indicated an overwhelming desire to have her come on for the fourth time, but the curiosity of the audience was not gratified.

Maggie was pale. From her eyes had been plucked all look of self-reliance. She leaned with a dependent air toward her companion. She was timid, as if fearing his anger or displeasure. She seemed to beseech tenderness of him.

Pete's air of distinguished valor had grown upon him until it threatened stupendous dimensions. He was infinitely gracious to the girl. It was apparent to her that his condescension was a marvel.

He could appear to strut even while sitting still and he showed that he was a lion of lordly characteristics by the air with which he spat.

With Maggie gazing at him wonderingly, he took pride in commanding the waiters who were, however, indifferent or deaf.

"Hi, you, git a russle on yehs! What deh hell yeh's lookin' at? Two more beehs, d'yeh hear?"

He leaned back and critically regarded the person of a girl with a straw-colored wig who upon the stage was flinging her heels in somewhat awkward imitation of a well-known danseuse.

At times Maggie told Pete long confidential tales of her former home life, dwelling upon the escapades of the other members of the family and the difficulties she had to combat in order to obtain a degree of comfort. He responded in tones of philanthropy. He pressed her arm with an air of reassuring proprietorship.

"Dey was damn jays," he said, denouncing the mother and brother.

The sound of the music which, by the efforts of the frowsy-headed leader, drifted to her ears through the smoke-filled atmosphere, made the girl dream. She thought of her former Rum Alley environment and turned to regard Pete's strong protecting fists. She thought of the collar and cuff manufactory and the eternal moan of the proprietor: "What een hell do you sink I pie fife dolla a week for?

Play? No, py damn." She contemplated Pete's man-subduing eyes and noted that wealth and prosperity was indicated by his clothes. She imagined a future, rose-tinted, because of its distance from all that she previously had experienced.

As to the present she perceived only vague reasons to be miserable. Her life was Pete's and she considered him worthy of the charge. She would be disturbed by no particular apprehensions, so long as Pete adored her as he now said he did. She did not feel like a bad woman. To her knowledge she had never seen any better.

At times men at other tables regarded the girl furtively. Pete, aware of it, nodded at her and grinned. He felt proud.

"Mag, yer a bloomin' good-looker," he remarked, studying her face through the haze. The men made Maggie fear, but she blushed at Pete's words as it became apparent to her that she was the apple of his eye.

Grey-headed men, wonderfully pathetic in their dissipation, stared at her through clouds. Smooth-cheeked boys, some of them with faces of stone and mouths of sin, not nearly so pathetic as the grey heads, tried to find the girl's eyes in the smoke wreaths. Maggie considered she was not what they thought her. She confined her glances to Pete and the stage.

The orchestra played negro melodies and a versatile drummer pounded, whacked, clattered and scratched on a dozen machines to make noise.

Those glances of the men, shot at Maggie from under half-closed lids, made her tremble. She thought them all to be worse men than Pete.

"Come, let's go," she said.

As they went out Maggie perceived two women seated at a table with some men. They were painted and their cheeks had lost their roundness. As she passed them the girl, with a shrinking movement, drew back her skirts.

～◎ XIII ◎～

Jimmie did not return home for a number of days after the fight with Pete in the saloon. When he did, he approached with extreme caution.

He found his mother raving. Maggie had not returned home. The parent continually wondered how her daughter could come to such a pass. She had never considered Maggie as a pearl dropped unstained into Rum Alley from Heaven, but she could not conceive how it was possible for her daughter to fall so low as to bring disgrace upon her family. She was terrific in denunciation of the girl's wickedness.

The fact that the neighbors talked of it, maddened her. When women came in, and in the course of their conversation casually asked, "Where's Maggie dese days?" the mother shook her fuzzy head at them and appalled them with curses. Cunning hints inviting confidence she rebuffed with violence.

"An' wid all deh bringin' up she had, how could she?" moaningly she asked of her son. "Wid all deh talkin' wid her I did an' deh t'ings I tol' her to remember? When a girl is bringed up deh way I bringed up Maggie, how kin she go teh deh devil?"

Jimmie was transfixed by these questions. He could not conceive how under the circumstances his mother's daughter and his sister could have been so wicked.

His mother took a drink from a squdgy* bottle that sat on the table. She continued her lament.

"She had a bad heart, dat girl did, Jimmie. She was wicked teh deh heart an' we never knowed it."

Jimmie nodded, admitting the fact.

"We lived in deh same house wid her an' I brought her up an' we never knowed how bad she was."

Jimmie nodded again.

---

*Short and stumpy; squashed.

"Wid a home like dis an' a mudder like me, she went teh deh bad," cried the mother, raising her eyes.

One day, Jimmie came home, sat down in a chair and began to wriggle about with a new and strange nervousness. At last he spoke shamefacedly.

"Well, look-a-here, dis t'ing queers us! See? We're queered! An' maybe it 'ud be better if I—well, I t'ink I kin look 'er up an'—maybe it 'ud be better if I fetched her home an—"

The mother started from her chair and broke forth into a storm of passionate anger.

"What! Let 'er come an' sleep under deh same roof wid her mudder agin! Oh, yes, I will, won't I? Sure? Shame on yehs, Jimmie Johnson, fer sayin' such a t'ing teh yer own mudder—teh yer own mudder! Little did I tink when yehs was a babby playin' about me feet dat ye'd grow up teh say sech a t'ing teh yer mudder—yer own mudder. I never taut—"

Sobs choked her and interrupted her reproaches.

"Dere ain't nottin teh raise sech hell about," said Jimmie. "I on'y says it 'ud be better if we keep dis t'ing dark, see? It queers us! See?"

His mother laughed a laugh that seemed to ring through the city and be echoed and re-echoed by countless other laughs. "Oh, yes, I will, won' I! Sure!"

"Well, yeh must take me fer a damn fool," said Jimmie, indignant at his mother for mocking him. "I didn't say we'd make 'er inteh a little tin angel, ner nottin, but deh way it is now she can queer us! Don' che see?"

"Aye, she'll git tired of deh life atter a while an' den she'll wanna be a-comin' home, won' she, deh beast! I'll let 'er in den, won' I?"

"Well, I didn' mean none of dis prod'gal bus'ness anyway," explained Jimmie.

"It wasn't no prod'gal dauter, yeh damn fool," said the mother. "It was prod'gal son, anyhow."

"I know dat," said Jimmie.

For a time they sat in silence. The mother's eyes gloated on a scene her imagination could call before her. Her lips were set in a vindictive smile.

"Aye, she'll cry, won' she, an' carry on, an' tell how Pete, or some odder feller, beats 'er an' she'll say she's sorry an' all dat an' she ain't happy, she ain't, an' she wants to come home agin, she does."

With grim humor, the mother imitated the possible wailing notes of the daughter's voice.

"Den I'll take 'er in, won't I, deh beast She kin cry 'er two eyes out on deh stones of deh street before I'll dirty deh place wid her. She abused an' ill-treated her own mudder—her own mudder what loved her an' she'll never git anodder chance dis side of hell."

Jimmie thought he had a great idea of women's frailty, but he could not understand why any of his kin should be victims.

"Damn her," he fervidly said.

Again he wondered vaguely if some of the women of his acquaintance had brothers. Nevertheless, his mind did not for an instant confuse himself with those brothers nor his sister with theirs. After the mother had, with great difficulty, suppressed the neighbors, she went among them and proclaimed her grief. "May Gawd forgive dat girl," was her continual cry. To attentive ears she recited the whole length and breadth of her woes.

"I bringed 'er up deh way a dauter oughta be bringed up an' dis is how she served me! She went teh deh devil deh first chance she got! May Gawd forgive her."

When arrested for drunkenness she used the story of her daughter's downfall with telling effect upon the police justices. Finally one of them said to her, peering down over his spectacles: "Mary, the records of this and other courts show that you are the mother of forty-two daughters who have been ruined. The case is unparalleled in the annals of this court, and this court thinks—"

The mother went through life shedding large tears of sorrow. Her red face was a picture of agony.

Of course Jimmie publicly damned his sister that he might appear on a higher social plane. But, arguing with himself, stumbling about in ways that he knew not, he, once, almost came to a conclusion that his sister would have been more firmly good had she better known why. However, he felt that he could not hold such a view. He threw it hastily aside.

~~℘~~ XIV ~~℘~~

IN A HILARIOUS HALL there were twenty-eight tables and twenty-eight women and a crowd of smoking men. Valiant noise was made on a stage at the end of the hall by an orchestra composed of men who looked as if they had just happened in. Soiled waiters ran to and fro, swooping down like hawks on the unwary in the throng; clattering along the aisles with trays covered with glasses; stumbling over women's skirts and charging two prices for everything but beer, all with a swiftness that blurred the view of the cocoanut palms and dusty monstrosities painted upon the walls of the room. A bouncer, with an immense load of business upon his hands, plunged about in the crowd, dragging bashful strangers to prominent chairs, ordering waiters here and there and quarreling furiously with men who wanted to sing with the orchestra.

The usual smoke cloud was present, but so dense that heads and arms seemed entangled in it. The rumble of conversation was replaced by a roar. Plenteous oaths heaved through the air. The room rang with the shrill voices of women bubbling o'er with drink-laughter. The chief element in the music of the orchestra was speed. The musicians played in intent fury. A woman was singing and smiling upon the stage, but no one took notice of her. The rate at which the piano, cornet and violins were going, seemed to impart wildness to the half-drunken crowd. Beer glasses were emptied at a gulp and conversation became a rapid chatter. The smoke eddied and swirled like a shadowy river hurrying toward some unseen falls. Pete and Maggie entered the hall and took chairs at a table near the door. The woman who was seated there made an attempt to occupy Pete's attention and, failing, went away.

Three weeks had passed since the girl had left home. The air of spaniel-like dependence had been magnified and showed its direct effect in the peculiar off-handedness and ease of Pete's ways toward her.[13]

53

She followed Pete's eyes with hers, anticipating with smiles gracious looks from him.

A woman of brilliance and audacity, accompanied by a mere boy, came into the place and took seats near them.

At once Pete sprang to his feet, his face beaming with glad surprise.

"By Gawd, there's Nellie," he cried.

He went over to the table and held out an eager hand to the woman.

"Why, hello, Pete, my boy, how are you," said she, giving him her fingers.

Maggie took instant note of the woman. She perceived that her black dress fitted her to perfection. Her linen collar and cuffs were spotless. Tan gloves were stretched over her well-shaped hands. A hat of a prevailing fashion perched jauntily upon her dark hair. She wore no jewelry and was painted with no apparent paint. She looked clear-eyed through the stares of the men.

"Sit down, and call your lady-friend over," she said cordially to Pete. At his beckoning Maggie came and sat between Pete and the mere boy.

"I thought yeh were gone away fer good," began Pete, at once. "When did yeh git back? How did dat Buff'lo bus'ness turn out?"

The woman shrugged her shoulders. "Well, he didn't have as many stamps* as he tried to make out, so I shook him, that's all."

"Well, I'm glad teh see yehs back in deh city," said Pete, with awkward gallantry.

He and the woman entered into a long conversation, exchanging reminiscences of days together. Maggie sat still, unable to formulate an intelligent sentence upon the conversation and painfully aware of it.

She saw Pete's eyes sparkle as he gazed upon the handsome stranger. He listened smilingly to all she said. The woman was familiar with all his affairs, asked him about mutual friends, and knew the amount of his salary.

---

*Slang for money, bank notes.

She paid no attention to Maggie, looking toward her once or twice and apparently seeing the wall beyond.

The mere boy was sulky. In the beginning he had welcomed with acclamations the additions.

"Let's all have a drink! What'll you take, Nell? And you, Miss what's-your-name. Have a drink, Mr.____, you, I mean."

He had shown a sprightly desire to do the talking for the company and tell all about his family. In a loud voice he declaimed on various topics. He assumed a patronizing air toward Pete. As Maggie was silent, he paid no attention to her. He made a great show of lavishing wealth upon the woman of brilliance and audacity.

"Do keep still, Freddie! You gibber like an ape, dear," said the woman to him. She turned away and devoted her attention to Pete.

"We'll have many a good time together again, eh?"

"Sure, Mike," said Pete, enthusiastic at once.

"Say," whispered she, leaning forward, "let's go over to Billie's and have a heluva time."

"Well, it's dis way! See?" said Pete. "I got dis lady frien' here."

"Oh, t'hell with her," argued the woman.

Pete appeared disturbed.

"All right," said she, nodding her head at him. "All right for you! We'll see the next time you ask me to go anywheres with you."

Pete squirmed.

"Say," he said, beseechingly, "come wid me a minit an' I'll tell yer why."

The woman waved her hand.

"Oh, that's all right, you needn't explain, you know. You wouldn't come merely because you wouldn't come, that's all there is of it."

To Pete's visible distress she turned to the mere boy, bringing him speedily from a terrific rage. He had been debating whether it would be the part of a man to pick a quarrel with Pete, or would he be justified in striking him savagely with his beer glass without warning. But he recovered himself when the woman turned to renew her smilings. He beamed upon her with an expression that was somewhat tipsy and inexpressibly tender.

"Say, shake that Bowery jay," requested he, in a loud whisper.

"Freddie, you are so droll," she replied.

Pete reached forward and touched the woman on the arm.

"Come out a minit while I tells yeh why I can't go wid yer. Yer doin' me dirt, Nell! I never taut ye'd do me dirt, Nell. Come on, will yer?" He spoke in tones of injury.

"Why, I don't see why I should be interested in your explanations," said the woman, with a coldness that seemed to reduce Pete to a pulp.

His eyes pleaded with her. "Come out a minit while I tells yeh,"

The woman nodded slightly at Maggie and the mere boy, "Scuse me."

The mere boy interrupted his loving smile and turned a shriveling glare upon Pete. His boyish countenance flushed and he spoke, in a whine, to the woman:

"Oh, I say, Nellie, this ain't a square deal, you know. You aren't goin' to leave me and go off with that duffer, are you? I should think—"

"Why, you dear boy, of course I'm not," cried the woman, affectionately. She bended over and whispered in his ear. He smiled again and settled in his chair as if resolved to wait patiently.

As the woman walked down between the rows of tables, Pete was at her shoulder talking earnestly, apparently in explanation. The woman waved her hands with studied airs of indifference. The doors swung behind them, leaving Maggie and the mere boy seated at the table.

Maggie was dazed. She could dimly perceive that something stupendous had happened. She wondered why Pete saw fit to remonstrate with the woman, pleading for forgiveness with his eyes. She thought she noted an air of submission about her leonine* Pete. She was astounded.

The mere boy occupied himself with cock-tails and a cigar. He was tranquilly silent for half an hour. Then he bestirred himself and spoke.

"Well," he said, sighing, "I knew this was the way it would be." There was another stillness. The mere boy seemed to be musing.

"She was pulling m'leg. That's the whole amount of it," he said,

---

*Having the qualities of a lion.

suddenly. "It's a bloomin' shame the way that girl does. Why, I've spent over two dollars in drinks to-night. And she goes off with that plug-ugly who looks as if he had been hit in the face with a coin-dye.* I call it rocky treatment for a fellah like me. Here, waiter, bring me a cock-tail and make it damned strong."

Maggie made no reply. She was watching the doors. "It's a mean piece of business," complained the mere boy. He explained to her how amazing it was that anybody should treat him in such a manner. "But I'll get square with her, you bet. She won't get far ahead of yours truly, you know," he added, winking. "I'll tell her plainly that it was bloomin' mean business. And she won't come it over me with any of her 'now-Freddie-dears.' She thinks my name is Freddie, you know, but of course it ain't. I always tell these people some name like that, because if they got onto your right name they might use it sometime. Understand? Oh, they don't fool me much."

Maggie was paying no attention, being intent upon the doors. The mere boy relapsed into a period of gloom, during which he exterminated a number of cock-tails with a determined air, as if replying defiantly to fate. He occasionally broke forth into sentences composed of invectives joined together in a long string.

The girl was still staring at the doors. After a time the mere boy began to see cobwebs just in front of his nose. He spurred himself into being agreeable and insisted upon her having a charlotte-russe† and a glass of beer.

"They's gone," he remarked, "they's gone." He looked at her through the smoke wreaths. "Shay, lil' girl, we mightish well make bes' of it. You ain't such bad lookin' girl, y'know. Not half bad. Can't come up to Nell, though. No, can't do it! Well, I should shay not! Nell fine-lookin' girl! F—i—n—ine. You look damn bad longsider her, but by y'self ain't so bad. Have to do anyhow. Nell gone. O'ny you left. Not half bad, though."

Maggie stood up.

"I'm going home," she said.

The mere boy started.

---

*Heavy piece of machinery used for stamping out coins.
†Frothy dessert consisting of custard and sponge cake.

"Eh? What? Home," he cried, struck with amazement. "I beg pardon, did hear say home?"

"I'm going home," she repeated.

"Great Gawd, what hava struck," demanded the mere boy of himself, stupefied.

In a semi-comatose state he conducted her on board an uptown car,* ostentatiously paid her fare, leered kindly at her through the rear window and fell off the steps.

〜❧ XV ❧〜

A FORLORN WOMAN WENT along a lighted avenue. The street was filled with people desperately bound on missions. An endless crowd darted at the elevated station stairs and the horse cars were thronged with owners of bundles.

The pace of the forlorn woman was slow. She was apparently searching for some one. She loitered near the doors of saloons and watched men emerge from them. She scanned furtively the faces in the rushing stream of pedestrians. Hurrying men, bent on catching some boat or train, jostled her elbows, failing to notice her, their thoughts fixed on distant dinners.

The forlorn woman had a peculiar face. Her smile was no smile. But when in repose her features had a shadowy look that was like a sardonic grin, as if some one had sketched with cruel forefinger indelible lines about her mouth.

Jimmie came strolling up the avenue. The woman encountered him with an aggrieved air.

"Oh, Jimmie, I've been lookin' all over fer yehs—," she began.

Jimmie made an impatient gesture and quickened his pace.

"Ah, don't bodder me! Good Gawd!" he said, with the savageness of a man whose life is pestered.

---

*Horse-drawn omnibus.

The woman followed him along the sidewalk in somewhat the manner of a suppliant.

"But, Jimmie," she said, "yehs told me ye'd—"

Jimmie turned upon her fiercely as if resolved to make a last stand for comfort and peace.

"Say, fer Gawd's sake, Hattie, don' foller me from one end of deh city teh deh odder. Let up, will yehs! Give me a minute's res', can't yehs? Yehs makes me tired, allus taggin' me. See? Ain' yehs got no sense? Do yehs want people teh get onto me? Go chase yerself, fer Gawd's sake."

The woman stepped closer and laid her fingers on his arm. "But, look-a here—"

Jimmie snarled. "Oh, go teh hell."

He darted into the front door of a convenient saloon and a moment later came out into the shadows that surrounded the side door. On the brilliantly lighted avenue he perceived the forlorn woman dodging about like a scout. Jimmie laughed with an air of relief and went away.

When he arrived home he found his mother clamoring. Maggie had returned. She stood shivering beneath the torrent of her mother's wrath.

"Well, I'm damned," said Jimmie in greeting.

His mother, tottering about the room, pointed a quivering forefinger.

"Lookut her, Jimmie, lookut her. Dere's yer sister, boy. Dere's yer sister. Lookut her! Lookut her!"

She screamed in scoffing laughter.

The girl stood in the middle of the room. She edged about as if unable to find a place on the floor to put her feet.

"Ha, ha, ha," bellowed the mother. "Dere she stands! Ain' she purty? Lookut her! Ain' she sweet, deh beast? Lookut her! Ha, ha, lookut her!"

She lurched forward and put her red and seamed hands upon her daughter's face. She bent down and peered keenly up into the eyes of the girl.

"Oh, she's jes' dessame as she ever was, ain' she? She's her mudder's purty darlin' yit, ain' she? Lookut her, Jimmie! Come here, fer Gawd's sake, and lookut her."

The loud, tremendous sneering of the mother brought the denizens of the Rum Alley tenement to their doors. Women came in the hallways. Children scurried to and fro.

"What's up? Dat Johnson party on anudder tear?"

"Naw! Young Mag's come home!"

"Deh hell yeh say?"

Through the open doors curious eyes stared in at Maggie. Children ventured into the room and ogled her, as if they formed the front row at a theatre. Women, without, bended toward each other and whispered, nodding their heads with airs of profound philosophy. A baby, overcome with curiosity concerning this object at which all were looking, sidled forward and touched her dress, cautiously, as if investigating a red-hot stove. Its mother's voice rang out like a warning trumpet. She rushed forward and grabbed her child, casting a terrible look of indignation at the girl.

Maggie's mother paced to and fro, addressing the doorful of eyes, expounding like a glib showman at a museum. Her voice rang through the building.

"Dere she stands," she cried, wheeling suddenly and pointing with dramatic finger. "Dere she stands! Lookut her! Ain' she a dindy? An' she was so good as to come home teh her mudder, she was! Ain' she a beaut'? Ain' she a dindy? Fer Gawd's sake!"

The jeering cries ended in another burst of shrill laughter.

The girl seemed to awaken. "Jimmie—"

He drew hastily back from her.

"Well, now, yer a hell of a t'ing, ain' yeh?" he said, his lips curling in scorn. Radiant virtue sat upon his brow and his repelling hands expressed horror of contamination.

Maggie turned and went.

The crowd at the door fell back precipitately. A baby falling down in front of the door, wrenched a scream like a wounded animal from its mother. Another woman sprang forward and picked it up, with a chivalrous air, as if rescuing a human being from an oncoming express train.

As the girl passed down through the hall, she went before open doors framing more eyes strangely microscopic, and sending broad beams of inquisitive light into the darkness of her path. On the second floor she met the gnarled old woman who possessed the music box.

"So," she cried, " 'ere yehs are back again, are yehs? An' dey've kicked yehs out? Well, come in an' stay wid me teh-night. I ain' got no moral standin'."

From above came an unceasing babble of tongues, over all of which rang the mother's derisive laughter.

～ XVI ～

PETE DID NOT CONSIDER that he had ruined Maggie. If he had thought that her soul could never smile again, he would have believed the mother and brother, who were pyrotechnic over the affair, to be responsible for it.

Besides, in his world, souls did not insist upon being able to smile. "What deh hell?"

He felt a trifle entangled. It distressed him. Revelations and scenes might bring upon him the wrath of the owner of the saloon, who insisted upon respectability of an advanced type.

"What deh hell do dey wanna raise such a smoke about it fer?" demanded he of himself, disgusted with the attitude of the family. He saw no necessity for anyone's losing their equilibrium merely because their sister or their daughter had stayed away from home.

Searching about in his mind for possible reasons for their conduct, he came upon the conclusion that Maggie's motives were correct, but that the two others wished to snare him. He felt pursued.

The woman of brilliance and audacity whom he had met in the hilarious hall showed a disposition to ridicule him.

"A little pale thing with no spirit," she said. "Did you note the expression of her eyes? There was something in them about pumpkin pie and virtue. That is a peculiar way the left corner of her mouth has of twitching, isn't it? Dear, dear, my cloud-compelling Pete, what are you coming to?"

Pete asserted at once that he never was very much interested in the girl. The woman interrupted him, laughing.

"Oh, it's not of the slightest consequence to me, my dear young man. You needn't draw maps for my benefit. Why should I be concerned about it?"

But Pete continued with his explanations. If he was laughed at for his tastes in women, he felt obliged to say that they were only temporary or indifferent ones.

The morning after Maggie had departed from home, Pete stood behind the bar. He was immaculate in white jacket and apron and his hair was plastered over his brow with infinite correctness. No customers were in the place. Pete was twisting his napkined fist slowly in a beer glass, softly whistling to himself and occasionally holding the object of his attention between his eyes and a few weak beams of sunlight that had found their way over the thick screens and into the shaded room.

With lingering thoughts of the woman of brilliance and audacity, the bartender raised his head and stared through the varying cracks between the swaying bamboo doors. Suddenly the whistling pucker faded from his lips. He saw Maggie walking slowly past. He gave a great start, fearing for the previously-mentioned eminent respectability of the place.

He threw a swift, nervous glance about him, all at once feeling guilty. No one was in the room.

He went hastily over to the side door. Opening it and looking out, he perceived Maggie standing, as if undecided, on the corner. She was searching the place with her eyes.

As she turned her face toward him Pete beckoned to her hurriedly, intent upon returning with speed to a position behind the bar and to the atmosphere of respectability upon which the proprietor insisted.

Maggie came to him, the anxious look disappearing from her face and a smile wreathing her lips.

"Oh, Pete—," she began brightly.

The bartender made a violent gesture of impatience.

"Oh, my Gawd," cried he, vehemently. "What deh hell do yeh wanna hang aroun' here fer? Do yeh wanna git me inteh trouble?" he demanded with an air of injury.

Astonishment swept over the girl's features. "Why, Pete! yehs tol' me—"

Pete glanced profound irritation. His countenance reddened with the anger of a man whose respectability is being threatened.

"Say, yehs makes me tired. See? What deh hell deh yeh wanna tag aroun' atter me fer? Yeh'll git me inteh trouble wid deh ol' man an' dey'll be hell teh pay! If he sees a woman roun' here he'll go crazy an' I'll lose me job! See? Ain' yehs got no sense? Don' be allus bodderin' me. See? Yer brudder come in here an' raised hell an' deh ol' man hada put up fer it! An' now I'm done! See? I'm done."

The girl's eyes stared into his face. "Pete, don' yeh remem—"

"Oh, hell," interrupted Pete, anticipating.

The girl seemed to have a struggle with herself. She was apparently bewildered and could not find speech. Finally she asked in a low voice: "But where kin I go?"

The question exasperated Pete beyond the powers of endurance. It was a direct attempt to give him some responsibility in a matter that did not concern him. In his indignation he volunteered information.

"Oh, go teh hell," cried he. He slammed the door furiously and returned, with an air of relief, to his respectability.

Maggie went away.[14]

She wandered aimlessly for several blocks. She stopped once and asked aloud a question of herself: "Who?"

A man who was passing near her shoulder, humorously took the questioning word as intended for him.

"Eh? What? Who? Nobody! I didn't say anything," he laughingly said, and continued his way.

Soon the girl discovered that if she walked with such apparent aimlessness, some men looked at her with calculating eyes. She quickened her step, frightened. As a protection, she adopted a demeanor of intentness as if going somewhere.

After a time she left rattling avenues and passed between rows of houses with sternness and stolidity stamped upon their features. She hung her head for she felt their eyes grimly upon her.

Suddenly she came upon a stout gentleman in a silk hat and a chaste black coat, whose decorous row of buttons reached from his chin to his knees. The girl had heard of the Grace of God and she decided to approach this man.

His beaming, chubby face was a picture of benevolence and kind-heartedness. His eyes shone good-will.

But as the girl timidly accosted him, he gave a convulsive movement and saved his respectability by a vigorous sidestep. He did not risk it to save a soul. For how was he to know that there was a soul before him that needed saving?

✎ XVII ✎

UPON A WET EVENING, several months after the last chapter, two interminable rows of cars, pulled by slipping horses, jangled along a prominent side-street. A dozen cabs, with coat-enshrouded drivers, clattered to and fro. Electric lights, whirring softly, shed a blurred radiance. A flower dealer, his feet tapping impatiently, his nose and his wares glistening with rain-drops, stood behind an array of roses and chrysanthemums. Two or three theatres emptied a crowd upon the storm-swept pavements. Men pulled their hats over their eyebrows and raised their collars to their ears. Women shrugged impatient shoulders in their warm cloaks and stopped to arrange their skirts for a walk through the storm. People having been comparatively silent for two hours burst into a roar of conversation, their hearts still kindling from the glowings of the stage.

The pavements became tossing seas of umbrellas. Men stepped forth to hail cabs or cars, raising their fingers in varied forms of polite request or imperative demand. An endless procession wended toward elevated stations. An atmosphere of pleasure and prosperity seemed to hang over the throng, born, perhaps, of good clothes and of having just emerged from a place of forgetfulness.

In the mingled light and gloom of an adjacent park, a handful of wet wanderers, in attitudes of chronic dejection, was scattered among the benches.

A girl of the painted cohorts of the city went along the street. She threw changing glances at men who passed her, giving smiling invitations to men of rural or untaught pattern and usually seeming sedately unconscious of the men with a metropolitan seal upon their faces.

Crossing glittering avenues, she went into the throng emerging from the places of forgetfulness. She hurried forward through the crowd as if intent upon reaching a distant home, bending forward in her handsome cloak, daintily lifting her skirts and picking for her well-shod feet the dryer spots upon the pavements.

The restless doors of saloons, clashing to and fro, disclosed animated rows of men before bars and hurrying barkeepers.

A concert hall gave to the street faint sounds of swift, machine-like music, as if a group of phantom musicians were hastening.

A tall young man, smoking a cigarette with a sublime air, strolled near the girl. He had on evening dress, a moustache, a chrysanthemum, and a look of ennui, all of which he kept carefully under his eye. Seeing the girl walk on as if such a young man as he was not in existence, he looked back transfixed with interest. He stared glassily for a moment, but gave a slight convulsive start when he discerned that she was neither new, Parisian, nor theatrical.[15] He wheeled about hastily and turned his stare into the air, like a sailor with a search-light.

A stout gentleman, with pompous and philanthropic whiskers, went stolidly by, the broad of his back sneering at the girl.

A belated man in business clothes, and in haste to catch a car, bounced against her shoulder. "Hi, there, Mary, I beg your pardon! Brace up, old girl." He grasped her arm to steady her, and then was away running down the middle of the street.

The girl walked on out of the realm of restaurants and saloons. She passed more glittering avenues and went into darker blocks than those where the crowd travelled.

A young man in light overcoat and derby hat received a glance shot keenly from the eyes of the girl. He stopped and looked at her, thrusting his hands in his pockets and making a mocking smile curl his lips. "Come, now, old lady," he said, "you don't mean to tell me that you sized me up for a farmer?"

A laboring man marched along with bundles under his arms. To her remarks, he replied: "It's a fine evenin', ain't it?"

She smiled squarely into the face of a boy who was hurrying by with his hands buried in his overcoat, his blonde locks bobbing on his youthful temples, and a cheery smile of unconcern upon his lips. He turned his head and smiled back at her, waving his hands.

"Not this eve—some other eve!"

A drunken man, reeling in her pathway, began to roar at her. "I ain' ga no money, dammit," he shouted, in a dismal voice. He lurched on up the street, wailing to himself, "Dammit, I ain' ga no money. Damn ba' luck. Ain' ga no more money."

The girl went into gloomy districts near the river, where the tall black factories shut in the street and only occasional broad beams of light fell across the pavements from saloons. In front of one of these places, from whence came the sound of a violin vigorously scraped, the patter of feet on boards and the ring of loud laughter, there stood a man with blotched features.

"Ah, there," said the girl.

"I've got a date," said the man.

Further on in the darkness she met a ragged being with shifting, blood-shot eyes and grimey hands. "Ah, what deh hell? Tink I'm a millionaire?"

She went into the blackness of the final block. The shutters of the tall buildings were closed like grim lips. The structures seemed to have eyes that looked over her, beyond her, at other things. Afar off the lights of the avenues glittered as if from an impossible distance. Street car bells jingled with a sound of merriment.

When almost to the river the girl saw a great figure. On going forward she perceived it to be a huge fat man in torn and greasy garments. His grey hair straggled down over his forehead. His small, bleared eyes, sparkling from amidst great rolls of red fat, swept eagerly over the girl's upturned face. He laughed, his brown, disordered teeth gleaming under a grey, grizzled moustache from which beer-drops dripped. His whole body gently quivered and shook like that of a dead jelly fish. Chuckling and leering, he followed the girl of the crimson legions.

At their feet the river appeared a deathly black hue. Some hidden factory sent up a yellow glare, that lit for a moment the waters lapping oilily against timbers. The varied sounds of life, made joyous by distance and seeming unapproachableness, came faintly and died away to a silence.

~❧ XVIII ❧~

IN A PARTITIONED-OFF SECTION of a saloon sat a man with a half dozen women, gleefully laughing, hovering about him. The man had arrived at that stage of drunkenness where affection is felt for the universe.

"I'm good f'ler, girls," he said, convincingly. "I'm damn good f'ler. An'body treats me right, I allus trea's zem right! See?"

The women nodded their heads approvingly. "To be sure," they cried in hearty chorus. "You're the kind of a man we like, Pete. You're outa sight! What yeh goin' to buy this time, dear?"

"An'thin' yehs wants, damn it," said the man in an abandonment of good will. His countenance shone with the true spirit of benevolence. He was in the proper mode of missionaries. He would have fraternized with obscure Hottentots.* And above all, he was overwhelmed in tenderness for his friends, who were all illustrious.

"An'thing yehs wants, damn it," repeated he, waving his hands with beneficent recklessness. "I'm good f'ler, girls, an' if an'body treats me right I—here," called he through an open door to a waiter, "bring girls drinks, damn it. What 'ill yehs have, girls? An'thing yehs want, damn it!"

The waiter glanced in with the disgusted look of the man who serves intoxicants for the man who takes too much of them. He nodded his head shortly at the order from each individual, and went.

"Damn it," said the man, "we're havin' heluva time. I like you girls! Damn'd if I don't! Yer right sort! See?"

He spoke at length and with feeling, concerning the excellencies of his assembled friends.

"Don' try pull man's leg, but have a heluva time! Das right! Das way teh do! Now, if I sawght yehs tryin' work me fer drinks, wouldn' buy damn t'ing! But yer right sort, damn it! Yehs know how ter treat

---

*Nomadic people indigenous to southwestern Africa, particularly the Kalahari Desert.

67

a f 'ler, an' I stays by yehs 'til spen' las' cent! Das right! I'm good f 'ler an' I knows when an'body treats me right!"

Between the times of the arrival and departure of the waiter, the man discoursed to the women on the tender regard he felt for all living things. He laid stress upon the purity of his motives in all dealings with men in the world and spoke of the fervor of his friendship for those who were amiable. Tears welled slowly from his eyes. His voice quavered when he spoke to them.

Once when the waiter was about to depart with an empty tray, the man drew a coin from his pocket and held it forth.

"Here," said he, quite magnificently, "here's quar'."

The waiter kept his hands on his tray.

"I don' want yer money," he said.

The other put forth the coin with tearful insistence.

"Here, damn it," cried he, "tak't! Yer damn goo' f 'ler an' I wan' yehs tak't!"

"Come, come, now," said the waiter, with the sullen air of a man who is forced into giving advice. "Put yer mon in yer pocket! Yer loaded an' yehs on'y makes a damn fool of yerself."

As the latter passed out of the door the man turned pathetically to the women.

"He don' know I'm damn goo' f 'ler," cried he, dismally.

"Never you mind, Pete, dear," said a woman of brilliance and audacity, laying her hand with great affection upon his arm. "Never you mind, old boy! We'll stay by you, dear!"

"Das ri'," cried the man, his face lighting up at the soothing tones of the woman's voice. "Das ri', I'm damn goo' f 'ler an' w'en anyone trea's me ri', I treats zem ri'! Shee!"

"Sure!" cried the women. "And we're not goin' back on you, old man."

The man turned appealing eyes to the woman of brilliance and audacity. He felt that if he could be convicted of a contemptible action he would die.

"Shay, Nell, damn it, I allus trea's yehs shquare, didn' I? I allus been goo' f 'ler wi' yehs, ain't I, Nell?"

"Sure you have, Pete," assented the woman. She delivered an oration to her companions. "Yessir, that's a fact. Pete's a square fellah, he is. He never goes back on a friend. He's the right kind an' we stay by him, don't we, girls?"

"Sure," they exclaimed. Looking lovingly at him they raised their glasses and drank his health.

"Girlsh," said the man, beseechingly, "I allus trea's yehs ri', didn' I? I'm goo' f'ler, ain' I, girlsh?"

"Sure," again they chorused.

"Well," said he finally, "le's have nozzer drink, zen."

"That's right," hailed a woman, "that's right. Yer no bloomin' jay! Yer spends yer money like a man. Dat's right."

The man pounded the table with his quivering fists.

"Yessir," he cried, with deep earnestness, as if someone disputed him. "I'm damn goo' f'ler, an' w'en anyone trea's me ri', I allus trea's—le's have nozzer drink."

He began to beat the wood with his glass.

"Shay," howled he, growing suddenly impatient. As the waiter did not then come, the man swelled with wrath.

"Shay," howled he again.

The waiter appeared at the door.

"Bringsh drinksh," said the man.

The waiter disappeared with the orders.

"Zat f'ler dam fool," cried the man. "He insul' me! I'm ge'man! Can' stan' be insul'! I'm goin' lickim when comes!"

"No, no," cried the women, crowding about and trying to subdue him. "He's all right! He didn't mean anything! Let it go! He's a good fellah!"

"Din' he insul' me?" asked the man earnestly.

"No," said they. "Of course he didn't! He's all right!"

"Sure he didn' insul' me?" demanded the man, with deep anxiety in his voice.

"No, no! We know him! He's a good fellah. He didn't mean anything."

"Well, zen," said the man, resolutely, "I'm go' 'pol'gize!"

When the waiter came, the man struggled to the middle of the floor.

"Girlsh shed you insul' me! I shay damn lie! I 'pol'gize!"

"All right," said the waiter.

The man sat down. He felt a sleepy but strong desire to straighten things out and have a perfect understanding with everybody.

"Nell, I allus trea's yeh shquare, din I? Yeh likes me, don' yehs, Nell? I'm goo' f 'ler?"

"Sure," said the woman of brilliance and audacity.

"Yeh knows I'm stuck on yehs, don' yehs, Nell?"

"Sure," she repeated, carelessly.

Overwhelmed by a spasm of drunken adoration, he drew two or three bills from his pocket, and, with the trembling fingers of an offering priest, laid them on the table before the woman.

"Yehs knows, damn it, yehs kin have all got, 'cause I'm stuck on yehs, Nell, damn't, I—I'm stuck on yehs, Nell—buy drinksh—damn't—we're havin' heluva time—w'en anyone trea's me ri'—I—damn't, Nell—we're havin' heluva—time."

Shortly he went to sleep with his swollen face fallen forward on his chest.

The women drank and laughed, not heeding the slumbering man in the corner. Finally he lurched forward and fell groaning to the floor.

The women screamed in disgust and drew back their skirts.

"Come ahn," cried one, starting up angrily, "let's get out of here."

The woman of brilliance and audacity stayed behind, taking up the bills and stuffing them into a deep, irregularly-shaped pocket. A guttural snore from the recumbent man caused her to turn and look down at him.

She laughed. "What a damn fool," she said, and went.

The smoke from the lamps settled heavily down in the little compartment, obscuring the way out. The smell of oil, stifling in its intensity, pervaded the air. The wine from an overturned glass dripped softly down upon the blotches on the man's neck.

≈ XIX ≈

IN A ROOM A woman sat at a table eating like a fat monk in a picture.

A soiled, unshaven man pushed open the door and entered.

"Well," said he, "Mag's dead."

"What?" said the woman, her mouth filled with bread.

"Mag's dead," repeated the man.

"Deh hell she is," said the woman. She continued her meal. When she finished her coffee she began to weep.

"I kin remember when her two feet was no bigger dan yer tumb, and she weared worsted* boots," moaned she.

"Well, whata dat?" said the man.

"I kin remember when she weared worsted boots," she cried.

The neighbors began to gather in the hall, staring in at the weeping woman as if watching the contortions of a dying dog. A dozen women entered and lamented with her. Under their busy hands the rooms took on that appalling appearance of neatness and order with which death is greeted.

Suddenly the door opened and a woman in a black gown rushed in with outstretched arms. "Ah, poor Mary," she cried, and tenderly embraced the moaning one.

"Ah, what ter'ble affliction is dis," continued she. Her vocabulary was derived from mission churches. "Me poor Mary, how I feel fer yehs! Ah, what a ter'ble affliction is a disobed'ent chile."

Her good, motherly face was wet with tears. She trembled in eagerness to express her sympathy. The mourner sat with bowed head, rocking her body heavily to and fro, and crying out in a high, strained voice that sounded like a dirge on some forlorn pipe.

"I kin remember when she weared worsted boots an' her two feets was no bigger dan yer tumb an' she weared worsted boots, Miss Smith," she cried, raising her streaming eyes.

"Ah, me poor Mary," sobbed the woman in black. With low, coddling cries, she sank on her knees by the mourner's chair, and put her arms about her. The other women began to groan in different keys.

"Yer poor misguided chil' is gone now, Mary, an' let us hope its fer deh bes'. Yeh'll fergive her now, Mary, won't yehs, dear, all her disobed'ence? All her tankless behavior to her mudder an' all her badness? She's gone where her ter'ble sins will be judged."

The woman in black raised her face and paused. The inevitable sunlight came streaming in at the windows and shed a ghastly cheerfulness

---

*Smooth yarn spun from wool, similar to silk but not as fine.

upon the faded hues of the room. Two or three of the spectators were sniffling, and one was loudly weeping. The mourner arose and staggered into the other room. In a moment she emerged with a pair of faded baby shoes held in the hollow of her hand.

"I kin remember when she used to wear dem," cried she. The women burst anew into cries as if they had all been stabbed. The mourner turned to the soiled and unshaven man.

"Jimmie, boy, go git yer sister! Go git yer sister an' we'll put deh boots on her feets!"

"Dey won't fit her now, yeh damn fool," said the man.

"Go git yer sister, Jimmie," shrieked the woman, confronting him fiercely.

The man swore sullenly. He went over to a corner and slowly began to put on his coat. He took his hat and went out, with a dragging, reluctant step.

The woman in black came forward and again besought the mourner.

"Yeh'll fergive her, Mary! Yeh'll fergive yer bad, bad chil'! Her life was a curse an' her days were black an' yeh'll fergive yer bad girl? She's gone where her sins will be judged."

"She's gone where her sins will be judged,"[16] cried the other women, like a choir at a funeral.

"Deh Lord gives and deh Lord takes away," said the woman in black, raising her eyes to the sunbeams.

"Deh Lord gives and deh Lord takes away," responded the others.

"Yeh'll fergive her, Mary!" pleaded the woman in black. The mourner essayed to speak but her voice gave way. She shook her great shoulders frantically, in an agony of grief. Hot tears seemed to scald her quivering face. Finally her voice came and arose like a scream of pain.

"Oh, yes, I'll fergive her! I'll fergive her!"

GEORGE'S MOTHER

I

IN THE SWIRLING RAIN that came at dusk the broad avenue glistened with that deep bluish tint which is so widely condemned when it is put into pictures. There were long rows of shops, whose fronts shone with full, golden light. Here and there, from druggists' windows, or from the red street-lamps that indicated the positions of fire-alarm boxes, a flare of uncertain, wavering crimson was thrown upon the wet pavements.

The lights made shadows, in which the buildings loomed with a new and tremendous massiveness, like castles and fortresses. There were endless processions of people, mighty hosts, with umbrellas waving, banner-like, over them. Horse-cars, aglitter with new paint, rumbled in steady array between the pillars that supported the elevated railroad. The whole street resounded with the tinkle of bells, the roar of iron-shod wheels on the cobbles, the ceaseless trample of the hundreds of feet. Above all, too, could be heard the loud screams of the tiny newsboys, who scurried in all directions. Upon the corners, standing in from the dripping eaves, were many loungers, descended from the world that used to prostrate itself before pageantry.

A brown young man went along the avenue. He held a tin lunch-pail under his arm in a manner that was evidently uncomfortable. He was puffing at a corn-cob pipe. His shoulders had a self-reliant poise, and the hang of his arms and the raised veins of his hands showed him to be a man who worked with his muscles.

As he passed a street-corner a man in old clothes gave a shout of surprise, and rushing impetuously forward, grasped his hand.

"Hello, Kelcey, ol' boy," cried the man in old clothes. "How's th' boy, anyhow? Where in thunder yeh been fer th' last seventeen years? I'll be hanged if you ain't th' last man I ever expected t' see."

The brown youth put his pail to the ground and grinned. "Well, if it ain't ol' Charley Jones," he said, ecstatically shaking hands. "How are yeh, anyhow? Where yeh been keepin' yerself? I ain't seen yeh fer a year!"

"Well, I should say so! Why, th' last time I saw you was up in Handyville!"

"Sure! On Sunday, we ——"

"Sure! Out at Bill Sickles's place. Let's go get a drink!"

They made toward a little glass-fronted saloon that sat blinking jovially at the crowds. It engulfed them with a gleeful motion of its two widely smiling lips.

"What'll yeh take, Kelcey?"

"Oh, I guess I'll take a beer."

"Gimme little whiskey, John."

The two friends leaned against the bar and looked with enthusiasm upon each other.

"Well, well, I'm thunderin' glad t' see yeh," said Jones.

"Well, I guess," replied Kelcey. "Here's to yeh, ol' man."

"Let 'er go."

They lifted their glasses, glanced fervidly at each other, and drank.

"Yeh ain't changed much, on'y yeh've growed like th' devil," said Jones, reflectively, as he put down his glass. "I'd know yeh anywheres!"

"Certainly yeh would," said Kelcey. "An' I knew you, too, th' minute I saw yeh. Yer changed, though!"

"Yes," admitted Jones, with some complacency, "I s'pose I am." He regarded himself in the mirror that multiplied the bottles on the shelf back of the bar. He should have seen a grinning face with a rather pink nose. His derby was perched carelessly on the back part of his head. Two wisps of hair straggled down over his hollow temples. There was something very worldly and wise about him. Life did not seem to confuse him. Evidently he understood its complications. His hand thrust into his trousers' pocket, where he jingled keys, and his hat perched back on his head expressed a young man of vast knowledge. His extensive acquaintance with bartenders aided him materially in this habitual expression of wisdom.

Having finished he turned to the barkeeper. "John, has any of th' gang been in t'-night yet?"

"No—not yet," said the barkeeper. "Ol' Bleecker was aroun' this afternoon about four. He said if I seen any of th' boys t' tell 'em he'd be up t'-night if he could get away. I saw Connor an' that other fellah goin' down th' avenyeh about an hour ago. I guess they'll be back after awhile."

"This is th' hang-out fer a great gang," said Jones, turning to Kelcey. "They're a great crowd, I tell yeh. We own th' place when we get started. Come aroun' some night. Any night, almost. T'-night, b' jiminy. They'll almost all be here, an' I'd like t' interduce yeh. They're a great gang! Gre-e-at!"

"I'd like teh," said Kelcey.

"Well, come ahead, then," cried the other, cordially. "Yeh'd like t' know 'em. It's an outa sight crowd. Come aroun' t'-night!"

"I will if I can."

"Well, yeh ain't got anything t' do, have yeh?" demanded Jones. "Well, come along, then. Yeh might just as well spend yer time with a good crowd 'a fellahs. An' it's a great gang. Great! Gre-e-at!"

"Well, I must make fer home now, anyhow," said Kelcey. "It's late as blazes. What'll yeh take this time, ol' man?"

"Gimme little more whiskey, John!"

"Guess I'll take another beer!"

Jones emptied the whiskey into his large mouth and then put the glass upon the bar. "Been in th' city long?" he asked. "Um—well, three years is a good deal fer a slick man. Doin' well? Oh, well, nobody's doin' well these days." He looked down mournfully at his shabby clothes. "Father's dead, ain't 'ee? Yeh don't say so? Fell off a scaffoldin', didn't 'ee? I heard it somewheres. Mother's livin', of course? I thought she was. Fine ol' lady—fi-i-ne. Well, you're th' last of her boys. Was five of yeh onct, wasn't there? I knew four m'self. Yes, five! I thought so. An' all gone but you, hey? Well, you'll have t' brace up an' be a comfort t' th' ol' mother. Well, well, well, who would 'a thought that on'y you'd be left out 'a all that mob 'a tow-headed kids. Well, well, well, it's a queer world, ain't it?"

A contemplation of this thought made him sad. He sighed and moodily watched the other sip beer.

"Well, well, it's a queer world—a damn queer world."

"Yes," said Kelcey, "I'm th' on'y one left!" There was an accent of discomfort in his voice. He did not like this dwelling upon a sentiment that was connected with himself.

"How is th' ol' lady, anyhow?" continued Jones. "Th' last time I remember she was as spry as a little ol' cricket, an' was helpeltin' aroun' th' country lecturin' before W.C.T.U.'s* an' one thing an' another."

---

*The Woman's Christian Temperance Union, the most prominent prohibition league at the time.

"Oh, she's pretty well," said Kelcey.

"An' outa five boys you're th' on'y one she's got left? Well, well—have another drink before yeh go."

"Oh, I guess I've had enough."

A wounded expression came into Jones's eyes. "Oh, come on," he said.

"Well, I'll take another beer!"

"Gimme little more whiskey, John!"

When they had concluded this ceremony, Jones went with his friend to the door of the saloon. "Good-by, ol' man," he said, genially. His homely features shone with friendliness. "Come aroun', now, sure. T'-night! See? They're a great crowd. Gre-e-at!"

II

A MAN WITH A red, mottled face put forth his head from a window and cursed violently. He flung a bottle high across two backyards at a window of the opposite tenement. It broke against the bricks of the house and the fragments fell crackling upon the stones below. The man shook his fist.[1]

A bare-armed woman, making an array of clothes on a line in one of the yards, glanced casually up at the man and listened to his words. Her eyes followed his to the other tenement. From a distant window, a youth with a pipe, yelled some comments upon the poor aim. Two children, being in the proper yard, picked up the bits of broken glass and began to fondle them as new toys.

From the window at which the man raged came the sound of an old voice, singing. It quavered and trembled out into the air as if a sound-spirit had a broken wing.

> "Should I be car-reed tew th' skies
> O-on flow'ry be-eds of ee-ease,
> While others fought tew win th' prize
> An' sailed through blood-ee seas."

The man in the opposite window was greatly enraged. He continued to swear.

A little old woman was the owner of the voice. In a fourth-story room of the red and black tenement she was trudging on a journey. In her arms she bore pots and pans, and sometimes a broom and dust-pan. She wielded them like weapons. Their weight seemed to have bended her back and crooked her arms until she walked with difficulty. Often she plunged her hands into water at a sink. She splashed about, the dwindled muscles working to and fro under the loose skin of her arms. She came from the sink, steaming and bedraggled as if she had crossed a flooded river.

There was the flurry of a battle in this room. Through the clouded dust or steam one could see the thin figure dealing mighty blows. Always her way seemed beset. Her broom was continually poised, lance-wise, at dust demons. There came clashings and clangings as she strove with her tireless foes.

It was a picture of indomitable courage. And as she went on her way her voice was often raised in a long cry, a strange war-chant, a shout of battle and defiance, that rose and fell in harsh screams, and exasperated the ears of the man with the red, mottled face.

> "Should I be car-reed tew th' skies
> O-on flow'ry be-eds of ee-ease ———"

Finally she halted for a moment. Going to the window she sat down and mopped her face with her apron. It was a lull, a moment of respite. Still it could be seen that she even then was planning skirmishes, charges, campaigns. She gazed thoughtfully about the room and noted the strength and position of her enemies. She was very alert.

At last, she turned to the mantel. "Five o'clock," she murmured, scrutinizing a little, swaggering, nickel-plated clock.

She looked out at chimneys growing thickly on the roofs. A man at work on one seemed like a bee. In the intricate yards below, vine-like lines had strange leaves of cloth. To her ears there came the howl of the man with the red, mottled face. He was engaged in a furious altercation with the youth who had called attention to his poor aim. They were like animals in a jungle.

In the distance an enormous brewery[2] towered over the other buildings. Great gilt letters advertised a brand of beer. Thick smoke came from funnels and spread near it like vast and powerful wings. The structure seemed a great bird, flying. The letters of the sign made a chain of gold hanging from its neck. The little old woman looked at the brewery. It vaguely interested her, for a moment, as a stupendous affair, a machine of mighty strength.

Presently she sprang from her rest and began to buffet with her shrivelled arms. In a moment the battle was again in full swing. Terrific blows were given and received. There arose the clattering uproar of a new fight. The little intent warrior never hesitated nor faltered. She fought with a strong and relentless will. Beads and lines of perspiration stood upon her forehead.

Three blue plates were leaning in a row on the shelf back of the stove. The little old woman had seen it done somewhere. In front of them swaggered the round nickel-plated clock. Her son had stuck many cigarette pictures in the rim of a looking-glass that hung near. Occasional chromos* were tacked upon the yellowed walls of the room. There was one in a gilt frame. It was quite an affair, in reds and greens. They all seemed like trophies.

It began to grow dark. A mist came winding. Rain plashed softly upon the window-sill. A lamp had been lighted in the opposite tenement; the strong orange glare revealed the man with a red, mottled face. He was seated by a table, smoking and reflecting.

The little old woman looked at the clock again. "Quarter 'a six."

She had paused for a moment, but she now hurled herself fiercely at the stove that lurked in the gloom, red-eyed, like a dragon. It hissed, and there was renewed clangor of blows. The little old woman dashed to and fro.

---

*Short for "chromolithograph"; cheap colored pictures, distributed free of charge by newspapers and churches, that usually depict patriotic or religious themes.

III

As it grew toward seven o'clock the little old woman became nervous. She often would drop into a chair and sit staring at the little clock.

"I wonder why he don't come," she continually repeated. There was a small, curious note of despair in her voice. As she sat thinking and staring at the clock the expressions of her face changed swiftly. All manner of emotions flickered in her eyes and about her lips. She was evidently perceiving in her imagination the journey of a loved person. She dreamed for him mishaps and obstacles. Something tremendous and irritating was hindering him from coming to her.

She had lighted an oil-lamp. It flooded the room with vivid yellow glare. The table, in its oil-cloth covering, had previously appeared like a bit of bare, brown desert. It now was a white garden, growing the fruits of her labor.

"Seven o'clock," she murmured, finally. She was aghast.

Then suddenly she heard a step upon the stair. She sprang up and began to bustle about the room. The little fearful emotions passed at once from her face. She seemed now to be ready to scold.

Young Kelcey entered the room. He gave a sigh of relief, and dropped his pail in a corner. He was evidently greatly wearied by a hard day of toil.

The little old woman hobbled over to him and raised her wrinkled lips. She seemed on the verge of tears and an outburst of reproaches.

"Hello!" he cried, in a voice of cheer. "Been gettin' anxious?"

"Yes," she said, hovering about him. "Where yeh been, George? What made yeh so late? I've been waitin' th' longest while. Don't throw your coat down there. Hang it up behind th' door."

The son put his coat on the proper hook, and then went to splatter water in a tin wash-basin at the sink.

"Well, yeh see, I met Jones—you remember Jones? Ol'

81

Handyville fellah. An' we had t' stop an' talk over ol' times. Jones is quite a boy."

The little old woman's mouth set in a sudden straight line. "Oh, that Jones," she said. "I don't like him."

The youth interrupted a flurry of white towel to give a glance of irritation. "Well, now, what's th' use of talkin' that way?" he said to her. "What do yeh know 'bout 'im? Ever spoke to 'im in yer life?"

"Well, I don't know as I ever did since he grew up," replied the little old woman. "But I know he ain't th' kind 'a man I'd like t' have you go around with. He ain't a good man. I'm sure he ain't. He drinks."

Her son began to laugh. "Th' dickens he does?" He seemed amazed, but not shocked at this information.

She nodded her head with the air of one who discloses a dreadful thing. "I'm sure of it! Once I saw 'im comin' outa Simpson's Hotel, up in Handyville, an' he could hardly walk. He drinks! I'm sure he drinks!"

"Holy smoke!" said Kelcey.

They sat down at the table and began to wreck the little white garden. The youth leaned back in his chair, in the manner of a man who is paying for things. His mother bended alertly forward, apparently watching each mouthful. She perched on the edge of her chair, ready to spring to her feet and run to the closet or the stove for anything that he might need. She was as anxious as a young mother with a babe. In the careless and comfortable attitude of the son there was denoted a great deal of dignity.

"Yeh ain't eatin' much t'-night, George?"

"Well, I ain't very hungry, t' tell th' truth."

"Don't yeh like yer supper, dear? Yeh must eat somethin', chile. Yeh mustn't go without."

"Well, I'm eatin' somethin', ain't I?"

He wandered aimlessly through the meal. She sat over behind the little blackened coffee-pot and gazed affectionately upon him.

After a time she began to grow agitated. Her worn fingers were gripped. It could be seen that a great thought was within her. She was about to venture something. She had arrived at a supreme moment. "George," she said, suddenly, "come t' prayer-meetin' with me t'-night."

The young man dropped his fork. "Say, you must be crazy," he said, in amazement.

"Yes, dear," she continued, rapidly, in a small pleading voice, "I'd like t' have yeh go with me onct in a while. Yeh never go with me any more, dear, an' I'd like t' have yeh go. Yeh ain't been anywheres at all with me in th' longest while."

"Well," he said, "well, but what th' blazes ———"

"Ah, come on," said the little old woman. She went to him and put her arms about his neck. She began to coax him with caresses.

The young man grinned. "Thunderation!" he said, "what would I do at a prayer-meetin'?"

The mother considered him to be consenting. She did a little antique caper.

"Well, yeh can come an' take care 'a yer mother," she cried, gleefully. "It's such a long walk every Thursday night alone, an' don't yeh s'pose that when I have such a big, fine, strappin' boy, I want 'im t' beau me aroun' some? Ah, I knew ye'd come."

He smiled for a moment, indulgent of her humor. But presently his face turned a shade of discomfort. "But—" he began, protesting.

"Ah, come on," she continually repeated.

He began to be vexed. He frowned into the air. A vision came to him of dreary blackness arranged in solemn rows. A mere dream of it was depressing.[3]

"But—" he said again. He was obliged to make great search for an argument. Finally he concluded, "But what th' blazes would I do at prayer-meetin'?"

In his ears was the sound of a hymn, made by people who tilted their heads at a prescribed angle of devotion. It would be too apparent that they were all better than he. When he entered they would turn their heads and regard him with suspicion. This would be an enormous aggravation, since he was certain that he was as good as they.

"Well, now, y' see," he said, quite gently, "I don't wanta go, an' it wouldn't do me no good t' go if I didn't wanta go."

His mother's face swiftly changed. She breathed a huge sigh, the counterpart of ones he had heard upon like occasions. She put a tiny black bonnet on her head, and wrapped her figure in an old shawl.

She cast a martyr-like glance upon her son and went mournfully away. She resembled a limited funeral procession.

The young man writhed under it to an extent. He kicked moodily at a table-leg. When the sound of her footfalls died away he felt distinctly relieved.

~ IV ~

THAT NIGHT, WHEN KELCEY arrived at the little smiling saloon, he found his friend Jones standing before the bar engaged in a violent argument with a stout man.

"Oh, well," this latter person was saying, "you can make a lot of noise, Charlie, for a man that never says anything—let's have a drink!"

Jones was waving his arms and delivering splintering blows upon some distant theories. The stout man chuckled fatly and winked at the bartender.

The orator ceased for a moment to say, "Gimme little whiskey, John." At the same time he perceived young Kelcey. He sprang forward with a welcoming cry. "Hello, ol' man, didn't much think ye'd come." He led him to the stout man.

"Mr. Bleecker—my friend Mr. Kelcey!"

"How d'yeh do!"

"Mr. Kelcey, I'm happy to meet you, sir; have a drink."

They drew up in line and waited. The busy hands of the bartender made glasses clink. Mr. Bleecker, in a very polite way, broke the waiting silence.

"Never been here before, I believe, have you, Mr. Kelcey?"

The young man felt around for a high-bred reply. "Er—no—I've never had that—er—pleasure," he said.

After a time the strained and wary courtesy of their manners wore away. It became evident to Bleecker that his importance slightly dazzled the young man. He grew warmer. Obviously, the youth was one whose powers of perception were developed. Directly, then, he launched forth into a tale of by-gone days, when the world was better. He had known all the great men of that age. He reproduced his conversations with them. There were traces of pride and of mournfulness in his voice. He rejoiced at the glory of the world of dead spirits. He grieved at the youth and flippancy of the present one. He lived with his head in the clouds of the past, and he seemed obliged to talk of what he saw there.

Jones nudged Kelcey ecstatically in the ribs. "You've got th' ol' man started in great shape," he whispered.

Kelcey was proud that the prominent character of the place talked at him, glancing into his eyes for appreciation of fine points.

Presently they left the bar, and going into a little rear room, took seats about a table. A gas-jet with a colored globe shed a crimson radiance. The polished wood of walls and furniture gleamed with faint rose-colored reflections. Upon the floor sawdust was thickly sprinkled.

Two other men presently came. By the time Bleecker had told three tales of the grand past, Kelcey was slightly acquainted with everybody.

He admired Bleecker immensely. He developed a brotherly feeling for the others, who were all gentle-spoken. He began to feel that he was passing the happiest evening of his life. His companions were so jovial and good-natured; and everything they did was marked by such courtesy.

For a time the two men who had come in late did not presume to address him directly. They would say: "Jones, won't your friend have so and so, or so and so?" And Bleecker would begin his orations: "Now, Mr. Kelcey, don't you think ——"

Presently he began to believe that he was a most remarkably fine fellow, who had at last found his place in a crowd of most remarkably fine fellows.

Jones occasionally breathed comments into his ear.

"I tell yeh, Bleecker's an ol'-timer. He was a husky guy in his day, yeh can bet. He was one 'a th' best known men in N' York once. Yeh ought to hear him tell about ——"

Kelcey listened intently. He was profoundly interested in these intimate tales of men who had gleamed in the rays of old suns.

"That O'Connor's a damn fine fellah," interjected Jones once, referring to one of the others. "He's one 'a th' best fellahs I ever knowed. He's always on th' dead level. An' he's always jest th' same as yeh see 'im now—good-natured an' grinnin'."

Kelcey nodded. He could well believe it.

When he offered to buy drinks there came a loud volley of protests. "No, no, Mr. Kelcey," cried Bleecker, "no, no. Tonight you are our guest. Some other time ———"

"Here," said O'Connor, "it's my turn now."

He called and pounded for the bartender. He then sat with a coin in his hand warily eying the others. He was ready to frustrate them if they offered to pay.

After a time Jones began to develop qualities of great eloquence and wit. His companions laughed. "It's the whiskey talking now," said Bleecker.

He grew earnest and impassioned. He delivered speeches on various subjects. His lectures were to him very imposing. The force of his words thrilled him. Sometimes he was overcome.

The others agreed with him in all things. Bleecker grew almost tender, and considerately placed words here and there for his use. As Jones became fiercely energetic the others became more docile in agreeing. They soothed him with friendly interjections.

His mood changed directly. He began to sing popular airs with enthusiasm. He congratulated his companions upon being in his society. They were excited by his frenzy. They began to fraternize in jovial fashion. It was understood that they were true and tender spirits. They had come away from a grinding world filled with men who were harsh.

When one of them chose to divulge some place where the world had pierced him, there was a chorus of violent sympathy. They rejoiced at their temporary isolation and safety.

Once a man, completely drunk, stumbled along the floor of the saloon. He opened the door of the little room and made a show of entering. The men sprang instantly to their feet. They were ready to throttle any invader of their island. They elbowed each other in rivalry as to who should take upon himself the brunt of an encounter.

"Oh!" said the drunken individual, swaying on his legs and blinking at the party, "oh! thish private room?"

"That's what it is, Willie," said Jones. "An' you git outa here er we'll throw yeh out."

"That's what we will," said the others.

"Oh," said the drunken man. He blinked at them aggrievedly for an instant and then went away.

They sat down again. Kelcey felt, in a way, that he would have liked to display his fidelity to the others by whipping the intruder.

The bartender came often. "Gee, you fellahs er tanks," he said, in a jocular manner, as he gathered empty glasses and polished the table with his little towel.

Through the exertions of Jones the little room began to grow clamorous. The tobacco-smoke eddied about the forms of the men in ropes and wreaths. Near the ceiling there was a thick gray cloud.

Each man explained, in his way, that he was totally out of place in the before-mentioned world. They were possessed of various virtues which were unappreciated by those with whom they were commonly obliged to mingle; they were fitted for a tree-shaded land, where everything was peace. Now that five of them had congregated it gave them happiness to speak their inmost thoughts without fear of being misunderstood.

As he drank more beer Kelcey felt his breast expand with manly feeling. He knew that he was capable of sublime things. He wished that some day one of his present companions would come to him for relief. His mind pictured a little scene. In it he was magnificent in his friendship.

He looked upon the beaming faces and knew that if at that instant there should come a time for a great sacrifice he would blissfully make it. He would pass tranquilly into the unknown, or into bankruptcy, amid the ejaculations of his companions upon his many virtues.

They had no bickerings during the evening. If one chose to momentarily assert himself, the others instantly submitted.

They exchanged compliments. Once old Bleecker stared at Jones for a few moments. Suddenly he broke out: "Jones, you're one of the finest fellows I ever knew!" A flush of pleasure went over the other's face, and then he made a modest gesture, the protest of an humble man. "Don't flim-flam me, ol' boy," he said, with earnestness. But

Bleecker roared that he was serious about it. The two men arose and shook hands emotionally. Jones bunted against the table and knocked off a glass.

Afterward a general hand-shaking was inaugurated. Brotherly sentiments flew about the room. There was an uproar of fraternal feeling.

Jones began to sing. He beat time with precision and dignity. He gazed into the eyes of his companions, trying to call music from their souls. O'Connor joined in heartily, but with another tune. Off in a corner old Bleecker was making a speech.

The bartender came to the door. "Gee, you fellahs er making a row. It's time fer me t' shut up th' front th' place, an' you mugs better sit on yerselves. It's one o'clock."

They began to argue with him. Kelcey, however, sprang to his feet. "One o'clock," he said. "Holy smoke, I mus' be flyin'!"

There came protesting howls from Jones. Bleecker ceased his oration. "My dear boy—" he began. Kelcey searched for his hat. "I've gota go t' work at seven," he said.

The others watched him with discomfort in their eyes. "Well," said O'Connor, "if one goes we might as well all go." They sadly took their hats and filed out.

The cold air of the street filled Kelcey with vague surprise. It made his head feel hot. As for his legs, they were like willow-twigs.

A few yellow lights blinked. In front of an all-night restaurant a huge red electric lamp hung and sputtered. Horse-car bells jingled far down the street. Overhead a train thundered on the elevated road.

On the sidewalk the men took fervid leave. They clutched hands with extraordinary force and proclaimed, for the last time, ardent and admiring friendships.

When he arrived at his home Kelcey proceeded with caution. His mother had left a light burning low. He stumbled once in his voyage across the floor. As he paused to listen he heard the sound of little snores coming from her room.

He lay awake for a few moments and thought of the evening. He had a pleasurable consciousness that he had made a good impression upon those fine fellows. He felt that he had spent the most delightful evening of his life.

V

KELCEY WAS CROSS IN the morning. His mother had been obliged to shake him a great deal, and it had seemed to him a most unjust thing. Also, when he, blinking his eyes, had entered the kitchen, she had said: "Yeh left th' lamp burnin' all night last night, George. How many times must I tell yeh never t' leave th' lamp burnin'?"

He ate the greater part of his breakfast in silence, moodily stirring his coffee and glaring at a remote corner of the room with eyes that felt as if they had been baked. When he moved his eyelids there was a sensation that they were cracking. In his mouth there was a singular taste. It seemed to him that he had been sucking the end of a wooden spoon. Moreover, his temper was rampant within him. It sought something to devour.

Finally he said, savagely: "Damn these early hours!"

His mother jumped as if he had flung a missile at her. "Why, George—" she began.

Kelcey broke in again. "Oh, I know all that—but this gettin' up in th' mornin' so early makes me sick. Jest when a man is gettin' his mornin' nap he's gota get up. I ——"

"George, dear," said his mother, "yeh know how I hate yeh t' swear, dear. Now please don't." She looked beseechingly at him.

He made a swift gesture. "Well, I ain't swearin', am I?" he demanded. "I was on'y sayin' that this gettin'-up business gives me a pain, wasn't I?"

"Well, yeh know how swearin' hurts me," protested the little old woman. She seemed about to sob. She gazed off retrospectively. She apparently was recalling persons who had never been profane.

"I don't see where yeh ever caught this way a' swearin' out at everything," she continued, presently. "Fred, ner John, ner Willie never swore a bit. Ner Tom neither, except when he was real mad."

The son made another gesture. It was directed into the air, as if he saw there a phantom injustice. "Oh, good thunder," he said, with an accent of despair. Thereupon, he relapsed into a mood of silence. He sombrely regarded his plate.

This demeanor speedily reduced his mother to meekness. When she spoke again it was in a conciliatory voice. "George, dear, won't yeh bring some sugar home t'-night?" It could be seen that she was asking for a crown of gold.

Kelcey aroused from his semi-slumber. "Yes, if I kin remember it," he said.

The little old woman arose to stow her son's lunch into the pail. When he had finished his breakfast he stalked for a time about the room in a dignified way. He put on his coat and hat, and taking his lunch-pail went to the door. There he halted, and without turning his head, stiffly said: "Well, good-by!"

The little old woman saw that she had offended her son. She did not seek an explanation. She was accustomed to these phenomena. She made haste to surrender.

"Ain't yeh goin' t' kiss me good-by," she asked in a little woful voice.

The youth made a pretence of going on, deaf-heartedly. He wore the dignity of an injured monarch.

Then the little old woman called again in forsaken accents: "George—George—ain't yeh goin' t' kiss me good-by?" When he moved he found that she was hanging to his coattails.

He turned eventually with a murmur of a sort of tenderness. "Why, 'a course I am," he said. He kissed her. Withal there was an undertone of superiority in his voice, as if he were granting an astonishing suit. She looked at him with reproach and gratitude and affection.

She stood at the head of the stairs and watched his hand sliding along the rail as he went down. Occasionally she could see his arm and part of his shoulder. When he reached the first floor she called to him: "Good-by!"

The little old woman went back to her work in the kitchen with a frown of perplexity upon her brow. "I wonder what was th' matter with George this mornin'," she mused. "He didn't seem a bit like himself!"

As she trudged to and fro at her labor she began to speculate. She was much worried. She surmised in a vague way that he was a sufferer from a great internal disease. It was something no doubt that devoured the kidneys or quietly fed upon the lungs. Later, she imagined a woman, wicked and fair, who had fascinated him and was turning his life into a bitter thing. Her mind created many wondrous influences that were swooping like green dragons at him. They were changing him to a morose man, who suffered silently. She longed to discover them, that she might go bravely to the rescue of her heroic son. She knew that he, generous in his pain, would keep it from her. She racked her mind for knowledge.

However, when he came home at night he was extraordinarily blithe. He seemed to be a lad of ten. He capered all about the room. When she was bringing the coffee-pot from the stove to the table, he made show of waltzing with her so that she spilled some of the coffee. She was obliged to scold him.

All through the meal he made jokes. She occasionally was compelled to laugh, despite the fact that she believed that she should not laugh at her own son's jokes. She uttered reproofs at times, but he did not regard them.

"Golly," he said once, "I feel fine as silk. I didn't think I'd get over feelin' bad so quick. It—" He stopped abruptly.

During the evening he sat content. He smoked his pipe and read from an evening paper. She bustled about at her work. She seemed utterly happy with him there, lazily puffing out little clouds of smoke and giving frequent brilliant dissertations upon the news of the day. It seemed to her that she must be a model mother to have such a son, one who came home to her at night and sat contented, in a languor of the muscles after a good day's toil. She pondered upon the science of her management.

The week thereafter, too, she was joyous, for he stayed at home each night of it, and was sunny-tempered. She became convinced that she was a perfect mother, rearing a perfect son. There came often a love-light into her eyes. The wrinkled, yellow face frequently warmed into a smile of the kind that a maiden bestows upon him who to her is first and perhaps last.

◦◦◦ VI ◦◦◦

THE LITTLE OLD WOMAN habitually discouraged all outbursts of youthful vanity upon the part of her son. She feared that he would get to think too much of himself, and she knew that nothing could do more harm. Great self-esteem was always passive, she thought, and if he grew to regard his qualities of mind as forming a dazzling constellation, he would tranquilly sit still and not do those wonders she expected of him. So she was constantly on the alert to suppress even a shadow of such a thing. As for him he ruminated with the savage, vengeful bitterness of a young man, and decided that she did not comprehend him.

But despite her precautions he often saw that she believed him to be the most marvellous young man on the earth. He had only to look at those two eyes that became lighted with a glow from her heart whenever he did some excessively brilliant thing. On these occasions he could see her glance triumphantly at a neighbor, or whoever happened to be present. He grew to plan for these glances. And then he took a vast satisfaction in detecting and appropriating them.

Nevertheless, he could not understand why, directly after a scene of this kind, his mother was liable to call to him to hang his coat on the hook under the mantel, her voice in a key of despair as if he were negligent and stupid in what was, after all, the only important thing in life.

"If yeh'll only get in the habit of doin' it, it'll be jest as easy as throwin' it down anywheres," she would say to him. "When yeh pitch it down anywheres, somebody's got t' pick it up, an' that'll most likely be your poor ol' mother. Yeh can hang it up yerself, if yeh'll on'y think." This was intolerable. He usually went then and hurled his coat savagely at the hook. The correctness of her position was maddening.

It seemed to him that anyone who had a son of his glowing attributes should overlook the fact that he seldom hung up his coat. It was impossible to explain this situation to his mother. She was unutterably narrow. He grew sullen.

There came a time, too, that, even in all his mother's tremendous admiration for him, he did not entirely agree with her. He was delighted that she liked his great wit. He spurred himself to new and flashing effort because of this appreciation. But for the greater part he could see that his mother took pride in him in quite a different way from that in which he took pride in himself. She rejoiced at qualities in him that indicated that he was going to become a white and looming king among men. From these she made pictures in which he appeared as a benign personage, blessed by the filled hands of the poor, one whose brain could hold massive thoughts and awe certain men about whom she had read. She was fêted as the mother of this enormous man. These dreams were her solace. She spoke of them to no one because she knew that, worded, they would be ridiculous. But she dwelt with them, and they shed a radiance of gold upon her long days, her sorry labor. Upon the dead altars of her life she had builded the little fires of hope for another.

He had a complete sympathy for as much as he understood of these thoughts of his mother. They were so wise that he admired her foresight. As for himself, however, most of his dreams were of a nearer time. He had many of the distant future when he would be a man with a cloak of coldness concealing his gentleness and his faults, and of whom the men and, more particularly, the women, would think with reverence. He agreed with his mother that at that time he would go through the obstacles to other men like a flung stone. And then he would have power and he would enjoy having his bounty and his wrath alike fall swiftly upon those below. They would be awed. And above all he would mystify them.

But then his nearer dreams were a multitude. He had begun to look at the great world revolving near to his nose. He had a vast curiosity concerning this city in whose complexities he was buried. It was an impenetrable mystery, this city. It was a blend of many enticing colors. He longed to comprehend it completely, that he might walk understandingly in its greatest marvels, its mightiest march of life, its sin. He dreamed of a comprehension whose pay was the admirable attitude of a man of knowledge. He remembered Jones. He could not help but admire a man who knew so many bartenders.

✠ VII ✠

AN INDEFINITE WOMAN WAS in all of Kelcey's dreams. As a matter of fact it was not he whom he pictured as wedding her. It was a vision of himself greater, finer, more terrible. It was himself as he expected to be. In scenes which he took mainly from pictures, this vision conducted a courtship, strutting, posing, and lying through a drama which was magnificent from glow of purple. In it he was icy, self-possessed; but she, the dream-girl, was consumed by wild, torrential passion. He went to the length of having her display it before the people. He saw them wonder at his tranquillity. It amazed them infinitely to see him remain cold before the glory of this peerless woman's love. She was to him as beseeching for affection as a pet animal, but still he controlled appearances and none knew of his deep abiding love. Some day, at the critical romantic time, he was going to divulge it. In these long dreams there were accessories of castle-like houses, wide lands, servants, horses, clothes.

They began somewhere in his childhood. When he ceased to see himself as a stern general pointing a sword at the nervous and abashed horizon, he became this sublime king of a vague woman's heart. Later when he had read some books, it all achieved clearer expression. He was told in them that there was a goddess in the world whose business it was to wait until he should exchange a glance with her. It became a creed, subtly powerful. It saved discomfort for him and for several women who flitted by him. He used her as a standard.

Often he saw the pathos of her long wait, but his faith did not faker. The world was obliged to turn gold in time. His life was to be fine and heroic, else he would not have been born. He believed that the common-place lot was the sentence, the doom of certain people who did not know how to feel. His blood was a tender current of life. He thought that the usual should fall to others whose nerves were of lead. Occasionally he wondered how fate was going to begin in making an enormous figure of him; but he had no doubt of the result. A chariot of pink clouds was coming for him. His faith was his reason for existence. Meanwhile he could dream of the indefinite woman and the fragrance of roses that came from her hair.

One day he met Maggie Johnson on the stairs.[4] She had a pail of beer in one hand and a brown-paper parcel under her arm. She glanced at him. He discovered that it would wither his heart to see another man signally successful in the smiles of her. And the glance that she gave him was so indifferent and so unresponsive to the sudden vivid admiration in his own eyes that he immediately concluded that she was magnificent in two ways.

As she came to the landing, the light from a window passed in a silver gleam over the girlish roundness of her cheek. It was a thing that he remembered.

He was silent for the most part at supper that night. He was particularly unkind when he did speak. His mother, observing him apprehensively, tried in vain to picture the new terrible catastrophe. She eventually concluded that he did not like the beef-stew. She put more salt in it.

He saw Maggie quite frequently after the meeting upon the stairs. He reconstructed his dreams and placed her in the full glory of that sun. The dream-woman, the goddess, pitched from her pedestal, lay prostrate, unheeded, save when he brought her forth to call her insipid and childish in the presence of his new religion.

He was relatively happy sometimes when Maggie's mother would get drunk and make terrific uproars. He used then to sit in the dark and make scenes in which he rescued the girl from her hideous environment.

He laid clever plans by which he encountered her in the halls, at the door, on the street. When he succeeded in meeting her he was always overcome by the thought that the whole thing was obvious to her. He could feel the shame of it burn his face and neck. To prove to her that she was mistaken he would turn away his head or regard her with a granite stare.

After a time he became impatient of the distance between them. He saw looming princes who would aim to seize her. Hours of his leisure and certain hours of his labor he spent in contriving. The shade of this girl was with him continually. With her he builded his grand dramas so that he trod in clouds, the matters of his daily life obscured and softened by a mist.

He saw that he need only break down the slight conventional barriers and she would soon discover his noble character. Sometimes he could see it all in his mind. It was very skilful. But then his courage flew away at the supreme moment. Perhaps the whole affair was humorous to her. Perhaps she was watching his mental contortions. She might laugh. He felt that he would then die or kill her. He could not approach the dread moment. He sank often from the threshold of knowledge. Directly after these occasions, it was his habit to avoid her to prove that she was a cipher to him.

He reflected that if he could only get a chance to rescue her from something, the whole tragedy would speedily unwind.

He met a young man in the halls one evening who said to him: "Say, me frien', where d' d' Johnson birds live in heh? I can't fin' me feet in dis bloomin' joint. I been battin' round heh fer a half-hour."

"Two flights up," said Kelcey stonily. He had felt a sudden quiver of his heart. The grandeur of the clothes, the fine worldly air, the experience, the self-reliance, the courage that shone in the countenance of this other young man made him suddenly sink to the depths of woe. He stood listening in the hall, flushing and ashamed of it, until he heard them coming down-stairs together. He slunk away then. It would have been a horror to him if she had discovered him there. She might have felt sorry for him.

They were going out to a show, perhaps. That pig of the world in his embroidered cloak was going to dazzle her with splendor. He mused upon how unrighteous it was for other men to dazzle women with splendor.

As he appreciated his handicap he swore with savage, vengeful bitterness. In his home his mother raised her voice in a high key of monotonous irritability. "Hang up yer coat, can't yeh, George?" she cried at him. "I can't go round after yeh all th' time. It's jest as easy t' hang it up as it is t' throw it down that way. Don't yeh ever git tired 'a hearin' me yell at yeh!"

"Yes," he exploded. In this word he put a profundity of sudden anger. He turned toward his mother a face, red, seamed, hard with hate and rage. They stared a moment in silence. Then she turned and staggered toward her room. Her hip struck violently against the corner of the table during this blind passage. A moment later the door closed.

Kelcey sank down in a chair with his legs thrust out straight and his hands deep in his trousers' pockets. His chin was forward upon his breast and his eyes stared before him. There swept over him all the self-pity that comes when the soul is turned back from a road.

VIII

DURING THE NEXT FEW days Kelcey suffered from his first gloomy conviction that the earth was not grateful to him for his presence upon it. When sharp words were said to him, he interpreted them with what seemed to be a lately acquired insight. He could now perceive that the universe hated him. He sank to the most sublime depths of despair.

One evening of this period he met Jones. The latter rushed upon him with enthusiasm. "Why, yer jest th' man I wanted t' see! I was comin' round t' your place t'-night. Lucky I met yeh! Ol' Bleecker's goin' t' give a blow-out t'-morrah night. Anything yeh want t' drink! All th' boys 'll be there an' everything. He tol' me expressly that he wanted yeh t' be there. Great time! Great! Can yeh come?"

Kelcey grasped the other's hand with fervor. He felt now that there was some solacing friendship in space. "You bet I will, ol' man," he said, huskily. "I'd like nothin' better in th' world!"

As he walked home he thought that he was a very grim figure. He was about to taste the delicious revenge of a partial self-destruction. The universe would regret its position when it saw him drunk.

He was a little late in getting to Bleecker's lodging. He was delayed while his mother read aloud a letter from an old uncle, who wrote in one place: "God bless the boy! Bring him up to be the man his father was." Bleecker lived in an old three-storied house on a side-street. A Jewish tailor lived and worked in the front parlor, and old Bleecker lived in the back parlor. A German, whose family took care of the house, occupied the basement. Another German, with a wife and eight children, rented the dining-room. The two upper floors were inhabited by tailors, dressmakers, a peddler, and mysterious people who were seldom seen. The door of the little hall-bedroom, at the foot of the second flight, was always open, and in there could be seen two bended men who worked at mending opera-glasses. The German woman in the dining-room was not friends with the little dressmaker in the rear room of the third floor, and frequently they yelled the vilest names up and down between the balusters.* Each part of the woodwork was scratched and rubbed by the contact of innumerable persons. In one wall there was a long slit with chipped edges, celebrating the time when a man had thrown a hatchet at his wife. In the lower hall there was an eternal woman, with a rag and a pail of suds, who knelt over the worn oilcloth. Old Bleecker felt that he had quite respectable and high-class apartments. He was glad to invite his friends.

Bleecker met Kelcey in the hall. He wore a collar that was cleaner and higher than his usual one. It changed his appearance greatly. He was now formidably aristocratic. "How are yeh, ol' man?" he shouted. He grasped Kelcey's arm, and, babbling jovially, conducted him down the hall and into the ex-parlor.

A group of standing men made vast shadows in the yellow glare of the lamp. They turned their heads as the two entered. "Why, hello, Kelcey, ol' man," Jones exclaimed, coming rapidly forward. "Good fer you! Glad yeh come! Yeh know O'Connor, 'a course! An' Schmidt! an' Woods! Then there's Zeusentell! Mr. Zeusentell—my friend Mr. Kelcey! Shake hands—both good fellows, damnitall! Then here is—oh, gentlemen, my friend Mr. Kelcey! A good fellow, he is, too! I've known 'im since I was a kid! Come, have a drink!" Everybody was excessively amiable. Kelcey felt that he had social standing. The strangers were cautious and respectful.

"By all means," said old Bleecker. "Mr. Kelcey, have a drink! An' by th' way, gentlemen, while we're about it, let's all have a drink!" There was much laughter. Bleecker was so droll at times.

With mild and polite gesturing they marched up to the table. There were upon it a keg of beer, a long row of whiskey bottles, a little heap of corn-cob pipes, some bags of tobacco, a box of cigars, and a mighty collection of glasses, cups, and mugs. Old Bleecker had

---

*Pillars supporting a banister rail on a staircase.

arranged them so deftly that they resembled a primitive bar. There was considerable scuffling for possession of the cracked cups. Jones politely but vehemently insisted upon drinking from the worst of the assortment. He was quietly opposed by others. Everybody showed that they were awed by Bleecker's lavish hospitality. Their demeanors expressed their admiration at the cost of this entertainment.

Kelcey took his second mug of beer away to a corner and sat down with it. He wished to socially reconnoitre. Over in a corner a man was telling a story, in which at intervals he grunted like a pig. A half dozen men were listening. Two or three others sat alone in isolated places. They looked expectantly bright, ready to burst out cordially if anyone should address them. The row of bottles made quaint shadows upon the table, and upon a side-wall the keg of beer created a portentous black figure that reared toward the ceiling, hovering over the room and its inmates with spectral stature. Tobacco-smoke lay in lazy cloud-banks overhead.

Jones and O'Connor stayed near the table, occasionally being affable in all directions. Kelcey saw old Bleecker go to them and heard him whisper: "Come, we must git th' thing started. Git th' thing started." Kelcey saw that the host was fearing that all were not having a good time. Jones conferred with O'Connor and then O'Connor went to the man named Zeusentell. O'Connor evidently proposed something. Zeusentell refused at once. O'Connor beseeched. Zeusentell remained implacable. At last O'Connor broke off his argument, and going to the centre of the room, held up his hand. "Gentlemen," he shouted loudly, "we will now have a recitation by Mr. Zeusentell, entitled 'Patrick Clancy's Pig'!" He then glanced triumphantly at Zeusentell and said: "Come on!" Zeusentell had been twisting and making pantomimic appeals. He said, in a reproachful whisper: "You son of a gun."

The men turned their heads to glance at Zeusentell for a moment and then burst into a sustained clamor. "Hurray! Let 'er go! Come— give it t' us! Spring it! Spring it! Let it come!" As Zeusentell made no advances, they appealed personally. "Come, ol' man, let 'er go! Whatter yeh 'fraid of? Let 'er go! Go ahn! Hurry up!"

Zeusentell was protesting with almost frantic modesty. O'Connor took him by the lapel and tried to drag him; but he leaned back, pulling at his coat and shaking his head. "No, no, I don't know it,

I tell yeh! I can't! I don't know it! I tell yeh I don't know it! I've forgotten it, I tell yeh! No—no—no—no. Ah, say, lookahere, le' go me, can't yeh? What's th' matter with yeh? I tell yeh I don't know it!" The men applauded violently. O'Connor did not relent. A little battle was waged until all of a sudden Zeusentell was seen to grow wondrously solemn. A hush fell upon the men. He was about to begin. He paused in the middle of the floor and nervously adjusted his collar and cravat. The audience became grave. " 'Patrick Clancy's Pig,' " announced Zeusentell in a shrill, dry, unnatural tone. And then he began in rapid sing-song:

> "Patrick Clancy had a pig
> Th' pride uv all th' nation,
> The half uv him was half as big
> As half uv all creation ——"

When he concluded the others looked at each other to convey their appreciation. They then wildly clapped their hands or tinkled their glasses. As Zeusentell went toward his seat a man leaned over and asked: "Can yeh tell me where I kin git that." He had made a great success. After an enormous pressure he was induced to recite two more tales. Old Bleecker finally led him forward and pledged him in a large drink. He declared that they were the best things he had ever heard.

The efforts of Zeusentell imparted a gayety to the company. The men having laughed together were better acquainted, and there was now a universal topic. Some of the party, too, began to be quite drunk.

The invaluable O'Connor brought forth a man who could play the mouth-organ.* The latter, after wiping his instrument upon his coat-sleeve, played all the popular airs. The men's heads swayed to and fro in the clouded smoke. They grinned and beat time with their feet. A valor, barbaric and wild, began to show in their poses and in their faces, red and glistening from perspiration. The conversation resounded in a hoarse roar. The beer would not run rapidly enough for

---

*Old-fashioned name for a harmonica.

Jones, so he remained behind to tilt the keg. This caused the black shadow on the wall to retreat and advance, sinking mystically to loom forward again with sudden menace, a huge dark figure controlled, as by some unknown emotion. The glasses, mugs, and cups travelled swift and regular, catching orange reflections from the lamp-light. Two or three men were grown so careless that they were continually spilling their drinks. Old Bleecker, cackling with pleasure, seized time to glance triumphantly at Jones. His party was going to be a success.

IX

OF A SUDDEN KELCEY felt the buoyant thought that he was having a good time. He was all at once an enthusiast, as if he were at a festival of a religion. He felt that there was something fine and thrilling in this affair isolated from a stern world, and from which the laughter arose like incense. He knew that old sentiment of brotherly regard for those about him. He began to converse tenderly with them. He was not sure of his drift of thought, but he knew that he was immensely sympathetic. He rejoiced at their faces, shining red and wrinkled with smiles. He was capable of heroisms.

His pipe irritated him by going out frequently. He was too busy in amiable conversations to attend to it. When he arose to go for a match he discovered that his legs were a trifle uncertain under him. They bended and did not precisely obey his intent. At the table he lit a match and then, in laughing at a joke made near him, forgot to apply it to the bowl of his pipe. He succeeded with the next match after annoying trouble. He swayed so that the match would appear first on one side of the bowl and then on the other. At last he happily got it directly over the tobacco. He had burned his fingers. He inspected them, laughing vaguely.

Jones came and slapped him on the shoulder. "Well, ol' man, let's take a drink fer ol' Handyville's sake!"

Kelcey was deeply affected. He looked at Jones with moist eyes. "I'll go yeh," he said. With an air of profound melancholy, Jones poured out some whiskey. They drank reverently. They exchanged a glistening look of tender recollections and then went over to where Bleecker was telling a humorous story to a circle of giggling listeners. The old man sat like a fat, jolly god. "—and just at that moment th' old woman put her head out of th' window an' said: 'Mike, yez lezy divil, fer phwat do yez be slapin' in me new geranium bid?' An' Mike woke up an' said: 'Domn a wash-woman thot do niver wash her own bidclues. Here do I be slapin' in nothin' but dhirt an' wades.'" The men slapped their knees, roaring loudly. They begged him to tell another. A clamor of comment arose concerning the anecdote, so that when old Bleecker began a fresh one nobody was heeding.

It occurred to Jones to sing. Suddenly he burst forth with a ballad that had a rippling waltz movement, and seizing Kelcey, made a furious attempt to dance. They sprawled over a pair of outstretched legs and pitched headlong. Kelcey fell with a yellow crash. Blinding lights flashed before his vision. But he arose immediately, laughing. He did not feel at all hurt. The pain in his head was rather pleasant.

Old Bleecker, O'Connor, and Jones, who now limped and drew breath through his teeth, were about to lead him with much care and tenderness to the table for another drink, but he laughingly pushed them away and went unassisted. Bleecker told him: "Great Gawd, your head struck hard enough t' break a trunk."

He laughed again, and with a show of steadiness and courage he poured out an extravagant portion of whiskey. With cold muscles he put it to his lips and drank it. It chanced that this addition dazed him like a powerful blow. A moment later it affected him with blinding and numbing power. Suddenly unbalanced, he felt the room sway. His blurred sight could only distinguish a tumbled mass of shadow through which the beams from the light ran like swords of flame. The sound of the many voices was to him like the roar of a distant river. Still, he felt that if he could only annul the force of these million winding fingers that gripped his senses, he was capable of most brilliant and entertaining things.

He was at first of the conviction that his feelings were only temporary. He waited for them to pass away, but the mental and physical pause only caused a new reeling and swinging of the room. Chasms with inclined approaches were before him; peaks leaned toward him.

And withal he was blind and numb with surprise. He understood vaguely in his stupefaction that it would disgrace him to fall down a chasm.

At last he perceived a shadow, a form, which he knew to be Jones. The adorable Jones, the supremely wise Jones, was walking in this strange land without fear or care, erect and tranquil. Kelcey murmured in admiration and affection, and fell toward his friend. Jones's voice sounded as from the shores of the unknown. "Come, come, ol' man, this will never do. Brace up." It appeared after all that Jones was not wholly wise. "Oh, I'm—all ri' Jones! I'm all ri'! I wan' shing song! Tha's all! I wan' shing song!"

Jones was stupid. "Come now, sit down an' shut up."

It made Kelcey burn with fury. "Jones, le' me alone, I tell yeh! Le' me alone! I wan' shing song er te' story! G'l'm'n, I lovsh girl live down my shtreet. Thash reason 'm drunk, 'tis! She ——"

Jones seized him and dragged him toward a chair. He heard him laugh. He could not endure these insults from his friend. He felt a blazing desire to strangle his companion. He threw out his hand violently, but Jones grappled him close and he was no more than a dried leaf. He was amazed to find that Jones possessed the strength of twenty horses. He was forced skilfully to the floor.

As he lay, he reflected in great astonishment upon Jones's muscle. It was singular that he had never before discovered it. The whole incident had impressed him immensely. An idea struck him that he might denounce Jones for it. It would be a sage thing. There would be a thrilling and dramatic moment in which he would dazzle all the others. But at this moment he was assailed by a mighty desire to sleep. Sombre and soothing clouds of slumber were heavily upon him. He closed his eyes with a sigh that was yet like that of a babe.

When he awoke, there was still the battleful clamor of the revel. He half arose with a plan of participating, when O'Connor came and pushed him down again, throwing out his chin in affectionate remonstrance and saying, "Now, now," as to a child.

The change that had come over these men mystified Kelcey in a great degree. He had never seen anything so vastly stupid as their idea of his state. He resolved to prove to them that they were dealing with one whose mind was very clear. He kicked and squirmed in O'Connor's arms, until, with a final wrench, he scrambled to his feet and stood tottering in the middle of the room. He would let them see that he had a strangely lucid grasp of events. "G'l'm'n, I lovsh girl! I ain' drunker'n yeh all are! She ——"

He felt them hurl him to a corner of the room and pile chairs and tables upon him until he was buried beneath a stupendous mountain. Far above, as up a mine's shaft, there were voices, lights, and vague figures. He was not hurt physically, but his feelings were unutterably injured. He, the brilliant, the good, the sympathetic had been thrust fiendishly from the party. They had had the comprehension of red lobsters. It was an unspeakable barbarism. Tears welled piteously from his eyes. He planned long diabolical explanations!

X

AT FIRST THE GRAY lights of dawn came timidly into the room, remaining near the windows, afraid to approach certain sinister corners. Finally, mellow streams of sunshine poured in, undraping the shadows to disclose the putrefaction, making pitiless revelation. Kelcey awoke with a groan of undirected misery. He tossed his stiffened arms about his head for a moment and then leaning heavily upon his elbow stared blinking at his environment. The grim truthfulness of the day showed disaster and death. After the tumults of the previous night the interior of this room resembled a decaying battle-field. The air hung heavy and stifling with the odors of tobacco, men's breaths, and beer half filling forgotten glasses. There was ruck of broken tumblers, pipes, bottles, spilled tobacco, cigar stumps. The chairs and tables were pitched this way and that way, as after some terrible struggle. In the midst of it all lay old Bleecker stretched upon a couch in deepest sleep, as abandoned in attitude, as motionless, as ghastly as if it were a corpse that had been flung there.

A knowledge of the thing came gradually into Kelcey's eyes. He looked about him with an expression of utter woe, regret, and loathing. He was compelled to lie down again. A pain above his eyebrows was like that from an iron-clamp.

As he lay pondering, his bodily condition created for him a bitter philosophy, and he perceived all the futility of a red existence. He saw his life problems confronting him like granite giants and he was no longer erect to meet them. He had made a calamitous retrogression in his war. Spectres were to him now as large as clouds.

Inspired by the pitiless ache in his head, he was prepared to reform and live a white life. His stomach informed him that a good man was the only being who was wise. But his perception of his future was hopeless. He was aghast at the prospect of the old routine. It was impossible. He trembled before its exactions.

Turning toward the other way, he saw that the gold portals of vice no longer enticed him. He could not hear the strains of alluring music. The beckoning sirens of drink had been killed by this pain in his head. The desires of his life suddenly lay dead like mullein stalks. Upon reflection, he saw, therefore, that he was perfectly willing to be virtuous if somebody would come and make it easy for him.

When he stared over at old Bleecker, he felt a sudden contempt and dislike for him. He considered him to be a tottering old beast. It was disgusting to perceive aged men so weak in sin. He dreaded to see him awaken lest he should be required to be somewhat civil to him.

Kelcey wished for a drink of water. For some time he had dreamed of the liquid, deliciously cool. It was an abstract, uncontained thing that poured upon him and tumbled him, taking away his pain like a kind of surgery. He arose and staggered slowly toward a little sink in a corner of the room. He understood that any rapid movement might cause his head to split.

The little sink was filled with a chaos of broken glass and spilled liquids. A sight of it filled him with horror, but he rinsed a glass with scrupulous care, and filling it, took an enormous drink. The water was an intolerable disappointment. It was insipid and weak to his scorched throat and not at all cool. He put down the glass with a gesture of despair. His face became fixed in the stony and sullen expression of a man who waits for the recuperative power of morrows.

Old Bleecker awakened. He rolled over and groaned loudly. For awhile he thrashed about in a fury of displeasure at his bodily stiffness and pain. Kelcey watched him as he would have watched a death agony. "Good Gawd," said the old man, "beer an' whiskey make th' devil of a mix. Did yeh see th' fight?"

"No," said Kelcey, stolidly.

"Why, Zeusentell an' O'Connor had a great old mill.* They were scrappin' all over th' place. I thought we were all goin' t' get pulled. Thompson, that fellah over in th' corner, though, he sat down on th' whole business. He was a dandy! He had t' poke Zeusentell! He was a bird! Lord, I wish I had a Manhattan!"†

Kelcey remained in bitter silence while old Bleecker dressed. "Come an' get a cocktail," said the latter briskly. This was part of his aristocracy. He was the only man of them who knew much about cocktails. He perpetually referred to them. "It'll brace yeh right up! Come along! Say, you get full too soon. You oughter wait until later, me boy! You're too speedy!" Kelcey wondered vaguely where his companion had lost his zeal for polished sentences, his iridescent mannerisms.

"Come along," said Bleecker.

Kelcey made a movement of disdain for cocktails, but he followed the other to the street. At the corner they separated. Kelcey attempted a friendly parting smile and then went on up the street. He had to reflect to know that he was erect and using his own muscles in walking. He felt like a man of paper, blown by the winds. Withal, the dust of the avenue was galling to his throat, eyes, and nostrils, and the roar of traffic cracked his head. He was glad, however, to be alone, to be rid of old Bleecker. The sight of him had been as the contemplation of a disease.

His mother was not at home. In his little room he mechanically undressed and bathed his head, arms, and shoulders. When he

---

*Term for a prizefight or wild brawl; from "windmill."
†Potent cocktail made from a mixture of bourbon whiskey and sweet vermouth.

crawled between the two white sheets he felt a first lifting of his misery. His pillow was soothingly soft. There was an effect that was like the music of tender voices.

When he awoke again his mother was bending over him giving vent to alternate cries of grief and joy. Her hands trembled so that they were useless to her. "Oh, George, George, where have yeh been? What has happened t' yeh? Oh, George, I've been so worried! I didn't sleep a wink all night."

Kelcey was instantly wide awake. With a moan of suffering he turned his face to the wall before he spoke. "Never mind, mother, I'm all right. Don't fret now! I was knocked down by a truck last night in th' street, an' they took me t' th' hospital; but it's all right now. I got out jest a little while ago. They told me I'd better go home an' rest up."

His mother screamed in pity, horror, joy, and self-reproach for something unknown. She frenziedly demanded the details. He sighed with unutterable weariness. "Oh—wait—wait—wait," he said shutting his eyes as from the merciless monotony of a pain. "Wait— wait—please wait. I can't talk now. I want t' rest."

His mother condemned herself with a little cry. She adjusted his pillow, her hands shaking with love and tenderness. "There, there, don't mind, dearie! But yeh can't think how worried I was—an' crazy. I was near frantic. I went down t' th' shop, an' they said they hadn't seen anything 'a yeh there. The foreman was awful good t' me. He said he'd come up this afternoon t' see if yeh had come home yet. He tol' me not t' worry. Are yeh sure yer all right? Ain't there anythin' I kin git fer yeh? What did th' docter say?"

Kelcey's patience was worn. He gestured, and then spoke querulously. "Now—now—mother, it's all right, I tell yeh! All I need is a little rest an' I'll be as well as ever. But it makes it all th' worse if yeh stand there an' ask me questions an' make me think. Jest leave me alone fer a little while, an' I'll be as well as ever. Can't yeh do that?"

The little old woman puckered her lips funnily. "My, what an old bear th' boy is!" She kissed him blithely. Presently she went out, upon her face a bright and glad smile that must have been a reminiscence of some charming girlhood.

~~ XI ~~

AT ONE TIME KELCEY had a friend who was struck in the head by the pole of a truck and knocked senseless. He was taken to the hospital, from which he emerged in the morning an astonished man, with rather a dim recollection of the accident. He used to hold an old brier-wood pipe in his teeth in a manner peculiar to himself, and, with a brown derby hat tilted back on his head, recount his strange sensations. Kelcey had always remembered it as a bit of curious history. When his mother cross-examined him in regard to the accident, he told this story with barely a variation. Its truthfulness was incontestable.

At the shop he was welcomed on the following day with considerable enthusiasm. The foreman had told the story and there were already jokes created concerning it. Mike O'Donnell, whose wit was famous, had planned a humorous campaign, in which he made charges against Kelcey, which were, as a matter of fact, almost the exact truth.[5] Upon hearing it, Kelcey looked at him suddenly from the corners of his eyes, but otherwise remained imperturbable. O'Donnell eventually despaired. "Yez can't goiy* that kid! He tekes ut all loike mate an' dhrink." Kelcey often told the story, his pipe held in his teeth peculiarly, and his derby tilted back on his head.

He remained at home for several evenings, content to read the papers and talk with his mother. She began to look around for the tremendous reason for it. She suspected that his nearness to death in the recent accident had sobered his senses and made him think of high things. She mused upon it continually. When he sat moodily pondering she watched him. She said to herself that she saw the light breaking in upon his spirit. She felt that it was a very critical period

---

*The term "guy" rendered in Irish dialect; it means to mock or make fun of someone.

of his existence. She resolved to use all her power and skill to turn his eyes toward the lights in the sky. Accordingly she addressed him one evening. "Come, go t' prayer-meetin' t'-night with me, will yeh, George?" It sounded more blunt than she intended.

He glanced at her in sudden surprise. "Huh?"

As she repeated her request, her voice quavered. She felt that it was a supreme moment. "Come, go t' prayer-meetin' t'-night, won't yeh?"

He seemed amazed. "Oh, I don't know," he began. He was fumbling in his mind for a reason for refusing. "I don't wanta go. I'm tired as th' dickens!" His obedient shoulders sank down languidly. His head mildly drooped.

The little old woman, with a quick perception of her helplessness, felt a motherly rage at her son. It was intolerable that she could not impart motion to him in a chosen direction. The waves of her desires were puny against the rocks of his indolence. She had a great wish to beat him. "I don't know what I'm ever goin' t' do with yeh," she told him, in a choking voice. "Yeh won't do anything I ask yeh to. Yeh never pay th' least bit 'a attention t' what I say. Yeh don't mind me any more than yeh would a fly. Whatever am I goin' t' do with yeh?" She faced him in a battleful way, her eyes blazing with a sombre light of despairing rage.

He looked up at her ironically. "I don't know," he said, with calmness. "What are yeh?" He had traced her emotions and seen her fear of his rebellion. He thrust out his legs in the easy scorn of a rapier-bravo.* "What are yeh?"

The little old woman began to weep. They were tears without a shame of grief. She allowed them to run unheeded down her cheeks. As she stared into space her son saw her regarding there the powers and influences that she had held in her younger life. She was in some way acknowledging to fate that she was now but withered grass, with no power but the power to feel the winds. He was smitten with a sudden shame. Besides, in the last few days he had gained quite a character for amiability. He saw something grand in relenting at this point. "Well," he said, trying to remove a sulky quality from his voice, "well, if yer bound t' have me go, I s'pose I'll have t' go."

---

*A cocky, arrogant, violent sword-for-hire of the Italian Renaissance.

His mother, with strange, immobile face, went to him and kissed him on the brow. "All right, George!" There was in her wet eyes an emotion which he could not fathom.

She put on her bonnet and shawl, and they went out together. She was unusually silent, and made him wonder why she did not appear gleeful at his coming. He was resentful because she did not display more appreciation of his sacrifice. Several times he thought of halting and refusing to go farther, to see if that would not wring from her some acknowledgment.

In a dark street the little chapel sat humbly between two towering apartment-houses. A red street-lamp stood in front. It threw a marvellous reflection upon the wet pavements. It was like the death-stain of a spirit. Farther up the brilliant lights of an avenue made a span of gold across the black street. A roar of wheels and a clangor of bells came from this point, interwoven into a sound emblematic of the life of the city. It seemed somehow to affront this solemn and austere little edifice. It suggested an approaching barbaric invasion. The little church, pierced, would die with a fine, illimitable scorn for its slayers.

When Kelcey entered with his mother he felt a sudden quaking. His knees shook. It was an awesome place to him. There was a menace in the red padded carpet and the leather doors, studded with little brass tacks that penetrated his soul with their pitiless glances. As for his mother, she had acquired such a new air that he would have been afraid to address her. He felt completely alone and isolated at this formidable time.

There was a man in the vestibule who looked at them blandly. From within came the sound of singing. To Kelcey there was a million voices. He dreaded the terrible moment when the doors should swing back. He wished to recoil, but at that instant the bland man pushed the doors aside and he followed his mother up the centre aisle of the little chapel. To him there was a riot of lights that made him transparent. The multitudinous pairs of eyes that turned toward him were implacable in their cool valuations.

They had just ceased singing. He who conducted the meeting motioned that the services should wait until the new-comers found seats. The little old woman went slowly on toward the first rows. Occasionally she paused to scrutinize vacant places, but they did not seem to meet her requirements. Kelcey was in agony. He thought the moment of her decision would never come. In his unspeakable haste he walked a little faster than his mother. Once she paused to glance in her calculating way at some seats and he forged ahead. He halted abruptly and returned, but by that time she had resumed her thoughtful march up the aisle. He could have assassinated her. He felt that everybody must have seen his torture, during which his hands were to him like monstrous swollen hides. He was wild with a rage in which his lips turned slightly livid. He was capable of doing some furious, unholy thing.

When the little old woman at last took a seat, her son sat down beside her slowly and stiffly. He was opposing his strong desire to drop.

When from the mists of his shame and humiliation the scene came before his vision, he was surprised to find that all eyes were not fastened upon his face. The leader of the meeting seemed to be the only one who saw him. He stared gravely, solemnly, regretfully. He was a pale-faced, but plump young man in a black coat that buttoned to his chin. It was evident to Kelcey that his mother had spoken of him to the young clergyman, and that the latter was now impressing upon him the sorrow caused by the contemplation of his sin. Kelcey hated the man.

A man seated alone over in a corner began to sing. He closed his eyes and threw back his head. Others, scattered sparsely throughout the innumerable light-wood chairs, joined him as they caught the air. Kelcey heard his mother's frail, squeaking soprano. The chandelier in the centre was the only one lighted, and far at the end of the room one could discern the pulpit swathed in gloom, solemn and mystic as a bier.* It was surrounded by vague shapes of darkness on which at times was the glint of brass, or of glass that shone like steel, until one could feel there the presence of the army of the unknown, possessors of the great eternal truths, and silent listeners at this ceremony. High up, the stained-glass windows loomed in leaden array like dull-hued banners, merely catching occasional splashes of dark wine-color from the lights. Kelcey fell to brooding concerning this indefinable presence which he felt in a church.

One by one people arose and told little tales of their religious

---

*Platform that supports a coffin during a funeral while the deceased is lying in state.

faith. Some were tearful and others calm, emotionless, and convincing. Kelcey listened closely for a time. These people filled him with a great curiosity. He was not familiar with their types.

At last the young clergyman spoke at some length. Kelcey was amazed, because, from the young man's appearance, he would not have suspected him of being so glib; but the speech had no effect on Kelcey, excepting to prove to him again that he was damned.

～◎ XII ◎～

KELCEY SOMETIMES WONDERED WHETHER he liked beer.[6] He had been obliged to cultivate a talent for imbibing it. He was born with an abhorrence which he had steadily battled until it had come to pass that he could drink from ten to twenty glasses of beer without the act of swallowing causing him to shiver. He understood that drink was an essential to joy, to the coveted position of a man of the world and of the streets. The saloons contained the mystery of a street for him. When he knew its saloons he comprehended the street. Drink and its surroundings were the eyes of a superb green dragon to him. He followed a fascinating glitter, and the glitter required no explanation.

Directly after old Bleecker's party he almost reformed. He was tired and worn from the tumult of it, and he saw it as one might see a skeleton emerged from a crimson cloak. He wished then to turn his face away. Gradually, however, he recovered his mental balance. Then he admitted again by his point of view that the thing was not so terrible. His headache had caused him to exaggerate. A drunk was not the blight which he had once remorsefully named it. On the contrary, it was a mere unpleasant incident. He resolved, however, to be more cautious.

When prayer-meeting night came again his mother approached him hopefully. She smiled like one whose request is already granted. "Well, will yeh go t' prayer-meetin' with me t'-night again?"

He turned toward her with eloquent suddenness, and then riveted his eyes upon a corner of the floor. "Well, I guess not," he said.

His mother tearfully tried to comprehend his state of mind. "What has come over yeh?" she said, tremblingly. "Yeh never used t' be this way, George. Yeh never used t' be so cross an' mean t' me ——"

"Oh, I ain't cross an' mean t' yeh," he interpolated, exasperated and violent.

"Yes, yeh are, too! I ain't hardly had a decent word from yeh in ever so long. Yer as cross an' as mean as yeh can be. I don't know what t' make of it. It can't be——" There came a look in her eyes that told that she was going to shock and alarm him with her heaviest sentence—— "it can't be that yeh've got t' drinkin'."

Kelcey grunted with disgust at the ridiculous thing. "Why, what an old goose yer gettin' t' be."

She was compelled to laugh a little, as a child laughs between tears at a hurt. She had not been serious. She was only trying to display to him how she regarded his horrifying mental state. "Oh, of course, I didn't mean that, but I think yeh act jest as bad as if yeh did drink. I wish yeh would do better, George!"

She had grown so much less frigid and stern in her censure that Kelcey seized the opportunity to try to make a joke of it. He laughed at her, but she shook her head and continued: "I do wish yeh would do better. I don't know what's t' become 'a yeh, George. Yeh don't mind what I say no more'n if I was th' wind in th' chimbly. Yeh don't care about nothin' 'cept goin' out nights. I can't ever get yeh t' prayer-meetin' ner church; yeh never go out with me anywheres unless yeh can't get out of it; yeh swear an' take on sometimes like everything, yeh never ——"

He gestured wrathfully in interruption. "Say, lookahere, can't yeh think 'a something I do?"

She ended her oration then in the old way. "An' I don't know what's goin' t' become 'a yeh."

She put on her bonnet and shawl and then came and stood near him, expectantly. She imparted to her attitude a subtle threat of unchangeableness. He pretended to be engrossed in his newspaper. The little swaggering clock on the mantel became suddenly evident, ticking with loud monotony. Presently she said, firmly: "Well, are yeh comin'?"

He was reading.

"Well, are yeh comin'?"

He threw his paper down, angrily. "Oh, why don't yeh go on an' leave me alone?" he demanded in supreme impatience. "What do yeh wanta pester me fer? Yeh'd think there was robbers. Why can't yeh go alone er else stay home? You wanta go an' I don't wanta go, an' yeh keep all time tryin' t' drag me. Yeh know I don't wanta go." He concluded in a last defiant wounding of her. "What do I care 'bout those ol' bags-'a-wind anyhow? They gimme a pain!"

His mother turned her face and went from him. He sat staring with a mechanical frown. Presently he went and picked up his newspaper.

Jones told him that night that everybody had had such a good time at old Bleecker's party that they were going to form a club. They waited at the little smiling saloon, and then amid much enthusiasm all signed a membership-roll. Old Bleecker, late that night, was violently elected president. He made speeches of thanks and gratification during the remainder of the meeting. Kelcey went home rejoicing. He felt that at any rate he would have true friends. The dues were a dollar for each week.

He was deeply interested. For a number of evenings he fairly gobbled his supper in order that he might be off to the little smiling saloon to discuss the new organization. All the men were wildly enthusiastic. One night the saloon-keeper announced that he would donate half the rent of quite a large room over his saloon. It was an occasion for great cheering. Kelcey's legs were like whalebone when he tried to go upstairs upon his return home, and the edge of each step was moved curiously forward.

His mother's questions made him snarl. "Oh, nowheres!" At other times he would tell her: "Oh, t' see some friends 'a mine! Where d' yeh s'pose?"

Finally, some of the women of the tenement concluded that the little old mother had a wild son. They came to condole with her. They sat in the kitchen for hours. She told them of his wit, his cleverness, his kind heart.

ᵗ XIII ᵗ

AT A CERTAIN TIME Kelcey discovered that some young men who stood in the cinders between a brick wall and the pavement, and near the side-door of a corner saloon, knew more about life than other people. They used to lean there smoking and chewing, and comment upon events and persons. They knew the neighborhood extremely well. They debated upon small typical things that transpired before them until they had extracted all the information that existence contained. They sometimes inaugurated little fights with foreigners or well-dressed men. It was here that Sapristi Glielmi, the pedler, stabbed Pete Brady to death, for which he got a life-sentence. Each patron of the saloon was closely scrutinized as he entered the place. Sometimes they used to throng upon the heels of a man and in at the bar assert that he had asked them in to drink. When he objected, they would claim with one voice that it was too deep an insult and gather about to thrash him. When they had caught chance customers and absolute strangers, the barkeeper had remained in stolid neutrality, ready to serve one or seven, but two or three times they had encountered the wrong men. Finally, the proprietor had come out one morning and told them, in the fearless way of his class, that their pastime must cease. "It quits right here! See? Right here! Th' nex' time yeh try t' work it, I come with th' bung-starter,* an' th' mugs I miss with it git pulled. See? It quits!" Infrequently, however, men did ask them in to drink.

The policeman of that beat grew dignified and shrewd whenever he approached this corner. Sometimes he stood with his hands behind his back and cautiously conversed with them. It was understood on both sides that it was a good thing to be civil.

In winter this band, a trifle diminished in numbers, huddled in their old coats and stamped little flat places in the snow, their faces turned always toward the changing life in the streets. In the summer they became more lively. Sometimes, then, they walked out to the curb to look up and down the street. Over in a trampled vacant lot, surrounded by high tenement-houses, there was a sort of a den among some bowlders. An old truck was made to form a shelter. The small hoodlums of that vicinity all avoided the spot. So many of them had been thrashed upon being caught near it. It was the summer-time lounging-place of the band from the corner.

They were all too clever to work. Some of them had worked, but

---

*Metal chisel used for making holes (bungs) in barrels of beer.

these used their experiences as stores from which to draw tales. They were like veterans with their wars. One lad in particular used to recount how he whipped his employer, the proprietor of a large grain and feed establishment. He described his victim's features and form and clothes with minute exactness. He bragged of his wealth and social position. It had been a proud moment of the lad's life. He was like a savage who had killed a great chief.

Their feeling for contemporaneous life was one of contempt. Their philosophy taught that in a large part the whole thing was idle and a great bore. With fine scorn they sneered at the futility of it. Work was done by men who had not the courage to stand still and let the skies clap together if they willed.

The vast machinery of the popular law indicated to them that there were people in the world who wished to remain quiet. They awaited the moment when they could prove to them that a riotous upheaval, a cloud-burst of destruction would be a delicious thing. They thought of their fingers buried in the lives of these people. They longed dimly for a time when they could run through decorous streets with crash and roar of war, an army of revenge for pleasures long possessed by others, a wild sweeping compensation for their years without crystal and gilt, women and wine. This thought slumbered in them, as the image of Rome might have lain small in the hearts of the barbarians.

Kelcey respected these youths so much that he ordinarily used the other side of the street. He could not go near to them, because if a passer-by minded his own business he was a disdainful prig and had insulted them; if he showed that he was aware of them they were likely to resent his not minding his own business and prod him into a fight if the opportunity were good. Kelcey longed for their acquaintance and friendship, for with it came social safety and ease; they were respected so universally.

Once in another street Fidsey Corcoran was whipped by a short, heavy man. Fidsey picked himself up, and in the fury of defeat hurled pieces of brick at his opponent. The short man dodged with skill and then pursued Fidsey for over a block. Sometimes he got near enough to punch him. Fidsey raved in maniacal fury. The moment the short man would attempt to resume his own affairs, Fidsey would turn upon him again, tears and blood upon his face, with the lashed rage of a vanquished animal. The short man used to turn about, swear madly, and make little dashes. Fidsey always ran and then returned as pursuit ceased. The short man apparently wondered if this maniac was ever going to allow him to finish whipping him. He looked helplessly up and down the street. People were there who knew Fidsey, and they remonstrated with him; but he continued to confront the short man, gibbering like a wounded ape, using all the eloquence of the street in his wild oaths.

Finally the short man was exasperated to black fury. He decided to end the fight. With low snarls, ominous as death, he plunged at Fidsey.

Kelcey happened there then. He grasped the short man's shoulder. He cried out in the peculiar whine of the man who interferes. "Oh, hol' on! Yeh don't wanta hit 'im any more! Yeh've done enough to 'im now! Leave 'im be!"

The short man wrenched and tugged. He turned his face until his teeth were almost at Kelcey's cheek: "Le' go me! Le' go me, you ———" The rest of his sentence was screamed curses.

Kelcey's face grew livid from fear, but he somehow managed to keep his grip. Fidsey, with but an instant's pause, plunged into the new fray.

They beat the short man. They forced him against a high board-fence where for a few seconds their blows sounded upon his head in swift thuds. A moment later Fidsey descried a running policeman. He made off, fleet as a shadow. Kelcey noted his going. He ran after him.

Three or four blocks away they halted. Fidsey said: "I'd 'a licked dat big stuff in 'bout a minute more," and wiped the blood from his eyes.

At the gang's corner, they asked: "Who soaked yeh, Fidsey?" His description was burning. Everybody laughed. "Where is 'e now?" Later they began to question Kelcey. He recited a tale in which he allowed himself to appear prominent and redoubtable. They looked at him then as if they thought he might be quite a man.

Once when the little old woman was going out to buy something for her son's supper, she discovered him standing at the side-door of the saloon engaged intimately with Fidsey and the others. She slunk away, for she understood that it would be a terrible thing to confront him and his pride there with youths who were superior to mothers.

When he arrived home he threw down his hat with a weary sigh, as if he had worked long hours, but she attacked him before he had time to complete the falsehood. He listened to her harangue with a curled lip. In defence he merely made a gesture of supreme exasperation. She never understood the advanced things in life. He felt the hopelessness of ever making her comprehend. His mother was not modern.

ᴥ XIV ᴥ

THE LITTLE OLD WOMAN arose early and bustled in the preparation of breakfast. At times she looked anxiously at the clock. An hour before her son should leave for work she went to his room and called him in the usual tone of sharpness, "George! George!"

A sleepy growl came to her.

"Come, come it's time t' git up," she continued. "Come now, git right up!"

Later she went again to the door. "George, are yeh gittin' up?"

"Huh?"

"Are yeh gittin' up?"

"Yes, I'll git right up!" He had introduced a valor into his voice which she detected to be false. She went to his bedside and took him by the shoulder. "George—George—git up!"

From the mist-lands of sleep he began to protest incoherently. "Oh, le' me be, won' yeh? 'M sleepy!"

She continued to shake him, "Well, it's time t' git up. Come—come—come on, now."

Her voice, shrill with annoyance, pierced his ears in a slender, piping thread of sound. He turned over on the pillow to bury his head in his arms. When he expostulated, his tones came half-smothered. "Oh le' me be, can't yeh? There's plenty 'a time! Jest fer ten minutes! 'M sleepy!"

She was implacable. "No, yeh must git up now! Yeh ain't got more'n time enough t' eat yer breakfast an' git t' work."

Eventually he arose, sullen and grumbling. Later he came to his breakfast, blinking his dry eyelids, his stiffened features set in a mechanical scowl.

Each morning his mother went to his room, and fought a battle to arouse him. She was like a soldier. Despite his pleadings, his threats, she remained at her post, imperturbable and unyielding. These affairs assumed large proportions in his life. Sometimes he grew beside himself with a bland, unformulated wrath. The whole thing was a consummate imposition. He felt that he was being cheated of his sleep. It was an injustice to compel him to arise morning after morning with bitter regularity, before the sleep-gods had at all loosened their grasp. He hated that unknown force which directed his life.

One morning he swore a tangled mass of oaths, aimed into the air, as if the injustice poised there. His mother flinched at first; then her mouth set in the little straight line. She saw that the momentous occasion had come. It was the time of the critical battle. She turned upon him valorously. "Stop your swearin', George Kelcey. I won't have yeh talk so before me! I won't have it! Stop this minute! Not another word! Do yeh think I'll allow yeh t' swear b'fore me like that? Not another word! I won't have it! I declare I won't have it another minute!"

At first her projected words had slid from his mind as if striking against ice, but at last he heeded her. His face grew sour with passion and misery. He spoke in tones dark with dislike. "Th' 'ell yeh won't? Whatter yeh goin' t' do 'bout it?" Then, as if he considered that he had not been sufficiently impressive, he arose and slowly walked over to her. Having arrived at point-blank range he spoke again. "Whatter yeh goin't' do 'bout it?" He regarded her then with an unaltering scowl, albeit his mien was as dark and cowering as that of a condemned criminal.

She threw out her hands in the gesture of an impotent one. He was acknowledged victor. He took his hat and slowly left her.

For three days they lived in silence. He brooded upon his mother's agony and felt a singular joy in it. As opportunity offered, he did little despicable things. He was going to make her abject. He was now uncontrolled, ungoverned; he wished to be an emperor. Her suffering was all a sort of compensation for his own dire pains.

She went about with a gray, impassive face. It was as if she had survived a massacre in which all that she loved had been torn from her by the brutality of savages.

One evening at six he entered and stood looking at his mother as she peeled potatoes. She had hearkened to his coming listlessly, without emotion, and at his entrance she did not raise her eyes.

"Well, I'm fired," he said, suddenly.

It seemed to be the final blow. Her body gave a convulsive movement in the chair. When she finally lifted her eyes, horror possessed her face. Her under jaw had fallen. "Fired? Outa work? Why—George?" He went over to the window and stood with his back to her. He could feel her gray stare upon him.

"Yep! Fired!"

At last she said, "Well—whatter yeh goin' t' do?"

He tapped the pane with his finger-nail. He answered in a tone made hoarse and unnatural by an assumption of gay carelessness, "Oh, nothin'!"

She began, then, her first weeping. "Oh—George—George— George ——"

He looked at her scowling. "Ah, whatter yeh givin' us? Is this all I git when I come home f'm being fired? Anybody 'ud think it was my fault. I couldn't help it."

She continued to sob in a dull, shaking way. In the pose of her head there was an expression of her conviction that comprehension of her pain was impossible to the universe. He paused for a moment, and then, with his usual tactics, went out, slamming the door. A pale flood of sunlight, imperturbable at its vocation, streamed upon the little old woman, bowed with pain, forlorn in her chair.

XV

KELCEY WAS STANDING ON the corner next day when three little boys came running. Two halted some distance away, and the other came forward. He halted before Kelcey, and spoke importantly.

"Hey, your ol' woman's sick."

"What?"

"Your ol' woman's sick."

"Git out!"

"She is, too!"

"Who tol' yeh?"

"Mis' Callahan. She said fer me t' run an' tell yeh. Dey want yeh."

A swift dread struck Kelcey. Like flashes of light little scenes from the past shot through his brain. He had thoughts of a vengeance from the clouds. As he glanced about him the familiar view assumed a meaning that was ominous and dark. There was prophecy of disaster in the street, the buildings, the sky, the people. Something tragic and terrible in the air was known to his nervous, quivering nostrils. He spoke to the little boy in a tone that quavered. "All right!"

Behind him he felt the sudden contemplative pause of his companions of the gang. They were watching him. As he went rapidly up the street he knew that they had come out to the middle of the walk and were staring after him. He was glad that they could not see his face, his trembling lips, his eyes wavering in fear. He stopped at the door of his home and stared at the panel as if he saw written thereon a word. A moment later he entered. His eye comprehended the room in a frightened glance.

His mother sat gazing out at the opposite walls and windows. She was leaning her head upon the back of the chair. Her face was overspread with a singular pallor, but the glance of her eyes was strong and the set of her lips was tranquil.

He felt an unspeakable thrill of thanksgiving at seeing her seated there calmly. "Why, mother, they said yeh was sick," he cried, going toward her impetuously. "What's th' matter?"

She smiled at him. "Oh, it ain't nothin'! I on'y got kinda dizzy, that's all." Her voice was sober and had the ring of vitality in it.

He noted her common-place air. There was no alarm or pain in her tones, but the misgivings of the street, the prophetic twinges of his nerves made him still hesitate. "Well—are you sure it ain't? They scared me 'bout t' death."

"No, it ain't anything, on'y some sorta dizzy feelin'. I fell down b'hind th' stove. Missis Callahan, she came an' picked me up. I must 'a laid there fer quite a while. Th' docter said he guessed I'd be all right in a couple 'a hours. I don't feel nothin'!"

Kelcey heaved a great sigh of relief. "Lord, I was scared." He began to beam joyously, since he was escaped from his fright. "Why, I couldn't think what had happened," he told her.

"Well, it ain't nothing" she said.

He stood about awkwardly, keeping his eyes fastened upon her in a sort of surprise, as if he had expected to discover that she had vanished. The reaction from his panic was a thrill of delicious contentment. He took a chair and sat down near her, but presently he jumped up to ask: "There ain't nothin' I can git fer yeh, is ther?" He looked at her eagerly. In his eyes shone love and joy. If it were not for the shame of it he would have called her endearing names.

"No, ther ain't nothin'," she answered. Presently she continued, in a conversational way, "Yeh ain't found no work yit, have yeh?"

The shadow of his past fell upon him then and he became suddenly morose. At last he spoke in a sentence that was a vow, a declaration of change. "No, I ain't, but I'm goin' t' hunt fer it hard, you bet."

She understood from his tone that he was making peace with her. She smiled at him gladly. "Yer a good boy, George!" A radiance from the stars lit her face.

Presently she asked, "D' yeh think yer old boss would take yeh on ag'in if I went t' see him?"

"No," said Kelcey, at once. "It wouldn't do no good! They got all th' men they want. There ain't no room there. It wouldn't do no good." He ceased to beam for a moment as he thought of certain disclosures. "I'm goin' t' try to git work everywheres. I'm goin' t' make a wild break t' git a job, an' if there's one anywheres I'll git it."

She smiled at him again. "That's right, George!"

When it came supper-time he dragged her in her chair over to the table and then scurried to and fro to prepare a meal for her. She laughed gleefully at him. He was awkward and densely ignorant. He exaggerated his helplessness sometimes until she was obliged to lean back in her chair to laugh. Afterward they sat by the window. Her hand rested upon his hair.

ᴥ XVI ᴥ

Wʜᴇɴ Kᴇʟᴄᴇʏ ᴡᴇɴᴛ ᴛᴏ borrow money from old Bleecker, Jones and the others, he discovered that he was below them in social position. Old Bleecker said gloomily that he did not see how he could loan money at that time. When Jones asked him to have a drink, his tone was careless. O'Connor recited at length some bewildering financial troubles of his own. In them all he saw that something had been reversed. They remained silent upon many occasions, when they might have grunted in sympathy for him.

As he passed along the street near his home he perceived Fidsey Corcoran and another of the gang. They made eloquent signs. "Are yen wid us?"

He stopped and looked at them. "What's wrong with yeh?"

"Are yeh wid us er not," demanded Fidsey. "New barkeep'! Big can! We got it over in d' lot. Big can, I tell yeh." He drew a picture in the air, so to speak, with his enthusiastic fingers.

Kelcey turned dejectedly homeward. "Oh, I guess not, this roun'."

"What's d' matter wi'che?" said Fidsey. "Yer gittin' t' be a reg'lar willie! Come ahn, I tell yeh! Youse gits one smoke at d' can b'cause yeh b'longs t' d' gang, an' yeh don't wanta give it up widout er scrap! See? Some udder john'll git yer smoke. Come ahn!"

When they arrived at the place among the bowlders in the vacant lot, one of the band had a huge and battered tin-pail tilted afar up. His throat worked convulsively. He was watched keenly and anxiously by five or six others. Their eyes followed carefully each fraction of distance that the pail was lifted. They were very silent.

Fidsey burst out violently as he perceived what was in progress. "Heh, Tim, yeh big sojer, le' go d' can! What 'a yeh tink! Wese er in dis! Le' go dat!"

He who was drinking made several angry protesting contortions of his throat. Then he put down the pail and swore. "Who's a big sojer? I ain't gittin' more'n me own smoke! Yer too bloomin' swift!

123

Yeh'd tink yeh was d' on'y mug what owned dis can! Close yer face while I gits me smoke!"

He took breath for a moment and then returned the pail to its tilted position. Fidsey went to him and worried and clamored. He interfered so seriously with the action of drinking that the other was obliged to release the pail again for fear of choking.

Fidsey grabbed it and glanced swiftly at the contents. "Dere! Dat's what I was hollerin' at! Lookut d' beer! Not 'nough t' wet yer t'roat! Yehs can't have not'in' on d' level wid youse damn' tanks! Youse was a reg'lar resevoiy, Tim Connigan! Look what yeh lef' us! Ah, say, youse was a dandy! What 'a yeh tink we ah? Willies? Don' we want no smoke? Say, lookut dat can! It's drier'n hell! What 'a yeh tink?"

Tim glanced in at the beer. Then he said: "Well, d' mug what come b'fore me, he on'y lef' me dat much. Blue Billee, he done d' swallerin'! I on'y had a tas'e!"

Blue Billie, from his seat near, called out in wrathful protest: "Yeh lie, Tim. I never had more'n a mouf-ful!" An inspiration evidently came to him then, for his countenance suddenly brightened, and, arising, he went toward the pail. "I ain't had me reg'lar smoke yit! Guess I come in aheader Fidsey, don' I?"

Fidsey, with a sardonic smile, swung the pail behind him. "I guess nit! Not dis minnet! Youse hadger smoke. If yeh ain't, yeh don't git none. See?"

Blue Billie confronted Fidsey determinedly. "D' 'ell I don't!"

"Nit," said Fidsey.

Billie sat down again.

Fidsey drank his portion. Then he manœuvred skilfully before the crowd until Kelcey and the other youth took their shares. "Youse er a mob 'a tanks," he told the gang. "Nobody 'ud git not'in' if dey wasn't on t' yehs!"

Blue Billie's soul had been smouldering in hate against Fidsey. "Ah, shut up! Youse ain't gota take care 'a dose two mugs, dough. Youse hadger smoke, ain't yeh? Den yer tr'u. G' home!"

"Well, I hate t' see er bloke use 'imself fer a tank," said Fidsey. "But youse don't wanta go jollyin' 'round 'bout d' can, Blue, er youse'll git done."

"Who'll do me?" demanded Blue Billie, casting his eye about him.

"Kel' will," said Fidsey, bravely.

"D' 'ell he will?"

"Dat's what he will!"

Blue Billie made the gesture of a warrior. "He never saw d' day 'a his life dat he could do me little finger. If 'e says much t' me, I'll push 'is face all over d' lot."

Fidsey called to Kelcey. "Say, Kel, hear what dis mug is chewin'?"

Kelcey was apparently deep in other matters. His back was half-turned.

Blue Billie spoke to Fidsey in a battleful voice. "Did 'e ever say 'e could do me?"

Fidsey said: "Soitenly 'e did. Youse is dead easy, 'e says. He says he kin punch holes in you, Blue!"

"When did 'e say it?"

"Oh—any time. Youse is a cinch, Kel' says."

Blue Billie walked over to Kelcey. The others of the band followed him exchanging joyful glances.

"Did youse say yeh could do me?"

Kelcey slowly turned, but he kept his eyes upon the ground. He heard Fidsey darting among the others telling of his prowess, preparing them for the downfall of Blue Billie. He stood heavily on one foot and moved his hands nervously. Finally he said, in a low growl, "Well, what if I did?"

The sentence sent a happy thrill through the band. It was the formidable question. Blue Billie braced himself. Upon him came the responsibility of the next step. The gang fell back a little upon all sides. They looked expectantly at Blue Billie.

He walked forward with a deliberate step until his face was close to Kelcey.

"Well, if you did," he said, with a snarl between his teeth, "I'm goin' t' t'ump d' life outa yeh right heh!"

A little boy, wild of eye and puffing, came down the slope as from an explosion. He burst out in a rapid treble, "Is dat Kelcey feller here? Say, yeh ol' woman's sick again. Dey want yeh! Yehs better run! She's awful sick!"

The gang turned with loud growls. "Ah, git outa here!" Fidsey threw a stone at the little boy and chased him a short distance, but he continued to clamor, "Youse better come, Kelcey feller! She's awful sick! She was hollerin'! Dey been lookin' fer yeh over'n hour!" In his eagerness he returned part way, regardless of Fidsey!

Kelcey had moved away from Blue Billie. He said: "I guess I'd better go!" They howled at him. "Well," he continued, "I can't—I don't wanta—I don't wanta leave me mother be—she———"

His words were drowned in the chorus of their derision. "Well, lookahere"—he would begin and at each time their cries and screams ascended. They dragged at Blue Billie. "Go fer 'im, Blue! Slug 'im! Go ahn!"

Kelcey went slowly away while they were urging Blue Billie to do a decisive thing. Billie stood fuming and blustering and explaining himself. When Kelcey had achieved a considerable distance from him, he stepped forward a few paces and hurled a terrible oath. Kelcey looked back darkly.

XVII

WHEN HE ENTERED THE chamber of death, he was brooding over the recent encounter and devising extravagant revenges upon Blue Billie and the others.

The little old woman was stretched upon her bed. Her face and hands were of the hue of the blankets. Her hair, seemingly of a new and wondrous grayness, hung over her temples in whips and tangles. She was sickeningly motionless, save for her eyes, which rolled and swayed in maniacal glances.

A young doctor had just been administering medicine. "There," he said, with a great satisfaction, "I guess that'll do her good!" As he went briskly toward the door he met Kelcey. "Oh," he said. "Son?"

Kelcey had that in his throat which was like fur. When he forced his voice, the words came first low and then high as if they had broken through something. "Will she—will she ———"

The doctor glanced back at the bed. She was watching them as she would have watched ghouls, and muttering. "Can't tell," he said. "She's wonderful woman! Got more vitality than you and I together! Can't tell! May—may not! Good-day! Back in two hours."

In the kitchen Mrs. Callahan was feverishly dusting the furniture, polishing this and that. She arranged everything in decorous rows. She was preparing for the coming of death. She looked at the floor as if she longed to scrub it.

The doctor paused to speak in an undertone to her, glancing at the bed. When he departed she labored with a renewed speed.

Kelcey approached his mother. From a little distance he called to her. "Mother—mother ——" He proceeded with caution lest this mystic being upon the bed should clutch at him.

"Mother—mother—don't yeh know me?" He put forth apprehensive, shaking fingers and touched her hand.

There were two brilliant steel-colored points upon her eyeballs. She was staring off at something sinister.

Suddenly she turned to her son in a wild babbling appeal. "Help me! Help me! Oh, help me! I see them coming."

Kelcey called to her as to a distant place. "Mother! Mother!" She looked at him, and then there began within her a struggle to reach him with her mind. She fought with some implacable power whose fingers were in her brain. She called to Kelcey in stammering, incoherent cries for help.

Then she again looked away. "Ah, there they come! There they come! Ah, look—look—loo—" She arose to a sitting posture without the use of her arms.

Kelcey felt himself being choked. When her voice pealed forth in a scream he saw crimson curtains moving before his eyes. "Mother—oh, mother—there's nothin'—there's nothin' ——"

She was at a kitchen-door with a dish-cloth in her hand. Within there had just been a clatter of crockery. Down through the trees of the orchard she could see a man in a field ploughing. "Bill—o-o-oh, Bill—have yeh seen Georgie? Is he out there with you? Georgie! Georgie! Come right here this minnet! Right—this—minnet!"

She began to talk to some people in the room. "I want t' know what yeh want here! I want yeh t' git out! I don't want yeh here! I don't feel good t'-day, an' I don't want yeh here! I don't feel good t'-day! I want yeh t' git out!" Her voice became peevish. "Go away! Go away! Go away!"

Kelcey lay in a chair. His nerveless arms allowed his fingers to sweep the floor. He became so that he could not hear the chatter from the bed, but he was always conscious of the ticking of the little clock out on the kitchen shelf.

When he aroused, the pale-faced but plump young clergyman was before him.

"My poor lad ———" began this latter.

The little old woman lay still with her eyes closed. On the table at the head of the bed was a glass containing a water-like medicine. The reflected lights made a silver star on its side. The two men sat side by side, waiting. Out in the kitchen Mrs. Callahan had taken a chair by the stove and was waiting.

Kelcey began to stare at the wall-paper. The pattern was clusters of brown roses. He felt them like hideous crabs crawling upon his brain.

Through the door-way he saw the oil-cloth covering of the table catching a glimmer from the warm afternoon sun. The window disclosed a fair, soft sky, like blue enamel, and a fringe of chimneys and roofs, resplendent here and there. An endless roar, the eternal trample of the marching city, came mingled with vague cries. At intervals the woman out by the stove moved restlessly and coughed.

Over the transom from the hall-way came two voices.

"Johnnie!"

"Wot!"

"You come right here t' me! I want yehs t' go t' d' store fer me!"

"Ah, ma, send Sally!"

"No, I will not! You come right here!"

"All right, in a minnet!"

"Johnnie!"

"In a minnet, I tell yeh!"

"Johnnie ———" There was the sound of a heavy tread, and later a boy squealed. Suddenly the clergyman started to his feet. He rushed forward and peered. The little old woman was dead.

≈ **OTHER WRITINGS**
ABOUT NEW YORK ≈

A NIGHT AT THE MILLIONAIRE'S CLUB.

A DOZEN OF THE members were enjoying themselves in the library. Their eyes were for the most part fixed in concrete stares at the ceiling where the decorations cost seventy-four dollars per square inch. An ecstatic murmur came from the remote corners of the apartment where each chair occupied two thousand dollars worth of floor. William C. Whitney was neatly arranged in a prominent seat to impart a suggestion of brains to the general effect. A clock had been chiming at intervals of ten minutes during the evening, and at each time of striking, Mr. Depew had made a joke, per agreement.

The last one, however, had smashed a seven-thousand dollar vase over by the window and Mr. Depew was hesitating. He had some doubt whether, after all, his jokes were worth that much commercially. His fellow members continued to ecstatically admire their isolation from the grimy vandals of the world. The soft breathing of the happy company made a sound like the murmur of pines in a summer wind. In the distance, a steward could be seen charging up seven thousand dollars to Mr. Depew's account; all, otherwise, was joy and perfect peace.

At this juncture, a seventeen-cent lackey upholstered in a three hundred dollar suit of clothes, made his appearance. He skated gracefully over the polished floor on snowshoes. Halting in the centre of the room, he made seven low bows and sang a little ode to Plutus.* Then he made a swift gesture, a ceremonial declaration that he was lower than the mud on the gaiters of the least wealthy of those before him, and spoke: "Sirs, there is a deputation of visitors in the hall who give their names as Ralph Waldo Emerson, Nathaniel Hawthorne, George Washington and Alexander Hamilton. They beg the favor of an audience."

A slumbering member in a large arm chair aroused and said: "Who?" And this pertinent interrogation was followed by others in

---

*Greek god of wealth.

various tones of astonishment and annoyance. "What's their names?" "Who did you say?" "What the devil do they want here?"

The lackey made seven more bows and sang another little ode. Then he spoke very distinctly: "Sirs, persons giving their names as Ralph Waldo Emerson, Nathaniel Hawthorne, George Washington and Alexander Hamilton desire the favor of an audience. They—"

But he was interrupted. "Don't know 'em!" "Who the deuce are these people anyhow!" "By Jove, here's a go! Want to see us, deuce take me!" "Well, I'm—"

It was at this point that Erroll Van Dyck Strathmore suddenly displayed those qualities which made his friends ever afterward look upon him as a man who would rise supreme at a crisis. He asked one question, but it was terse, sharp, and skillful, a master-piece of a man with presence of mind:

"Where are they from?"

"Sir," said the lackey, "they said they were from America!"

Strathmore paused but a moment to formulate his second searching question. His friends looked at him with admiration and awe. "Do they look like respectable people?"

The lackey arched his eyebrows. "Well—I don't know, sir." He was very discreet.

This reply created great consternation among the members. There was a wild scramble for places of safety. There were hurried commands given to the lackey. "Don't bring 'em in here!" "Throw 'em out!" "Kill 'em!" But over all the uproar could be heard the voice of the imperturbably Strathmore. He was calmly giving orders to the servant.

"You will tell them that as we know no one in America, it is not possible that we have had the honor of their acquaintance, but that nevertheless it is our pleasure to indulge them a little, as it is possible that they are respectable people. However, they must not construe this into permission to come again. You will say to them that if they will repair quietly to any convenient place, wash their hands and procure rubber bibs, they may return and look at the remains of a cigarette which I carelessly threw upon the door-step. Tell the steward to provide each man with a recipe for Mr. Jones-Jones Smith-Jones' terrapin stew and a gallery ticket for the Kilanyi living pictures, then bid them go in safety. Afterward, you will sponge off the front steps and give the door-mat to one of those down-town clubs. You may go."

As the servant skated forth on his errand, Mr. Whitney fell in a death-like swoon, unnoticed, as the company thronged about the adroit, the brave Erroll Van Dyck Strathmore. "Bravo, old man, you saved us!" "What skill, what diplomacy!" "Egad, but you have courage!"

Suddenly the clock noted the time of ten minutes after twelve. Mr. Depew sprang to his feet. A broad smile illuminated his face.

"Say, fellows, the other day—" But he was surrounded by slumbering figures. His smile changed then to a glare of bitter disappointment. In a burst of rage he hurled a champagne bottle at the clock and broke it to smithereens. Its cost was $4,675. He strode over to the ex-secretary. When Mr. Whitney had become aroused, the following conversation ensued:

"Say, Willie, what are we doing here?"

"I don't know, Chauncey!"

"Well, let's float,* then!"

"Float it is, Chauncey!"

On the sidewalk they turned to regard each other.

"An antidote, Willie?"

"Well, I should say, Chauncey!"

They started on a hard run down the avenue.

---

*Leave; depart.

AN EXPERIMENT IN MISERY

AN EVENING, A NIGHT AND A MORNING WITH THOSE CAST OUT. THE TRAMP LIVES LIKE A KING BUT HIS ROYALTY, TO THE NOVITIATE, HAS DRAWBACKS OF SMELLS AND BUGS. LODGED WITH AN ASSASSIN. A WONDERFULLY VIVID PICTURE OF A STRANGE PHASE OF NEW YORK LIFE, WRITTEN FOR "THE PRESS" BY THE AUTHOR OF "MAGGIE."

TWO MEN STOOD REGARDING a tramp.

"I wonder how he feels," said one, reflectively. "I suppose he is homeless, friendless, and has, at the most, only a few cents in his pocket. And if this is so, I wonder how he feels."

The other being the elder, spoke with an air of authoritative wisdom. "You can tell nothing of it unless you are in that condition yourself. It is idle to speculate about it from this distance."

"I suppose so," said the younger man, and then he added as from an inspiration: "I think I'll try it. Rags and tatters, you know, a couple of dimes, and hungry, too, if possible. Perhaps I could discover his point of view or something near it."

"Well, you might," said the other, and from those words begins this veracious narrative of an experiment in misery.

The youth went to the studio of an artist friend, who, from his store, rigged him out in an aged suit and a brown derby hat that had been made long years before. And then the youth went forth to try to eat as the tramp may eat, and sleep as the wanderers sleep. It was late at night, and a fine rain was swirling softly down, covering the pavements with a bluish luster. He began a weary trudge toward the downtown places, where beds can be hired for coppers. By the time he had reached City Hall Park he was so completely plastered with yells of "bum" and "hobo," and with various unholy epithets that small boys had applied to him at intervals that he was in a state of profound dejection, and looked searchingly for an outcast of high degree that the two might share miseries. But the lights threw a quivering glare over rows and circles of deserted benches that glistened damply, showing patches of wet sod behind them. It seemed that their usual freights of sorry humanity had fled on this night to better things. There were only squads of well dressed Brooklyn people, who swarmed toward the Bridge.*

He Finds His Field.

The young man loitered about for a time, and then went shuffling off down Park row.† In the sudden descent in style of the dress of the crowd he felt relief. He began to see others whose tatters matched his tatters. In Chatham square‡ there were aimless men strewn in front of saloons and lodging houses. He aligned himself with these men, and turned slowly to occupy himself with the pageantry of the street.

The mists of the cold and damp night made an intensely blue haze, through which the gaslights in the windows of stores and saloons shone with a golden radiance. The street cars rumbled softly, as if going upon carpet stretched in the aisle made by the pillars of the elevated road. Two interminable processions of people went along the wet pavements, spattered with black mud that made each shoe leave a scar-like impression. The high buildings lurked a-back, shrouded in shadows. Down a side street there were mystic curtains of purple and black, on which lamps dully glittered like embroidered flowers.

A saloon stood with a voracious air on a corner. A sign leaning against the front of the doorpost announced: "Free hot soup to-night." The swing doors snapping to and fro like ravenous lips, made gratified smacks, as if the saloon were gorging itself with plump men.

Caught by the delectable sign, the young man allowed himself to be swallowed. A bartender placed a schooner of dark and portentous

---

*Brooklyn Bridge
†Street in lower Manhattan located at the foot of City Hall Park.
‡Confluence of several major thoroughfares in lower Manhattan; today Chatham Square is the heart of Chinatown.

beer on the bar. Its monumental form up-reared until the froth a-top was above the crown of the young man's brown derby.

He Finds His Supper.

"Soup over there, gents," said the bartender, affably. A little yellow man in rags and the youth grasped their schooners and went with speed toward a lunch counter, where a man with oily but imposing whiskers ladled genially from a kettle until he had furnished his two mendicants with a soup that was steaming hot and in which there were little floating suggestions of chicken. The young man, sipping his broth, felt the cordiality expressed by the warmth of the mixture, and he beamed at the man with oily but imposing whiskers, who was presiding like a priest behind an altar. "Have some more, gents?" he inquired of the two sorry figures before him. The little yellow man accepted with a swift gesture, but the youth shook his head and went out, following a man whose wondrous seediness promised that he would have a knowledge of cheap lodging houses.

On the sidewalk he accosted the seedy man. "Say, do you know a cheap place t' sleep?"

The other hesitated for a time, gazing sideways. Finally he nodded in the direction of up the street. "I sleep up there," he said, "when I've got th' price."

"How much?"

"Ten cents."

The young man shook his head dolefully. "That's too rich for me."

Enter The Assassin.

At that moment there approached the two a reeling man in strange garments. His head was a fuddle of bushy hair and whiskers from which his eyes peered with a guilty slant. In a close scrutiny it was possible to distinguish the cruel lines of a mouth, which looked as if its lips had just closed with satisfaction over some tender and piteous morsel. He appeared like an assassin steeped in crime performed awkwardly.

But at this time his voice was tuned to the coaxing key of an affectionate puppy. He looked at the men with wheedling eyes and began to sing a little melody for charity.

"Say, gents, can't yeh give a poor feller a couple of cents t' git a bed. Now, yeh know how a respecter'ble gentlem'n feels when he's down on his luck an' I—"

The seedy man, staring with imperturbable countenance at a train which clattered overhead, interrupted in an expressionless voice: "Ah, go t' h—!"

But the youth spoke to the prayerful assassin in tones of astonishment and inquiry. "Say, you must be crazy! Why don't yeh strike somebody that looks as if they had money?"

The assassin, tottering about on his uncertain legs, and at intervals brushing imaginary cobwebs from before his nose, entered into a long explanation of the psychology of the situation. It was so profound that it was unintelligible.

When he had exhausted the subject the young man said to him: "Let's see th' five cents."

The assassin wore an expression of drunken woe at this sentence, filled with suspicion of him. With a deeply pained air he began to fumble in his clothing, his red hands trembling. Presently he announced in a voice of bitter grief, as if he had been betrayed: "There's on'y four."

He Finds His Bed.

"Four," said the young man thoughtfully. "Well, look-a-here, I'm a stranger here, an' if ye'll steer me to your cheap joint I'll find the other three."

The assassin's countenance became instantly radiant with joy. His whiskers quivered with the wealth of his alleged emotions. He seized the young man's hand in a transport of delight and friendliness.

"B'gawd," he cried, "if ye'll do that, b'gawd, I'd say yeh was a damned good feller, I would, an' I'd remember yeh all m' life, I would, b'gawd, an' if I ever got a chance I'd return th' compliment"—he spoke with drunken dignity—"b'gawd, I'd treat yeh white, I would, an' I'd allus remember yeh—"

The young man drew back, looking at the assassin coldly. "Oh, that's all right," he said. "You show me th' joint—that's all you've got t' do."

The assassin, gesticulating gratitude, led the young man along a dark street. Finally he stopped before a little dusty door. He raised his hand impressively. "Look-a-here," he said, and there was a thrill of deep and ancient wisdom upon his face, "I've brought yeh here, an' that's my part, ain't it? If th' place don't suit yeh yeh needn't git mad at me, need yeh? There won't be no bad feelin', will there?"

"No," said the young man.

The assassin waved his arm tragically and led the march up the steep stairway. On the way the young man furnished the assassin with three pennies. At the top a man with benevolent spectacles looked at them through a hole in the board. He collected their money, wrote some names on a register, and speedily was leading the two men along a gloom shrouded corridor.

A Place of Smells.

Shortly after the beginning of this journey the young man felt his liver turn white, for from the dark and secret places of the building there suddenly came to his nostrils strange and unspeakable odors that assailed him like malignant diseases with wings. They seemed to be from human bodies closely packed in dens; the exhalations from a hundred pairs of reeking lips; the fumes from a thousand bygone debauches; the expression of a thousand present miseries.

A man, naked save for a little snuff colored undershirt, was parading sleepily along the corridor. He rubbed his eyes, and, giving vent to a prodigious yawn, demanded to be told the time.

"Half past one."

The man yawned again. He opened a door, and for a moment his form was outlined against a black, opaque interior. To this door came the three men, and as it was again opened the unholy odors rushed out like released fiends, so that the young man was obliged to struggle as against an overpowering wind.

It was some time before the youth's eyes were good in the intense gloom within, but the man with benevolent spectacles led him skillfully, pausing but a moment to deposit the limp assassin upon a cot. He took the youth to a cot that lay tranquilly by the window, and, showing him a tall locker for clothes that stood near the head with the ominous air of a tombstone, left him.

To The Polite, Horrors.

The youth sat on his cot and peered about him. There was a gas jet in a distant part of the room that burned a small flickering orange hued flame. It caused vast masses of tumbled shadows in all parts of the place, save where, immediately about it, there was a little gray haze. As the young man's eyes became used to the darkness he could see upon the cots that thickly littered the floor the forms of men sprawled out, lying in deathlike silence or heaving and snoring with tremendous effort, like stabbed fish.

The youth locked his derby and his shoes in the mummy case near him and then lay down with his old and familiar coat around his shoulders. A blanket he handled gingerly, drawing it over part of the coat. The cot was leather covered and cold as melting snow. The youth was obliged to shiver for some time on this affair, which was like a slab. Presently, however, his chill gave him peace, and during this period of leisure from it he turned his head to stare at his friend, the assassin, whom he could dimly discern where he lay sprawled on a cot in the abandon of a man filled with drink. He was snoring with incredible vigor. His wet hair and beard dimly glistened and his inflamed nose shone with subdued luster like a red light in a fog.

Within reach of the youth's hand was one who lay with yellow breast and shoulders bare to the cold drafts. One arm hung over the side of the cot and the fingers lay full length upon the wet cement floor of the room. Beneath the inky brows could be seen the eyes of the man exposed by the partly opened lids. To the youth it seemed that he and this corpse-like being were exchanging a prolonged stare and that the other threatened with his eyes. He drew back, watching this neighbor from the shadows of his blanket edge. The man did not move once through the night, but lay in this stillness as of death, like a body stretched out, expectant of the surgeon's knife.

Men Lay Like The Dead.

And all through the room could be seen the tawny hues of naked flesh, limbs thrust into the darkness, projecting beyond the cots; up-reared knees; arms hanging, long and thin, over the cot edges. For the most part they were statuesque, carven, dead. With the curious lockers standing all about like tombstones there was a strange effect of a graveyard, where bodies were merely flung.

Yet occasionally could be seen limbs wildly tossing in fantastic nightmare gestures, accompanied by guttural cries, grunts, oaths. And there was one fellow off in a gloomy corner, who in his dreams was oppressed by some frightful calamity, for of a sudden he began to utter long wails that went almost like yells from a hound, echoing wailfully and weird through this chill place of tombstones, where men lay like the dead.

The sound, in its high piercing beginnings that dwindled to final melancholy moans, expressed a red and grim tragedy of the unfathomable possibilities of the man's dreams. But to the youth these were not merely the shrieks of a vision pierced man. They were an utterance of the meaning of the room and its occupants. It was to him the protest of the wretch who feels the touch of the imperturbably granite wheels and who then cries with an impersonal eloquence, with a strength not from him, giving voice to the wail of a whole section, a class, a people. This, weaving into the young man's brain and mingling with his views of these vast and somber shadows that like mighty black fingers curled around the naked bodies, made the young man so that he did not sleep, but lay carving biographies for these men from his meager experience. At times the fellow in the corner howled in a writhing agony of his imaginations.

Then Morning Came.

Finally a long lance point of gray light shot through the dusty panes of the window. Without, the young man could see roofs drearily white in the dawning. The point of light yellowed and grew brighter, until the golden rays of the morning sun came in bravely and strong. They touched with radiant color the form of a small, fat man, who snored in stuttering fashion. His round and shiny bald head glowed suddenly with the valor of a decoration. He sat up, blinked at the sun, swore fretfully and pulled his blanket over the ornamental splendors of his head.

The youth contentedly watched this rout of the mystic shadows before the bright spears of the sun and presently he slumbered. When he awoke he heard the voice of the assassin raised in valiant curses. Putting up his head he perceived his comrade seated on the side of the cot engaged in scratching his neck with long finger nails that rasped like files.

"Hully* Jee dis is a new breed. They've got can openers on their feet," he continued in a violent tirade.

The young man hastily unlocked his closet and took out his clothes. As he sat on the side of the cot, lacing his shoes, he glanced about and saw that daylight had made the room comparatively commonplace and uninteresting. The men, whose faces seemed stolid, serene or absent, were engaged in dressing, while a great crackle of bantering conversation arose.

A few were parading in unconcerned nakedness. Here and there were men of brawn, whose skins shone clear and ruddy. They took splendid poses, standing massively, like chiefs. When they had dressed in their ungainly garments there was an extraordinary change. They then showed bumps and deficiencies of all kinds.

There were others who exhibited many deformities. Shoulders were slanting, bumped, pulled this way and pulled that way. And notable among these latter men was the little fat man who had refused to allow his head to be glorified. His pudgy form, builded like a pear, bustled to and fro, while he swore in fishwife fashion. It appeared that some article of his apparel had vanished.

---

*Holy (dialect).

The young man, attired speedily, went to his friend, the assassin. At first the latter looked dazed at the sight of the youth. This face seemed to be appealing to him through the cloud wastes of his memory. He scratched his neck and reflected. At last he grinned, a broad smile gradually spreading until his countenance was a round illumination. "Hello, Willie," he cried, cheerily.

"Hello," said the young man. "Are yeh ready t' fly?"

"Sure." The assassin tied his shoe carefully with some twine and came ambling.

When he reached the street the young man experienced no sudden relief from unholy atmospheres. He had forgotten all about them, and had been breathing naturally and with no sensation of discomfort or distress.

He was thinking of these things as he walked along the street, when he was suddenly startled by feeling the assassin's hand, trembling with excitement, clutching his arm, and when the assassin spoke, his voice went into quavers from a supreme agitation.

"I'll be hully, bloomin' blowed, if there wasn't a feller with a nightshirt on up there in that joint!"

The youth was bewildered for a moment, but presently he turned to smile indulgently at the assassin's humor.

"Oh, you're a d—liar," he merely said.

Whereupon the assassin began to gesture extravagantly and take oath by strange gods. He frantically placed himself at the mercy of remarkable fates if his tale were not true. "Yes, he did! I cross m' heart thousan' times!" he protested, and at the time his eyes were large with amazement, his mouth wrinkled in unnatural glee. "Yessir! A nightshirt! A hully white nightshirt!"

"You lie!"

"Nosir! I hope ter die b'fore I kin git anudder ball if there wasn't a jay wid a hully, bloomin' white nightshirt!"

His face was filled with the infinite wonder of it. "A hully white nightshirt," he continually repeated.

The young man saw the dark entrance to a basement restaurant. There was a sign which read, "No mystery about our hash," and there were other age stained and world battered legends which told him that the place was within his means. He stopped before it and spoke to the assassin. "I guess I'll git somethin' t' eat."

Breakfast.

At this the assassin, for some reason, appeared to be quite embarrassed. He gazed at the seductive front of the eating place for a moment. Then he started slowly up the street. "Well, goodby, Willie," he said, bravely.

For an instant the youth studied the departing figure. Then he called out, "Hol' on a minnet." As they came together he spoke in a certain fierce way, as if he feared that the other could think him to be weak. "Look-a-here, if yeh wanta git some breakfas' I'll lend yeh three cents t' do it with. But say, look-a-here, you've gota git out an' hustle. I ain't goin' t' support yeh, or I'll go broke b'fore night. I ain't no millionaire."

"I take me oath, Willie," said the assassin, earnestly, "th' on'y thing I really needs is a ball. Me t'roat feels like a fryin' pan. But as I can't git a ball, why, th' next bes' thing is breakfast, an' if yeh do that fer me, b'gawd, I'd say yeh was th' whitest lad I ever see."

They spent a few moments in dexterous exchanges of phrases, in which they each protested that the other was, as the assassin had originally said, a "respecter'ble gentlem'n." And they concluded with mutual assurances that they were the souls of intelligence and virtue. Then they went into the restaurant.

There was a long counter, dimly lighted from hidden sources. Two or three men in soiled white aprons rushed here and there.

A Retrospect.

The youth bought a bowl of coffee for two cents and a roll for one cent. The assassin purchased the same. The bowls were webbed with brown seams, and the tin spoons wore an air of having emerged from the first pyramid. Upon them were black, moss like encrustations of age, and they were bent and scarred from the attacks of long forgotten teeth. But over their repast the wanderers waxed warm and mellow. The assassin grew affable as the hot mixture went soothingly down his parched throat, and the young man felt courage flow in his veins.

Memories began to throng in on the assassin, and he brought forth long tales, intricate, incoherent, delivered with a chattering swiftness as from an old woman. "—great job out'n Orange. Boss keep yeh hustlin', though, all time. I was there three days, and then I went an' ask'im t' lend me a dollar. 'G-g-go ter the devil,' he ses, an' I lose me job."

—"South no good. Damn niggers work for twenty-five an' thirty cents a day. Run white man out. Good grub, though. Easy livin'."

—"Yas; useter work little in Toledo, raftin' logs. Make two or three dollars er day in the spring. Lived high. Cold as ice, though, in the winter"—

"I was raised in northern N'York. O-o-o-oh, yeh jest oughto live there. No beer ner whisky, though, way off in the woods. But all th' good hot grub yeh can eat., B'gawd, I hung around there long as I could till th' ol' man fired me. 'Git t'hell outa here, yeh wuthless skunk, git t'hell outa here an' go die,' he ses. 'You're a fine father,' I ses, 'you are,' an' I quit 'im."

As they were passing from the dim eating place they encountered an old man who was trying to steal forth with a tiny package of food, but a tall man with an indomitable mustache stood dragon fashion, barring the way of escape. They heard the old man raise a plaintive protest. "Ah, you always want to know what I take out, and you never see that I usually bring a package in here from my place of business."

The Life of a King.

As the wanderers trudged slowly along Park row, the assassin began to expand and grow blithe. "B'gawd, we've been livin' like kings," he said, smacking appreciative lips.

"Look out or we'll have t' pay fer it t' night," said the youth, with gloomy warning.

But the assassin refused to turn his gaze toward the future. He went with a limping step, into which he injected a suggestion of lamblike gambols. His mouth was wreathed in a red grin.

In the City Hall Park the two wanderers sat down in the little circle of benches sanctified by traditions of their class. They huddled in their old garments, slumbrously conscious of the march of the hours which for them had no meaning.

The people of the street hurrying hither and thither made a blend of black figures, changing, yet frieze like. They walked in their good clothes as upon important missions, giving no gaze to the two wanderers seated upon the benches. They expressed to the young man his infinite distance from all that he valued. Social position, comfort, the pleasures of living, were unconquerable kingdoms. He felt a sudden awe.

And in the background a multitude of buildings, of pitiless hues and sternly high, were to him emblematic of a nation forcing its regal head into the clouds, throwing no downward glances; in the sublimity of its aspirations ignoring the wretches who may flounder at its feet. The roar of the city in his ear was to him the confusion of strange tongues, babbling heedlessly; it was the clink of coin, the voice of the city's hopes which were to him no hopes.

He confessed himself an outcast, and his eyes from under the lowered rim of his hat began to glance guiltily, wearing the criminal expression that comes with certain convictions.

"Well," said the friend, "did you discover his point of view?"

"I don't know that I did," replied the young man; "but at any rate I think mine own has undergone a considerable alteration."

AN EXPERIMENT IN LUXURY

THE EXPERIENCES OF A YOUTH WHO SOUGHT OUT CROESUS. IN THE GLITTER OF WEALTH. A FUZZY ACROBATIC KITTEN WHICH HELD GREAT RICHNESS AT BAY. LIFE OF THE WOMAN OF GOLD. ARE THERE, AFTER ALL, BURRS UNDER EACH FINE CLOAK AND BENEFITS IN ALL BEGGARS' GARB?

"IF YOU ACCEPT THIS invitation you will have an opportunity to make another social study," said the old friend.

The youth laughed. "If they caught me making a study of them they'd attempt a murder. I would be pursued down Fifth avenue by the entire family."

"Well," persisted the old friend who could only see one thing at a time, "it would be very interesting. I have been told all my life that millionaires have no fun, and I know that the poor are always assured that the millionaire is a very unhappy person. They are informed that miseries swarm around all wealth, that all crowned heads are heavy with care, and—"

"But still—" began the youth.

"And, in the irritating, brutalizing, enslaving environment of their poverty, they are expected to solace themselves with these assurances," continued the old friend. He extended his gloved palm and began to tap it impressively with a finger of his other hand. His legs were spread apart in a fashion peculiar to his oratory. "I believe that it is mostly false. It is true that wealth does not release a man from many things from which he would gladly purchase release. Consequences cannot be bribed. I suppose that every man believes steadfastly that he has a private tragedy which makes him yearn for other existences. But it is impossible for me to believe that these things equalize themselves; that there are burrs under all rich cloaks and benefits in all ragged jackets, and the preaching of it seems wicked to me. There are those who have opportunities; there are those who are robbed of—"

"But look here," said the young man; "what has this got to do with my paying Jack a visit?"

"It has got a lot to do with it," said the old friend sharply. "As I said, there are those who have opportunities; there are those who are robbed—"

"Well, I won't have you say Jack ever robbed anybody of anything, because he's as honest a fellow as ever lived," interrupted the youth, with warmth. "I have known him for years, and he is a perfectly square fellow. He doesn't know about these infernal things. He isn't criminal because you say he is benefited by a condition which other men created."

"I didn't say he was," retorted the old friend. "Nobody is responsible for anything. I wish to Heaven somebody was, and then we could all jump on him. Look here, my boy, our modern civilization is—"

"Oh, the deuce!" said the young man.

The old friend then stood very erect and stern. "I can see by your frequent interruptions that you have not yet achieved sufficient pain in life. I hope one day to see you materially changed. You are yet—"

"There he is now," said the youth, suddenly. He indicated a young man who was passing. He went hurriedly toward him, pausing once to gesture adieu to his old friend.

*   *   *   *

The house was broad and brown and stolid like the face of a peasant. It had an inanity of expression, an absolute lack of artistic strength that was in itself powerful because it symbolized something. It stood, a homely pile of stone, rugged, grimly self reliant, asserting its quality as a fine thing when in reality the beholder usually wondered why so much money had been spent to obtain a complete negation. Then from another point of view it was important and mighty because it stood as a fetish, formidable because of traditions of worship.

At The Portals of Luxury.

When the great door was opened the youth imagined that the footman who held a hand on the knob looked at him with a quick, strange stare. There was nothing definite in it; it was all vague and elusive, but a suspicion was certainly denoted in some way. The youth felt that he, one of the outer barbarians, had been detected to be a barbarian by the guardian of the portal, he of the refined nose, he of the exquisite sense, he who must be more atrociously aristocratic than any that he serves. And the youth, detesting himself for it, found that he would rejoice to take a frightful revenge upon this lackey who, with a glance of his eyes, had called him a name. He would have liked to have been for a time a dreadful social perfection whose hand, waved lazily, would cause hordes of the idolatrous imperfect to be smitten in the eyes. And in the tumult of his imagination he did not think it strange that he should plan in his vision to come around to this house and with the power of his new social majesty, reduce this footman to ashes.

He had entered with an easy feeling of independence, but after this incident the splendor of the interior filled him with awe. He was a wanderer in a fairy land, and who felt that his presence marred certain effects. He was an invader with a shamed face, a man who had come to steal certain colors, forms, impressions that were not his. He had a dim thought that some one might come to tell him to begone.

His friend, unconscious of this swift drama of thought, was already upon the broad staircase. "Come on," he called. When the youth's foot struck from a thick rug and clanged upon the tiled floor he was almost frightened.

There was cool abundance of gloom. High up stained glass caught the sunlight, and made it into marvelous hues that in places touched the dark walls. A broad bar of yellow gilded the leaves of lurking plants. A softened crimson glowed upon the head and shoulders of a bronze swordsman, who perpetually strained in a terrific lunge, his blade thrust at random into the shadow, piercing there an unknown something.

An immense fire place was at one end, and its furnishings gleamed until it resembled a curious door of a palace, and on the threshold, where one would have to pass, a fire burned redly. From some remote place came the sound of a bird twittering busily. And from behind heavy portieres came a subdued noise of the chatter of three, twenty or a hundred women.

He could not relieve himself of this feeling of awe until he had reached his friend's room. There they lounged carelessly and smoked pipes. It was an amazingly comfortable room. It expressed to the visitor that he could do supremely as he chose, for it said plainly that in it the owner did supremely as he chose. The youth wondered if there had not been some domestic skirmishing to achieve so much beautiful disorder. There were various articles left about defiantly, as if the owner openly flaunted the feminine ideas of precision. The disarray of a table that stood prominently defined the entire room. A set of foils, a set of boxing gloves, a lot of illustrated papers, an inkstand and a hat lay entangled upon it. Here was surely a young man, who, when his menacing mother, sisters or servants knocked, would open a slit in the door like a Chinaman in an opium joint, and tell them to leave him to his beloved devices. And yet, withal, the effect was good, because the disorder was not necessary, and because there are some things that when flung down, look to have been flung by an artist. A baby can create an effect with a guitar. It would require genius to deal with the piled up dishes in a Cherry street sink.

"The World of Chance."

The youth's friend lay back upon the broad seat that followed the curve of the window and smoked in blissful laziness. Without one could see the windowless wall of a house overgrown with a green, luxuriant vine. There was a glimpse of a side street. Below were the stables. At intervals a little fox terrier ran into the court and barked tremendously.

The youth, also blissfully indolent, kept up his part of the conversation on the recent college days, but continually he was beset by a stream of sub-conscious reflection. He was beginning to see a vast wonder in it that they two lay sleepily chatting with no more apparent responsibility than rabbits, when certainly there were men, equally fine perhaps, who were being blackened and mashed in the churning life of the lower places. And all this had merely happened; the great secret hand had guided them here and had guided others there. The eternal mystery of social condition exasperated him at this time. He wondered if incomprehensible justice were the sister of open wrong.

And, above all, why was he impressed, awed, overcome by a mass of materials, a collection of the trophies of wealth, when he knew that to him their dominant meaning was that they represented a lavish expenditure? For what reason did his nature so deeply respect all this? Perhaps his ancestors had been peasants bowing heads to the heel of appalling pomp of princes or rows of little men who stood to watch a king kill a flower with his cane. There was one side of him that said there were finer things in life, but the other side did homage.

The Glory of Gold.

Presently he began to feel that he was a better man than many— entitled to a great pride. He stretched his legs like a man in a garden, and he thought that he belonged to the garden. Hues and forms had smothered certain of his comprehensions. There had been times in his life when little voices called to him continually from the darkness; he heard them now as an idle, half-smothered babble on the horizon edge. It was necessary that it should be so, too. There was the horizon, he said, and, of course, there should be a babble of pain on it. Thus it was written; it was a law, he thought. And, anyway, perhaps it was not so bad as those who babbled tried to tell.

In this way and with this suddenness he arrived at a stage. He was become a philosopher, a type of the wise man who can eat but three meals a day, conduct a large business and understand the purposes of infinite power. He felt valuable. He was sage and important.

There were influences, knowledges that made him aware that he was idle and foolish in his new state, but he inwardly reveled like a barbarian in his environment. It was delicious to feel so high and mighty, to feel that the unattainable could be purchased like a penny bun. For a time, at any rate, there was no impossible. He indulged in monarchical reflections.

Parental Portraits.

As they were dressing for dinner his friend spoke to him in this wise: "Be sure not to get off anything that resembles an original thought before my mother. I want her to like you, and I know that when any one says a thing cleverly before her he ruins himself with her forever. Confine your talk to orthodox expressions. Be dreary and unspeakably commonplace in the true sense of the word. Be damnable."

"It will be easy for me to do as you say," remarked the youth.

"As far as the old man goes," continued the other, "he's a blooming good fellow. He may appear like a sort of a crank if he happens to be in that mood, but he's all right when you come to know him. And besides he doesn't dare do that sort of thing with me, because I've got nerve enough to bully him. Oh, the old man is all right."

On their way down the youth lost the delightful mood that he had enjoyed in his friend's rooms. He dropped it like a hat on the stairs. The splendor of color and form swarmed upon him again. He bowed before the strength of this interior; it said a word to him which he believed he should despise, but instead he crouched. In the distance shone his enemy, the footman.

"There will be no people here to-night, so you may see the usual evening row between my sister Mary and me, but don't be alarmed or uncomfortable, because it is quite an ordinary matter," said his friend, as they were about to enter a little drawing room that was well apart from the grander rooms.

The Joys of a Millionaire.

The head of the family, the famous millionaire, sat on a low stool before the fire. He was deeply absorbed in the gambols of a kitten who was plainly trying to stand on her head that she might use all four paws in grappling with an evening paper with which her playmate was poking her ribs. The old man chuckled in complete glee. There was never such a case of abstraction, of want of care. The map of millions was in a far land where mechanics and bricklayers go, a mystic land of little, universal emotions, and he had been guided to it by the quaint gestures of a kitten's furry paws.

His wife, who stood near, was apparently not at all a dweller in thought lands. She was existing very much in the present. Evidently she had been wishing to consult with her husband on some tremendous domestic question, and she was in a state of rampant irritation, because he refused to acknowledge at this moment that she or any such thing as a tremendous domestic question was in existence. At intervals she made savage attempts to gain his attention.

As the youth saw her she was in a pose of absolute despair. And her eyes expressed that she appreciated all the tragedy of it. Ah, they said, hers was a life of terrible burden, of appalling responsibility; her pathway was beset with unsolved problems, her horizon was lined with tangled difficulties, while her husband—the man of millions, continued to play with the kitten. Her expression was an admission of heroism.

The Gold Woman.

The youth saw that here at any rate was one denial of his oratorical old friend's statement. In the face of this woman there was no sign that life was sometimes a joy. It was impossible that there could be any pleasure in living for her. Her features were as lined and creased with care and worriment as those of an apple woman. It was as if the passing of each social obligation, of each binding form of her life, had left its footprints, scarring her face.

Somewhere in her expression there was terrible pride, that kind of pride which, mistaking the form for the real thing, worships itself because of its devotion to the form.

In the lines of the mouth and the set of the chin could be seen the might of a grim old fighter. They denoted all the power of machination of a general, veteran of a hundred battles. The little scars at the corners of her eyes made a wondrously fierce effect, baleful, determined, without regard somehow to ruck of pain. Here was a savage, a barbarian, a spear woman of the Philistines, who fought battles to excel in what are thought to be the refined and worthy things in life; here was a type of Zulu chieftainess who scuffled and scrambled for place before the white altars of social excellence. And woe to the socially weaker who should try to barricade themselves against that dragon.

It was certain that she never rested in the shade of the trees. One could imagine the endless churning of that mind. And plans and other plans coming forth continuously, defeating a rival here, reducing a family there, bludgeoning a man here, a maid there. Woe and wild eyes followed like obedient sheep upon her trail.

Too, the youth thought he could see that here was the true abode of conservatism—in the mothers, in those whose ears displayed their diamonds instead of their diamonds displaying their ears, in the ancient and honorable controllers who sat in remote corners and pulled wires and respected themselves with a magnitude of respect that heaven seldom allows on earth. There lived tradition and superstition. They were perhaps ignorant of that which they worshipped, and, not comprehending it at all, it naturally followed that the fervor of their devotion could set the sky ablaze.

As he watched, he saw, that the mesmeric power of a kitten's waving paws was good. He rejoiced in the spectacle of the little fuzzy cat trying to stand on its head, and by this simple antic defeating some intention of a great domestic Napoleon.

The Business of Being Beautiful.

The three girls of the family were having a musical altercation over by the window. Then and later the youth thought them adorable. They were wonderful to him in their charming gowns. They had time and opportunity to create effects, to be beautiful. And it would have been a wonder to him if he had not found them charming, since making themselves so could but be their principal occupation.

Beauty requires certain justices, certain fair conditions. When in a field no man can say: "Here should spring up a flower; here one should not." With incomprehensible machinery and system, nature sends them forth in places both strange and proper, so that, somehow, as we see them each one is a surprise to us. But at times, at places, one can say: "Here no flower can flourish." The youth wondered then why he had been sometimes surprised at seeing women fade, shrivel, their bosoms flatten, their shoulders crook forward, in the heavy swelter and wrench of their toil. It must be difficult, he thought, for a woman to remain serene and uncomplaining when she contemplated the wonder and the strangeness of it.

The lights shed marvelous hues of softened rose upon the table. In the encircling shadows the butler moved with a mournful, deeply solemn air. Upon the table there was color of pleasure, of festivity, but this servant in the background went to and fro like a slow religious procession.

The youth felt considerable alarm when he found himself involved in conversation with his hostess. In the course of this talk he discovered the great truth that when one submits himself to a thoroughly conventional conversation he runs risks of being most amazingly stupid. He was glad that no one cared to overhear it.

The millionaire, deprived of his kitten, sat back in his chair and laughed at the replies of his son to the attacks of one of the girls. In the rather good wit of his offspring he took an intense delight, but he laughed more particularly at the words of the son.

Croesus Dines.

Indicated in this light chatter about the dinner table there was an existence that was not at all what the youth had been taught to see. Theologians had for a long time told the poor man that riches did not bring happiness, and they had solemnly repeated this phrase until it had come to mean that misery was commensurate with dollars, that each wealthy man was inwardly a miserable wretch. And when a wail of despair of rage had come from the night of the slums they had stuffed this epigram down the throat of he who cried out and told him that he was a lucky fellow. They did this because they feared.

The youth, studying this family group, could not see that they had great license to be pale and haggard. They were no doubt fairly good, being not strongly induced toward the bypaths. Various worlds turned open doors toward them. Wealth in a certain sense is liberty. If they were fairly virtuous he could not see why they should be so persistently pitied.

And no doubt they would dispense their dollars like little seeds upon the soil of the world if it were not for the fact that since the days of the ancient great political economist, the more exalted forms of virtue have grown to be utterly impracticable.

MR. BINKS' DAY OFF

A STUDY OF A CLERK'S HOLIDAY

WHEN BINKS WAS COMING up town in a Broadway cable car one afternoon he caught some superficial glimpses of Madison square* as he ducked his head to peek through between a young woman's bonnet and a young man's newspaper. The green of the little park vaguely astonished Binks. He had grown accustomed to a white and brown park; now, all at once, it was radiant green. The grass, the leaves, had

---

*Small park at Fifth Avenue and East Twenty-third Street in Manhattan; the original home of Madison Square Garden.

come swiftly, silently, as if a great green light from the sky had shone suddenly upon the little desolate hued place.

The vision cheered the mind of Binks. It cried to him that nature was still supreme; he had begun to think the banking business to be the pivot on which the universe turned. Produced by this wealth of young green, faint, faraway voices called to him. Certain subtle memories swept over him. The million leaves looked into his soul and said something sweet and pure in an unforgotten song, the melody of his past. Binks began to dream.

When he arrived at the little Harlem* flat he sat down to dinner with an air of profound dejection, which Mrs. Binks promptly construed into an insult to her cooking, and to the time and thought she had expended in preparing the meal. She promptly resented it. "Well, what's the matter now?" she demanded. Apparently she had asked this question ten thousand times.

"Nothin'," said Binks, shortly, filled with gloom. He meant by this remark that his ailment was so subtle that her feminine mind would not be enlightened by any explanation.

The head of the family was in an ugly mood. The little Binkses suddenly paused in their uproar and became very wary children. They knew that it would be dangerous to do anything irrelevant to their father's bad temper. They studied his face with their large eyes, filled with childish seriousness and speculation. Meanwhile they ate with the most extraordinary caution. They handled their little forks with such care that there was barely a sound. At each slight movement of their father they looked apprehensively at him, expecting the explosion.

The meal continued amid a somber silence. At last, however, Binks spoke, clearing his throat of the indefinite rage that was in it and looking over at his wife. The little Binkses seemed to inwardly dodge, but he merely said: "I wish I could get away into the country for awhile!"

His wife bristled with that brave anger which agitates a woman

---

*Neighborhood in northern Manhattan; in Crane's day Harlem was a middle-class neighborhood.

when she sees fit to assume that her husband is weak spirited. "If I worked as hard as you do, if I slaved over those old books the way you do, I'd have a vacation once in awhile or I'd tear their old office down." Upon her face was a Roman determination. She was a personification of all manner of courages and rebellions and powers.

Binks felt the falsity of her emotion in a vague way, but at that time he only made a sullen gesture. Later, however, he cried out in a voice of sudden violence: "Look at Tommie's dress! Why the dickens don't you put a bib on that child?"

His wife glared over Tommie's head at her husband, as she leaned around in her chair to tie on the demanded bib. The two looked as hostile as warring redskins. In the wife's eyes there was an intense opposition and defiance, an assertion that she now considered the man she had married to be beneath her in intellect, industry, valor. There was in this glance a jeer at the failures of his life. And Binks, filled with an inexpressible rebellion at what was to him a lack of womanly perception and sympathy in her, replied with a look that called his wife a drag, an uncomprehending thing of vain ambitions, the weight of his existence.

The baby meanwhile began to weep because his mother, in her exasperation, had yanked him and hurt his neck. Her anger, groping for an outlet, had expressed itself in the nervous strength of her fingers. "Keep still, Tommie," she said to him. "I didn't hurt you. You neen't cry the minute anybody touches you!" He made a great struggle and repressed his loud sobs, but the tears continued to fall down his cheeks and his under lip quivered from a baby sense of injury, the anger of an impotent child who seems as he weeps to be planning revenges.

"I don't see why you don't keep that child from eternally crying," said Binks, as a final remark. He then arose and went away to smoke, leaving Mrs. Binks with the children and the dishevelled table.

Later that night, when the children were in bed, Binks said to his wife: "We ought to get away from the city for awhile at least this spring. I can stand it in the summer, but in the spring—" He made a motion with his hand that represented the new things that are born in the heart when spring comes into the eyes.

"It will cost something, Phil," said Mrs. Binks.

"That's true," said Binks. They both began to reflect, contemplating the shackles of their poverty. "And besides, I don't believe I could get off," said Binks after a time.

Nothing more was said of it that night. In fact, it was two or three days afterward that Binks came home and said: "Margaret, you get the children ready on Saturday noon and we'll all go out and spend Sunday with your Aunt Sarah!"

When he came home on Saturday his hat was far back on the back of his head from the speed he was in. Mrs. Binks was putting on her bonnet before the glass, turning about occasionally to admonish the little Binkses, who, in their new clothes, were wandering around, stiffly, and getting into all sorts of small difficulties. They had been ready since 11 o'clock. Mrs. Binks had been obliged to scold them continually, one after the other, and sometimes three at once.

"Hurry up," said Binks, immediately, "ain't got much time. Say, you ain't going to let Jim wear that hat, are you? Where's his best one? Good heavens, look at Margaret's dress! It's soiled already! Tommie, stop that, do you hear? Well, are you ready?"

Indeed, it was not until the Binkses had left the city far behind and were careering into New Jersey that they recovered their balances.[1] Then something of the fresh quality of the country stole over them and cooled their nerves. Horse cars and ferryboats were maddening to Binks when he was obliged to convoy a wife and three children. He appreciated the vast expanses of green, through which ran golden hued roads. The scene accented his leisure and his lack of responsibility.

Near the track a little river jostled over the stones. At times the cool thunder of its roar came faintly to the ear. The Ramapo Hills* were in the background, faintly purple, and surrounded with little peaks that shone with the luster of the sun. Binks began to joke heavily with the children. The little Binkses, for their part, asked the most superhuman questions about details of the scenery. Mrs. Binks leaned

---

*Picturesque chain of rocky hills stretching from central New Jersey into New York State.

contentedly back in her seat and seemed to be at rest, which was a most extraordinary thing.

When they got off the train at the little rural station they created considerable interest. Two or three loungers began to view them in a sort of concentrated excitement. They were apparently fascinated by the Binkses and seemed to be indulging in all manner of wild and intense speculation. The agent, as he walked into his station, kept his head turned. Across the dusty street, wide at this place, a group of men upon the porch of a battered grocery store shaded their eyes with their hands. The Binkses felt dimly like a circus and were a trifle bewildered by it. Binks gazed up and down, this way and that; he tried to be unaware of the stare of the citizens. Finally, he approached the loungers, who straightened their forms suddenly and looked very expectant.

"Can you tell me where Miss Pattison lives?"

The loungers arose as one man. "It's th' third house up that road there."

"It's a white house with green shutters!"

"There, that's it—yeh can see it through th' trees!" Binks discerned that his wife's aunt was a well known personage, and also that the coming of the Binkses was an event of vast importance. When he marched off at the head of his flock, he felt like a drum-major. His course was followed by the unwavering, intent eyes of the loungers.

The street was lined with two rows of austere and solemn trees. In one way it was like parading between the plumes on an immense hearse. These trees, lowly sighing in a breath-like wind, oppressed one with a sense of melancholy and dreariness. Back from the road, behind flower beds, controlled by box-wood borders, the houses were asleep in the drowsy air. Between them one could get views of the fields lying in a splendor of gold and green. A monotonous humming song of insects came from the regions of sunshine, and from some hidden barnyard a hen suddenly burst forth in a sustained cackle of alarm. The tranquillity of the scene contained a meaning of peace and virtue that was incredibly monotonous to the warriors from the metropolis. The sense of a city is battle. The Binkses were vaguely irritated and astonished at the placidity of this little town. This life spoke to them of no absorbing nor even interesting thing.

There was something unbearable about it. "I should go crazy if I had to live here," said Mrs. Binks. A warrior in the flood-tide of his blood, going from the hot business of war to a place of utter quiet, might have felt that there was an insipidity in peace. And thus felt the Binkses from New York. They had always named the clash of the swords of commerce as sin, crime, but now they began to imagine something admirable in it. It was high wisdom. They put aside their favorite expressions: "The curse of gold," "A mad passion to get rich," "The rush for the spoils." In the light of their contempt for this stillness, the conflicts of the city were exalted. They were at any rate wondrously clever.

But what they did feel was the fragrance of the air, the radiance of the sunshine, the glory of the fields and the hills. With their ears still clogged by the tempest and fury of city uproars, they heard the song of the universal religion, the mighty and mystic hymn of nature, whose melody is in each landscape. It appealed to their elemental selves. It was as if the earth had called recreant and heedless children and the mother world, of vast might and significance, brought them to sudden meekness. It was the universal thing whose power no one escapes. When a man hears it he usually remains silent. He understands then the sacrilege of speech.

When they came to the third house, the white one with the green blinds, they perceived a woman, in a plaid sun bonnet, walking slowly down a path. Around her was a riot of shrubbery and flowers. From the long and tangled grass of the lawn grew a number of cherry trees. Their dark green foliage was thickly sprinkled with bright red fruit. Some sparrows were scuffling among the branches. The little Binkses began to whoop at the sight of the woman in the plaid sun bonnet.

"Hay-oh, Aunt Sarah, hay-oh!" they shouted.

The woman shaded her eyes with her hand. "Well, good gracious, if it ain't Marg'ret Binks! An' Phil, too! Well, I am surprised!"

She came jovially to meet them. "Why, how are yeh all? I'm awful glad t' see yeh!"

The children, filled with great excitement, babbled questions and ejaculations while she greeted the others.

"Say, Aunt Sarah, gimme some cherries!"

"Look at th' man over there!"

"Look at th' flowers!"

"Gimme some flowers, Aunt Sarah!"

And little Tommie, red faced from the value of his information, bawled out: "Aunt Sah-wee, dey have horse tars where I live!" Later he shouted: "We come on a twain of steam tars!"

Aunt Sarah fairly bristled with the most enthusiastic hospitality. She beamed upon them like a sun. She made desperate attempts to gain possession of everybody's bundles that she might carry them to the house. There was a sort of a little fight over the baggage. The children clamored questions at her; she tried heroically to answer them. Tommie, at times, deluged her with news.

The curtains of the dining room were pulled down to keep out the flies. This made a deep, cool gloom in which corners of the old furniture caught wandering rays of light and shone with a mild luster. Everything was arranged with an unspeakable neatness that was the opposite of comfort. A branch of an apple tree moved by the gentle wind, brushed softly against the closed blinds.

"Take off yer things," said Aunt Sarah.

Binks and his wife remained talking to Aunt Sarah, but the children speedily swarmed out over the farm, raiding in countless directions. It was only a matter of seconds before Jimmie discovered the brook behind the barn. Little Margaret roamed among the flowers, bursting into little cries at sight of new blossoms, new glories. Tommie gazed at the cherry trees for a few moments in profound silence. Then he went and procured a pole. It was very heavy, relatively. He could hardly stagger under it, but with infinite toil he dragged it to the proper place and somehow managed to push it erect. Then with a deep earnestness of demeanor he began a little onslaught upon the trees. Very often his blow missed the entire tree and the pole thumped on the ground. This necessitated the most extraordinary labor. But then at other times he would get two or three cherries at one wild swing of his weapon.

Binks and his wife spent the larger part of the afternoon out under the apple trees at the side of the house. Binks lay down on his back, with his head in the long lush grass. Mrs. Binks moved lazily to and fro in a rocking chair that had been brought from the house. Aunt Sarah, sometimes appearing, was strenuous in an account of relatives, and the Binkses had only to listen. They were glad of it, for this warm, sleepy air, pulsating with the sounds of insects, had enchained them in a great indolence.

It was to this place that Jimmie ran after he had fallen into the brook and scrambled out again. Holding his arms out carefully from his dripping person, he was roaring tremendously. His new sailor suit was a sight. Little Margaret came often to describe the wonders of her journeys, and Tommie, after a frightful struggle with the cherry trees, toddled over and went to sleep in the midst of a long explanation of his operations. The breeze stirred the locks on his baby forehead. His breath came in long sighs of content. Presently he turned his head to cuddle deeper into the grass. One arm was thrown in childish abandon over his head. Mrs. Binks stopped rocking to gaze at him. Presently she bended and noiselessly brushed away a spear of grass that was troubling the baby's temple. When she straightened up she saw that Binks, too, was absorbed in a contemplation of Tommie. They looked at each other presently, exchanging a vague smile. Through the silence came the voice of a plowing farmer berating his horses in a distant field.

The peace of the hills and the fields came upon the Binkses. They allowed Jimmie to sit up in bed and eat cake while his clothes were drying. Uncle Daniel returned from a wagon journey and recited them a ponderous tale of a pig that he had sold to a man with a red beard. They had no difficulty in feeling much interest in the story.

Binks began to expand with enormous appreciation. He would not go into the house until they compelled him. And as soon as the evening meal was finished he dragged his wife forth on a trip to the top of the hill behind the house. There was a great view from there, Uncle Daniel said.

The path, gray with little stones in the dusk, extended above them like a pillar. The pines were beginning to croon in a mournful key, inspired by the evening winds. Mrs. Binks had great difficulty in climbing this upright road. Binks was obliged to assist her, which he did with a considerable care and tenderness. In it there was a sort of a reminiscence of their courtship. It was a repetition of old days. Both enjoyed it because of this fact, although they subtly gave each other to understand that they disdained this emotion as an altogether un-American thing, for she, as a woman, was proud, and he had great esteem for himself as a man.

At the summit they seated themselves upon a fallen tree, near the edge of a cliff. The evening silence was upon the earth below them. Far in the west the sun lay behind masses of corn colored clouds, tumbled and heaved into crags, peaks and canyons. On either hand stood the purple hills in motionless array. The valley lay wreathed in somber shadows. Slowly there went on the mystic process of the closing of the day. The corn colored clouds faded to yellow and finally to a faint luminous green, inexpressibly vague. The rim of the hills was then an edge of crimson. The mountains became a profound blue. From the night, approaching in the east, came a wind. The trees of the mountain raised plaintive voices, bending toward the faded splendors of the day.

This song of the trees arose in low, sighing melody into the still air. It was filled with an infinite sorrow—a sorrow for birth, slavery, death. It was a wail telling the griefs, the pains of all ages. It was the symbol of agonies. It celebrated all suffering. Each man finds in this sound the expression of his own grief. It is the universal voice raised in lamentation.

As the trees huddled and bended as if to hide from their eyes a certain sight the green tints became blue. A faint suggestion of yellow replaced the crimson. The sun was dead.

The Binkses had been silent. These songs of the trees awe. They had remained motionless during this ceremony, their eyes fixed upon the mighty and indefinable changes which spoke to them of the final thing—the inevitable end. Their eyes had an impersonal expression. They were purified, chastened by this sermon, this voice calling to them from the sky. The hills had spoken and the trees had crooned their song. Binks finally stretched forth his arm in a wondering gesture.

"I wonder why," he said; "I wonder why the dickens it—why it—why—"

Tangled in the tongue was the unformulated question of the centuries, but Mrs. Binks had stolen forth her arm and linked it with his. Her head leaned softly against his shoulder.

CONEY ISLAND'S FAILING DAYS

WHAT ONE OF THEM HELD FOR A STROLLING PHILOSOPHER. NOT WHOLLY WITHOUT JOY. THE ADVANTAGES OF GREAT TOYS AND THE UNIMPORTANCE OF BUGS.

"DOWN HERE AT YOUR Coney Island,* toward the end of the season, I am made to feel very sad," said the stranger to me. "The great mournfulness that settles upon a summer resort at this time always depresses me exceedingly. The mammoth empty buildings, planned by extraordinarily optimistic architects, remind me in an unpleasant manner of my youthful dreams. In those days of visions I erected huge castles for the reception of my friends and admirers, and discovered later that I could have entertained them more comfortably in a small two story frame structure. There is a mighty pathos in these gaunt and hollow buildings, impassively and stolidly suffering from an enormous hunger for the public. And the unchangeable, ever imperturbable sea pursues its quaint devices blithely at the feet of these mournful wooden animals, gabbling and frolicking, with no thought for absent man nor maid!"

As the stranger spoke, he gazed with considerable scorn at the emotions of the sea; and the breeze from the far Navesink hills† gently stirred the tangled, philosophic hair upon his forehead. Presently he went on: "The buildings are in effect more sad than the men, but I assure you that some of the men look very sad. I watched a talented and persuasive individual who was operating in front of a tintype‡ gallery, and he had only the most marvelously infrequent

---

*Spit of land on the Atlantic shore of Brooklyn, famed for its amusement parks and honky-tonks.
†Low hills on the New Jersey side of Lower New York Bay.
‡Inexpensive form of photography; the picture is printed on a thin sheet of tin instead of paper.

opportunities to display his oratory and finesse. The occasional stragglers always managed to free themselves before he could drag them into the gallery and take their pictures. In the long intervals he gazed about him with a bewildered air, as if he felt his world dropping from under his feet. Once I saw him spy a promising youth afar off. He lurked with muscles at a tension, and then at the proper moment he swooped. 'Look-a-here,' he said, with tears of enthusiasm in his eyes, 'the best picture in the world! An' on'y four fer a quarter. O'ny jest try it, an' you'll go away perfectly satisfied!'

" 'I'll go away perfectly satisfied without trying it," replied the promising youth, and he did. The tintype man wanted to dash his samples to the ground and whip the promising youth. He controlled himself, however, and went to watch the approach of two women and a little boy who were nothing more than three dots, away down the board walk.

"At one place I heard the voice of a popcorn man raised in a dreadful note, as if he were chanting a death hymn. It made me shiver as I felt all the tragedy of the collapsed popcorn market. I began to see that it was an insult to the pain and suffering of these men to go near to them without buying anything. I took new and devious routes sometimes.

"As for the railroad guards and station men, they were so tolerant of the presence of passengers that I felt it to be an indication of their sense of relief from the summer's battle. They did not seem so greatly irritated by patrons of the railroad as I have seen them at other times. And in all the beer gardens the waiters had opportunity to indulge that delight in each other's society and conversation which forms so important a part in a waiter's idea of happiness. Sometimes the people in a sparsely occupied place will fare more strange than those in a crowded one. At one time I waited twenty minutes for a bottle of the worst beer in Christendom while my waiter told a charmingly naive story to a group of his compatriots. I protested sotto voice at the time that such beer might at least have the merit of being brought quickly.

Crabs That Seemed Fresh.

"The restaurants, however, I think to be quite delicious, being in a large part thoroughly disreputable and always provided with huge piles of red boiled crabs. These huge piles of provision around on the floor and on the oyster counters always give me the opinion that I am dining on the freshest food in the world, and I appreciate the sensation. If need be, it also allows a man to revel in dreams of unlimited quantity.

"I found countless restaurants where I could get things almost to my taste, and, as I ate, watch the grand, eternal motion of the sea and have the waiter come up and put the pepper castor on the menu card to keep the salt breeze from interfering with my order for dinner.

"And yet I have an occasional objection to the sea when dining in sight of it; for a man with a really artistic dining sense always feels important as a duke when he is indulging in his favorite pastime, and, as the sea always makes me feel that I am a trivial object, I cannot dine with absolute comfort in its presence. The conflict of the two perceptions disturbs me. This is why I have grown to prefer the restaurants down among the narrow board streets. I tell you this because I think an explanation is due to you."

As we walked away from the beach and around one of those huge buildings whose pathos had so aroused the stranger's interest, we came into view of two acres of merry-go-rounds, circular swings, roller coasters, observation wheels* and the like. The stranger paused and regarded them.

"Do you know," he said, "I am deeply fascinated by all these toys. For, of course, I perceive that they are really enlarged toys. They reinforce me in my old opinion that humanity only needs to be provided for ten minutes with a few whirligigs and things of the sort, and it can forget at least four centuries of misery. I rejoice in these whirligigs,"† continued the stranger, eloquently, "and as I watch here and there a person going around and around or up and down, or over and over, I say to myself that whirligigs must be made in heaven.

---

*Ferris wheels.
†Merry-go-rounds.

"It is a mystery to me why some man does not provide a large number of wooden rocking horses and let the people sit and dreamfully rock themselves into temporary forgetfulness. There could be intense quiet enforced by special policemen, who, however, should allow subdued conversation on the part of the patrons of the establishment. Deaf mutes should patrol to and fro selling slumberous drinks. These things are none of them insane. They are particularly rational. A man needs a little nerve quiver, and he gets it by being flopped around in the air like a tailess kite. He needs the introduction of a reposeful element, and he procures it upon a swing that makes him feel like thirty-five emotional actresses all trying to swoon upon one rug. There are some people who stand apart and deride these machines. If you could procure a dark night for them and the total absence of their friends they would smile, many of them. I assure you that I myself would indulge in these forms of intoxication if I were not a very great philosopher."

Dreariness in The Music Halls.

We strolled in the music hall district, where the sky lines of the row of buildings are wondrously near to each other, and the crowded little thoroughfares resemble the eternal "Street Scene in Cairo." There was an endless strumming and tooting and shrill piping in clamor and chaos, while at all times there were interspersed the sharp cracking sounds from the shooting galleries and the coaxing calls of innumerable fakirs. At the stand where one can throw at wooden cats and negro heads and be in danger of winning cigars, a self reliant youth bought a whole armful of base balls, and missed with each one. Everybody grinned. A heavily built man openly jeered. "You couldn't hit a church!" "Couldn't I?" retorted the young man, bitterly. Near them three bad men were engaged in an intense conversation. The fragment of a sentence suddenly dominated the noises. "He's got money to burn." The sun, meanwhile, was muffled in the clouds back of Staten Island* and the Narrows.† Softened tones

---

*Large island located between Upper New York Bay and New Jersey.
†Entrance to Upper New York Bay; the Narrows are just north of Coney Island.

of sapphire and carmine touched slantingly the sides of the buildings. A view of the sea, to be caught between two of the houses, showed it to be of a pale, shimmering green. The lamps began to be lighted, and shed a strong orange radiance. In one restaurant the only occupants were a little music hall singer and a youth. She was laughing and chatting in a light hearted way not peculiar to music hall girls. The youth looked as if he desired to be at some other place. He was singularly wretched and uncomfortable. The stranger said he judged from appearances that the little music hall girl must think a great deal of that one youth. His sympathies seemed to be for the music hall girl. Finally there was a sea of salt meadow, with a black train shooting across it.

"I have made a discovery in one of these concert halls," said the stranger, as we retraced our way. "It is an old gray haired woman, who occupies proudly the position of chief pianiste. I like to go and sit and wonder by what mighty process of fighting and drinking she achieved her position. To see her, you would think she was leading an orchestra of seventy pieces, although she alone composes it. It is a great reflection to watch that gray head. At those moments I am willing to concede that I must be relatively happy, and that is a great admission from a philosopher of my attainments.

"How seriously all these men out in front of the dens take their vocations. They regard people with a voracious air, as if they contemplated any moment making a rush and a grab and mercilessly compelling a great expenditure. This scant and feeble crowd must madden them. When I first came to the part of the town I was astonished and delighted, for it was the nearest approach to a den of wolves that I had encountered since leaving the West. Oh, no, of course the Coney Island of to-day is not the Coney Island of the ancient days. I believe you were about to impale me upon that sentence, were you not?"

The Philosophy of Frankfurters.

We walked along for some time in silence until the stranger went to buy a frankfurter. As he returned, he said: "When a man is respectable he is fettered to certain wheels, and when the chariot of fashion moves, he is dragged along at the rear. For his agony, he can console himself with the law that if a certain thing has not yet been respectable, he need only wait a sufficient time and it will eventually be so. The only disadvantage is that he is obliged to wait until other people wish to do it, and he is likely to lose his own craving. Now I have a great passion for eating frankfurters on the street, and if I were respectable I would be obliged to wait until the year 3365, when man will be able to hold their positions in society only by consuming immense quantities of frankfurters on the street. And by that time I would have undoubtedly developed some new pastime. But I am not respectable. I am a philosopher. I eat frankfurters on the street with the same equanimity that you might employ toward a cigarette.

"See those three young men enjoying themselves. With what rakish, daredevil airs they smoke those cigars. Do you know, the spectacle of three modern young men enjoying themselves is something that I find vastly interesting and instructive. I see revealed more clearly the purposes of the inexorable universe which plans to amuse us occasionally to keep us from the rebellion of suicide. And I see how simply and drolly it accomplishes its end. The insertion of a mild quantity of the egotism of sin into the minds of these young men causes them to wildly enjoy themselves. It is necessary to encourage them, you see, at this early day. After all, it is only great philosophers who have the wisdom to be utterly miserable."

The End of it All.

As we walked toward the station the stranger stopped often to observe types which interested him. He did it with an unconscious calm insolence as if the people were bugs. Once a bug* threatened to beat him. "What 'cher lookin' at?" he asked of him. "My friend," said the stranger, "if any one displays real interest in you in this world, you should take it as an occasion for serious study and reflection. You should be supremely amazed to find that a man can be interested in anybody but himself!" The belligerent seemed quite abashed. He

---

*Irritable person.

explained to a friend: "He ain't right! What? I dunno. Something 'bout 'study' er something! He's got wheels in his head!"

On the train the cold night wind blew transversely across the reeling cars, and in the dim light of the lamps one could see the close rows of heads swaying and jolting with the motion. From directly in front of us peanut shells fell to the floor amid a regular and interminable crackling. A stout man, who slept with his head forward upon his breast, crunched them often beneath his uneasy feet. From some unknown place a drunken voice was raised in song.

"This return of the people to their battles always has a stupendous effect upon me," said the stranger. "The gayety which arises upon these Sunday night occasions is different from all other gayeties. There is an unspeakable air of recklessness and bravado and grief about it. The train load is going toward that inevitable, overhanging, devastating Monday. That singer there tomorrow will be a truckman, perhaps, and swearing ingeniously at his horses and other truckmen. He feels the approach of this implacable Monday. Two hours ago he was ingulfed in whirligigs and beer and had forgotten that there were Mondays. Now he is confronting it, and as he can't battle it, he scorns it. You can hear the undercurrent of it in that song, which is really as grievous as the cry of a child. If he had no vanity—well, it is fortunate for the world that we are not all great thinkers."

We sat on the lower deck of the Bay Ridge boat* and watched the marvelous lights of New York looming through the purple mist. The little Italian band situated up one stairway, through two doors and around three corners from us, sounded in beautiful, faint and slumberous rhythm. The breeze fluttered again in the stranger's locks. We could hear the splash of the waves against the bow. The sleepy lights looked at us with hue of red and green and orange. Overhead some dust-colored clouds scudded across the deep indigo sky. "Thunderation," said the stranger, "if I did not know of so many yesterdays and have such full knowledge of to-morrows, I should be perfectly happy at this moment, and that would create a sensation among philosophers all over the world."

---

*Ferryboat linking Bay Ridge, in Brooklyn, with Manhattan.

IN A PARK ROW RESTAURANT

THE NEVADAN SHERIFF WENT THERE FOR EXCITEMENT. LIKE A BATTLE OF BAD MEN. HE SUGGESTS THAT REPEATING RIFLES MIGHT TAKE THE PLACE OF SPOONS.

"WHENEVER I COME INTO a place of this sort, I am reminded of the battle of Gettysburg," remarked the stranger. To make me hear him he had to raise his voice considerably, for we were seated in one of the Park Row restaurants during the noon hour rush. "I think that if a squadron of Napoleon's dragoons charged into this place they would be trampled under foot before they could get a biscuit. They were great soldiers, no doubt, but they would at once perceive that there were many things about sweep and dash and fire of war of which they were totally ignorant.

"I come in here for the excitement. You know, when I was Sheriff, long ago, of one of the gayest counties of Nevada, I lived a life that was full of thrills, for the citizens could not quite comprehend the uses of a sheriff, and did not like to see him busy himself in other people's affairs continually. One man originated a popular philosophy, in which he asserted that if a man required pastime, it was really better to shoot the sheriff than any other person, for then it would be quite impossible for the sheriff to organize a posse and pursue the assassin. The period which followed the promulgation of this theory gave me habits which I fear I can never outwear. I require fever and exhilaration in life, and when I come in here it carries me back to the old days."

I was obliged to put my head far forward, or I could never have heard the stranger's remarks. Crowds of men were swarming in from streets and invading the comfort of seated men in order that they might hang their hats and overcoats upon the long rows of hooks that lined the sides of the room. The finding of vacant chairs became a serious business. Men dashed to and fro in swift searches. Some of those already seated were eating with terrible speed, or else casting impatient or tempestuous glances at the waiters.

Like Distracted Water Bugs.

Meanwhile the waiters dashed about the room as if a monster pursued them, and they sought escape wildly through the walls. It was like the scattering and scampering of a lot of water bugs, when one splashes the surface of the brook with a pebble. Withal, they carried incredible masses of dishes and threaded their swift ways with rare skill. Perspiration stood upon their foreheads, and their breaths came strainedly. They served customers with such speed and violence that it often resembled a personal assault. The crumbs from the previous diner were swept off with one fierce motion of a napkin. A waiter struck two blows at the table and left there a knife and a fork. And then came the viands in a volley, thumped down in haste, causing men to look sharp to see if their trousers were safe.

There was in the air an endless clatter of dishes, loud and bewilderingly rapid, like the gallop of a thousand horses. From afar back, at the places of communication to the kitchen, there came the sound of a continual roaring altercation, hoarse and vehement, like the cries of the officers of a regiment under attack. A mist of steam fluttered where the waiters crowded and jostled about the huge copper coffee urns. Over in one corner a man who toiled there like a foundryman was continually assailed by sharp cries. "Brown th' wheat!" An endless string of men were already filing past the cashier, and, even in those moments, this latter was a marvel of self possession and deftness. As the spring doors clashed to and fro, one heard the interminable thunder of the street, and through the window, partially obscured by displayed vegetables and roasts and pies, could be seen the great avenue, a picture in gray tones, save where a bit of green park gleamed, the foreground occupied by this great typical turmoil of car and cab, truck and mail van, wedging their way through an opposing army of the same kind and surrounded on all sides by the mobs of hurrying people.

The Habit of Great Speed.

"A man might come in here with a very creditable stomach and lose his head and get indigestion," resumed the stranger, thoughtfully. "It is astonishing how fast a man can eat when he tries. This air is surcharged with appetites. I have seen very orderly, slow moving men become possessed with the spirit of this rush, lose control of themselves and all at once begin to dine like madmen. It is impossible not to feel the effect of this impetuous atmosphere.

"When consommé grows popular in these places all breweries will have to begin turning out soups. I am reminded of the introduction of canned soup into my town in the West. When the boys found that they could not get full on it they wanted to lynch the proprietor of the supply store for selling an inferior article, but a drummer who happened to be in town explained to them that it was a temperance drink.

"It is plain that if the waiters here could only be put upon a raised platform and provided with repeating rifles that would shoot corn muffins, butter cakes, Irish stews or any delicacy of the season, the strain of this strife would be greatly lessened. As long as the waiters were competent marksmen the meals here would be conducted with great expedition. The only difficulty would be when, for instance, a waiter made an error and gave an Irish stew to the wrong man. The latter would have considerable difficulty in passing it along to the right one. Of course the system would cause awkward blunders for a time. You can imagine an important gentleman in a white waistcoat getting up to procure the bill of fare from an adjacent table and by chance intercepting a Hamburger steak bound for a man down by the door. The man down by the door would refuse to pay for a steak that had never come into his possession.

To Save Time.

"In some such manner thousands of people could be accommodated in restaurants that at present during the noon hour can feed only a few hundred. Of course eloquent pickets would have to be stationed in the distance to intercept any unsuspecting gentleman from the West who might consider the gunnery of the waiters in a personal way and resent what would look to them like an assault. I remember that my old friend Jim Wilkinson, the ex-sheriff of Tin Can, Nevada, got very drunk one night and wandered into the business end of the bowling alley there. Of course he thought that they were shooting at him, and in reply he killed three of the best bowlers in Tin Can."

THE MEN IN THE STORM

AT ABOUT THREE O'CLOCK of the February afternoon, the blizzard began to swirl great clouds of snow along the streets, sweeping it down from the roofs and up from the pavements until the faces of pedestrians tingled and burned as from a thousand needle-prickings. Those on the walks huddled their necks closely in the collars of their coats and went along stooping like a race of aged people. The drivers of vehicles hurried their horses furiously on their way. They were made more cruel by the exposure of their positions, aloft on high seats. The street cars, bound up-town, went slowly, the horses slipping and straining in the spongy brown mass that lay between the rails. The drivers, muffled to the eyes, stood erect and facing the wind, models of grim philosophy. Overhead the trains rumbled and roared, and the dark structure of the elevated railroad, stretching over the avenue, dripped little streams and drops of water upon the mud and snow beneath it.

All the clatter of the street was softened by the masses that lay upon the cobbles until, even to one who looked from a window, it became important music, a melody of life made necessary to the ear by the dreariness of the pitiless beat and sweep of the storm. Occasionally one could see black figures of men busily shovelling the white drifts from the walks. The sounds from their labor created new recollections of rural experiences which every man manages to have in a measure. Later, the immense windows of the shops became aglow with light, throwing great beams of orange and yellow upon the pavement. They were infinitely cheerful, yet in a way they accented the force and discomfort of the storm, and gave a meaning to the pace of the people and the vehicles, scores of pedestrians and drivers, wretched with cold faces, necks and feet, speeding for scores of unknown doors and entrances, scattering to an infinite variety of shelters, to places which the imagination made warm with the familiar colors of home.

There was an absolute expression of hot dinners in the pace of the people. If one dared to speculate upon the destination of those who came trooping, he lost himself in a maze of social calculations; he might fling a handful of sand and attempt to follow the flight of each particular grain. But as to the suggestion of hot dinners, he was in firm lines of thought, for it was upon every hurrying face. It is a matter of tradition; it is from the tales of childhood. It comes forth with every storm.

However, in a certain part of a dark West-side street, there was a collection of men to whom these things were as if they were not. In this street was located a charitable house where for five cents the homeless of the city could get a bed at night and, in the morning, coffee and bread.

During the afternoon of the storm, the whirling snows acted as drivers, as men with whips, and at half-past three, the walk before the closed doors of the house was covered with wanderers of the street, waiting. For some distance on either side of the place they could be seen lurking in doorways and behind projecting parts of buildings, gathering in close bunches in an effort to get warm. A covered wagon drawn up near the curb sheltered a dozen of them. Under the stairs that led to the elevated railway station, there were six or eight, their hands stuffed deep in their pockets, their shoulders stooped, jiggling their feet. Others always could be seen coming, a strange procession, some slouching along with the characteristic hopeless gait of professional strays, some coming with hesitating steps wearing the air of men to whom this sort of thing was new.

It was an afternoon of incredible length. The snow, blowing in twisting clouds, sought out the men in their meagre hiding-places and skilfully beat in among them, drenching their persons with showers of fine, stinging flakes. They crowded together, muttering, and fumbling in their pockets to get their red, inflamed wrists covered by the cloth.

Newcomers usually halted at one of the groups and addressed a question, perhaps much as a matter of form, "Is it open yet?"

Those who had been waiting inclined to take the questioner seriously and become contemptuous. "No; do yeh think we'd be standin' here?"

The gathering swelled in numbers steadily and persistently. One could always see them coming, trudging slowly through the storm.

Finally, the little snow plains in the street began to assume a leaden hue from the shadows of evening. The buildings upreared gloomily save where various windows became brilliant figures of light that made shimmers and splashes of yellow on the snow. A street lamp on the curb struggled to illuminate, but it was reduced to impotent blindness by the swift gusts of sleet crusting its panes.

In this half-darkness, the men began to come from their shelter places and mass in front of the doors of charity. They were of all types, but the nationalities were mostly American, German and Irish. Many were strong, healthy, clear-skinned fellows with that stamp of countenance which is not frequently seen upon seekers after charity. There were men of undoubted patience, industry and temperance, who in time of ill-fortune, do not habitually turn to rail at the state of society, snarling at the arrogance of the rich and bemoaning the cowardice of the poor, but who at these times are apt to wear a sudden and singular meekness, as if they saw the world's progress marching from them and were trying to perceive where they had failed, what they had lacked, to be thus vanquished in the race. Then there were others of the shifting, Bowery lodging-house element who were used to paying ten cents for a place to sleep, but who now came here because it was cheaper.

But they were all mixed in one mass so thoroughly that one could not have discerned the different elements but for the fact that the laboring men, for the most part, remained silent and impassive in the blizzard, their eyes fixed on the windows of the house, statues of patience.

The sidewalk soon became completely blocked by the bodies of the men. They pressed close to one another like sheep in a winter's gale, keeping one another warm by the heat of their bodies. The snow came down upon this compressed group of men until, directly from above, it might have appeared like a heap of snow-covered merchandise, if it were not for the fact that the crowd swayed gently with a unanimous, rhythmical motion. It was wonderful to see how the snow lay upon the heads and shoulders of these men, in little ridges an inch thick perhaps in places, the flakes steadily adding drop and drop, precisely as they fall upon the unresisting grass of the fields. The feet of the men were all wet and cold and the wish to warm them accounted for the slow, gentle, rhythmical motion. Occasionally some man whose ears or nose tingled acutely from the cold winds would wriggle down until his head was protected by the shoulders of his companions.

There was a continuous murmuring discussion as to the probability of the doors being speedily opened. They persistently lifted their eyes toward the windows. One could hear little combats of opinion.

"There's a light in th' winder!"

"Naw; it's a reflection f 'm across th' way."

"Well, didn't I see 'em lite it?"

"You did?"

"I did!"

"Well, then, that settles it!"

As the time approached when they expected to be allowed to enter, the men crowded to the doors in an unspeakable crush, jamming and wedging in a way that it seemed would crack bones. They surged heavily against the building in a powerful wave of pushing shoulders. Once a rumor flitted among all the tossing heads.

"They can't open th' doors! Th' fellers er smack up ag'in 'em."

Then a dull roar of rage came from the men on the outskirts; but all the time they strained and pushed until it appeared to be impossible for those that they cried out against to do anything but be crushed to pulp.

"Ah, git away f 'm th' door!"

"Git outa that!"

"Throw 'em out!"

"Kill 'em!"

"Say, fellers, now, what th' 'ell? Give 'em a chanct t' open th' door!"

"Yeh damned pigs, give 'em a chanct t' open th' door!"

Men in the outskirts of the crowd occasionally yelled when a boot-heel of one of frantic trampling feet crushed on their freezing extremities.

"Git off me feet, yeh clumsy tarrier!"

"Say, don't stand on me feet! Walk on th' ground!"

A man near the doors suddenly shouted: "O-o-oh! Le' me out— le' me out!" And another, a man of infinite valor, once twisted his head so as to half face those who were pushing behind him. "Quit yer shovin', yeh"—and he delivered a volley of the most powerful and singular invective straight into the faces of the men behind him. It was as if he was hammering the noses of them with curses of triple brass. His face, red with rage, could be seen; upon it, an expression of sublime disregard of consequences. But nobody cared to reply to his imprecations; it was too cold. Many of them snickered and all continued to push.

In occasional pauses of the crowd's movement the men had opportunity to make jokes; usually grim things, and no doubt very uncouth. Nevertheless, they are notable—one does not expect to find the quality of humor in a heap of old clothes under a snowdrift.

The winds seemed to grow fiercer as time wore on. Some of the gusts of snow that came down on the close collection of heads cut like knives and needles, and the men huddled, and swore, not like dark assassins, but in a sort of an American fashion, grimly and desperately, it is true, but yet with a wondrous under-effect, indefinable and mystic, as if there was some kind of humor in this catastrophe, in this situation in a night of snow-laden winds.

Once, the window of the huge dry-goods shop across the street furnished material for a few moments of forgetfulness. In the brilliantly-lighted space appeared the figure of a man. He was rather stout and very well clothed. His whiskers were fashioned charmingly after those of the Prince of Wales. He stood in an attitude of magnificent reflection. He slowly stroked his moustache with a certain grandeur of manner, and looked down at the snow-encrusted mob. From below, there was denoted a supreme complacence in him. It seemed that the sight operated inversely, and enabled him to more clearly regard his own environment, delightful relatively.

One of the mob chanced to turn his head and perceive the figure in the window. "Hello, lookit 'is whiskers," he said genially.

Many of the men turned then, and a shout went up. They called to him in all strange keys. They addressed him in every manner, from familiar and cordial greetings to carefully-worded advice concerning changes in his personal appearance. The man presently fled, and the mob chuckled ferociously like ogres who had just devoured something.

They turned then to serious business. Often they addressed the stolid front of the house.

"Oh, let us in fer Gawd's sake!"

"Let us in or we'll all drop dead!"

"Say, what's th' use o' keepin' all us poor Indians out in th' cold?"

And always some one was saying, "Keep off me feet."

The crushing of the crowd grew terrific toward the last. The men, in keen pain from the blasts, began almost to fight. With the pitiless whirl of snow upon them, the battle for shelter was going to the strong. It became known that the basement door at the foot of a little steep flight of stairs was the one to be opened, and they jostled and heaved in this direction like laboring fiends. One could hear them panting and groaning in their fierce exertion.

Usually some one in the front ranks was protesting to those in the rear: "O—o—ow! Oh, say, now, fellers, let up, will yeh? Do yeh wanta kill somebody?"

A policeman arrived and went into the midst of them, scolding and berating, occasionally threatening, but using no force but that of his hands and shoulders against these men who were only struggling to get in out of the storm. His decisive tones rang out sharply: "Stop that pushin' back there! Come, boys, don't push! Stop that! Here, you, quit yer shovin'! Cheese that!"

When the door below was opened, a thick stream of men forced a way down the stairs, which were of an extraordinary narrowness and seemed only wide enough for one at a time. Yet they somehow went down almost three abreast. It was a difficult and painful operation. The crowd was like a turbulent water forcing itself through one tiny outlet. The men in the rear, excited by the success of the others, made frantic exertions, for it seemed that this large band would more than fill the quarters and that many would be left upon the pavements. It would be disastrous to be of the last, and accordingly men with the snow biting their faces, writhed and twisted with their might. One expected that from the tremendous pressure, the narrow passage to the basement door would be so choked and clogged with human limbs and bodies that movement would be impossible. Once indeed the crowd was forced to stop, and a cry went along that a man had been injured at the foot of the stairs. But presently the slow movement began again, and the policeman fought at the top of the flight to ease the pressure on those who were going down.

A reddish light from a window fell upon the faces of the men when they, in turn, arrived at the last three steps and were about to enter. One could then note a change of expression that had come over their features. As they thus stood upon the threshold of their hopes, they looked suddenly content and complacent. The fire had passed from their eyes and the snarl had vanished from their lips. The very force of the crowd in the rear, which had previously vexed them, was regarded from another point of view, for it now made it inevitable that they should go through the little doors into the place that was cheery and warm with light.

The tossing crowd on the sidewalk grew smaller and smaller. The snow beat with merciless persistence upon the bowed heads of those who waited. The wind drove it up from the pavements in frantic forms of winding white, and it seethed in circles about the huddled forms, passing in, one by one, three by three, out of the storm.

WHEN EVERY ONE IS PANIC STRICKEN

A REALISTIC PEN PICTURE OF A FIRE IN A TENEMENT. THE
PHILOSOPHY OF WOMEN. FRIGHT AND FLIGHT—THE MISSING
BABY—A COMMONPLACE HERO.

Fire!

We were walking on one of the shadowy side streets, west of Sixth
avenue. The midnight silence and darkness was upon it save where at
the point of intersection with the great avenue, there was a broad span
of yellow light. From there came the steady monotonous jingle of
streetcar bells and the weary clatter of hoofs on the cobbles. While
the houses in this street turned black and mystically silent with the
night, the avenue continued its eternal movement and life, a great
vein that never slept nor paused. The gorgeous orange-hued lamps
of a saloon flared plainly, and the figures of some loungers could be
seen as they stood on the corner. Passing to and fro, the tiny black
figures of people made an ornamental border on this fabric of yellow light.

The stranger was imparting to me some grim midnight reflections upon existence, and in the heavy shadows and in the great stillness pierced only by the dull thunder of the avenue, they were very
impressive.

Suddenly the muffled cry of a woman came from one of those
dark, impassive houses near us. There was the sound of the splinter
and crash of broken glass, falling to the pavement. "What's that,"
gasped the stranger. The scream contained that ominous quality, that
weird timbre which denotes fear of imminent death.

A policeman, huge and panting, ran past us with glitter of buttons
and shield in the darkness. He flung himself upon the fire alarm box
at the corner where the lamp shed a flicker of carmine tints upon the
pavement. "Come on," shouted the stranger. He dragged me excitedly

down the street. We came upon an old four story structure, with a long sign of a bakery over the basement windows, and the region about the quaint front door plastered with other signs. It was one of those ancient dwellings which the churning process of the city had changed into a hive of little industries.

At this time some dull gray smoke, faintly luminous in the night, writhed out from the tops of the second story windows, and from the basement there glared a deep and terrible hue of red, the color of satanic wrath, the color of murder. "Look! Look!" shouted the stranger.

It was extraordinary how the street awakened. It seemed but an instant before the pavements were studded with people. They swarmed from all directions, and from the dark mass arose countless exclamations, eager and swift.

"Where is it? Where is it?"

"No. 135."

"It's that old bakery."

"Is everybody out?"

"Look—gee—say, lookut 'er burn, would yeh?"

The windows of almost every house became crowded with people, clothed and partially clothed, many having rushed from their beds. Here were many women, and as their eyes fastened upon that terrible growing mass of red light one could hear their little cries, quavering with fear and dread. The smoke oozed in greater clouds from the spaces between the sashes of the windows, and urged by the fervor of the heat within, ascended in more rapid streaks and curves.

Upon the sidewalk there had been a woman who was fumbling mechanically with the buttons at the neck of her dress. Her features were lined in anguish; she seemed to be frantically searching her memory—her memory, that poor feeble contrivance that had deserted her at the first of the crisis, at the momentous time. She really struggled and tore hideously at some frightful mental wall that upreared between her and her senses, her very instincts. The policeman, running back from the fire alarm box, grabbed her, intending to haul her away from danger of falling things. Then something came to her like a bolt from the sky. The creature turned all grey, like an ape. A loud shriek rang out that made the spectators bend their bodies, twisting as if they were receiving sword thrusts.

"My baby! My baby! My baby!"

The policeman simply turned and plunged into the house. As the woman tossed her arms in maniacal gestures about her head, it could then be seen that she waved in one hand a little bamboo easel, of the kind which people sometimes place in corners of their parlors. It appeared that she had with great difficulty saved it from the flames. Its cost should have been about 30 cents.

A long groaning sigh came from the crowd in the street, and from all the thronged windows. It was full of distress and pity, and a sort of cynical scorn for their impotency. Occasionally the woman screamed again. Another policeman was fending her off from the house, which she wished to enter in the frenzy of her motherhood, regardless of the flames. These people of the neighborhood, aroused from their beds, looked at the spectacle in a half-dazed fashion at times, as if they were contemplating the ravings of a red beast in a cage. The flames grew as if fanned by tempests, a sweeping, inexorable appetite of a thing, shining, with fierce, pitiless brilliancy, gleaming in the eyes of the crowd that were upturned to it in an ecstasy of awe, fear and, too, half barbaric admiration. They felt the human helplessness that comes when nature breaks forth in passion, overturning the obstacles, emerging at a leap from the position of a slave to that of a master, a giant. There became audible a humming noise, the buzzing of curious machinery. It was the voices of the demons of the flame. The house, in manifest heroic indifference to the fury that raged in its entrails, maintained a stolid and imperturbable exterior, looming black and immovable against the turmoil of crimson.

Eager questions were flying to and fro in the street.

"Say, did a copper go in there?"

"Yeh! He come out again, though."

"He did not! He's in there yet!"

"Well, didn't I see 'im?"

"How long ago was the alarm sent it?"

" 'Bout a minute."

A woman leaned perilously from a window of a nearby apartment house and spoke querulously into the shadowy, jostling crowd beneath her, "Jack!"

And the voice of an unknown man in an unknown place answered her gruffly and short in the tones of a certain kind of downtrodden husband who revels upon occasion, "What?"

"Will you come up here?" cried the woman, shrilly irritable. "Supposin' this house should get afire"—It came to pass that during the progress of the conflagration these two held a terse and bitter domestic combat, infinitely commonplace in language and mental maneuvers.

The blaze had increased with a frightful vehemence and swiftness. Unconsciously, at times, the crowd dully moaned, their eyes fascinated by this exhibition of the strength of nature, their master after all, that ate them and their devices at will whenever it chose to fling down their little restrictions. The flames changed in color from crimson to lurid orange as glass was shattered by the heat, and fell crackling to the pavement. The baker, whose shop had been in the basement, was running about, weeping. A policeman had fought interminably to keep the crowd away from the front of the structure.

"Thunderation!" yelled the stranger, clutching my arm in a frenzy of excitement, "did you ever see anything burn so? Why, it's like an explosion. It's only been a matter of seconds since it started."

In the street, men had already begun to turn toward each other in that indefinite regret and sorrow, as if they were not quite sure of the reason of their mourning.

"Well, she's a goner!"

"Sure—went up like a box of matches!"

"Great Scott, lookut 'er burn!"

Some individual among them furnished the inevitable grumble. "Well, these—" It was a half-coherent growling at conditions, men, fate, law.

Then, from the direction of the avenue there suddenly came a tempestuous roar, a clattering, rolling rush and thunder, as from the headlong sweep of a battery of artillery. Wild and shrill, like a clangorous noise of war, arose the voice of a gong.

One could see a sort of a delirium of excitement, of ardorous affection, go in a wave of emotion over this New York crowd, usually so stoical. Men looked at each other. "Quick work, eh?" They crushed back upon the pavements, leaving the street almost clear. All eyes were turned toward the corner, where the lights of the avenue glowed.

The roar grew and grew until it was as the sound of an army, charging. That policeman's hurried fingers sending the alarm from the box at the corner had aroused a tornado, a storm of horses, machinery, men. And now they were coming in clamor and riot of hoofs and wheels, while over all rang the piercing cry of the gong, tocsin-like, a noise of barbaric fights.

It thrilled the blood, this thunder. The stranger jerked his shoulders nervously and kept up a swift muttering. "Hear 'em come!" he said, breathlessly.

Then in an instant a fire patrol wagon, as if apparitional, flashed into view at the corner. The lights of the avenue gleamed for an instant upon the red and brass of the wagon, the helmets of the crew and the glassy sides of the galloping horses. Then it swung into the dark street and thundered down upon its journey, with but a half-view of a driver making his reins to be steel ribbons over the backs of his horses, mad from the fervor of their business.

The stranger's hand tightened convulsively upon my arm. His enthusiasm was like the ardor of one who looks upon the pageantry of battles. "Ah, look at 'em! Look at 'em! Ain't that great? Why it hasn't been any time at all since the alarm was sent in, and now look!" As this clanging, rolling thing, drawn swiftly by the beautiful might of the horses, clamored through the street, one could feel the cheers, wild and valorous, at the very lips of these people habitually so calm, cynical, impassive. The crew tumbled from their wagon and ran toward the house. A hoarse shout arose high above the medley of noises.

Other roars, other clangings, were to be heard from all directions. It was extraordinary, the loud rumblings of wheels and the pealings of gongs aroused by a movement of the policeman's fingers.

Of a sudden, three white horses dashed down the street with their engine, a magnificent thing of silver-like glitter, that sent a storm of red sparks high into the air and smote the heart with the wail of its whistle.

A hosecart swept around the corner and into the narrow lane, whose close walls made the reverberations like the crash of infantry volleys. There was shine of lanterns, of helmets, of rubber coats, of the bright, strong trappings of the horses. The driver had been confronted by a dreadful little problem in street cars and elevated railway pillars just as he was about to turn into the street, but there had been no pause, no hesitation. A clever dodge, a shrill grinding of the wheels in the street-car tracks, a miss of this and an escape of that by a beautifully narrow margin, and the hosecart went on its headlong way. When the gleam-white and gold of the cart stopped in the shadowy street it was but a moment before a stream of water, of a cold steel color, was plunging through a window into the yellow glare, into this house which was now a den of fire wolves, lashing, carousing, leaping, straining. A wet snakelike hose trailed underfoot to where the steamer was making the air pulsate with its swift vibrations.

From another direction had come another thunder that developed into a crash of sounds, as a hook-and-ladder truck, with long and graceful curves, spun around the other corner, with the horses running with steady leaps toward the place of the battle. It was always obvious that these men who drove were drivers in blood and fibre, charioteers incarnate.

When the ladders were placed against the side of the house, firemen went slowly up them, dragging their hose. They became outlined like black beetles against the red and yellow expanses of flames. A vast cloud of smoke, sprinkled thickly with sparks, went coiling heavily toward the black sky. Touched by the shine of the blaze, the smoke sometimes glowed dull red, the color of bricks. A crowd that, it seemed, had sprung from the cobbles, born at the sound of the wheels rushing through the night, thickly thronged the walks, pushed here and there by the policemen who scolded them roundly, evidently in an eternal state of injured surprise at their persistent desire to get a view of things.

As we walked to the corner we looked back and watched the red glimmer from the fire shine on the dark surging crowd over which towered at times the helmets of police. A billow of smoke swept away from the structure. Occasionally, burned out sparks, like fragments of dark tissue, fluttered in the air. At the corner a streamer was throbbing, churning, shaking in its power as if overcome with rage. A fireman was walking tranquilly about it scrutinizing the mechanism. He wore a blasé air. They all, in fact, seemed to look at fires with the calm, unexcited vision of veterans. It was only the populace with their new nerves, it seemed, who could feel the thrill and dash of these attacks, these furious charges made in the dead of night, at high noon, at any time, upon the common enemy, the loosened flame.

WHEN MAN FALLS, A CROWD GATHERS

A GRAPHIC STUDY OF NEW YORK HEARTLESSNESS. GAZING WITH PITILESS EYES. "WHAT'S THE MATTER?" THAT TOO FAMILIAR QUERY.

A MAN AND A boy were trudging slowly along an East Side street. It was nearly 6 o'clock in the evening and this street which led to one of the East River ferries* was crowded with laborers, shop men and shop women hurrying to their dinners. The store windows were a-glare.

The man and the boy conversed in Italian mumbling the soft syllables and making little quick egostitical gestures. They walked with the lumbering peasant's gait, slowly, and blinking their black eyes at the passing show of the street.

Suddenly the man wavered on his limbs and glared bewildered and helpless as if some blinding light had flashed before his vision. Then he swayed like a drunken man and fell. The boy grasped his companion's arm frantically and made an attempt to support him so that the limp form slid to the sidewalk with an easy motion as a body sinks in the sea. The boy screamed.

Instantly, from all directions, people turned their gaze upon the prone figure. In a moment there was a dodging, pushing, peering group about the man. A volley of questions, replies, speculations flew to and fro above all the bobbing heads.

"What's th' matter? What's th' matter?"

Two streams of people coming from different directions met at this point to form a crowd. Others came from across the street.

---

*Ferryboats that carried passengers between Brooklyn and Manhattan even after the construction of the Brooklyn Bridge.

Down under their feet, almost lost under this throng, lay the man, hidden in the shadows caused by their forms, which, in fact, barely allowed a particle of light to pass between them. Those in the foremost rank bended down, shouldering each other, eager, anxious to see everything. Others, behind them, crowded savagely for a place like starving men fighting for bread. Always the question could be heard flying in the air: "What's the matter?" Some near to the body and perhaps feeling the danger of being forced over upon it, twisted their heads and protested violently to those unheeding ones who were scuffling in the rear. "Say, quit yer shovin', can't yeh? Wat d' yeh want, anyhow? Quit!"

A man back in the crowd suddenly said: "Say, young feller, you're a peach wid dose feet o' yours. Keep off me!"

Another voice said, "Well, dat's all right!"

The boy who had been walking with the man who fell was standing helplessly, a terrified look in his eyes. He held the man's hand. Sometimes he gave it a little jerk that was at once an appeal, a reproach, a caution. And, withal, it was a timid calling to the limp and passive figure as if he half expected to arouse it from its coma with a pleading touch of his fingers. Occasionally he looked about him with swift glances of indefinite hope, as if assistance might come from the clouds. The men near him questioned him, but he did not seem to understand. He answered them "Yes" or "No," blindly, with no apparent comprehension of their language. They frequently jostled him until he was obliged to put his hand upon the breast of the body to maintain his balance.

Those that were nearest to the man upon the sidewalk at first saw his body go through a singular contortion. It was as if an invisible hand had reached up from the earth and had seized him by the hair. He seemed dragged slowly, relentlessly backward, while his body stiffened convulsively; his hand clenched, and his arms swung rigidly upward. A slight froth was upon his chin. Through his pallid, half closed lids could be seen the steel colored gleam of his eyes that were turned toward all the bending, swaying faces and this inanimate thing upon the pavement burned threateningly, dangerously, whining with a mystic light, as a corpse might glare at those live ones who seemed about to trample it under foot.

As for the men near, they hung back, appearing as if they expected it to spring erect and clutch at them. Their eyes, however, were held in a spell of fascination. They seemed scarcely to breathe. They were contemplating a depth into which a human being had sunk, and the marvel of this mystery of life or death held them chained.

Occasionally from the rear a man came thrusting his way impetuously, satisfied that there was a horror to be seen and apparently insane to get a view of it. Less curious persons swore at these men when they trod upon their toes. The loaded street cars jingled past this scene in endless parade. Occasionally, from where the elevated railroad crossed the street, there came a rhythmical roar, suddenly begun and suddenly ended. Over the heads of the crowd hung an immovable canvas sign, "Regular dinner, twenty cents."

After the first spasm of curiosity had passed away there were those in the crowd who began to consider ways to help. A voice called: "Rub his wrists." The boy and some one on the other side of the man began to rub his wrists and slap his palms, but still the body lay inert, rigid. When a hand was dropped the arm fell like a stick. A tall German suddenly appeared and resolutely began to push the crowd back. "Get back there—get back," he continually repeated as he pushed them. He had psychological authority over this throng: they obeyed him. He and another knelt by the man in the darkness and loosened his shirt at the throat. Once they struck a match and held it close to the man's face. This livid visage suddenly appearing under their feet in the light of the match's yellow glare made the throng shudder. Half articulate exclamations could be heard. There were men who nearly created a battle in the madness of their desire to see the thing.

Meanwhile others with magnificent passions for abstract statistical information were questioning the boy. "What's his name?" "Where does he live?"

Then a policeman appeared. The first part of the little play had gone on without his assistance, but now he came swiftly, his helmet towering above the multitude of black derbys and shading that confident, self reliant police face. He charged the crowd as if he were a squadron of Irish lancers. The people fairly withered before this onslaught. He shouted: "Come, make way there! Make way!" He was evidently a man whose life was half pestered out of him by the inhabitants of the city who were sufficiently unreasonable and stupid as to insist on being in the streets. His was the rage of a placid cow, who wishes to lead a life of tranquility, but who is eternally besieged by flies that hover in clouds.

When he arrived at the center of the crowd he first demanded, threateningly: "Well, what's th' matter here?" And then, when he saw that human bit of wreckage at the bottom of the sea of men, he said to it: "Come, git up out a-that! Git out a-here!"

Whereupon hands were raised in the crowd and a volley of decorated information was blazed at the officer.

"Ah, he's got a fit! Can't yeh see?"

"He's got a fit!"

"He's sick!"

"What yeh doin'? Leave 'm be!"

The policeman menaced with a glance the crowd from whose safe interior the defiant voices had emerged.

A doctor had come. He and the policeman bended down at the man's side. Occasionally the officer upreared to create room. The crowd fell way before his threats, his admonitions, his sarcastic questions and before the sweep of those two huge buckskin gloves.

At last the peering ones saw the man on the sidewalk begin to breathe heavily, with the strain of overtaxed machinery, as if he had just come to the surface from some deep water. He uttered a low cry in his foreign tongue. It was a babyish squeal, or like the sad wail of a little storm-tossed kitten. As this cry went forth to all those eager ears, the jostling and crowding recommenced until the doctor was obliged to yell warningly a dozen times. The policeman had gone to send an ambulance call.

When a man struck another match and in its meager light the doctor felt the skull of the prostrate one to discover if any wound or fracture had been caused by his fall to the stone sidewalk, the crowd pressed and crushed again. It was as if they fully anticipated a sight of blood in the gleam of the match and they scrambled and dodged for positions. The policeman returned and fought with them. The doctor looked up frequently to scold at them and to sharply demand more space.

At last out of the golden haze made by the lamps far up the street, there came the sound of a gong beaten rapidly, impatiently. A monstrous truck loaded to the sky with barrels scurried to one side with marvelous agility. And then the black ambulance with its red light, its galloping horse, its dull gleam of lettering and bright shine of gong clattered into view. A young man, as imperturbable always as if he were going to a picnic, sat thoughtfully upon the rear seat.

When they picked up the limp body, from which came little moans and howls, the crowd almost turned into a mob, a silent mob, each member of which struggled for one thing. Afterward some resumed their ways with an air of relief, as if they themselves had been in pain and were at last recovered. Others still continued to stare at the ambulance on its banging, clanging return journey until it vanished into the golden haze. It was as if they had been cheated. Their eyes expressed discontent at this curtain which had been rung down in the midst of the drama. And this impenetrable fabric, suddenly intervening between a suffering creature and their curiosity, seemed to appear to them as an injustice.

OPIUM'S VARIED DREAMS.

THE HABIT, THE VICTIM, THE RELIEF, AND THE DESPAIR. THIS CITY'S 25,000 OPIUM SMOKERS AND THEIR WAYS SINCE REFORM BROKE UP THEIR RESORTS—THE PIPE AND ITS HANDLING, AND THE HABITUE'S DEFENCE.

OPIUM SMOKING IN THIS country is believed to be more particularly a pastime of the Chinese, but in truth the greater number of the smokers are white men and white women. Chinatown furnishes the pipe, lamp, and yen-nock,* but let a man once possess a layout, and a common American drug store furnishes him with the opium, and China is discernible only in the traditions that cling to the habit.

---

*Long, sharpened shaft used for holding opium over an open flame prior to smoking it.

There are 25,000 opium smokers in the city of New York alone. At one time there were two great colonies, one in the Tenderloin, one, of course, in Chinatown. This was before the hammer of reform struck them. Now the two colonies are splintered into something less than 25,000 fragments. The smokers are disorganized, but they still exist.

The Tenderloin district of New York fell an early victim to opium. That part of the population which is known as the "sporting" class adopted the habit quickly. Cheap actors, race track touts, gamblers, and the different kinds of confidence men took to it generally. Opium raised its yellow banner over the Tenderloin, attaining the dignity of a common vice.

Splendid joints were not uncommon then in New York. There was one on Forty-second street which would have been palatial if it were not for the bad taste of the decorations. An occasional man from Fifth avenue or Madison avenue would have there his private layout, an elegant equipment of silver, ivory, and gold. The bunks which lined all sides of the two rooms were nightly crowded, and some of the people owned names which are not altogether unknown to the public. This place was raided because of sensational stories in the newspapers, and the little wicket no longer opens to allow the fiend to enter.

Upon the appearance of reform, opium retired to private flats. Here it now reigns, and it will be undoubtedly an extremely long century before the police can root it from these little strongholds. Once Billie Hostetter got drunk on whiskey and emptied three scuttles of coal down the dumb-waiter shaft. This made a noise, and, Billie, naturally, was arrested. But opium is silent. The smokers do not rave. They dream, or talk in low tones.

People who declare themselves able to pick out opium smokers on the street usually are deluded. An opium smoker may look like a deacon or a deacon may look like an opium smoker. The fiends easily conceal their vice. They get up from the layout, adjust their cravats, straighten their coat tails, and march off like ordinary people, and the best kind of an expert would not be willing to bet that they were or were not addicted to the habit.

It would be very hard to say just exactly what constitutes a habit.

With the fiends it is an elastic word. Ask a smoker if he has a habit and he will deny it. Ask him if some one who smokes the same amount has a habit and he will admit it. Perhaps the ordinary smoker consumes 25 cents' worth of opium each day. There are others who smoke $1 worth. This is rather extraordinary, and in this case at least it is safe to say that it is a habit. The $1 smokers usually indulge in high hats, which is the term for a large pill. The ordinary smoker is satisfied with pinheads. Pinheads are of about the size of a French pea.

Habit smokers have a contempt for the sensation smoker, who has been won by the false glamour which surrounds the vice, and goes about really pretending that he has a ravenous hunger for the pipe. There are more sensation smokers than one would imagine.

It is said to take one year of devotion to the pipe before one can contract a habit; but probably it does not take any such long time. Sometimes an individual who has smoked only a few months will speak of nothing but pipe, and when a man talks pipe persistently it is a pretty sure sign that the drug has fastened its grip so that he is not able to stop its use easily. When a man arises from his first trial of the pipe, the nausea that clutches him is something that can give cards and spades and big casino to seasickness. If he had swallowed a live chimney sweep he could not feel more like dying. The room and everything in it whirls like the inside of an electric light plant. There comes a thirst, a great thirst, and this thirst is so sinister and so misleading that if the novice drank spirits to satisfy it he would presently be much worse. The one thing that will make him feel again that life may be a joy is a cup of strong black coffee.

If there is a sentiment in the pipe for him, he returns to it after this first unpleasant trial. Gradually the power of the drug sinks into his heart. It absorbs his thought. He begins to lie with more and more grace to cover the shortcomings and little failures of his life. And then, finally, he may become a full-fledged pipe fiend, a man with a yen-yen.

A yen-yen, be it known, is the hunger, the craving. It comes to a fiend when he separates himself from his pipe and it takes him by the heart strings. If, indeed, he will not buck through a brick wall to get to the pipe, he at least will become the most disagreeable, sour-tempered person on earth until he finds a way to satisfy his craving.

When the victim arrives at the point where his soul calls for the drug, he usually learns to cook. The operation of rolling the pill and cooking it over the little lamp is a delicate task, and it takes time to learn it. When a man can cook for himself and buys his own layout, he is gone, probably. He has placed upon his shoulders an elephant which he may carry to the edge of forever. The Chinese have a preparation which they call a cure, but the first difficulty is to get the fiend to take the preparation, and the second difficulty is to cure anything with this cure.

The fiend will defend opium with eloquence and energy. He very seldom drinks spirits, and so he gains an opportunity to make the most ferocious parallels between the effects of rum and the effects of opium. Ask him to free his mind and he will probably say:

"Opium does not deprive you of your senses. It does not make a madman of you. But drink does. See? Who ever heard of a man committing murder when full of hop. Get him full of whiskey and he might kill his father. I don't see why people kick so about opium smoking. If they knew anything about it, they wouldn't talk that way. Let anybody drink rum who cares to, but as for me, I would rather be what I am."

As before mentioned, there were at one time gorgeous opium dens in New York, but now there is probably not a den with any pretence to splendid decoration. The Chinamen will smoke in a cellar, bare, squalid, occupied by an odor that will float wooden ships. The police took the adornments from the vice and left nothing but the pipe itself. Yet the pipe is sufficient for its slant-eyed lover.

When prepared for smoking purposes, opium is a heavy liquid much like molasses. Ordinarily it is sold in hollow li-shi nuts or in little round tins resembling the old percussion cap boxes. The pipe is a curious affair, particularly notable for the way in which it does not resemble the drawings of it that appear in print. The stem is of thick bamboo, the mouthpiece usually of ivory. The bowl crops out suddenly about four inches from the end of the stem. It is a heavy affair of clay or stone. The cavity is a mere hole, of the diameter of a lead pencil, drilled through the centre. The yen-nock is a sort of sharpened darning needle. With it the cook takes the opium from the box. He twirls it dexterously with his thumb and forefinger until enough of the gummy substance adheres to the sharp point. Then he holds it over the tiny flame of the lamp which burns only peanut oil or sweet oil. The pill now exactly resembles boiling molasses. The clever fingers of the cook twirl it above the flame. Lying on his side comfortably, he takes the pipe in his left hand and transfers the cooked pill from the yen-nock to the bowl of the pipe, where he again moulds it with the yen-nock until it is a little button-like thing with a hole in the centre fitting squarely over the hole in the bowl. Dropping the yen-nock, the cook now uses two hands for the pipe. He extends the mouthpiece toward the one whose turn it is to smoke, and as the smoker leans forward in readiness, the cook draws the bowl toward the flame until the heat sets the pill to boiling. Whereupon the smoker takes a long, deep draw at the pipe, the pill sputters and fries, and a moment later the smoker sinks back tranquilly. An odor, heavy, aromatic, agreeable, and yet disagreeable, hangs in the air and makes its way with peculiar powers of penetration. The group about the layout talk in low voices, and watch the cook deftly moulding another pill. The little flame casts a strong yellow light on their faces as they huddle about the layout. As the pipe passes and passes around the circle, the voices drop to a mere indolent cooing, and the eyes that so lazily watch the cook at his work, glisten and glisten from the influence of the drug until they resemble flashing bits of silver.

There is a similarity in coloring and composition in a group of men about a midnight camp fire in a forest and a group of smokers about the layout tray with its tiny light. Everything, of course, is on a smaller scale with the smoking. The flame is only an inch and a half, perhaps, in height, and the smokers huddle closely in order that every person may smoke undisturbed. But there is something in the abandon of the poses, the wealth of light on the faces, and the strong mystery of shadow at the backs of the people that bring the two scenes into some kind of artistic resemblance. And just as the lazy eyes about a camp fire fasten themselves dreamfully upon the blaze of logs, so do the lazy eyes about an opium layout fasten themselves upon the little flame.

There is but one pipe, one lamp, and one cook to each smoking layout. Pictures of nine or ten persons sitting in armchairs and smoking various kinds of curiously carved tobacco pipes probably serve well enough, but when they are named "Interior of an Opium Den" and that sort of thing, it is absurd. Opium could not be smoked like tobacco, A pill is good for one long draw. After that the cook moulds another. A smoker would just as soon choose a gallows as an armchair for smoking purposes. He likes to curl down on a mattress placed on the floor in the quietest corner of a Tenderloin flat, and smoke there with no light but the tiny yellow spear from the layout lamp.

It is a curious fact that it is rather the custom to purchase for a layout tray one of those innocent black tin affairs which are supposed to be placed before a baby as he takes his high chair for dinner.

If a beginner expects to have dreams of an earth dotted with white porcelain towers and a sky of green silk, he will be much mistaken. "The Opium Smoker's Dream" seems to be mostly a mistake. The influence of dope is evidently a fine languor, a complete mental rest. The problems of life no longer appear. Existence is peace. The virtues of a man's friends, for instance, loom beautifully against his own sudden perfection. The universe is readjusted. Wrong departs, injustice vanishes: there is nothing but a quiet harmony of all things— until the next morning.[2]

And who should invade this momentary land of rest, this dream country, if not the people of the Tenderloin; they who are at once supersensitive and hopeless, the people who think more upon death and the mysteries of life, the chances of the hereafter than any other class, educated or uneducated? Opium holds out to them its lie, and they embrace it eagerly, expecting to find a consummation of peace, but they awake to find the formidable labors of life grown more formidable. And if the pipe should happen to ruin their lives they cling the more closely to it because then it stands between them and thought.

NEW YORK'S BICYCLE SPEEDWAY

THE BOULEVARD, ONCE A QUIET AVENUE, NOW THE SCENE OF NIGHTLY CARNIVALS—HERE ALL GOTHAM COMES TOGETHER AND ROLLS ALONG IN AN ENDLESS, SHIMMERING PANORAMA. BY STEPHEN CRANE.

NEW YORK, JULY 3, 1896.—The Bowery has had its day as a famous New York street. It is now a mere tradition. Broadway will long hold its place as the chief vein of the city's life. No process of expansion can ever leave it abandoned to the cheap clothing dealers and dime museum robbers. It is too strategic in position. But lately the Western Boulevard which slants from the Columbus monument at the southwest corner of Central Park to the river has vaulted to a startling prominence and is now one of the sights of New York. This is caused by the bicycle. Once the Boulevard was a quiet avenue whose particular distinctions were its shade trees and its third foot-walk which extended in Parisian fashion down the middle of the street. Also it was noted for its billboards and its huge and slumberous apartment hotels. Now, however, it is the great thoroughfare for bicycles. On these gorgeous spring days they appear in thousands. All mankind is a-wheel apparently and a person on nothing but legs feels like a strange animal. A mighty army of wheels streams from the brick wilderness below Central Park and speeds over the asphalt. In the cool of the evening it returns with swaying and flashing of myriad lamps.

The bicycle crowd has completely subjugated the street. The glittering wheels dominate it from end to end. The cafes and dining rooms or the apartment hotels are occupied mainly by people in bicycle clothes. Even the billboards have surrendered. They advertise wheels and lamps and tires and patent saddles with all the flaming vehemence of circus art. Even when they do condescend to still advertise a patent medicine, you are sure to confront a lithograph of a young person in bloomers who is saying in large type: "Yes, George, I find that Willowrum always refreshes me after these long rides."

Down at the Circle where stands the patient Columbus, the stores are crowded with bicycle goods. There are innumerable repair shops. Everything is bicycle. In the afternoon the parade begins. The great discoverer, erect on his tall grey shaft, must feel his stone head whirl when the battalions come swinging and shining around the curve.

It is interesting to note the way in which the blasphemous and terrible truck-drivers of the lower part of the city will hunt a bicyclist. A truck-driver, of course, believes that a wheelman is a pest. The average man could not feel more annoyance if nature had suddenly invented some new kind of mosquito. And so the truck-driver resolves in his dreadful way to make life as troublous and thrilling for the wheelman as he possibly can. The wheelman suffers under a great handicap. He is struggling over the most uneven cobbles which bless a metropolis. Twenty horses threaten him and forty wheels miss his shoulder by an inch. In his ears there is a hideous din. It surrounds him, envelopes him.

Add to this trouble, then, a truckman with a fiend's desire to see dead wheelmen. The situation affords deep excitement for everyone concerned.

But when a truck-driver comes to the Boulevard the beautiful balance of the universe is apparent. The teamster sits mute, motionless, casting sidelong glances at the wheels which spin by him. He still contrives to exhibit a sort of a sombre defiance, but he has no oath nor gesture nor wily scheme to drive a 3 ton wagon over the prostrate body of some unhappy cyclist. On the Boulevard this roaring lion from down town is so subdued, so isolated that he brings tears to the sympathetic eye.

There is a new game on the Boulevard. It is the game of Bicycle Cop and Scorcher. When the scorcher scorches beyond the patience of the law, the bicycle policeman, if in sight, takes after him. Usually the scorcher has a blissful confidence in his ability to scorch and thinks it much easier to just ride away from the policeman than to go to court and pay a fine. So they go flying up the Boulevard with the

whole mob of wheelmen and wheelwomen, eager to see the race,
sweeping after them. But the bicycle police are mighty hard riders
and it takes a flier to escape them. The affair usually ends in calamity
for the scorcher, but in the meantime fifty or sixty cyclists have had
a period of delirious joy.

Bicycle Cop and Scorcher is a good game, but after all it is not as
good as the game that was played in the old days when the suggestion of a corps of bicycle police in neat knickerbockers would have
scandalized Mulberry street.* This was the game of Fat Policeman on
Foot Trying to Stop a Spurt. A huge, unwieldy officer rushing out into
the street and wildly trying to head off and grab some rider who was
spinning along in just one silver flash was a sight that caused the populace to turn out in a body. If some madman started at a fierce gait
from the Columbus monument, he could have the consciousness that
at frequent and exciting intervals, red-faced policemen would gallop
out at him and frenziedly clutch at his coat-tails. And owing to a curious dispensation, the majority of the policemen along the boulevard were very stout and could swear most graphically in from two
to five languages.

But they changed all that. The un-police-like bicycle police are
wonderfully clever and the vivid excitement of other days is gone.
Even the scorcher seems to feel depressed and narrowly looks over
the nearest officer before he starts on his frantic career.

The girl in bloomers is, of course, upon her native heath when
she steers her steel steed into the Boulevard. One becomes conscious
of a bewildering variety in bloomers. There are some that fit and
some that do not fit. There are some that were not made to fit and
there are some that couldn't fit anyhow. As a matter of fact the
bloomer costume is now in one of the primary stages of its evolu-
tion. Let us hope so at any rate. Of course every decent citizen con-
cedes that women shall wear what they please and it is supposed that
he covenants with himself not to grin and nudge his neighbor when
anything particularly amazing passes him on the street but resolves

---

*Street in lower Manhattan; in Crane's day it was where the headquarters of the New
York City Police Department was located.

to simply and industriously mind his own affairs. Still the situation no doubt harrows him greatly. No man was ever found to defend bloomers. His farthest statement, as an individual, is to advocate them for all women he does not know and cares nothing about. Most women become radical enough to say: "Why shouldn't I wear 'em, if I choose." Still, a second look at the Boulevard convinces one that the world is slowly, solemnly, inevitably coming to bloomers. We are about to enter an age of bloomers, and the bicycle, that machine which has gained an economic position of the most tremendous importance, is going to be responsible for more than the bruises on the departed fat policemen of the Boulevard.

ADVENTURES OF A NOVELIST.

BY STEPHEN CRANE. THE DISTINGUISHED AUTHOR'S NARRATIVE OF HOW HE SOUGHT "MATERIAL" IN REAL LIFE IN THE "TENDERLOIN" AND FOUND MORE THAN HE BARGAINED FOR.

LAST WEEK THE JOURNAL arranged with Mr. Stephen Crane, the novelist whose "Red Badge of Courage" everybody has read, to write a series of studies of life in New York. He chose the police courts as his first subject.

Bright and early Monday morning Mr. Crane took a seat beside Magistrate Cornell at the Jefferson Market Police Court, and observed the machinery of justice in full operation. The novelist felt, however, that he had seen but a kaleidoscopic view of the characters who passed rapidly before the judicial gaze of the presiding Magistrate. He must know more of that throng of unfortunates; he must study the police court victims in their haunts.

With the scenes of the forenoon still flitting through his mind, the novelist sought out a Broadway resort that evening. He was soon deeply interested in the women who had gathered at his table—two chorus girls and a young woman of uncertain occupation. The novelist cared not who they were. It was enough that he had found the types of character that he was after.

Later in the evening the party separated, and the novelist courteously escorted one of the women to a Broadway car. While his back was turned for a moment a policeman seized one of the party—Dora Wilkins. Mr. Crane at once protested, and, following the officer to the station house, explained that a mistake had been made.

Bright and early next morning the novelist was once more at Jefferson Market Court. This time he was a witness. The novelist had sought a closer knowledge of the unfortunate creatures of the courts, and he found himself in the midst of them.

This is a plain tale of two chorus girls, a woman of the streets and a reluctant laggard witness. The tale properly begins in a resort on Broadway, where the two chorus girls and the reluctant witness sat the entire evening. They were on the verge of departing their several ways when a young woman approached one of the chorus girls, with outstretched hand.

"Why, how do you do?" she said. "I haven't seen you for a long time."

The chorus girl recognized some acquaintance of the past, and the young woman then took a seat and joined the party. Finally they left the table in this resort, and the quartet walked down Broadway together. At the corner of Thirty-first street one of the chorus girls said that she wished to take a car immediately for home, and so the reluctant witness left one of the chorus girls and the young woman on the corner of Thirty-first street while he placed the other chorus girl aboard an uptown cable car. The two girls who waited on the corner were deep in conversation.

The reluctant witness was returning leisurely to them. In the semi-conscious manner in which people note details which do not appear at the time important, he saw two men passing along Broadway. They passed swiftly, like men who are going home. They paid attention to none, and none at the corner of Thirty-first street and Broadway paid attention to them.

The two girls were still deep in conversation. They were standing at the curb facing the street. The two men passed unseen—in all human probability—by the two girls. The reluctant witness continued his leisurely way. He was within four feet of these two girls when suddenly and silently a man appeared from nowhere in particular and grabbed them both.

The astonishment of the reluctant witness was so great for the ensuing seconds that he was hardly aware of what transpired during that time, save that both girls screamed. Then he heard this man, who was now evidently an officer, say to them: "Come to the station house. You are under arrest for soliciting two men."

With one voice the unknown woman, the chorus girl and the reluctant witness cried out: "What two men?"

The officer said: "Those two men who have just passed."

And here began the wildest and most hysterical sobbing of the two girls, accompanied by spasmodic attempts to pull their arms away from the grip of the policeman. The chorus girl seemed nearly insane with fright and fury. Finally she screamed:

"Well, he's my husband." And with her finger she indicated the reluctant witness. The witness at once replied to the swift, questioning glance of the officer, "Yes; I am."

If it was necessary to avow a marriage to save a girl who is not a prostitute from being arrested as a prostitute, it must be done, though the man suffer eternally. And then the officer forgot immediately—without a second's hesitation, he forgot that a moment previously he had arrested this girl for soliciting, and so, dropping her arm, released her.

"But," said he, "I have got this other one." He was as picturesque as a wolf.

"Why arrest her, either?" said the reluctant witness.

"For soliciting those two men."

"But she didn't solicit those two men."

"Say," said the officer, turning, "do you know this woman?"

The chorus girl had it in mind to lie then for the purpose of saving this woman easily and simply from the palpable wrong she seemed to be about to experience. "Yes; I know her"—"I have seen her two or three times"—"Yes; I have met her before"—But the reluctant witness said at once that he knew nothing whatever of the girl.

"Well," said the officer, "she's a common prostitute."

There was a short silence then, but the reluctant witness presently said: "Are you arresting her as a common prostitute? She has been perfectly respectable since she has been with us. She hasn't done anything wrong since she has been in our company."

"I am arresting her for soliciting those two men," answered the officer, "and if you people don't want to get pinched, too, you had better not be seen with her."

Then began a parade to the station house—the officer and his prisoner ahead and two simpletons following.

At the station house the officer said to the sergeant behind the desk that he had seen the woman come from the resort on Broadway alone, and on the way to the corner of Thirty-first street solicit two men, and that immediately afterward she had met a man and a woman—meaning the chorus girl and the reluctant witness—on the said corner, and was in conversation with them when he arrested her. He did not mention to the sergeant at this time the arrest and release of the chorus girl.

At the conclusion of the officer's story the sergeant said, shortly: "Take her back." This did not mean to take the woman back to the corner of Thirty-first street and Broadway. It meant to take her back to the cells, and she was accordingly led away.

The chorus girl had undoubtedly intended to be an intrepid champion; she had avowedly come to the station house for that purpose, but her entire time had been devoted to sobbing in the wildest form of hysteria. The reluctant witness was obliged to devote his entire time to an attempt to keep her from making an uproar of some kind. This paroxysm of terror, of indignation, and the extreme mental anguish caused by her unconventional and strange situation, was so violent that the reluctant witness could not take time from her to give any testimony to the sergeant.

After the woman was sent to the cell the reluctant witness reflected a moment in silence; then he said:

"Well, we might as well go."

On the way out of Thirtieth street the chorus girl continued to sob. "If you don't go to court and speak for that girl you are no man!" she cried. The arrested woman had, by the way, screamed out a request to appear in her behalf before the Magistrate.

"By George! I cannot," said the reluctant witness. "I can't afford to do that sort of thing. I—I—"

After he had left this girl safely, he continued to reflect: "Now this arrest I firmly believe to be wrong. This girl may be a courtesan, for anything that I know at all to the contrary. The sergeant at the station house seemed to know her as well as he knew the Madison square tower. She is then, in all probability, a courtesan. She is arrested, however, for soliciting those two men. If I have ever had a conviction in my life, I am convinced that she did not solicit those two men. Now, if these affairs occur from time to time, they must be witnessed occasionally by men of character. Do these reputable citizens interfere? No, they go home and thank God that they can still attend piously to their own affairs. Suppose I were a clerk and I interfered in this sort of a case. When it became known to my employers they would say to me: 'We are sorry, but we cannot have men in our employ who stay out until 2:30 in the morning in the company of chorus girls.'

"Suppose, for instance, I had a wife and seven children in Harlem. As soon as my wife read the papers she would say: 'Ha! You told me you had a business engagement! Half-past two in the morning with questionable company!'

"Suppose, for instance, I were engaged to the beautiful Countess of Kalamazoo. If she were to hear it, she could write: 'All is over between us. My future husband cannot rescue prostitutes at 2:30 in the morning.'

"These, then, must be three small general illustrations of why men of character say nothing if they happen to witness some possible affair of this sort, and perhaps these illustrations could be multiplied to infinity. I possess nothing so tangible as a clerkship, as a wife and seven children in Harlem, as an engagement to the beautiful Countess of Kalamazoo; but all that I value may be chanced in this affair. Shall I take this risk for the benefit of a girl of the streets?

"But this girl, be she prostitute or whatever, was at this time manifestly in my escort, and—Heaven save the blasphemous philosophy—a wrong done to a prostitute must be as purely a wrong as a wrong done to a queen," said the reluctant witness—this blockhead.

"Moreover, I believe that this officer has dishonored his obligation as a public servant. Have I a duty as a citizen, or do citizens have duty, as a citizen, or do citizens have no duties? Is it a mere myth that there was at one time a man who possessed a consciousness of civic responsibility, or has it become a distinction of our munic-

ipal civilization that men of this character shall be licensed to
depredate in such a manner upon those who are completely at their
mercy?"

He returned to the sergeant at the police station, and, after asking if he could send anything to the girl to make her more comfortable for the night, he told the sergeant the story of the arrest, as he
knew it.

"Well," said the sergeant, "that may be all true. I don't defend the
officer. I do not say that he was right, or that he was wrong, but it
seems to me that I have seen you somewhere before and know you
vaguely as a man of good repute; so why interfere in this thing? As
for this girl, I know her to be a common prostitute. That's why I sent
her back."

"But she was not arrested as a common prostitute. She was arrested for soliciting two men, and I know that she didn't solicit the
two men."

"Well," said the sergeant, "that, too, may all be true, but I give
you the plain advice of a man who has been behind this desk for
years, and knows how these things go, and I advise you simply to stay
home. If you monkey with this case, you are pretty sure to come out
with mud all over you."

"I suppose so," said the reluctant witness. "I haven't a doubt of
it. But don't see how I can, in honesty, stay away from court in the
morning."

"Well, do it anyhow," said the sergeant.

"But I don't see how I can do it."

The sergeant was bored. "Oh, I tell you, the girl is nothing but a
common prostitute," he said, wearily.

The reluctant witness on reaching his room set the alarm clock
for the proper hour.

In the court at 8:30 he met a reporter acquaintance. "Go
home," said the reporter, when he had heard the story. "Go home;
your own participation in the affair doesn't look very respectable.
Go home."

"But it is a wrong," said the reluctant witness.

"Oh, it is only a temporary wrong," said the reporter. The
definition of a temporary wrong did not appear at that time to the

reluctant witness, but the reporter was too much in earnest to consider terms. "Go home," said he.

Thus—if the girl was wronged—it is to be seen that all circumstances, all forces, all opinions, all men were combined to militate against her. Apparently the united wisdom of the world declared that no man should do anything but throw his sense of justice to the winds in an affair of this description. "Let a man have a conscience for the daytime," said wisdom. "Let him have a conscience for the daytime, but it is idiocy for a man to have a conscience at 2:30 in the morning, in the case of an arrested prostitute."

IN THE TENDERLOIN

A DUEL BETWEEN AN ALARM CLOCK AND A SUICIDAL PURPOSE.

EVERYBODY KNOWS ALL ABOUT the Tenderloin district of New York.

There is no man that has the slightest claim to citizenship that does not know all there is to know concerning the Tenderloin. It is wonderful—this amount of truth which the world's clergy and police forces have collected concerning the Tenderloin. My friends from the stars obtain all this information, if possible, and then go into this wilderness and apply it. Upon observing you, certain spirits of the jungle will term you a wise guy, but there is no gentle humor in the Tenderloin, so you need not fear that this remark is anything but a tribute to your knowledge.

Once upon a time there was fought in the Tenderloin a duel between an Alarm Clock and a Suicidal Purpose. That such a duel was fought is a matter of no consequence, but it may be worth a telling, because it may be the single Tenderloin incident about which every man in the world has not exhaustive information.

It seems that Swift Doyer and his girl quarreled. Swift was jealous in the strange and devious way of his kind, and at midnight, his voice burdened with admonition, grief and deadly menace, roared through the little flat and conveyed news of the strife up the air-shaft and down the air-shaft.

"Lied to me, didn't you?" he cried. "Told me a lie and thought I wouldn't get unto you. Lied to me! There's where I get crazy. If you hadn't lied to me in one thing, and I hadn't collared you flat in it, I might believe all the rest, but now—how do I know you ever tell the truth? How do I know I ain't always getting a game? Hey? How do I know?"

To the indifferent people whose windows opened on the air-shaft there came the sound of a girl's low sobbing, while into it at times burst wildly the hoarse bitterness and rage of the man's tone. A grim thing is a Tenderloin air-shaft.

Swift arose and paused his harangue for a moment while he lit a cigarette. He puffed at it vehemently and scowled, black as a storm-god, in the direction of the sobbing.

"Come! Get up out of that," he said, with ferocity. "Get up and look at me and let me see you lie!"

There was a flurry of white in the darkness, which was no more definite to the man than the ice-floes which your reeling ship passes in the night. Then, when the gas glared out suddenly, the girl stood before him. She was a wondrous white figure in her vestal-like robe. She resembled the priestess in paintings of long-gone Mediterranean religions. Her hair fell wildly on her shoulder. She threw out her arms and cried to Swift in a woe that seemed almost as real as the woe of good people.

"Oh, oh, my heart is broken! My heart is broken!"

But Swift knew as well as the rest of mankind that these girls have no hearts to be broken, and this acting filled him with a new rage. He grabbed an alarm clock from the dresser and banged her heroically on the head with it.

She fell and quivered for a moment. Then she arose, and, calm and dry-eyed, walked to the mirror. Swift thought she was taking an account of the bruises, but when he resumed his cyclonic tirade, she said: "I've taken morphine, Swift."

Swift leaped at a little red pill box. It was empty. Eight quarter-grain pills make two grains. The Suicidal Purpose was distinctly ahead of the Alarm Clock. With great presence of mind Swift now took the empty pill box and flung it through the window.

At this time a great battle was begun in the dining-room of the little flat. Swift dragged the girl to the sideboard, and in forcing her to drink whisky he almost stuffed the bottle down her throat. When the girl still sank to the depths of an infinite drowsiness, sliding limply in her chair like a cloth figure, he dealt her furious blows, and our decorous philosophy knows little of the love and despair that was in those caresses. With his voice he called the light into her eyes, called her from the sinister slumber which her senses welcomed, called her soul back from the verge.

He propped the girl in a chair and ran to the kitchen to make coffee. His fingers might have been from a dead man's hands, and his senses confused the coffee, the water, the coffee-pot, the gas stove, but by some fortune he managed to arrange them correctly. When he lifted the girlish figure and carried her to the kitchen, he was as wild, haggard, gibbering, as a man of midnight murders, and it is only because he was not engaged in the respectable and literary assassination of a royal duke that almost any sensible writer would be ashamed of this story. Let it suffice, then, that when the steel-blue dawn came and distant chimneys were black against a rose sky, the girl sat at the dining-room table chattering insanely and gesturing. Swift, with his hands pressed to his temples, watched her from the other side of the table, with all his mind in his eyes, for each gesture was still a reminiscence, and each tone of her voice a ballad to him. And yet he could not half measure his misery. The tragedy was made of homeliest details. He had to repeat to himself that he, worn-out, stupefied from his struggle, was sitting there awaiting the moment when the unseen hand should whirl this soul into the abyss, and that then he should be alone.

The girl saw a fly alight on a picture. "Oh," she said, "there's a little fly." She arose and thrust out her finger. "Hello, little fly," she said, and touched the fly. The insect was perhaps too cold to be alert, for it fell at the touch of her finger. The girl gave a cry of remorse, and, sinking to her knees, searched the floor, meanwhile uttering apologies.

At last she found the fly, and, taking it, [in] her palm went to the gas-jet which still burned weirdly in the dawning. She held her hand close to the flame. "Poor little fly," she said, "I didn't mean to hurt you. I wouldn't hurt you for anything. There now—p'r'aps when you get warm you can fly away again. Did I crush the poor little bit of fly? I'm awful sorry—honest. I am. Poor little thing! Why I wouldn't hurt you for the world, poor little fly—"

Swift was woefully pale and so nerve-weak that his whole body felt a singular coolness. Strange things invariably come into a man's head at the wrong time, and Swift was aware that this scene was defying his preconceptions. His instruction had been that people when dying behaved in a certain manner. Why did this girl occupy herself with an accursed fly? Why in the name of the gods of the drama did she not refer to her past? Why, by the shelves of the saints of literature, did she not clutch her brow and say: "Ah, once I was an innocent girl?" What was wrong with this death scene? At one time he thought that his sense of propriety was so scandalized that he was upon the point of interrupting the girl's babble.

But here a new thought struck him. The girl was not going to die. How could she under these circumstances? The form was not correct.

All this was not relevant to the man's love and despair, but, behold, my friend, at the tragic, the terrible point in life there comes an irrelevancy to the human heart direct from the Wise God. And this is why Swift Doyer thought those peculiar thoughts.

The girl chattered to the fly minute after minute, and Swift's anxiety grew dim and more dim until his head fell forward on the table and he slept as a man who has moved mountains, altered rivers, caused snow to come because he wished it to come, and done his duty.

For an hour the girl talked to the fly, the gas-jet, the walls, the distant chimneys. Finally she sat opposite the slumbering Swift and talked softly to herself.

When broad day came they were both asleep, and the girl's fingers had gone across the table until they had found the locks on the man's forehead. They were asleep, and this after all is a human action, which may safely be done by characters in the fiction of our time.

THE "TENDERLOIN" AS IT REALLY IS

BY STEPHEN CRANE. THE FIRST OF A SERIES OF STRIKING SKETCHES OF NEW YORK LIFE BY THE FAMOUS NOVELIST.

MANY REQUIEMS HAVE BEEN sung over the corpse of the Tenderloin. Dissipated gentlemen with convivial records burn candles to its memory each day at the corner of Twenty-eighth street and Broadway. On the great thoroughfare there are 4,000,000 men who at all times recite loud anecdotes of the luminous past.

They say: "Oh, if you had only come around when the old Haymarket was running!" They relate the wonders of this prehistoric time and fill the mind of youth with poignant regret. Everybody on earth must have attended regularly at this infernal Haymarket. The old gentlemen with convivial records do nothing but relate the glories of this place. To be sure, they tell of many other resorts, but the old gentlemen really do their conjuring with this one simple name—"the old Haymarket."

The Haymarket is really responsible for half the tales that are in the collections of these gay old boys of the silurian period. Some time a man will advertise "The Haymarket Restored," and score a clamoring, popular success. The interest in a reincarnation of a vanished Athens must pale before the excitement caused by "The Haymarket Restored."

Let a thing become a tradition, and it becomes half a lie. These moss-grown columns that support the sky over Broadway street corners insist that life in this dim time was a full joy. Their descriptions are short, but graphic.

One of this type will cry: "Everything wide open, my boy; everything wide open! You should have seen it. No sneaking in side doors. Everything plain as day. Ah, those were the times! Reubs from the West used to have their bundles lifted every night before your eyes. Always somebody blowing champagne for the house. Great! Great! Diamonds, girls, lights, music. Well, maybe it wasn't smooth. Fights all over Sixth avenue. Wasn't room enough. Used to hold over-flow fights in the side streets. Say, it was great!"

Then the type heaves a sigh and murmurs: "But now? Dead—dead as a mackerel. The Tenderloin is a graveyard. Quiet as a tomb. Say, you ought to have been around here when the old Haymarket was running."

Perchance they miss in their definition of the Tenderloin. They describe it as a certain condition of affairs in a metropolitan district. But probably it is in truth something more dim, an essence, an emotion—something superior to the influences of politics or geographies, a thing unchangeable. It represents a certain wild impulse, and a wild impulse is yet more lasting than an old Haymarket. And so we come to reason that the Tenderloin is not dead at all and that the old croakers on the corners are men who have mistaken the departure of their own youth for the death of the Tenderloin, and that there still exists the spirit that flings beer bottles, jumps debts and makes havoc for the unwary; also sings in a hoarse voice at 3 A.M.

There is one mighty fact, however, that the croakers have clinched. In the old days there was a great deal of money and few dress clothes exhibited in the Tenderloin. Now it is all clothes and no money. The spirit is garish, for display, as are the flaming lights that advertise theatres and medicines. In those days long ago there might have been freedom and fraternity.

*   *   *   *

Billie Maconnigle is probably one of the greatest society leaders that the world has produced. Seventh avenue is practically one voice in this matter.

He asked Flossie to dance with him, and Flossie did, seeming to enjoy the attentions of this celebrated cavalier. He asked her again, and she accepted again. Johnnie, her fellow, promptly interrupted the dance.

"Here!" he said, grabbing Maconnigle by the arm. "Dis is me own private snap! Youse gitaway f 'm here an' leggo d' loidy!"

"A couple a nits," rejoined Maconnigle swinging his arm clear of his partner. "Youse go chase yerself. I'm spieling wit' dis loidy when I likes, an' if youse gits gay, I'll knock yer block off—an dat's no dream!"

"Youse'll knock nuttin' off."

"Won't I?"

"Nit. An' if yeh say much I'll make yeh look like a lobster, you fresh mug. Leggo me loidy!"

"A couple a nits."

"Won't?"

"Nit."

Blim! Blam! Crash!

The orchestra stopped playing and the musicians wheeled in their chairs, gazing with that semi-interest which only musicians in a dance hall can bring to bear upon such a scene. Several waiters ran forward, crying "Here, gents, quit dat!" A tall, healthy individual with no coat slid from behind the bar at the far end of the hall, and came with speed. Two well-dressed youths, drinking bottled beer at one end of the tables, nudged each other in ecstatic delight, and gazed with all their eyes at the fight. They were seeing life. They had come purposely to see it.

The waiters grabbed the fighters quickly. Maconnigle went through the door some three feet ahead of his hat, which came after him with a battered crown and a torn rim. A waiter with whom Johnnie had had a discussion over the change had instantly seized this opportunity to assert himself. He grappled Johnnie from the rear and flung him to the floor, and the tall, healthy person from behind the bar, rushing forward, kicked him in the head. Johnnie didn't say his prayers. He only wriggled and tried to shield his head with his arms, because every time that monstrous foot struck it made red lightning flash in his eyes.

But the tall, healthy man and his cohort of waiters had forgotten one element. They had forgotten Flossie. She could worry Johnnie; she could summon every art to make him wildly jealous; she could cruelly, wantonly harrow his soul with every device known to her kind, but she wouldn't stand by and see him hurt by gods nor men.

Blim! As the tall person drew back for his fourth kick, a beer mug landed him just back of his ear. Scratch! The waiter who had grabbed Johnnie from behind found that fingernails had made a ribbon of blood down his face as neatly as if a sign painter had put it there with a brush.

This cohort of waiters was, however, well drilled. Their leader was prone, but they rallied gallantly, and flung Johnnie and Flossie into the street, thinking no doubt that these representatives of the lower classes could get their harmless pleasure just as well outside.

The crowd at the door favored the vanquished. "Sherry!" said a voice. "Sherry! Here comes a cop!" Indeed a helmet and brass buttons shone brightly in the distance. Johnnie and Flossie sherried with all the promptitude allowed to a wounded man and a girl whose sole anxiety is the man. They ended their flight in a little dark alley.

Flossie was sobbing as if her heart was broken. She hung over her wounded hero, wailing and making moan to the sky, weeping with the deep and impressive grief of gravesides, when he swore because his head ached.

"Dat's all right," said Johnnie. "Nex' time youse needn't be so fresh wit' every guy what comes up."

"Well, I was only kiddin', Johnnie," she cried, forlornly.

"Well, yeh see what yeh done t' me wit'cher kiddin," replied Johnnie.

They came forth cautiously from their alley and journeyed homeward. Johnnie had had enough of harmless pleasure.

However, after a considerable period of reflective silence, he paused and said: "Say, Floss, youse couldn't a done a t'ing t' dat guy."

"I jest cracked 'im under d' ear," she explained. "An it laid 'im flat out, too."

A complacence for their victory here came upon them, and as they walked out of the glow of Seventh avenue into a side street it could have been seen that their self satisfaction was complete.

*   *   *   *

Five men flung open the wicket doors of a brilliant cafe on Broadway and, entering, took seats at a table. They were in evening dress, and each man held his chin as if it did not belong to him.

"Well, fellows, what'll you drink?" said one. He found out, and after the ceremony there was a period of silence. Ultimately another man cried, "Let's have another drink." Following this outburst and its attendant ceremony there was another period of silence.

At last a man murmured: "Well, let's have another drink." Two members of the party discussed the state of the leather market. There was an exciting moment when a little newsboy slid into the place, crying a late extra, and was ejected by the waiter. The five men gave the incident their complete attention.

"Let's have a drink," said one afterward.

At an early hour of the morning one man yawned and said: "I'm going home. I've got to catch an early train, and—"

The four others awoke. "Oh, hold on, Tom. Hold on. Have another drink before you go. Don't go without a last drink."

He had it. Then there was a silence. Then he yawned again and said: "Let's have another drink."

They settled comfortably once more around the table. From time to time somebody said: "Let's have a drink."

*   *   *   *

Yes, the Tenderloin is more than a place. It is an emotion. And this spirit seems still to ring true for some people. But if one is ever obliged to make explanation to any of the old croakers, it is always possible to remark that the Tenderloin has grown too fine. Therein lies the cause of the change.

To the man who tries to know the true things there is something hollow and mocking about this Tenderloin of to-day, as far as its outward garb is concerned. The newer generation brought new clothes with them. The old Tenderloin is decked out. And wherever there are gorgeous lights, massive buildings, dress clothes and theatrical managers, there is very little nature, and it may be no wonder that the old spirit of the locality chooses to lurk in the darker places.

IN THE "TENDERLOIN"

BY STEPHEN CRANE. THE SECOND OF A SERIES OF SKETCHES OF NEW YORK LIFE BY THE FAMOUS NOVELIST

THE WAITERS WERE VERY wise. Every man of them had worked at least three years in a Tenderloin restaurant, and this must be equal to seven centuries and an added two decades in Astoria. Even the man who opened oysters wore an air of accumulated information. Here the science of life was perfectly understood by all.

At 10 o'clock the place was peopled only by waiters and the man behind the long bar. The innumerable tables represented a vast white field, and the glaring electric lamps were not obstructed in their mission of shedding a furious orange radiance upon the cloths. An air of such peace and silence reigned that one might have heard the ticking of a clock. It was as quiet as a New England sitting room.

As 11 o'clock passed, however, and time marched toward 12, the place was suddenly filled with people. The process was hardly to be recognized. One surveyed at one moment a bare expanse of tables with groups of whispering waiters and at the next it was crowded with men and women attired gorgeously and plainly and splendidly and correctly. The electric glare swept over a region of expensive bonnets. Frequently the tall pride of a top hat—a real top hat—could be seen on its way down the long hall, and the envious said with sneers that the theatrical business was booming this year.

Without, the cable cars moved solemnly toward the mysteries of Harlem, and before the glowing and fascinating refrigerators displayed at the front of the restaurant a group of cabmen engaged in their singular diplomacy.

If there ever has been in a New York cafe an impulse from the really Bohemian religion of fraternity it has probably been frozen to death. A universal suspicion, a thing of so austere a cast that we mistake it for a social virtue, is the quality that generally oppresses us. But the hand of a bartender is a supple weapon of congeniality. In the small hours a man may forget the formulae which prehistoric fathers invented for him. Usually social form as practised by the stupid is not a law. It is a vital sensation. It is not temporary, emotional; it is fixed and, very likely, the power that makes the rain, the sunshine, the wind, now recognizes social form as an important element in the curious fashioning of the world. It is as solid, as palpable as a fort, and if you regard any landscape, you may see it in the foreground.

Therefore a certain process which moves in this restaurant is very instructive. It is a process which makes constantly toward the obliteration of the form. It never dangerously succeeds, but it is joyous and frank in the attempt.

*   *   *   *

A man in race-track clothing turned in his chair and addressed a stranger at the next table. "I beg your pardon—will you tell me the time please?"

The stranger was in evening dress, very correct indeed. At the question, he stared at the man for a moment, particularly including his tie in this look of sudden and subtle contempt. After a silence he drew forth his watch, looked at it, and returned it to his pocket. After another silence he drooped his eyes with peculiar significance, puffed his cigar and, of a sudden, remarked: "Why don't you look at the clock?"

The race-track man was a genial soul. He promptly but affably directed the kind gentleman to a place supposed to be located at the end of the Brooklyn trolley lines.

And yet at 4:30 A.M. the kind gentleman overheard the race-track man telling his experience in London in 1886, and as he had experiences similar in beauty, and as it was 4:30 A.M. and as he had completely forgotten the incident of the earlier part of the evening, he suddenly branched into the conversation, and thereafter it took ten strong men to hold him from buying a limitless ocean of wine.

*   *   *   *

A curious fact of upper Broadway is the man who knows everybody, his origin, wealth, character and tailor. His knowledge is always from personal intercourse, too, and, without a doubt, he must have lived for ten thousand years to absorb all the anecdotes which he has at the tip of his tongue. If it were a woman, now, most of the stories would be weird resurrections of long-entombed scandals. The trenches for the dead on medieval battle fields would probably be clawed open to furnish evidence of various grim truths, or of untruths, still more grim. But if, according to a rigid definition, these men are gossips, it is in a kinder way than is usually denominated by the use of the word. Let a woman once take an interest in the shortcomings of her neighbors, and she immediately and naturally begins to magnify events in a preposterous fashion, until one can imagine that the law of proportion is merely a legend. There is one phrase which she uses eternally. "They say"—Herein is the peculiar terror of the curse. "They say"—It is so vague that the best spear in the world must fail to hit this shadow. The charm of it is that a woman seldom relates from personal experience. It is nearly always some revolving tale from a hundred tongues.

But it is evident in most cases that the cafe historians of upper Broadway speak from personal experience. The dove that brought the olive branch to Noah was one of their number. Another was in Hades at the time that Lucifer made his celebrated speech against the street-lighting system there. Another is an ex-member of the New Jersey Legislature. All modes, all experiences, all phases of existence are chronicled by these men. They are not obliged to fall back upon common report for their raw material. They possess it in the original form.

A cafe of the kind previously described is a great place for the concentration of the historians. Here they have great opportunities.

"See that fellow going there? That's young Jimmie Lode. Knew his father well. Denver people, you know. Old man had a strange custom of getting drunk on the first Friday after the first Thursday in June. Indian reservation near his house. Used to go out and fist-fight the Indians. Gave a twenty-dollar gold piece to every Indian he licked. Indians used to labor like thunder to get licked. Well, sir, one time the big chief of the whole push was trying to earn his money, and, by

Jove, no matter what he did, he couldn't seem to fix it so the old man could lick him. So finally he laid down flat on the ground and the old man jumped on him and stove in his bulwarks. Indian said it was all right, but he thought forty dollars was a better figure for stove-in bulwarks. But the old man said he had agreed to pay twenty dollars, and he wouldn't give up another sou. So they had a fight—a real fight, you know—and the Indian killed him.

"Well, that's the son over there. Father left him a million and a half. Maybe Jack ain't spending it. Say! He just pours it out. He's crushed on Dollie Bangle, you know. She plays over here at the Palais de Glace. That's her now he's talking to. Ain't she a peach. Say? Am I right? Well, I should say so. She don't do a thing to his money. Burns it in an open grate. She's on the level with him, though. That's one thing. Well, I say she is. Of course, I'm sure of it."

In the meantime others pass before the historian's watchful vi-sion, and he continues heroically to volley his traditions.

*　　*　　*　　*

The babble of voices grew louder and louder. The heavy smoke clouds eddied above the shining countenances. Into the street came the clear, cold blue of impending day-light, and over the cobbles roared a milk wagon.

STEPHEN CRANE IN MINETTA LANE

ONE OF GOTHAM'S MOST NOTORIOUS THOROUGHFARES. THE NOVELIST TELLS WHAT HE SAW AND HEARD ON A STREET WHERE THE INHABITANTS HAVE BEEN FAMOUS FOR EVIL DEEDS, WHERE THE BURGLAR AND THE SHOPLIFTER AND THE MURDERER LIVE SIDE BY SIDE. THE NOVEL RESORT OF MAMMY ROSS AND OTHERS OF HER KIND.

MINETTA LANE IS A small and becobbled valley between hills of dingy brick. At night the street lamps, burning dimly, cause the shadows to be important, and in the gloom one sees groups of qui-etly conversant negroes with occasionally the gleam of a passing growler.* Everything is vaguely outlined and of uncertain identity unless indeed it be the flashing buttons and shield of the policeman on post. The Sixth Avenue horse cars jingle past one end of the Lane and, a block eastward, the little thoroughfare ends in the darkness of MacDougal Street.

One wonders how such an insignificant alley could get such an absurdly large reputation, but, as a matter of fact, Minetta Lane, and Minetta Street, which leads from it southward to Bleecker Street, MacDougal Street and nearly all the streets thereabouts were most unmistakably bad, but when the Minettas started out the other streets went away and hid. To gain a reputation in Minetta Lane, in those days, a man was obliged to commit a number of furious crimes, and no celebrity was more important than the man who had a good honest killing to his credit. The inhabitants, for the most part, were negroes, and they represented the very worst elements of their race. The razor habit clung to them with the tenacity of an epidemic, and every night the uneven cobbles felt blood. Minetta Lane was not a public thoroughfare at this period. It was a street set apart, a refuge for criminals. Thieves came here preferably with their gains, and almost any day peculiar sentences passed among the inhabitants. "Big Jim turned a thousand last night." "No Toe's made another haul." And the worshipful citizens would make haste to be present at the consequent revel.

Not Then a Thoroughfare.

As has been said, Minetta Lane was then no thoroughfare. A peaceable citizen chose to make a circuit rather than venture through this place, that swarmed with the most dangerous people in the city. Indeed, the thieves of the district used to say: "Once get in the Lane and you're all right." Even a policeman in chase of a criminal would probably shy away instead of pursuing him into the lane. The odds were too great against a lone officer.

---

*Slang for a beer truck.

Sailors, and many men who might appear to have money about them, were welcomed with all proper ceremony at the terrible dens of the Lane. At departure, they were fortunate if they still retained their teeth. It was the custom to leave very little else to them. There was every facility for the capture of coin, from trapdoors to plain ordinary knockout drops.

And yet Minetta Lane is built on the grave of Minetta Brook, where, in olden times, lovers walked under the willows of the bank, and Minetta Lane, in later times, was the home of many of the best families of the town.

A negro named Bloodthirsty was perhaps the most luminous figure of Minetta Lane's aggregation of desperadoes. Bloodthirsty, supposedly, is alive now, but he has vanished from the Lane. The police want him for murder. Bloodthirsty is a large negro and very hideous. He has a rolling eye that shows white at the wrong time and his neck, under the jaw, is dreadfully scarred and pitted.

Bloodthirsty was particularly eloquent when drunk, and in the wildness of a spree he would rave so graphically about gore, that even the habituated wool of old timers would stand straight. Bloodthirsty meant most of it, too. That is why his orations were impressive. His remarks were usually followed by the wide lightning sweep of his razor. None cared to exchange epithets with Bloodthirsty. A man in a boiler iron suit would walk down to City Hall and look at the clock before he would ask the time of day from single minded and ingenuous Bloodthirsty.

No Toe Charley.

After Bloodthirsty, in combative importance, came No Toe Charley. Singularly enough Charley was called No Toe solely because he did not have a toe to his feet. Charley was a small negro and his manner of amusement was not Bloodthirsty's simple ways. As befitting a smaller man, Charley was more wise, more sly, more roundabout than the other man. The path of his crimes was like a corkscrew, in architecture, and his method led him to make many tunnels. With all his cleverness, however, No Toe was finally induced to pay a visit to the gentlemen in the grim gray building up the river.

Black-Cat was another famous bandit who made the Lane his home. Black-Cat is dead. It is within some months that Jube Tyler has been sent to prison, and after mentioning the recent disappearance of Old Man Spriggs, it may be said that the Lane is now destitute of the men who once crowned it with a glory of crime. It is hardly essential to mention Guinea Johnson. Guinea is not a great figure. Guinea is just an ordinary little crook. Sometimes Guinea pays a visit to his friends, the other little crooks who make homes in the Lane, but he himself does not live there, and with him out of it, there is now no one whose industry in unlawfulness has yet earned him the dignity of a nickname. Indeed, it is difficult to find people now who remember the old gorgeous days, although it is but two years since the Lane shone with sin like a new headlight. But after a search the reporter found three.

Mammy Ross is one of the last relics of the days of slaughter still living there. Her weird history also reaches back to the blossoming of the first members of the Whyo* gang in the old Sixth Ward, and her mind is stored with bloody memories. She at one time kept a sailor's boarding house near the Tombs Prison,† and accounts of all the festive crimes of that neighborhood in ancient years roll easily from her tongue. They killed a sailor man every day, and the pedestrians went about the streets wearing stoves for fear of the handy knives. At the present day the route to Mammy's home is up a flight of grimy stairs that is pasted on the outside of an old and tottering frame house. Then there is a hall blacker than a wolf's throat, and this hall leads to a little kitchen where Mammy usually sits groaning by the fire. She is, of course, very old, and she is also very fat. She seems always to be in great pain. She says she is suffering from "de very las' dregs of de yaller fever."

---

*Name of a notoriously bloodthirsty gang in nineteenth-century New York.
†Nickname for the Manhattan House of Detention; the original structure was said to resemble an Egyptian tomb.

A Picture of Suffering.

During the first part of a reporter's recent visit old Mammy seemed most dolefully oppressed by her various diseases. Her great body shook and her teeth clicked spasmodically during her long and painful respirations. From time to time she reached her trembling hand and drew a shawl closer about her shoulders. She presented as true a picture of a person undergoing steady, unchangeable, chronic pain as a patent medicine firm could wish to discover for miraculous purposes. She breathed like a fish thrown out on the bank, and her old head continually quivered in the nervous tremors of the extremely aged and debilitated person. Meanwhile her daughter hung over the stove and placidly cooked sausages.

Appeals were made to the old woman's memory. Various personages who had been sublime figures of crime in the long-gone days were mentioned to her, and presently her eyes began to brighten. Her head no longer quivered. She seemed to lose for a period her sense of pain in the gentle excitement caused by the invocation of the spirits of her memory.

It appears that she had had a historic quarrel with Apple Mag. She first recited the prowess of Apple Mag; how this emphatic lady used to argue with paving stones, carving knives and bricks. Then she told of the quarrel; what Mag said; what she said; what Mag said; what she said: It seems that they cited each other as spectacles of sin and corruption in more fully explanatory terms than are commonly known to be possible. But it was one of Mammy's most gorgeous recollections, and, as she told it, a smile widened over her face.

Finally she explained her celebrated retort to one of the most illustrious thugs that had blessed the city in bygone days. "Ah says to 'im, Ah says: 'You—you'll die in yer boots like Gallopin' Thompson—dat's what you'll do.' [Slug missing from newsprint here.] one chile an' he ain't nuthin' but er cripple, but le'me tel' you, man, dat boy'll live t' pick de feathers f 'm de goose dat'll eat de grass dat grows over your grave, man! Dat's what I tol' 'm. But—lan's sake—how I know dat in less'n three day, dat man be lying in de gutter wif a knife stickin' out'n his back. Lawd, no, I sholy never s'pected nothing like dat."

Memories of the Past.

These reminiscences, at once maimed and reconstructed, have been treasured by old Mammy as carefully, as tenderly, as if they were the various little tokens of an early love. She applies the same back-handed sentiment to them, and, as she sits groaning by the fire, it is plainly to be seen that there is only one food for her ancient brain, and that is the recollection of the beautiful fights and murders of the past.

On the other side of the Lane, but near Mammy's house, Pop Babcock keeps a restaurant. Pop says it is a restaurant, and so it must be one, but you could pass there ninety times each day and never know that you were passing a restaurant. There is one obscure little window in the basement and if you went close and peered in, you might, after a time, be able to make out a small, dusty sign, lying amid jars on a shelf. This sign reads: "Oysters in every style." If you are of a gambling turn of mind, you will probably stand out in the street and bet yourself black in the face that there isn't an oyster within a hundred yards. But Pop Babcock made that sign and Pop Babcock could not tell an untruth. Pop is a model of all the virtues which an inventive fate has made for us. He says so.

As far as goes the management of Pop's restaurant, it differs from Sherry's. In the first place the door is always kept locked. The wardmen* of the Fifteenth Precinct have a way of prowling through the restaurant almost every night, and Pop keeps the door locked in order to keep out the objectionable people that cause the wardmen's visits. He says so. The cooking stove is located in the main room of the restaurant, and it is placed in such a strategic manner that it occupies about all the space that is not already occupied by a table, a bench and two chairs. The table will, on a pinch, furnish room for the plates of two people if they are willing to crowd. Pop says he is the best cook in the world.

---

*Neighborhood policemen under the control of the local politico known as the "ward boss."

"Pop's" View of It.

When questioned concerning the present condition of the Lane, Pop said: "Quiet? Quiet? Lo'd save us, maybe it ain't! Quiet? Quiet?" His emphasis was arranged crescendo, until the last word was really a vocal explosion. "Why, dis her' Lane ain't nohow like what it useter be—no indeed, it ain't. No, sir! 'Deed it ain't! Why, I kin remember dey was a-cuttin' an' a'slashin' 'long yere all night. 'Deed dey was! My—my, dem times was different! Dat dar Kent, he kep' de place at Green Gate Cou't—down yer ol' Mammy's—an' he was a hard baby—'deed, he was—an' ol' Black-Cat an' ol' Bloodthirsty, dey was a-roamin' round yere a-cuttin' an' a-slashin'. Didn't dar' say boo to a goose in dose days, dat you didn't, less'n you lookin' fer a scrap. No, sir!" Then he gave information concerning his own prowess at that time. Pop is about as tall as a picket on an undersized fence. "But dey didn't have nothin' ter say to me! No, sir! 'Deed, dey didn't! I wouldn't lay down fer none of 'em. No, sir! Dey knew my gait, 'deed, dey did! Man, man, many's de time I buck up agin 'em. Yes, sir!"

At this time Pop had three customers in his place, one asleep on the bench, one asleep on the two chairs, and one asleep on the floor behind the stove.

But there is one man who lends dignity of the real bevel-edged type to Minetta Lane, and that man is Hank Anderson. Hank, of course, does not live in the Lane, but the shadow of his social perfections falls upon it as refreshingly as a morning dew. Hank gives a dance twice in each week, at a hall hard by in MacDougal Street, and the dusky aristocracy of the neighborhood know their guiding beacon. Moreover, Hank holds an annual ball in Forty-fourth Street. Also he gives a picnic each year to the Montezuma Club, when he again appears as a guiding beacon. This picnic is usually held on a barge and the occasion is a very joyous one. Some years ago it required the entire reserve squad of an up-town police precinct to properly control the enthusiasm of the gay picnickers, but that was an exceptional exuberance and no measure of Hank's ability for management.

He is really a great manager. He was Boss Tweed's body-servant in the days when Tweed was a political prince, and anyone who saw Bill Tweed through a spyglass learned the science of leading, pulling, driving and hauling men in a way to keep men ignorant of it. Hank imbibed from this fount of knowledge and he applied his information in Thompson Street. Thompson Street salaamed. Presently he bore a proud title: "The Mayor of Thompson Street." Dignities from the principal political organization of the city adorned his brow and he speedily became illustrious.

Keeping in Touch.

Hank knew the Lane well in its direful days. As for the inhabitants, he kept clear of them and yet in touch with them according to a method that he might have learned in the Sixth Ward. The Sixth Ward was a good place in which to learn that trick. Anderson can tell many strange tales and good of the Lane, and he tells them in the graphic way of his class. "Why, they could steal your shirt without moving a wrinkle on it."

The killing of Joe Carey was the last murder that happened in the Minettas. Carey had what might be called a mixed ale difference with a man named Kenny. They went out to the middle of Minetta Street to affably fight it out and determine the justice of the question. In the scrimmage Kenny drew a knife, thrust quickly and Carey fell. Kenny had not gone a hundred feet before he ran into the arms of a policeman.

There is probably no street in New York where the police keep closer watch than they do in Minetta Lane. There was a time when the inhabitants had a profound and reasonable contempt for the public guardians, but they have it no longer apparently. Any citizen can walk through there at any time in perfect safety unless, perhaps, he should happen to get too frivolous. To be strictly accurate, the change began under the reign of Police Captain Chapman. Under Captain Groo, the present commander of the Fifteenth Precinct, the Lane has donned a complete new garb. Its denizens brag now of its peace precisely as they once bragged of its war. It is no more a bloody lane. The song of the razor is seldom heard. There are still toughs and semi-toughs galore in it, but they can't get a chance with the copper looking the other way. Groo has got the poor old Lane by the throat. If a man should insist on becoming a victim of the badger game he could probably succeed upon search in Minetta Lane, as indeed, he could on any of the great avenues; but then Minetta Lane is not supposed to be a pearly street in Paradise.

In the meantime the Italians have begun to dispute possession of the Lane with the negroes. Green Gate Court is filled with them now, and a row of houses near the MacDougal Street corner is occupied entirely by Italian families. None of them seems to be overfond of the old Mulberry Bend fashion of life, and there are no cutting affrays among them worth mentioning. It is the original negro element that makes the trouble when there is trouble.

But they are happy in this condition, are these people. The most extraordinary quality of the negro is his enormous capacity for happiness under most adverse circumstances. Minetta Lane is a place of poverty and sin, but these influences cannot destroy the broad smile of the negro, a vain and simple child but happy. They all smile here, the most evil as well as the poorest. Knowing the negro, one always expects laughter from him, be he ever so poor, but it was a new experience to see a broad grin on the face of the devil. Even old Pop Babcock had a laugh as fine and mellow as would be the sound of falling glass, broken saints from high windows, in the silence of some great cathedral's hollow.

ENDNOTES

Maggie: A Girl of the Streets

1. (p. 7) *for the honor of Rum Alley . . . howling urchins from Devil's Row*: As far as can be determined there was neither a Rum Alley nor a Devil's Row in Manhattan. Crane used these unpleasant names to underscore the squalor in which he had set his story. Rum Alley could be construed as a gentle dig at his mother's devotion to the cause of temperance.

2. (p. 7) *a dock at the river*: The river mentioned here is the East River, which is not a river at all, but a tidal estuary that connects Upper New York Bay with Long Island Sound.

3. (p. 7) *Over on the Island*: This is a reference to Blackwell's Island (now Roosevelt Island), which has been home to prisons, a quarantine hospital, and a potter's field. Because the island can be seen from Rum Alley, we know that the action of the story takes place in a slum on the east side of Manhattan known as Dutch Hill, roughly where the United Nations building stands today.

4. (p. 18) *The babe, Tommie, died*: These four simple words are typical of Crane's writing style. This clipped, emotionless, technique was the antithesis of the more flowery style of the day.

5. (p. 19) *His father died and his mother's years were divided up into periods of thirty days*: This is another example of Crane's dispassionate voice. ("Thirty days" is a reference to the fact that she is living month to month in her hovel.) It is interesting to note that there is no mention of extravagant grief over the death of a husband and child, as opposed to Mary Johnson's lamentations following the death of her daughter.

6. (p. 21) *Yet he achieved a respect for a fire engine*: The thundering of fire engines through the chaotic streets stopped even the most jaded New Yorkers in their tracks. Jimmie, who respects very little, respects the firemen in their rigs because they are stronger and even greater daredevils than he is.

7. (p. 22) *"Deh moon looks like hell, don't it?"*: This is perhaps the most famous line in the book, and the inarticulate limit of Jimmie's appreciation of life beyond the gutter.

8. (p. 22) *"Mag, I'll tell yeh dis!"* Here Jimmie explains Maggie's options, the two choices of slum women—hell (prostitution) or the presumed reward of heaven that comes with monotonous, unhealthy, poorly paid labor.

9. (p. 23) *to a boxing match in Williamsburg:* Williamsburg was a separate city from New York and Brooklyn. Presumably going to far-off Williamsburg was something of an adventure. Williamsburg was later incorporated into the city of Brooklyn, which in turn became a borough of New York City in 1898.

10. (p. 29) *nationalities of the Bowery:* As the legitimate theater moved uptown, the Bowery, which had once been the great entertainment center of New York, was given over to tawdry dance halls and music halls such as the one described here.

11. (p. 33) *She began to see the bloom:* This is almost the only example in the book of Maggie's sense of her own worth.

12. (p. 42) *"Anybody what had eyes could see dat dere was somethin' wrong wid dat girl. I didn't like her actions":* The neighbors in the tenement function as a chorus commenting on the action of the story. They are by turns mocking, appalled, offended, and, as this line illustrates, almost always wrong.

13. (p. 53) *ease of Pete's ways toward her:* This is a simple suggestion that Pete is bored with Maggie and ready to move on. His excitement at seeing Nell a few lines later only compounds this.

14. (p. 63) *Maggie went away:* With these three words Crane tells the reader, but not Maggie, that this is the beginning of the end for her.

15. (p. 65) *she was neither new, Parisian, nor theatrical:* Although we get the impression that Maggie was the most naive, inept prostitute to walk the streets of New York, this line suggests that she must have gained some worldly knowledge in the course of her brief career.

16. (p. 72) *"She's gone where her sins will be judged":* Here is another example of the tenement dwellers acting as commentators on the action of the story.

George's Mother

1. (p. 78) *A man with a red, mottled face . . . shook his fist:* This paragraph tells us that although we are now in the world of the upright, hardworking Kelceys, we are back in the slums, back in Maggie's milieu.

2. (p. 80) *In the distance an enormous brewery:* Here Crane includes a simple bit of foreshadowing. This brewery, snorting smoke like some kind of monster, is the creature that suffuses the entire story and is the source of George's downfall.

3. (p. 83) *He began to be vexed. . . . it was depressing:* This paragraph and the others describing the imagined prayer meeting are so vivid that they must have been based on Crane's own experiences in his ultrareligious childhood home. The religious regimen of his youth consisted of going to church twice on Sundays and once on Wednesdays, as well as twice-daily Bible readings at home.

4. (p. 95) *One day he met Maggie Johnson on the stairs:* One can only say "poor George" and "poorer still Maggie." If only they had stopped to chat . . .

5. (p. 108) *almost the exact truth:* In other words, at least one of George's co-workers knew what had happened earlier. George had gotten blind drunk somewhere and passed out.

6. (p. 112) *Kelcey sometimes wondered whether he liked beer:* This is one of the most telling lines in the book, and certainly the funniest. If George had thought a bit harder about the question he would have realized that he probably didn't like beer and would be happier without it.

Other Stories

1. (p. 157) *Indeed, it was not until the Binkses had left the city . . . recovered their balances:* Given that New Jersey has now become the punch line of jokes about urban sprawl and air pollution, it is hard to recall that until recently, the state of New Jersey was considered a verdant paradise compared with the smoky and cobble-bound New York City. Just across the Hudson River were green fields, fresh water, and the quiet of rural life. New Jersey supplied most of the fresh vegetables for New York and Philadelphia. It is no coincidence that New Jersey is called the "Garden State."

2. (p. 195) *If a beginner expects . . . until the next morning:* Crane steadfastly maintained that he had never smoked opium. The vividness of this paragraph suggests otherwise. When asked in open court about his opium use, Crane took cover behind the Fifth Amendment.

AN INSPIRATION FOR
CRANE'S WRITINGS ABOUT NEW YORK:
JACOB RIIS'S *HOW THE OTHER HALF LIVES*
AND MUCKRAKING

Stephen Crane's *Maggie: A Girl of the Streets* (1893) was the first major work of naturalism in American fiction. The novel's vivid, unflinching narrative, set in the inhumane living conditions in the tenements of New York City, inspired scores of other American writers to record their observations with a near-photographic realism. Crane's material for his remarkably true-to-life novel came from firsthand experience. He had immersed himself in the very conditions he describes in *Maggie* and his newspaper articles, several of which appear in the present volume.

Three years before *Maggie* appeared, social activist Jacob Riis published an unfaltering depiction of life in New York City with *How the Other Half Lives: Studies Among the Tenements of New York* (1890), a groundbreaking work of nonfiction and photography. Riis, who like Crane had a background in journalism, wrote a startling exposé of the squalid existence of New York's immigrant poor. Riis's work, well-received from the start, had a tremendous impact on social policy. With its publication, officials recognized the appalling living conditions of many of the city's residents and made tenement reform a priority on the political agenda. Theodore Roosevelt, at the time New York City's police commissioner, called Riis "the most useful citizen of New York."

Much of the emotional appeal of *How the Other Half Lives* arose from Riis's unforgettable photographs of the extreme misery of people living in tenements. The pictures forced readers to confront head-on the staggering circumstances of large numbers of people in a manner that prose could not possibly convey. Riis's explicit photographs allowed him to maintain a more subdued tone in his writing that lent credibility to his call for reform. The success of his work paved the way for Stephen Crane, who in many ways tried to replicate the photographic impact of *How the Other Half Lives*. Crane's narrative style is often referred to as "imagistic," and in *Maggie*, his first mature work, Crane compensates for a lack of actual images with his colorful, even lurid prose impressions.

Crane and Riis are associated with the tradition of American journalism known as "muckraking." The loose term refers to journalists who wrote exposé and reform stories in the period between the 1890s and World War I. Overly sensational, condescending, and truth-distorting accounts by some journalists lent muckraking a dubious reputation, although many writers made their cases for reform with integrity. Notable "muckraking" journalists include Lincoln Steffens, Ray Stannard Baker, and Ida Tarbell. Riis's *How the Other Half Lives* inspired socialist-leaning author Jack London to write an analogous depiction of London's East End, titled *The People of the Abyss* (1903).

Upton Sinclair's muckraking novel *The Jungle* (1906) is singular among works of fiction for its positive effect on the real world. The novel's horrifying descriptions of the unsanitary handling of food in Chicago's meatpacking district caused public outrage, and the reality of rotten and diseased food being offered to consumers was confirmed by Chicago newspapers. In response to the furor caused by *The Jungle*, Roosevelt, who had become president of the United States, ordered the Department of Agriculture to investigate conditions in the stockyards, and Congress passed the Food and Drug Act and the Meat Inspection Act just months after the novel's publication.

The term "muckraking," ironically, was coined as a pejorative by Roosevelt in 1906, more than a decade after he had praised Riis's work. The word comes from John Bunyan's Christian allegory *The Pilgrim's Progress* (part I, 1678; part II, 1684), which refers to the Man with the Muck-rake: "the man who could look no way but downward, with the muck-rake in his hand; who was offered a celestial crown for his muck-rake, but who would neither look up nor regard the crown he was offered, but continued to rake to himself the filth of the floor." In coining the term in its modern application, Roosevelt meant to discourage the sort of reckless journalism that, rather than responsibly exposing injustices, attempted to increase circulation with negative stories dependent upon hyperbole and sensationalism—methods both Crane and Riis avoided. In signing the reform legislation, however, and in his praise of Riis, Roosevelt implicitly acknowledged the usefulness of ethical muckrakers.

Later "muckrakers" include civil-rights activist Angela Davis, feminist and political activist Gloria Steinem, *Fast Food Nation* (2001) author Eric Schlosser, and filmmaker Michael Moore, whose films include *Roger & Me* (1989), *Bowling for Columbine* (2002), and *Fahrenheit 9/11* (2004).

COMMENTS & QUESTIONS

In this section, we aim to provide the reader with an array of perspectives on the texts, as well as questions that challenge those perspectives. The commentary has been culled from sources as diverse as reviews contemporaneous with the works, letters written by the author, literary criticism of later generations, and appreciations written throughout the works' histories. Following the commentary, a series of questions seeks to filter Stephen Crane's Maggie: A Girl of the Streets and Other Writings About New York through a variety of points of view and bring about a richer understanding of these enduring works.

Comments

HAMLIN GARLAND

['Maggie'] is of more interest to me, both because it is the work of a young man, and also because it is a work of astonishingly good style. It deals with poverty and vice and crime also, but it does so, not out of curiosity, not out of salaciousness, but because of a distinct art impulse, the desire to utter in truthful phrase a certain rebellious cry. It is the voice of the slums. It is not written by a dilettante; it is written by one who has lived the life. The young author, Stephen Crane, is a native of the city, and has grown up in the very scenes he describes. His book is the most truthful and unhackneyed study of the slums I have yet read, fragment though it is. It is pictorial, graphic, terrible in its directness. It has no conventional phrases. It gives the dialect of the slums as I have never before seen it written—crisp, direct, terse. It is another locality finding voice. . . .

The dictum is amazingly simple and fine for so young a writer. Some of the words illuminate like flashes of light. Mr. Crane is only twenty-one years of age, and yet he has met and grappled with the actualities of the street in almost unequalled grace and strength. With such a technique already at command, with life mainly before him, Stephen Crane is to be henceforth reckoned with.

—from *Arena* (June 1893)

NEW YORK TIMES

Mr. Crane pictures Maggie's home with colors now lurid and now black, but always with the hand of an artist. And the various stages of her career, until in despair at being neglected she, we are led to believe, commits suicide by jumping into the river, are shown with such vivid and terrible accuracy as to make one believe they are photographic. Mr. Crane cannot have seen all that he describes, and yet the reader feels that he must have seen it all. This, perhaps, is the highest praise one can give the book. Mr. Crane is a master of slum slang. His dialogues are surprisingly effective and natural. The talk Pete indulges in while intoxicated makes one see in his mind's eye the very figure of the loathsome beast for the loss of whom Maggie died. . . . Mr. Crane's story should be read for the fidelity with which it portrays a life that is potent on this island, along with the life of the best of us. It is a powerful portrayal, and, if sombre and repellent, none the less true, none the less freighted with appeal to those who are able to assist in righting wrongs.

—May 31, 1896

MORNING ADVERTISER

A Girl of the Streets, Stephen Crane's latest novel, is a picture of the lowest stratum of society in its gloomiest form. It is as realistic as anything that Emile Zola has ever written. Though some of its chapters are enough to give one the 'creeps,' none can deny that the characters which he draws with such a master hand are absolutely true to life. The dialect is also natural, and nothing is lacking to give Devil's Row and Rum Alley, slums of the darker New York, such prominence as they never had before. It may, in fact, be said that Mr. Crane has discovered those localities and revealed them to the astonished gaze of the world for the first time. The reader, in going over the pages of *A Girl of the Streets*, is reminded of nothing so much as the slimy things that crawl and blink when a long undisturbed stone is removed and the light is thrown upon them. The hero and heroine, if such they may be called, are Jimmie and Maggie Johnson, brother and sister, residents of Devil's Row. Maggie is the only redeeming character in the book, and even she does not redeem to any extent. She is betrayed and she dies, and the mourning of Devil's Row at her wake is fearfully grewsome. Analytical powers are the chief feature of the novel.

It is free from maudlin sentiment. No missionary ever ventures near Rum Alley. Its denizens are left to their own resources, and they simmer in them.

—June 1, 1896

WILLIAM DEAN HOWELLS

I think that what strikes me most in the story of *Maggie* is that quality of fatal necessity which dominates Greek tragedy. From the conditions it all had to be, and there were the conditions. I felt this in Mr. Hardy's *Jude*, where the principle seems to become conscious in the writer; but there is apparently no consciousness of any such motive in the author of *Maggie*. Another effect is that of an ideal of artistic beauty which is as present in the working out of this poor girl's squalid romance as in any classic fable. This will be foolishness, I know, to the foolish people who cannot discriminate between the material and the treatment in art, and who think that beauty is inseparable from daintiness and prettiness, but I do not speak to them. I appeal rather to such as feel themselves akin with every kind of human creature, and find neither high nor low when it is a question of inevitable suffering, or of a soul struggling vainly with an inexorable fate.

My rhetoric scarcely suggests the simple terms the author uses to produce the effect which I am trying to report again. They are simple, but always most graphic, especially when it comes to the personalities of the story; the girl herself, with her bewildered wish to be right and good; with her distorted perspective; her clinging and generous affections; her hopeless environments; the horrible old drunken mother, a cyclone of violence and volcano of vulgarity; the mean and selfish lover; a dandy tough, with his gross ideals and ambitions; her brother, an Ishmaelite from the cradle, who with his warlike instincts beaten back into cunning, is what the b'hoy of former times has become in our more strenuously policed days. He is indeed a wonderful figure in a group which betrays no faltering in the artist's hand. He, with his dull hates, his warped good-will, his cowed ferocity, is almost as fine artistically as Maggie, but he could not have been so hard to do, for all the pathos of her fate is rendered without one maudlin touch.

So is that of the simple-minded and devoted and tedious old

woman who is George's mother in the book of that name. This is scarcely a study at all, while Maggie is really and fully so. It is the study of a situation merely: a poor, inadequate woman, of a commonplace religiosity, whose son goes to the bad. The wonder of it is the courage which deals with persons so absolutely average, and the art that graces them with the beauty of the author's compassion for everything that errs and suffers. Without this feeling the effects of his mastery would be impossible, and if it went further or put itself into the pitying phrases it would annul the effects. But it never does this; it is notable how in all respects the author keeps himself well in hand. He is quite honest with his reader. He never shows his characters or his situations in any sort of sentimental glamour; if you will be moved by the sadness of common fates you will feel his intention, but he does not flatter his portraits of people or conditions to take your fancy.

In George and his mother he has to do with folk of country origin as the city affects them, and the son's decadence is admirably studied; he scarcely struggles against temptation, and his mother's only art is to cry and to scold. Yet he loves her, in a way, and she is devotedly proud of him. These simple country folk are contrasted with simple city folk of varying degrees of badness. Mr. Crane has the skill to show how evil is greatly the effect of ignorance and imperfect civilization. The club of friends, older men than George, whom he is asked to join, is portrayed with extraordinary insight, and the group of young toughs whom he finally consorts with is done with even greater mastery. The bulldog motive of one of them, who is willing to fight to the death, is most impressively rendered.

—from *New York World* (July 26, 1896)

H. G. WELLS

The relative merits of the *Red Badge of Courage* and *Maggie* are open to question. To the present reviewer it seems that in *Maggie* we come nearer to Mr. Crane's individuality. Perhaps where we might expect strength we get merely stress, but one may doubt whether we have not been hasty in assuming Mr. Crane to be a strong man in fiction. Strength and gaudy colour rarely go together; tragic and sombre are well nigh inseparable. One gets an impression from the *Red Badge* that at the end Mr. Crane could scarcely have had a gasp left in him—that he must have been mentally hoarse for weeks after it. But here he works chiefly for pretty effects, for gleams of sunlight on the stagnant puddles he paints. He gets them, a little consciously perhaps, but, to the present reviewer's sense, far more effectively than he gets anger and fear. And he has done his work, one feels, to please himself. His book is a work of art, even if it is not a very great or successful work of art—it ranks above the novel of commerce, if only on that account.

—from *Saturday Review* (December 19, 1896)

JOSEPH CONRAD

[Stephen Crane] had indeed a wonderful power of vision, which he applied to the things of this earth and of our mortal humanity with a penetrating force that seemed to reach, within life's appearances and forms, the very spirit of life's truth. His ignorance of the world at large—he had seen very little of it—did not stand in the way of his imaginative grasp of facts, events, and picturesque men.

His manner was very quiet, his personality at first sight interesting, and he talked slowly with an intonation which on some people, mainly Americans, had, I believe, a jarring effect. But not on me. Whatever he said had a personal note, and he expressed himself with a graphic simplicity which was extremely engaging. He knew little of literature, either of his own country or of any other, but he was himself a wonderful artist in words whenever he took a pen into his hand. Then his gift came out—and it was seen to be much more than mere felicity of language. His impressionism of phrase went really deeper than the surface. In his writing he was very sure of his effects. I don't think he was ever in doubt about what he could do. Yet it often seemed to me that he was but half aware of the exceptional quality of his achievement.

This achievement was curtailed by his early death. It was a great loss to his friends, but perhaps not so much to literature. I think he had given his measure fully in the few books he had the time to write. Let me not be misunderstood: the loss was great, but it was the loss of the delight his art could give, not the loss of any further possible revelation. As to himself, who can say how much he gained or lost by quitting so early this world of the living, which he knew how to set before us in the terms of his own artistic vision? Perhaps he did not lose a great deal.

—from *Notes on Life and Letters* (1921)

EDWARD GARNETT

Two qualities in especial combined to form Crane's unique quality, viz his wonderful insight into, and mastery of, the primary passions, and his irony deriding the swelling emotions of the self. It is his irony that checks the emotional intensity of his delineation, and suddenly reveals passion at high tension in the clutch of the implacable tides of life. It is the perfect fusion of these two forces of passion and irony that creates Crane's spiritual background, and raises his work, at its finest, into the higher zone of man's tragic conflict with the universe. . . . In "Maggie," 1896, that little masterpiece which drew the highest tribute from the veteran, W. D. Howells, again it is the irony that keeps in right perspective Crane's remorseless study of New York slum and Bowery morals. The code of herd law by which the inexperienced girl, Maggie, is pressed to death by her family, her lover and the neighbours, is seen working with strange finality. The Bowery inhabitants, as we, can be nothing other than what they are; their human nature responds inexorably to their brutal environment; the curious habits and code of the most primitive savage tribes could not be presented with a more impartial exactness, or with more sympathetic understanding.

"Maggie" is not a story *about* people; it is primitive human nature itself set down with perfect spontaneity and grace of handling. For pure aesthetic beauty and truth no Russian, not Tchekhov himself, could have bettered this study, which, as Howells remarks, has the quality of Greek tragedy.

—from *Friday Nights: Literary Criticism and Appreciation* (1922)

SHERWOOD ANDERSON

Writers in America who do not know their Stephen Crane are missing a lot.

—from his Introduction to Volume 11 of
The Work of Stephen Crane, edited by Wilson Follett (1925–1926)

JOHN BERRYMAN

No American work of [*Maggie's*] length had driven the reader so hard; in none had the author remained so persistently invisible behind his creation.

—from *Stephen Crane* (1950)

Questions

1. The French phrase *nostalgie de la boue* can be roughly translated as a hankering for the gutter, the lower depths, the slums. Crane seems to have had it. Can you sympathize? Is the attraction to the gutter simply that it stimulates a fantasy of throwing off the burden of respectability? What else motivates this attraction? A strange sense of purity?

2. People who read *Maggie* are not likely to have much direct experience with the lower depths of life in the slums or with the down-and-out. Yet from the beginning, readers have called the novel realistic or naturalistic, even without being able to compare the actual scene to Crane's version of it. How does Crane achieve the *effect* of realism, whether or not he actually captures a reality in words?

3. The nineteenth century was a great period for novels about fallen women. Think of *Madame Bovary* and *Anna Karenina*. What is distinctive about Crane's treatment of this theme? Is there anything fundamentally American about it?

4. What attitude do you think Crane wanted to create in the minds of his readers? Righteous indignation? Repugnance? A desire to ameliorate the conditions of the urban poor? A desire to call people like Maggie and her friends to a prayer meeting? Scientific detachment? A sense of superiority? Something else?

FOR FURTHER READING

Biographies and Related Materials

The first biography of Stephen Crane appeared in 1923. It was Thomas Beer's *Stephen Crane: A Study in American Letters*. Almost as soon as it was published, though, there was some doubt about the veracity of much of the book. Nevertheless, for many years it remained the only source of knowledge about Crane. However, as scholars became more interested in Stephen Crane, doubts about Beer's biography increased. As a recent Crane scholar, Christopher Benfey, delicately put it: "In the writing of biography, invention is supposed to play a subsidiary role; in Beer's *Stephen Crane* it was primary" (*The Double Life of Stephen Crane*, p. 8). Nevertheless, I include Beer's biography in this bibliography and will let readers draw their own conclusions.

Beer, Thomas. *Stephen Crane: A Study in American Letters*. New York: Alfred A. Knopf, 1923.

Benfey, Christopher. *The Double Life of Stephen Crane*. New York: Alfred A. Knopf, 1992. An interesting, unorthodox take on the life of the author. Along with Wertheim and Sorrentino, Benfey did much to discredit Beer's biography.

Berryman, John. *Stephen Crane: A Critical Biography*. 1950. Revised edition. New York: Cooper Square Press, 2001. As the subtitle suggests, this book focuses on the works of Crane, placing them in literary and historical context.

Davis, Linda H. *Badge of Courage: The Life of Stephen Crane*. Boston and New York: Houghton Mifflin, 1998. This is the most recent and most comprehensive biography of Stephen Crane. Davis was relentless in ferreting out heretofore unknown facts about Crane, and the volume includes a number of photographs not previously published. Although a piece of serious scholarship, it is not dry but very readable and entertaining.

Gandal, Keith. *The Virtues of the Vicious: Jacob Riis, Stephen Crane, and the Spectacle of the Slum*. New York: Oxford University Press, 1997. An interesting study of fact and fiction about the nineteenth-century slum.

Linson, Corwin. *My Stephen Crane.* Syracuse, NY: Syracuse University Press, 1958. An anecdote-filled memoir of Crane written by a close friend. Although written shortly after Crane's death, it lay unpublished for fifty years.

Stallman, R. W. *Stephen Crane: A Biography.* New York: George Braziller, 1968. A good, solid piece of scholarship, Stallman published the first biography of Crane after Beer.

Wertheim, Stanley, and Paul Sorrentino. *The Crane Log: A Documentary Life of Stephen Crane, 1871–1900.* American Author's Log Series. New York: G. K. Hall, 1994. A thorough investigation of Stephen Crane's life, this book went far toward discrediting much of the Beer biography.

Selected Critical Studies

Bergon, Frank. *Stephen Crane's Artistry.* New York: Columbia University Press, 1975.

Berryman, John. *Stephen Crane.* New York: Sloane, 1950.

Cady, Edwin H. *Stephen Crane.* Revised edition. Boston: Twayne Publishers, 1980.

Campbell, Donna M. *Resisting Regionalism: Gender and Naturalism in American Fiction, 1885–1915.* Athens: Ohio University Press, 1997.

Dooley, Patrick K. *The Pluralistic Philosophy of Stephen Crane.* Urbana: University of Illinois Press, 1993.

LaFrance, Marston. *A Reading of Stephen Crane.* Oxford: Clarendon Press, 1971.

Nagel, James. *Stephen Crane and Literary Impressionism.* University Park: Pennsylvania State University Press, 1980.

Pizer, Donald, ed. *Critical Essays on Stephen Crane's* The Red Badge of Courage. Boston: G. K. Hall, 1990.

Solomon, Eric. *Stephen Crane: From Parody to Realism.* Cambridge, MA: Harvard University Press, 1966.